DON'T TELL A SOUL

BOOKS BY D.K. HOOD

DON'T TELL A SOUL

D.K. HOOD

bookouture

Published by Bookouture in 2017

An imprint of StoryFire Ltd.
Carmelite House
50 Victoria Embankment
London EC4Y 0DZ

www.bookouture.com

ISBN: 978-1-78681-274-2
eBook ISBN: 978-1-78681-273-5

To Gary for providing a constant flow of coffee.

PROLOGUE

Kill me. One blood-splattered cowboy boot crunched on the chipped cement floor inches away from his cheek. A sick chuckle followed by a nerve-shattering kick to broken ribs brought back the tremors. A lightning bolt of white-hot agony shot down his spine. In a desperate attempt to pull precious air through swollen lips, he spat blood and gasped precious air. Lungs burning with effort, he writhed like a worm in the dirt waiting for the death blow. His vision blurred and pain pierced his eyes. He'd lost all sense of direction, and his tormentor's peals of satanic laughter played tricks with his confused mind. Night had drifted into another day of endless torture. He tried to crawl away and puffed out a spray of red, stirring the straw on the dusty floor.

How long had it been since he walked into the stables? One day? Five days? Time had become the periods between attacks. He'd suffered unimaginable torture from a man well skilled at inflicting misery, but he'd somehow survived. At first, he tried to reason with his captor and gave him the information he demanded, but he'd fallen into a lunatic's sadistic fantasy. He'd had no time to retaliate, no time to bargain for his life. The first hammer blow knocked him senseless and he came out of oblivion into a world of pain, tied hand and foot at the mercy of a monster.

He hovered between reality and delusion. The mind is a wonderful organ, and his tried to compensate by taking him on trips to the beach with his family. At times, he floated into another dimension on marshmallow clouds but reality came crashing back with each round of torment. He soon discovered crying or begging for mercy made the sessions last longer. Biting back moans and pretending to be unconscious gave the wielder of pain no satisfaction.

Under him, the cold floor acted as a balm to his injuries, numbing the agony, and when darkness came, he'd crawl beneath a pile of stinking straw. The fermenting horse dung kept him warm, kept him alive. He'd spent the first hours in captivity gnawing at the ropes around his wrists, using his teeth to loosen the knot, but one swing of the lunatic's hammer put paid to any hope of escape. A shadow passed over him. A boot pressed down on his spine, the heel twisting to part the vertebrae in bone-jarring agony. Sensation left his legs. *He's paralyzed me.* Determined not to give him the satisfaction of crying out, he remained silent. One more night naked on the freezing ground would finish him, and he'd welcome the release.

A vehicle engine hummed in the distance and Cowboy Boots bent over him, grabbed his legs, and dragged him into a stall. Straw tumbled over him, coating his eyelashes with dust. Through the golden strands, he peered out of the open door and his heart pounded in anticipation. A sheriff's department cruiser pulled up in the driveway and two uniformed officers climbed out. A female with the logo: SHERIFF across her jacket handed his captor a piece of paper. He edged forward on his elbows, dragging his useless legs behind him. Sucking in a deep breath, he screamed through his shredded lips but only a long whine escaped his throat. The sheriff glanced in his direction and he clawed at the ground, edging inch by inch from the stall. He must get her attention, and fighting back waves of nausea, he tried again. "*Aaaaarh.*"

The sheriff indicated toward the barn with her chin and then moved in his direction, but Cowboy Boots blocked her way and shook his head. A grin spread across his face with the cunning of a gargoyle, evil personified. The sheriff spoke again but her muffled words dissipated in the wind and his tormentor's attention moved back to the paper in his hand. Somehow, he'd convinced her all was well. *I have a chance to escape.* He dug for his last ounce of strength and bucked to move forward one painful inch at a time.

I must crawl into the open. Spitting blood, he pushed sound through his shattered mouth. *Hear me. Please hear me.* "*Aaaaarh.*"

The sheriff flicked a look his way, squeezed Cowboy Boots' arm in a comforting gesture and then followed the other officer back to the car. Despair enveloped him, and all hope lost, he allowed the tears stinging his eyes to run down his cheeks. Footsteps came tapping on the cement floor like the ringing of a death knell. His cries for help had enraged the maniac.

"How dare you try to alert the sheriff? I *own* you." Cowboy Boots spat a hot, slimy globule on his cheek. "It's your fault she scanned my yard. You are so gonna pay."

Blows rained down on him, searing pain exploded in his head, and his vision blinked. A strange fog surrounded him and he embraced the peace of darkness.

ONE

"It's official. I'm crazy, nuts, certifiable." David Kane peered through the frost-covered windshield into the inky darkness closing around his truck. The tricked out, bombproof black monster he'd affectionately named the Beast, cut through the ice and snow like a hot knife through butter. "Only a madman drives overnight in a blizzard." Alone in the truck, his voice seemed louder than usual.

The headlights illuminated a strip of blacktop like a glossy, ice-covered snake winding through snow-covered fields. An uncomplicated life in a small, sleepy town in Montana had looked good during his ten-month stint in the Walter Reed National Military Medical Center, but after four hours of driving deeper into oblivion, he'd started to have doubts. "Talking to yourself is the first sign."

Yawning, he opened a window to clear his head. A blast of freezing wind slapped his face, jerking his concentration to full alert. "That's better." He pulled down his black woolen cap to cover his ears and then tapped the GPS screen. "Are you awake?"

The robotic female voice keeping him company had remained silent since her last set of directions. In the distance, he caught the intermittent glow of taillights and accelerated. Following a vehicle through the treacherous, unfamiliar roads would make life easier, and if it dropped out of sight, he doubted another would come by any time soon. Isolated and far from civilization, only idiots like him visited the backwoods town of Black Rock Falls during a blizzard.

He rounded a long curve and gained on the bobbing red lights. Snow piled on the wipers and left a frozen trail on the windshield, distorting the view. He slowed to keep pace, remaining at a distance, not wanting to tailgate or disturb the driver, but the fact someone else had braved the weather gave him comfort. When a road loomed up on the right with a stop sign peppered with bullet holes and sagging at a jaunty angle, he sighed with relief. The headlights picked out a white barn, fences, and a driveway leading to darkness. *At last, signs of life.*

The roar of an engine cut through the silence and light hit the rear-vision mirror. Twin halogen beams cut into his corneas, blinding him. The vehicle shot past at high speed, showering his black truck with ice and gravel. He blinked away red spots in time to make out a mud-covered license plate on a dark pickup carrying a large black barrel secured by ropes. *Jerk!* The speeding maniac bore down on the vehicle in front and both disappeared around a tight bend. A wave of apprehension hit him. A loud bang and grinding shattered the still night and he slowed his pace. Taking the sweeping turn with caution, he gaped in dismay at the pieces of twisted metal littering the bank of fresh snow.

Vivid memories of life-changing seconds slammed into his mind. The image of his wife's lifeless eyes staring into nothingness. The blood on her forehead. The anger knowing the bad guys had won. He shook his thoughts back into the now and scanned the road for wreckage. The ruts in the snow indicated one vehicle had left the road. He inched the Beast forward and stared into the distance.

Two red taillights disappeared into the darkness.

The pickup had appeared out of nowhere as if the driver had been holed up behind the barn and then rammed the other vehicle with no regard to human life. What a great start to his new job. He'd arrive in Black Rock Falls as the sole witness to attempted murder and leaving the scene of an accident. *This is all I need.* Using the headlights to scan the area, he crawled forward, searching the gray packed snow along the edge of the road for the other vehicle. A plume of smoke shimmered in a nearby grassland and a deep groove in the soil showed the car's trajectory. He turned his vehicle to flood the area with light. Leaving the engine running, he grabbed a flashlight from the glove compartment and slid from the seat.

Sleet stung his cheeks and an icy chill cut through his clothes. He zipped his thick winter hoodie and shivered. Gut clenching with apprehension of finding death in the crushed metal, he ran, boots crunching on ice, toward a cruiser with the BLACK ROCK FALLS COUNTY SHERIFF'S DEPART-MENT logo on the door. The cruiser revolved on its roof, wheels spinning and cloaked in a haze of mist. As it came to a stop, he jumped the drainage gully along the roadside, dropped the flashlight and then slid on his knees toward the driver's side. A cloud of fumes billowed around him and gas dripped from the wreck pooling in the snow. One spark and the fuel would ignite. Placing one boot on the side panel, he grabbed the handle and gently levered open the door. He reached for the flashlight and aimed the beam on the face of a woman in uniform suspended upside down by the seatbelt, her face flush with the airbag. She glared at him, dark eyes flashing. She appeared alert and, from her expression, as mad as hell. *She's alive.*

As he moved the flashlight over her, the deputy squinted

and then lifted the muzzle of a Glock 22 and aimed it at his face.

TWO

Kane gaped at her in disbelief, the offer of help frozen on his lips. *Okay, what is going on here?*

Blood oozed from her hairline but her hand remained steady. She narrowed her gaze at him.

"Take the light out of my eyes. Step away from the vehicle and get your hands where I can see them."

"Yes, ma'am." Kane laid the flashlight on the ground and raised his hands. He kept his manner calm and professional to avoid her splattering his brains all over the snow. "Do you want me to call this in and notify the paramedics? You're injured."

"No, I don't need medical assistance. It's just a scratch." As cool as a combat-trained field officer, she didn't as much as blink and just glared at him. "Give me your name."

"I'm David Kane, Black Rock Falls' new deputy sheriff. Can I show you my creds or license? They're in my inside pocket and I'm carrying a revolver in a shoulder holster." He stared into eyes as cold as ice. She wore the stark expression of a trained killer and one as familiar as his own reflection. "I don't have a badge. I'm due to collect one and my uniform on arrival."

"The creds they sent you will do just fine." Her gaze

moved over him but the Glock remained aimed at his forehead. "One hand on your head, leave the gun holstered then take out your ID real slow. I don't take people's word for granted."

Wondering how he'd had the misfortune to relocate to a town with a deputy ready to take him down, he gave her a nod. She had no idea he'd spent years in DC's Special Forces Investigation Command—or that she could trust him. He complied and then flipped open the wallet and turned it upside down to display his ID. "The Black Rock Falls County Sheriff's Department is a small office—I'm sure you've heard about my appointment? I'm due to report at zero eight hundred on Monday to Sheriff Jenna Alton."

"Put some light on that ID." She blinked away the trickle of blood seeping into one eye. "No sudden moves."

He held the wallet holding his photograph and creds as deputy sheriff in front of the flashlight. "Now you know who I am, can I help you, ma'am? Can I call someone to take a look at your head?"

She didn't offer her name but gave him a curt nod and then winced. "It's nothing and I don't require the paramedics."

Moving his gaze over her ashen face, he leaned closer to push away black bangs from an inch-long scratch oozing blood at the hairline. The gun didn't waver but her finger slid away from above the trigger and curled around the grip. He swallowed the command to insist she holster her weapon. "I'll need to lift you out of the vehicle so I can dress the wound. Any other injuries?"

"No. I'm just peachy." She gave him a sarcastic smile. "There's a knife strapped to my right ankle. Grab it and cut through the seatbelt."

Kane went for his own knife and her eyes widened. He ignored her and punctured the airbag on the underside, away from her face. The deflated balloon allowed him more space to check her injuries. "Take the gun out of my face. If it misfires, we'll both be toast. The gas tank is leaking."

"Do you see my finger on the trigger? I'm not a rookie. Here, take it." She dropped the muzzle of the weapon and offered it to him butt-first. "Get me out of here."

He pushed the Glock into the back of his belt. "Okay, tell me if anything hurts when I move you."

Sliding his left arm around her waist for support, he sliced through the seatbelt then lifted her out of the vehicle and placed her on the ground a safe distance away. He collected the flashlight and then returned. He offered his hand. "Can you stand?"

"Just a minute." She touched her head gingerly, stared at her bloodstained fingers, then turned away and vomited.

Concerned, Kane crouched beside her. "You're showing signs of a concussion. I'm calling nine-one-one."

She wiped her mouth with a handful of snow and glared at him.

"It's not the head injury. It was the vehicle spinning." She gagged and crawled away from him on hands and knees. "I've had a concussion before and I'm lucid, my vision is fine. I'm not going into shock. Give me a second."

She wasn't reacting like someone who'd just had a near-death experience. Although she'd gone on the offensive the moment he'd arrived on scene, she'd remained in complete control. Why had she pulled her weapon on a potential Good Samaritan unless she believed him to be a threat? He scratched his chin and caught the slight tremble of her gloved hands. Yeah, it was freezing but she seemed adept at blocking all signs of emotion. He'd worked in the Special Forces Investigation Command long enough to recognize specialized training, and his mind reeled with the implications. *Why would the SFIC put me slap bang in the middle of an ongoing undercover mission?*

Getting more confused by the second, Kane moved back to

the cruiser and kicked a pile of snow over the spreading patch of fuel. He pulled out his phone and took a few photographs of the scene then called nine-one-one. One of the other deputies would have to secure the scene. His priority was getting her to safety. When a dog-barking ringtone came from the deputy's phone, he turned to stare at her.

"Yeah, that's right, nine-one-one calls go straight to my phone. Consider the accident reported." She pressed a handful of snow to the oozing cut on her head and winced. "I'll get someone out here in the morning. Just secure the vehicle."

"Yes, ma'am."

Rounding the vehicle, he went to the open door and peered inside. The interior was devoid of the usual take-away coffee lids and wrappers. He slid across the front seat and opened the glove compartment. Inside was a pile of statement books and a Thermos. He collected the items, snatched the keys from the ignition and climbed out, shutting the door behind him with care. The beep from the key toggle sounded loud in the darkness. Wind blasted him, and a bone-numbing chill hit the metal plate in his head and sent a shiver across the back of his neck. A familiar throb set up a painful beat in his temple, spreading to the backs of his eyes. In the few minutes since the accident, the sleet had turned into a blizzard. The deputy was on her knees spewing. He needed to move her into his vehicle before she went into shock.

He tossed the items into the back seat of his truck and then returned to her side. He crouched beside her. "Any weapons in the trunk?"

"No." She did not look at him.

Shrugging, he ignored her protests, scooped her up, and headed for his truck. "Okay, let's get you out of the cold."

She was heavier than expected and had the kind of muscular body that took years to perfect. The fact that she had the same physique as many of the female agents he'd worked beside for the last ten years raised more red flags. He could be wrong; not everyone was in the same position as him. People wanted him dead. Although the media reported his death in a wreck along with his wife, Annie, he would need to watch his back twenty-four-seven. His commander had organized the escape to the country right down to the demotion to deputy sheriff. Changing identities came with the job, and after spending months in recovery perfecting his cover story, he had expected to have time to mourn the loss of his wife in a lazy rural town. Instead, he'd marched into trouble yet again. *I seem to attract crime.*

Holding her close, he crunched through the snow and her inquiring gaze fixed on him as if she'd read his mind. He indicated toward his vehicle with his chin. "I have a first aid kit in my truck. I'll see to your head wound before we leave."

"Do you usually dash in and take charge of situations?"

Kane pushed down the urge to roll his eyes. "It's part of the job and it's not like you're in any shape to take charge." He juggled her in one arm, pulled open the passenger door, and eased her inside. "Here." He handed back her pistol. "Just don't shoot me—okay?" He shut the door and headed around the hood of the truck.

Snatching the first aid kit from the back seat, he climbed in beside her. To his surprise, she sat motionless and allowed him to clean and dress the wound. She'd been correct; the cut was small but he still had concerns. "I know you've refused medical treatment but will you allow me to check your pupils?"

"If you must."

He picked up the flashlight then flicked the beam across her eyes. When both pupils reacted in unison, he sighed with relief. "All good."

"Copy that. Now can we get going?" Moving as if in pain, she leaned back in the seat and secured the belt.

He tossed the first aid kit into the back and turned to her. "You know my name. How would you like me to address you?"

"Sheriff Alton will do just fine for now." The twinkle of amusement in her eyes reflected his disbelief.

Kane guessed by her cool-headed response to the accident that she'd spent time in the field, but holding the position of Black Rock Falls' sheriff hadn't entered his mind. For the first time, he took in her features. Too young to have the experience necessary for such a high-profile position. Her uniform was pristine apart from the blood spatters and she wore her hair in a short yet fashionable style. Dark blue eyes set off an attractive face and he wondered what division of the military had trained her. The question burned on his lips but he pushed it aside and gave her a nod. "Do you know who ran you off the road and why?" He moved the truck into drive and turned onto the highway.

"No, I was kind of busy trying to survive. Did *you* get a plate?"

He glanced at her and shook his head. "The number had mud smeared over it but I made out one digit, a nine."

"Make?"

"Yeah, it was a Ford pickup, maybe a seventies model, dark paint, maybe blue or green with a torn sticker next to the taillight. It was carrying a beat-up black drum with molasses written on the side. I'm sure I'd recognize the vehicle again. I assume the driver came out from behind the barn some ways back because I had nobody following me." He cleared his throat. "Do you have any enemies?"

"Who doesn't in Black Rock Falls?" Jenna snorted. "If it's not members of the Town Council at each other's throats, it's the drifters or cowboys doing the rodeo circuit. Then we have the fights between the rival hockey teams and the fans. We have a stadium on the other side of town and this weekend is a home game. Trust me, even bad weather doesn't keep them away. The

majority of hockey fans arrive early and stay for the weekend."
She shrugged. "They tend to overindulge, and if the driver was
under the influence, he wouldn't stop to help a law enforcement
officer and risk prosecution."

"I guess, but the mud on the plate seems a little too convenient for me." He considered the implications of investigating a
horde of visitors in town and shrugged. "At least we have a
partial and the make and model of the vehicle."

"There are dozens of Ford pickups in Black Rock Falls
without considering those from the other towns." She gave him
a long, considering stare as if assessing him. "As to personal
enemies, I could give you a list of maybe five people who'd
prefer to have a man in my job. It's just as well women have the
vote."

So, not the quiet little town I had envisioned. He sucked in a
breath. "So what emergency had you out at this time of night?"

"It was a prank call." She pressed trembling fingers to the
white dressing on her head. "They didn't leave a name and said
they'd seen a wreck near the Simpson place. That's about a mile
past the barn you mentioned. I crawled five miles in either
direction but found nothing and was heading home at the time
of the accident."

He stared at her, confused by her calmness. "I wouldn't
class what happened as an 'accident.' The vehicle came out of
nowhere. I think the driver was the prank caller and waited for
you to pass. At the speed the pickup was traveling, hitting you
was deliberate. I'll track down the vehicle and haul them in for
questioning."

"You're very motivated." Jenna pulled up her collar and he
noticed her fingers shaking. "Have you worked many hit-and-
run cases?"

"One or two." He flicked a glance in her direction. "Do you
make a habit of going out on patrol in the middle of the night
without backup?"

"I *usually* take Rowley or one of the other deputies." Jenna's mouth twitched as if in amusement. "Now *you're* here maybe you'll volunteer for *permanent* night duty?"

"Maybe later, when I get to know the area." The headlights picked up groups of buildings stacked along the road. "I'll drop you home then I'll need directions to the O'Reilly Ranch. I've arranged to stay there until I can find a place of my own."

"Hang a right at the next crossroads. The O'Reilly Ranch is about a mile away. Look out for a white arch with a bull's skull on top." Her lips twitched into a semblance of a smile. "You're staying with me. I own the O'Reilly Ranch."

THREE

The last thing Kane needed was company. "I do appreciate the gesture but it won't be for more than a night or two. I prefer to live alone."

"You *will* be alone. I don't like roommates either and I'm sure you'll find the accommodation I've arranged more than adequate." She gave him an indignant look then pointed into the distance. "The entrance is just ahead, white fence. Turn in and follow the driveway."

Ten feet inside the gate, a row of lights flashed on, illuminating the outline of a snow-covered driveway. Kane spotted CT cameras set high on posts below the floodlights, and swept his gaze in all directions. The land surrounding the old ranch-style house contained an open yard, with a corral to one side and a substantial barn. A substantial cottage was on its own beside a small garage. He pulled up on a gravel driveway recently cleared of snow and shot a glance at her. "Have you lived here long?"

"Two years or so." Jenna pointed to the cottage sitting about thirty yards from the main house. "You'll be staying over there. I've stocked the refrigerator with enough food to keep you going for at least the weekend. I've left your uniforms, badge and cards on the kitchen table." She dug a set of keys out of her jacket pocket and handed them to him with a flourish. "Welcome to Black Rock Falls County." She slid out of the door and strode toward the ranch house without a backward glance.

"Oh, this is going to be a blast." He turned the Beast toward the cottage.

Snatching his bags from the back seat, he headed toward the front door, found the key, and turned on the lights. The house smelled of furniture polish with a hint of bleach. He glanced around, taking in the plain, furnished family room comprising of one single chair, a coffee table, and a sofa set before a flat-screen TV. The room was surprisingly warm. He shucked his coat and dropped it over the back of the sofa, and then pulled the bug catcher from his bag. Using the earbuds, he made a room-by-room sweep of the house. *I'll see if you are paranoid enough to have installed surveillance devices.*

After a systematic search, he shook his head in disbelief at the pile of listening devices and cameras collected from strategic positions throughout the house. He strolled along the passageway then turned into the kitchen area complete with granite bench tops and aluminum appliances. He cleared the room of devices and placed the pile of bugs on the table beside three neat stacks of uniforms, three winter jackets, three pairs of boots, and a shiny new shield.

His handler had given him zero intel on Black Rock Falls County or Sheriff Alton, yet it seemed Jenna had information on him right down to the size of his pants. Sure, she had his cover story of a cop injured in the line of duty, but it would be impossible for her to discover the truth of his identity. The agency had sealed his service record and she'd require his real name and a presidential clearance to get a hint of his last position. Depending on her reason for being in Black Rock Falls, she might have perceived him as a potential threat. If so, she had an excuse for the listening devices and cameras. *You're not on my hit list.*

Then again, if Jenna hadn't planted the devices, he could have marched slap bang into a trap. He pulled off his woolen cap and ran a fingertip over the six-inch scar on his head. The hairs on the back of his neck tingled and he rested one hand on the butt of his pistol. His razor-sharp survival instinct had saved his life many a time, and right now it was firing on all cylinders.

FOUR

Jenna shot bolt upright in bed and blinked at the light coming through the curtains. One hand went for the pistol on the nightstand. The Glock slid into her palm, as familiar as breathing. She fixed her attention on the bedroom door and listened. Someone had found her. Three years had passed since giving evidence against underworld kingpin Viktor Carlos. The thug had threatened to kill her during his trial for manufacturing drugs and trafficking in child sex slaves. Believing she would be safe once he was behind bars had been a stupid mistake. Like an octopus, Carlos had long arms, and following the brutal murder of her fellow undercover agent, the FBI had relocated her to Black Rock Falls. Although her new identity should be rock solid, Carlos had hackers and she remained on alert waiting for the other shoe to drop. Seeing Kane's black truck and a man running toward her after a near-fatal accident had convinced her a paid assassin had found her. On instinct, she'd reached for her weapon, and although he appeared to be legit, the incident had shattered her nerves.

The noise came again and, fully alert, she slid from the bed and crouched in combat position. When a loud hammering came on the front door, relief shot through her. Someone must be dead for one of her deputies to disturb her on a Saturday morning before seven. All of them had the sense to call first and not arrive on her doorstep unannounced. *All of them except Kane.*

Pushing her feet into her favorite pink slippers, she dragged on her robe and pocketed her weapon. Glancing down the hallway, she sucked in a breath at the sight of blinking green lights on the security panel. *Stupid. I didn't set the alarm.* She slipped into her office and turned on the bank of screens. The black views inside Kane's cottage matched the furious expression on his face. He glared into the camera mounted on her front porch with one arm resting on the doorframe.

She moved down the hallway and threw open the front door. "Yes?" She looked up, way up, into his strained expression.

"I think we need to talk." Kane opened his hand to reveal a pile of surveillance devices.

Jenna blocked the doorway and gave him a look to stop normal men in their tracks. "Later, when I'm dressed and I've eaten."

"I need to speak to you, right now, ma'am. This can't wait. Are you going to invite me inside, or do we talk in the cold?"

What has you so upset? Jenna shrugged and stepped to one side. "Fine, come in if you want to talk. The kitchen is the second on the left. I'll put on a pot of coffee."

As Jenna filled the coffee pot, she shot a glance at Kane over one shoulder. The colonial-style kitchen chair creaked under the weight of him. He appeared bigger than her memories from the previous evening, with a rugged, handsome appearance and piercing blue eyes. Without doubt, criminals would fold immediately under his glare.

After reading his impressive qualifications, she had wondered why he'd taken a position in Black Rock Falls

County. Now he'd discovered her well-hidden surveillance devices her suspicious mind went into overdrive. The weight of the Glock in her pocket gave some comfort and she forced her face into a neutral expression. Trusting people didn't come easy and a nagging voice in the back of her mind was telling her to be wary of him. She took two cups from the overhead cupboard and placed them on the table. "Sugar and cream?"

"Information." Kane gave her a level stare. "I want to know why you have me under surveillance." He stared at her, his face set in stone. He opened one hand, poured the surveillance devices on the table, leaned back in his chair, and stared at her. "I don't know too many local sheriffs who go to the trouble of bugging their deputy sheriff's residence or answer the door carrying a weapon—unless I'm mistaken and you're carrying a particularly heavy bundle of tissues in your pocket. I want to know what's happening here and why you figure I'm a threat to you."

Jenna straightened and deliberately hardened her expression, although she couldn't quite exert seniority over him wearing a robe and pink slippers. She cleared her throat and glared back at him. "I don't need to give you an excuse. I'm the law in Black Rock Falls County."

"Perhaps, but you don't have the power to change the U.S. Constitution." A nerve in Kane's cheek twitched and his steel-hard gaze did not leave her face. "I have the right to read the warrant you obtained to contravene my Fourth Amendment rights." His mouth twitched into a wry smile. "Don't have one? Well, maybe instead of sitting here I should be visiting the mayor and writing up a complaint against you." He went to rise then leaned toward her. "*Unless* you want to come clean about the attempt on your life last night and the need for all the surveillance?" Placing both hands flat on the table, he met her gaze. "If you're not a voyeur, and don't figure I'm a threat to you, why didn't you set the alarm? I could have broken in and slit your throat in seconds."

Annoyed that he'd noticed her stupid mistake, she swallowed the lump in her throat. "I guess the accident shook me up more than I figured. I forgot to set the alarm, okay?"

"Have you been threatened?"

"Not lately." Stuck between a rock and a hard place, Jenna turned toward the refrigerator. She took out a jug of cream and placed it on the table then collected the coffee pot and sat opposite him with her professional persona firmly in place. "I'm fully aware of the law but I had a good reason to suspect you." She poured two cups of coffee and pushed one toward him.

"We've only just met. How could you possibly form an opinion about my character in such a short space of time? Or is there something we need to discuss?" Kane flicked her an angry glance, reached for the sugar and scooped four teaspoons into his cup, then reached for the cream. "I'm sure you've read my qualifications and references for deputy sheriff or you wouldn't have accepted me."

Jenna pushed hair from her eyes and shrugged. "I have and you came highly recommended but not many men of thirty-five with your previous rank would take a demotion, not to mention half the pay, and move to a town like Black Rock Falls." She shrugged. "It wasn't personal. I was just being careful."

"I'm sorry but that excuse doesn't come close to an explanation." He shook his head, and his shoulders slumped. "If we're going to work together, we'll need a modicum of trust between us."

She needed a plausible excuse in a hurry. "Did the mayor headhunt you to take my job?"

"No. I haven't met the mayor." Kane shook his head and sipped his coffee. "I answered the advertisement in the newspaper. I took this position because I received a gunshot wound to the head in the line of duty. The nice titanium plate covering the hole in my skull sets off security scans and precludes me from working in my chosen field." He dropped his lashes to cover his eyes. "I wanted to remain in law enforcement and Black Rock Falls seemed a nice quiet place to work." He snorted. "Obviously I was mistaken. Now, why don't you explain what is going on here?"

Jenna had no reason to disbelieve his story; she had checked him out and his creds appeared legitimate. Although, not many detective sergeants swept their rooms for bugs or had the body of a marine. Her mind went to the previous night. The moment he'd turned his vehicle onto her property, his attention had flicked from side to side, taking full account of her well-hidden surveillance. His head had not moved, and the familiar ploy had her inner alarm bell ringing loud and clear. She would bet her last dollar he was ex-secret service and had a past he wanted hidden. If she poked too hard, he'd start looking into her background and could easily have the clearance to discover her secrets. Her excuse would have to be a good one to pass his scrutiny. She shrugged. "Nothing unusual is going on. I came here to get far away from an abusive relationship. He was a cop, so my trust is limited and I'm not foolish enough to let my guard down."

"What else has spooked you? This setup is overkill."

She chewed on her bottom lip, and he noticed her hesitation and raised a brow. Glaring at him, she lifted her chin. "Okay, fine. Many locals don't hide the fact they hate a woman doing a man's job and want to see the back of me." She sipped her coffee and considered him over the rim. "I believe last night was one of the disgruntled residents trying to frighten me in the hope I'd leave town. The council elections are coming up soon and my position here is on the line."

"I see." Kane toyed with his coffee cup, turning it with the tips of his fingers. "If you'd agree, ma'am, I'll investigate the incident and discover who tried to kill you last night. If you believe anyone in town is a potential threat, then I want a list of names along with any open cases you're investigating. If you know of anything concerning you or your safety, I need to know." He waved a hand toward the front door. "You shouldn't have to live like this. I could rig up a silent alarm that goes straight to my phone?"

She rolled her eyes. "I have an alarm and it's usually activated."

"That won't save you if you believe your life is in danger. This ranch is isolated and I can be here in minutes." Kane's gaze roamed over her face. "If you want, I can fit a chip into one of your earrings, then if you get into trouble out on patrol, squeeze it and I'll be able to track your whereabouts." His mouth twitched into a small smile. "It's obvious you're a tech head, so if you'd rather make one, I could give you the specifications. I'm not suggesting this to keep tabs on you. I'm offering my help, is all. If I wanted to kill you I've had ample opportunity in the past eight hours."

Every word he'd said made sense, and the idea of twenty-four-seven personal protection eased her nerves. She nodded in agreement. "Okay, I'll take you up on your offer and thank you." She sucked in a breath. "Look, we're going to be sharing down-time together, seeing as you're living on my ranch for a time. Can we leave the formalities at work? Call me Jenna."

"Sure, I'd like that." Kane nodded in approval. "I'm Dave."

As she removed the diamond stud from her ear and handed it over, she stared at the capable man sitting at her table. Having someone like him to watch her back would be a dream come true, but he could be a plant sent to arrange a fatal accident for her. *I would like to trust you, Dave Kane—but not just yet.*

FIVE

Kane leaned back in his chair at Jenna's kitchen table, trying to unravel why she was acting so defensive. By the strain on her face, whatever was troubling her had caused considerable worry. The moment he'd walked through the front door, he'd scanned the interior of her house. The complete lack of personal items—well, apart from the pink slippers—raised a red flag. The family photographs and personal knickknacks most people displayed in their homes were missing, and it was unusual for a woman living in a secluded rural area not to own a dog. He assumed Jenna was like him before he'd made the mistake of marrying Annie—not that he hadn't loved his wife; he still did but he'd exposed her to danger. Men coming for him had killed her, and he blamed himself. Back then, he'd preferred to be devoid of attachments and ready to leave at a moment's notice. He'd been in Jenna's position, lived through the sleepless nights waiting for the silent assassin. That had changed when he'd married. Living in DC, he'd started to feel safe and that had been a fatal mistake. His wife had died and his carelessness carried the blame. He should have discovered the bomb in his vehicle. His commander refused to ignore the hit and ordered him to vanish. Watching the video of his empty coffin buried beside Annie had been surreal. He'd accepted the chance of a new life for one reason—revenge. One day, he would seek justice for Annie and it would be brutal.

He understood Jenna's fear. The world believed him dead, but his survival kit was packed and ready for a quick getaway. Yet she'd lived in Black Rock Falls for at least two years, apparently without a problem. He didn't buy the battered woman story, not her; she could take a man down with one hand tied behind her back. The threat to her life last evening, might have shaken her but she'd broken the first rule of survival —to head for the hills. Why hadn't she left town, if she believed him to be a threat? Right now, she wouldn't confide in him and his questions would have to wait until he gained her trust. "What else is bothering you? If anyone in town is a problem, I need to know. I can't protect you if I'm kept out of the loop."

"I'll give you the access code to view the department's files but apart from neighborhood disputes and the like there are three main cases." Jenna placed her cup on the table and the tip of her tongue flicked across her lips. "People are going missing, and if there's a killer on the loose as I'm living alone, then my extra precautions are valid."

Kane stared at her in disbelief. "So why bug *my* room?"

"I was watching my back is all. Just in case my ex paid someone to take revenge or check out my vulnerability." She shrugged in a dismissive gesture. "You see, for the last two years, I've asked the mayor for a deputy sheriff without success. Then, without notice, he suddenly receives funding to create the position, and the only person to apply was *you*. Kind of suspicious, don't you agree?"

Letting out a long sigh, Kane shook his head. "Not at all."

"Yeah, it is." Jenna's troubled gaze settled on his face. "What's the probability of you seeing the advertisement I placed in the Black Rock Falls County news?" She leaned back in her chair and gave him a long, concerned look. "You worry me."

Then you have something to hide. "Do I? I'm sorry if you don't believe me."

"Maybe you should explain just how you came to apply for the job?" She ran a hand through her hair and then refilled her cup and pushed the pot toward him. "Help yourself."

Kane refilled his coffee cup and slowly added the fixings. She intrigued him and he wanted to call his contact at HQ and get intel on her. He chuckled to clear the tension in the room. "It was fate. When I was recovering in hospital, the social worker at the hospital found the position online and suggested I apply. After being shot in the head all I wanted was a quiet life, and for the record, I'm not after your job." He sipped his coffee and then placed the cup on the table. "If you figure I might be a problem, why did you accept my application?"

"I have three deputies. Rowley is twenty-five and as solid as a rock, Daniels is fresh out of college, and Walters is old enough to be my grandpa." Her cheeks pinked. "I needed an experienced officer to be my deputy. Trust me, I checked you out and you came up clean... maybe too clean."

He stretched, acting as nonchalant as possible under her scrutiny, something he'd perfected over the years. "It sounds like I have the experience you need. I'm street-smart and I'll watch your six. Bring me up to speed on the missing persons' cases?"

She tossed her head in an action he guessed she'd once used to flick long hair over one shoulder, then as if remembering her short bob, pushed a few strands behind one ear.

"We have itinerant workers drifting in and out of town depending on the season but over the last couple of months two people have arrived and vanished." Her brow wrinkled. "Trust me, Black Rock Falls isn't a place most people would want to visit in winter."

I wonder if you've had plastic surgery like me. Kane added more sugar to his coffee. "I agree. So who or what alerted you to the problem?"

"A young woman came into the office to file a missing persons' report. Her name is Sarah Woodward." Jenna fingered the bandage on her forehead and pressed the dark blue bruise under her eye. "She arrived two weeks ago looking for her grandma, Samantha Woodward. Apparently, the grandma is a spry and healthy sixty-eight year old. Nine months ago, after her husband died, she sold up and informed Sarah she'd be traveling around the state. Last Sarah had heard, she'd planned to visit Black Rock Falls." Jenna chewed on her bottom lip. "We know she arrived, opened a post office box and then dropped off the earth."

Kane raised a brow. "Maybe she moved on. Did you pass on the information to the sheriff of the next county?"

"No, because Sarah mentioned her grandma planned to purchase a small ranch here. Many years ago, her father owned land in the area and I guess she wanted to recapture her youth. Sarah's mother received letters from her on a regular basis, then two months ago the letters stopped and Sarah became worried. She checked hospitals along the route she'd taken, and when she couldn't find any trace of her, she ended up in Black Rock Falls. Her grandma mentioned the town but no specific area." Jenna sighed and pushed her fingers through her short hair. "She ran into brick walls trying to get help from the locals and came in to report her grandma missing last Tuesday."

Kane blew out along breath. "Do people still write letters?"

"Apparently so." Jenna shrugged and her mouth turned down. "She was old-school, and preferred to write letters. She refused to own a phone. Sarah told me she believed them to be intrusive and preferred to speak to people in person."

"Okay. How was she picking up her mail?" Kane removed his woolen cap and scratched his head. He missed his buzz cut but the longer style covered the ugly scar.

"She'd collect them from post office boxes along the way. Before you ask, she used her daughter's address to hire them. The postmaster in town says he doesn't keep tabs on people collecting their mail but did mention Woodward's lease expires at the end of the month." She held up one hand like a police officer conducting traffic. "And yes, I did ask Sarah if her grandma ever mentioned if she'd worked in the area, and came up empty. Sarah said her letters were brief and usually about the history of the places she'd stopped at along the way, and personal matters. All I know is she came into town about a month ago, banked cash, and picked up her mail. We've made inquiries at the local ranches in the area but no one recalls seeing her."

He stirred his coffee, mulling over what she had said. "You mentioned others are missing?"

"*One* other." She refilled her cup then ran the tip of one finger absently through a drop spilled on the table. "I had an inquiry about a missing person from Father Maguire out of Atlanta. He's concerned about one of his parishioners, John Helms. The last time he heard from him, Helms was heading into Black Rock Falls to attend a game of hockey. That was two weeks ago. Father Maguire hasn't made contact with him since he notified him to say his vehicle had died and he'd planned to take the bus. Apparently, he called regularly." She sighed and leaned back in the chair, coffee cup in hand. "This one is tricky because Helms took the vacation after marriage counseling. Apparently, he needed a break from his wife."

Kane tried to get his head around the problem. It didn't sound like too much of a problem just yet. "Have you considered he might have run off with his lover?"

"The thought has crossed my mind but Father Maguire is tight-lipped about the circumstances of the couple's problems." Jenna raised both eyebrows. "I have a phone number for Mr. Helms but the service has been disconnected. As this was yesterday, I haven't gotten very far with my inquiries and have no reason to suspect the two cases are linked."

Kane drummed his fingers on the table. The missing persons' cases should not be serious enough to put her this much on edge. She'd mentioned three ongoing cases and he waited as she sipped her coffee for her to continue.

"Then there's the guy in the lock-up." She placed her cup carefully on the table and lifted her gaze. "There was a fight Thursday evening at the Cattleman's Hotel. I was on duty with Deputy Rowley and we picked up three men for public intoxication. Two of them accused Billy Watts, the detainee, of stealing chips during a poker game. I'm trying to determine whether Mr. Watts is a suspect or a victim. When arrived on scene, he was carrying two hundred dollars and had cashed in a few minutes before the fight started." She cleared her throat and gave him an apologetic look. "I released the other men in the morning. They're local boys and one is the mayor's son. They're members of the local hockey team, and with a home game this weekend their coach will keep them in line."

The mayor's son? "Did you give special consideration because of their connection to the mayor?"

"I most certainly did not." She gaped at him with an aghast expression, pushed back the chair, and stood with her fists balled on her waist. "Trust me, I don't bend the rules for anyone, least of all Mayor Rockford."

Kane swallowed the laugh crawling up his throat. She had guts to challenge him, and by the flash of anger in her eyes, she was serious. "Okay, okay, that's good to know. How did the arrests go down? Would one of them be upset enough to commit vehicular homicide?"

"What you really mean is, 'Did they lose face in front of their friends after being arrested by a woman?'" She chuckled and her face softened. "Probably, but enough to attempt murder? No, I don't think so."

Kane's stomach rumbled. "Please tell me you have a place in town that serves a good breakfast."

"Aunt Betty's Café is the best if you want good honest food, but you have fixings in your cottage."

"Yeah, I know, but I figure it would be good to get the layout of the town before I start work on Monday." He pushed slowly to his feet and smiled at her. "Would you consider coming along to show me around?"

She blinked a few times as if trying to compute what he had said then waved a hand toward her dressing gown.

"Why not? But I'll need a few minutes to shower and change." She lifted her chin and gave him a long, considering stare. "I guess I can give you the tour."

"Thanks, see you out front when you're ready." Kane smiled at her confused expression. "Before I go, could I have the web address and password for the files? I'll take a look before we leave and if you give me the number of one of the deputies on duty this weekend, I'll send him out to photograph the scene of your accident and arrange a tow truck."

"You're welcome to look over the files. I need fresh eyes on the cases." Jenna's lips flattened into a thin line as she turned to a notepad on the bench beside the telephone. Taking a pen attached by a string, she wrote a combination of numbers beside a URL. She frowned as if deciding her next move then handed him the slip of paper. "I'll call Rowley. He won't know who you are and you're not an official member of Black Rock Falls County Sheriff's Department until Monday morning. Rowley is the best one to send out to the scene of an accident and will handle the case for now." She tapped her bottom lip then wiggled her eyebrows. "*Unless* you want to start today?"

"Sure." He turned toward the front door. "Thanks for the coffee."

. . .

Once back inside his cottage, he went to the bedroom and pulled out his escape kit. It contained burner phones, six credit cards in different identities, cash, his backup pistol, ammunition, and a few changes of clothes. He dug out one of the phones and punched in his contact's number. "Ninety-eight H requesting information on Sheriff Jenna Alton of Black Rock Falls County."

He listened to the tapping of fingers on computer keys followed by an intake of breath.

"We have no records of interest under that name. I must advise you to stand down on any further inquiries on this subject and enjoy your new position."

Kane grimaced. There should be information available on a county sheriff, no matter how inconsequential, so his instincts about her had been correct. "Copy that." He flicked the phone shut, turned it over, and removed the SIM card, then strolled into the kitchen and nuked it in the microwave.

SIX

The *chug, chug, chug* of heavy machinery from the front of the cottage grabbed Kane's attention. He strolled to the front door and stepped outside into an icy breeze. A snowplow turned in front of the sheriff's house. The operator moved the machinery past his front door and peeled away the fresh top coat of snow. The red-faced man inside gave him a cheery wave then continued along the driveway. Kane lifted his hand in a mock salute and watched the spray of snow pile up each side of the driveway. The chill of winter cut through his thick sweater and he turned inside, kicking the door shut with his foot.

Checking through Black Rock Falls County Sheriff's Department arrest files could wait until later. The tracker in Jenna's earring had been his first priority. He grabbed a winter coat from his bag and walked back to the door. Outside, he locked the deadbolt behind him and then crunched through the ice-covered driveway to his truck. He slipped inside, turned on the engine to allow the motor to idle, and pushed the heater up a few notches before pulling on his gloves. He'd lived in cold places but not in the West. Climate change made the winters brutal in many states and he expected freezing temperatures but the wind in Black Rock Falls was wicked. Rather than wait, he backed out of the garage and drove to the front of Jenna's house. Moments later, she emerged.

The sheriff had dressed in a padded jacket with a fur-trimmed hood worn over blue jeans and ankle boots. Carefully applied makeup covered the bruise on her face. She headed down the steps and rounded the hood of his vehicle to open the passenger door. Settled inside, she clicked in her seatbelt before looking at him expectantly with a raised eyebrow.

"Oh, I guess you'll be needing directions to Aunt Betty's?" She waved a hand nonchalantly toward the entrance to the property "You can't miss it. It's on the main street. The café has a slice of apple pie on a sign out front."

He slanted a glance in her direction. "Copy that, but before we leave, here you go." He fished her earring out of his pocket. "Just squeeze it and it will call my phone. I'll be able to track you on my app. Later, I'll set up a silent alarm for the house but this will work in an emergency."

"Thank you." Jenna attached the earring then her brow crinkled into a frown. "I'm afraid I'm going to need you as my ride for a couple days until my cruiser is repaired." She tucked a strand of hair inside her hood and a small smile curled her lips. "I could commandeer your vehicle but I'd appreciate your coop-eration as you're a member of my department. All expenses paid, of course."

"Not a problem." He turned the vehicle onto the main road and headed toward the center of town, trailing behind the snowplow. "Do you have the snow cleared every morning?"

"Jim lives next door and does my driveway as a courtesy before heading into town." Jenna smiled in a flash of white teeth. "He says if I can't get to town, I can't assist anyone who needs help."

Kane took in his surroundings. Black Rock Falls was not the small town he imagined. The county spread out in every direction, attached to the main town by a spiderweb of back roads. Signposts and bunting directed traffic to Black Rock Falls Stadium, home of the Larks, and the showgrounds. As they drove closer to town, snow-covered houses nestled in clusters. The main street showed prosperity and a thriving community. The cold had not kept the locals indoors. People lined up outside the bakery, chatting beneath a cloud of steam, and vehicles lined the curb. He glanced at Jenna. "Is it usually so busy at this time of the morning?"

"It's the Larks' home game tonight." She flicked a glance at him. "The away weekends are quieter in the hockey season because the fans from here follow the team. We're on the rodeo circuit too, and as soon as the snow melts, the cowboys come to town. Trust me, the visitors and locals keep us on our toes."

Jenna impressed him. Protecting Black Rock Falls County with a handful of officers would be a nightmare. He rubbed his temple in anticipation of the torment to come. His plans to vegetate in a backwoods town had disintegrated like snowflakes on a heated windshield. The familiar pain in his head returned with a wave of nausea. Agony shot through his back teeth and he relaxed his jaw in a practiced move to gain control. He needed a meal and a gallon of strong coffee if he planned to make it through the day.

"Are you okay?" Jenna turned in her seat and an expression of concern crossed her face. "You're sheet white."

"It's just a headache." He pushed his lips into what he hoped was some semblance of a smile and decided to be honest. "I mentioned the plate in my head? Well, the cold doesn't do me any favors." He kept his gaze on the road. "As long as I keep the hat on, I'll be fine."

"You have a choice, you know." Jenna leaned back in her seat but the concern had not left her expression. "Why not start on Monday and take the weekend to rest after your trip?"

Why wasn't she taking the attempt on her life seriously? "Ah, someone tried to kill you, and in my book the attempted murder of a sheriff is priority one on my list."

"Don't be so dramatic." Jenna let out a long patient sigh. "I'd like to view the evidence before I decide. You didn't *actually* witness the incident, did you?"

"I didn't see the impact." Kane stared at her in disbelief. "But I'm a witness to dangerous driving causing an accident and to the suspect leaving the scene without so much as slowing down to see if he'd injured you."

"You're law enforcement all the way." She tucked a strand of black hair into her hood. "Don't you ever stand down?"

Kane shook his head. "Nope."

As they drove through town, he noted the general store and gas office. A large park, with snow encrusted swings and a carousel offered the local kids a safe place to play. Next came a real estate office with frozen red and white flags hanging from the gutters and set back on one side of the road. It was conveniently opposite a red-brick building with a shingle denoting a lawyer's office. In the middle of town, he found Aunt Betty's Café wedged between a medical center and an optometrist. He pulled the Beast to the curb and they stomped through the snow toward the café's doorway.

The delicious smell of ham, eggs, hotcakes, and coffee wafted toward him in a wall of welcoming succulent heat. When Jenna moved in front of him and dropped into a blue plastic seat at a wooden table in front of the window toward the back of the room, he followed, glancing around. The diner was spotless, and popular, judging by the number of people enjoying their meals. A low hum of conversation filled the room and many people glanced in his direction. He shucked his coat and dropped it over the back of the chair before sitting. Two men in their twenties shot to their feet and, disregarding the food piled on their plates, headed out the door. Kane followed their progress down the street and made a mental note of their descriptions. Inhaling the aromas of the delights on offer, his attention went to the glossy colored illustrations of meals pinned to the wall behind the counter. "What do you recommend?"

"Everything." Jenna's face lit up with a grin at the young woman approaching with a coffee pot in hand. "Morning, Susie."

"Mornin', Sheriff." The woman filled two cups with coffee and placed the pot on the table then pulled a notebook out of her pocket. "What can I get you?" Her inquisitive brown eyes moved over Kane. "Good mornin' to you too. You must be new in town?"

"This is Deputy Kane." Jenna shot him an amused stare. "Say hello to Susie Hartwig. Her grandma started this establishment in 1960."

Kane nodded. "Nice to meet you, Ms. Hartwig."

After ordering, he leaned back in his chair and stretched his legs. His gaze flicked over two men sitting in a secluded corner and sending furtive glances their way. Lifting the coffee to his lips, he regarded Jenna over the rim. She appeared at ease but her attention moved around the room, resting on each person before moving on to the next. He dropped the cup back into the saucer and met her gaze. "I find it hard to believe two visitors have vanished in Black Rock Falls without a trace and yet the moment I arrived the locals picked me as a stranger." He cleared his throat. "It doesn't make sense."

"It does." Jenna rubbed her hands together. She spooned sugar into her cup then lifted the creamer. "It's common knowledge Mayor Rockford hired a new deputy. The moment you walked in here with me, you became a person of interest. The two missing persons may have worked on the outlying ranches. If Mrs. Woodward came into town to pick up her mail, she might have avoided Aunt Betty's Café. We've spent a good deal of time showing her photograph around the ranches without luck but a teller at the local bank remembers her. She came into town one time to do her banking, so she might have worked somewhere in the area as a housekeeper, perhaps." She sipped her coffee, and her lips curled up in contentment. "Many people visit Black Rock Falls and unless they cause trouble or call attention to themselves, I doubt many people would remember them."

Allowing the information to percolate into his mind, Kane turned the cup of excellent coffee around in his fingers. "So I gather Mrs. Woodward wasn't staying in town?"

"Not at the Cattleman's Hotel or the Black Rock Falls Motel." Jenna unzipped her coat with a flourish and shrugged out of it. "Apparently, she has several vehicles but her granddaughter believes she was driving a pickup." She raised both dark eyebrows. "Oh, don't give me that look. Hers would be one of possibly a hundred passing through town at any given weekend. I haven't met the woman, let alone upset her enough to try to kill me."

Everyone is a suspect until we prove otherwise. "Okay." He lifted his chin toward the men across the room on their right. "Any problems with the men sitting at two o' clock?"

"Nope. They breed horses and own a ranch out past the Triple Z Roadhouse." Jenna waited for Susie to place plates piled high with food on the table. "Thank you."

"Enjoy! I'll be straight back with fresh coffee." Susie collected the coffee pot then bounced toward the kitchen humming and came back a few moments later to refill their cups.

Kane eyeballed the men again in his periphery. "Those men seem a bit nervous around law enforcement. Known them long?"

"About two years or so." Jenna's smile reached her eyes. "One of my deputies, Pete Daniels, is their brother so they have no reason to be nervous around law enforcement."

Kane shrugged. "Uh-huh, so what's their story?"

"Pete wasn't raised here. When their mother died, his father sent him to live with an aunt. Pete has his own place in town." Jenna's lips turned down at the edges. "Pete was glad to be with his aunt, he mentioned their father was a hard person to live with."

Kane moved his attention to the men then back to her. "What happened to their father? Is he in jail?"

"No, he fell under a tractor, as far as I know, some years before I arrived in town." Jenna pushed a stray black hair from her face and shook her head. "I don't know the details."

Interesting. "Was there an investigation?"

"I believe it was an accident. Wow! You're intense and the way you're looking at them I'm not surprised they're nervous." Jenna's eyes flashed with annoyance. "You're an unknown quantity in town and intimidated me when we first met. Adding the fact, you arrived the same time as I've been conducting a door-to-door would put anyone on edge. I'd say many people believe they're under scrutiny and I'm sure a few people have something to hide."

Kane shrugged and leaned back in his chair. "Maybe but with a brother in the department, they'd be aware of the reason you've been asking questions." He shook his head. "It's unlikely they'd have something to hide unless Deputy Daniels is covering for them. Can he be trusted?"

"He's a rookie. Sometimes he acts like a jerk and I've had to speak to him about discussing cases with his girlfriends but he's shaping up okay now. Would he report his brothers for breaking the law? I really couldn't say but honestly, the Daniels boys are the least of my worries. They keep to themselves and don't cause trouble. I think you can take them off your radar." She picked up a fork, scooped up fluffy scrambled eggs, popped them in her mouth, then lifted an amused gaze to him. "In case you're wondering, the two men that high-tailed it out of here are

Josh Rockford and Dan Beal, the men I arrested for being a public nuisance. They tend to overindulge and Rockford figures he's God's gift to women, which could turn into a problem as half of his fans are teenage girls—not that any have complained." She raised a dark eyebrow. "I noticed Rockford was on his phone when we arrived. I 'd guess they're probably late for hockey practice. I held them up yesterday and the coach probably fined them for being late. The Larks' coach has rules about players missing training sessions."

"Okay." Kane ate with leisure and mulled over what they had discussed earlier. He wanted to investigate Jenna's accident before the trail went cold. "Do you happen to know what vehicles they drive?"

"Not Beal but Josh Rockford drives a decked-out truck. Red with plenty of chrome. He's the peacock of the team, if you know what I mean?"

"Then it wasn't him—or it wasn't his vehicle."

"It could easily be Rockford." Jenna cleared her throat and her cheeks colored. "He believes being the mayor's son is a get out of jail free card. He's disrespectful toward me in a suggestive way."

"He doesn't appreciate being rejected?"

"No." Jenna met his gaze with a frown. "He's the 'women should be barefoot and pregnant' type and no doubt expects to marry a virgin."

"I'll keep an eye on him." Kane stirred his coffee. "Did you contact Rowley?"

"Yeah, and he should be reporting in soon. I told him to drop in here on his way to the office and bring the images of the scene. With what you have, we'll be able to see if anyone else disturbed the area after we left." She stared thoughtfully at the table, poured cream into her fresh coffee, added sugar, and stirred. "Are you sure you want to sign on today? If you'd prefer we can discuss the accident at the office on Monday?"

"I'd rather start today. I'd like to find the person who caused the accident before they have time to repair the damage to their vehicle." He narrowed his gaze. "Why aren't you making the attempt on your life a priority?"

"Trust me, I am." She gingerly touched the dressing on her forehead. "I had Rowley on scene as soon as possible. You have a description of the other vehicle and took photographs before the snow covered any tracks. I believe we're well on the way to finding a suspect."

Kane leaned forward and lowered his voice. "Then give me the case so I can investigate."

"As I am involved it would be the sensible thing to do. Rowley doesn't have the experience but he works well under instruction." Jenna turned and her face broke into a smile as the door to the shop swung open and a ruddy-faced young man wearing a deputy's jacket over blue jeans removed his hat and ambled toward them. "Ah, here is Deputy Rowley now."

"Ma'am." Deputy Rowley strolled to the table with a camera in one hand.

"Rowley, meet Deputy Sheriff David Kane. He is taking the lead in my apparent hit-and-run." Jenna gave a dismissive wave in his direction. "Take a seat and show me what you have."

Kane offered his hand. "Did you notice any paint residue on the damage to the sheriff's vehicle?"

"Yes, sir. I took a video and stills." Rowley's handshake was firm. "I remained on scene until the tow truck arrived and informed the operator to take the vehicle to Miller's Garage and not touch it until further notice." He placed the camera on the table.

"Do you mind?" Kane looked at Jenna and indicated toward the camera.

"Go ahead."

He flicked through the images, zooming in on anything suspicious. The scrape to the rear side appeared to have collected paint residue. He showed the image to Jenna. "We'll need a sample."

"I'll collect a forensics kit from the office then we'll head down to the garage." A frown wrinkled her brow and she rubbed her temples. "It can wait until after we've finished eating."

Kane smiled. "I have one in my truck." He glanced at Rowley. "Go to the garage and remain there. Make sure no one goes near the cruiser. We'll relieve you in about ten minutes."

"Yes, sir." Rowley jumped to his feet and headed for the door.

"He seems efficient." Kane cut into a slice of succulent honey ham and pushed it into his mouth.

"He's getting there." Jenna lifted a slice of toast and sighed. "It amazes me. Without fail, every Saturday something comes along to spoil my day."

Kane reached for his coffee and smiled. "I'm sure this won't take more than an hour." He finished his coffee. "I'd like to chase down the pickup ASAP."

"If *you* want to go through the DMV records be my guest, but take me home first." Jenna puffed out a tired sigh that lifted her bangs. She pushed her plate to one side and stared at him. "I have two officers on duty this weekend and I'll need to introduce you. If the headache becomes a problem, you can access the DMV records from home when you recover but I'd suggest delegating the task to one of the other deputies."

Kane bit back a smile as he imagined her slipping back into her pink slippers and leaving her sheriff's persona at the door. "I'm fine now and I'd prefer to work at the office. I want to familiarize myself with the missing person cases as well." He stood and reached for his wallet. "Ready?"

"Yeah." Jenna pulled bills from the pocket of her jeans and tossed them on the table. "My treat, to say welcome to Black Rock Falls."

Surprised, Kane smiled at her. "Thanks."

"Don't get used to it." She picked up the camera, then, head erect and eyes front, marched toward the door. "Don't forget to grab the forensics kit from your truck. The garage is right across the street."

He grinned at her and snatched his coat from the back of the chair. "Yes, ma'am."

SEVEN

The cold seeped through Jenna's coat, as if attacking the aches and pains from the wreck. She made her way across the street to Miller's Garage and stamped the snow from her boots before entering. Realization of how close she'd come to dying hit her at the sight of the crumpled cruiser. She bit her bottom lip. How had she escaped the wreck without serious injury? She turned as Deputy Rowley ambled up to her and gave her a boyish smile.

"George will fill out a damage report for the insurance company but he thinks you'll need a replacement." Rowley wiggled his eyebrows. "You did mention wanting a new cruiser."

Jenna shook her head, annoyed at his insinuation. "I wouldn't risk my life for a new vehicle, and spinning upside down in the snow in the middle of the night wasn't my idea of fun."

"Someone driving a dark Ford pickup caused the accident." Kane moved to her side and his intent stare at Rowley made the young man's cheeks color. "I can identify the vehicle. What is the name of the road with the barn on the corner, not far from the scene? The one with the shot-up stop sign."

"That would be Smith's Road." Rowley rubbed his chin as if in deep thought. "There are a ton of Ford pickups in town, but from the paint scrape the vehicle is dark blue. That might narrow our search a bit and I can name a few owners."

"Make a list of everyone you know in the area with the same vehicle and check them for damage. If you're delayed getting back to the office, send me a list of those we can discount." Kane straightened to his full six-five, took a card out of his wallet, and handed it to him. "I'm going to be checking the DMV records this afternoon and we can follow up any leads when you return."

"Yes, sir." Rowley glanced at the card. "If you don't need me here, I'll get at it."

Jenna smiled at him. "Okay thanks. I'm heading home soon, and before you hear any gossip, Kane is living in the cottage on my ranch until he finds somewhere else to live." She flicked a glance in Kane's direction. "Unless he decides to stay."

"The cottage suits me fine." Kane took his time walking around the wreck, and examining every inch. "Rowley, wait until I collect the paint samples. I'll need you to countersign the sealed baggies; the sheriff can't touch the evidence." He grimaced. "Conflict of interest."

"I understand." Rowley's brow crinkled into a frown. "Oh yeah, I almost forgot, Sarah Woodward called late yesterday afternoon. She said she had some more information about her grandmother and wanted to drop by the office this morning." He met her gaze "Do you want me to interview her?"

"Yeah." Jenna remembered the prisoner in the lock-up. "And then, when you've checked out the Ford pickups, go down to the Cattleman's Hotel and get a list of the other men involved in the poker game on Thursday night. Go and speak with them, and if Billy Watts' story checks out, release him with a warning."

"Yes, ma'am."

Her attention moved to Kane bent over inspecting the back of the cruiser. He impressed her by the meticulous way he collected and bagged the paint samples. When he straightened and moved away to label each piece of evidence, she moved to his side. "What do you think? Accident or attempted murder?"

"Attempted murder." Kane passed the bags to Rowley for his signature. "The paint evidence and the scene photographs disprove the accident theory. The vehicle couldn't have accidentally slid into your cruiser." He took a notepad out of his pocket and drew a diagram. "The road at the point of impact is a tight left-hand bend, and at the speed the driver took the corner, the centrifugal force would pull the back end of the pickup to the right *away* from your vehicle. I saw no evidence that the driver had lost control or left the road. He didn't fishtail into the cruiser, that was for darn sure. The driver was in control when he clipped the back of your vehicle."

"It sounds like an ambush to me." Deputy Rowley flashed her a look of concern.

Concerned by the evidence, Jenna chewed on her bottom lip. "I can't say for sure. I didn't see a thing and only caught the flash of his headlights before he hit me. It sure looks like an attempt on my life. The thing is I haven't upset anyone in town enough to make them want to murder me." She pushed her hair back and stared at Kane's diagram. "Sure, I've ruffled a few feathers but there aren't any crime syndicates operating in Black Rock Falls."

"Okay, leave the investigation with me until you're back on duty." Kane's mouth turned down and he glanced at Rowley. "You'd better get going."

"I'll send you the information you need as soon as possible, sir." Rowley turned on his heel and strolled out the door.

"Is there anything you're not telling me?" Kane raised both eyebrows in question. "Love affairs gone wrong, jealous wives?"

"In Black Rock Falls? The mayor wouldn't allow any scandal in the sheriff's department, not that I've time for more than the odd dinner date, and adultery isn't my style."

"Then I guess the reason will come out when we find the other vehicle. I'll send the paint samples away for analysis. A match and my testimony will be enough to send the driver away for jail time." Kane leaned his shoulder against the damaged cruiser and cleared his throat. "I'd like to sit in on the interview with Miss Woodward. I'd be interested to see what information she has discovered about her grandmother's disappearance. Would you mind if I dropped you home, changed into my uniform, and then headed back to the office?"

Jenna smothered the smile threatening to burst across her face. She'd not met anyone so keen to give up a weekend, let alone after a long journey and a late night. "Sure. I'll send the mayor's office an email to let them know you've started today, so you'll get paid." She waved a hand toward the cruiser. "Do you need anything else from the wreck? I'd like to get the insurance claim underway as soon as possible."

"We've covered every angle." Kane indicated toward the street with his chin. "Which way to the office?"

"It's at the other end of town." She edged to the door. "We'll need to drive but let's make it a short stop. I've things to do at home and I'm on duty tonight after the game."

"Okay, but I'll want time to log the paint scrapings and send a sample away before we leave. I don't want to give anyone the impression we've had time to tamper with the evidence." He shrugged. "That's why I took the precaution of collecting the samples in front of Rowley and getting him to sign across the seals of the baggies."

Professional and slick. I'm starting to like this guy. "It's normal procedure—well, it is for me. I'm glad we're on the same page."

"So am I." Kane grinned and his eyes sparkled with amusement. "It will sure make life easier."

EIGHT

Kane followed Jenna into the sheriff's office and glanced around. A young woman and two men sat apart in the waiting area. He strolled behind Jenna past the people and into one large room. Partitioned areas took up most of the main floor where deputies conducted interviews in cubicles. An impressive show of flat-screens embellished the work areas. A door to one side held a large copper plate with the name "Sheriff Alton" embossed in silver. At the other end of the room, another door hung open to display a passageway. The aroma of freshly brewed coffee and bagels moved his attention to a small kitchenette complete with coffee maker and stainless-steel refrigerator. A whiteboard covered with some type of chart hung beside a notice showing the way to the bathrooms. He waited for Jenna to introduce him to the deputies on duty but, before she'd opened her mouth, an elderly deputy in his sixties offered his hand and gave him a warm smile.

"Welcome to Black Rock Falls, I'm Duke Walters and this is Pete Daniels." Walters indicated to the tall man in his twenties beside him. "It's about time we had another sheriff's deputy. I'm getting too close to retirement to be taking over in an emergency."

"Jake said you planned to drop by today." Daniels shook his hand then looped his thumbs into the belt on his pants and leaned against a desk.

"Jake?" Kane met the condescending stare of Daniels and shrugged off the wave of insolence coming from the younger man. "I don't believe I've met anyone by that name."

"He's referring to Jake Rowley." Jenna smiled at him. "Daniels here is our latest acquisition, straight out of college. I'm sure he'll benefit from your knowledge and experience."

I hope so. Kane turned to Walters. "I have paint samples from the sheriff's accident to log into the evidence locker." He pulled the baggies from his pocket and turned to Daniels. "You come too. I want two officers' signatures on the evidence book."

"The room requires two keys to unlock the cage." Jenna pulled a ring of keys from her pocket. "I have one and Walters has the other, as he was the senior officer before you arrived." She gave the older man a long, considering stare. "I guess that honor goes to Kane now."

Kane looked at the older man. "I'll value Deputy Walters' expertise to settle in." He took the bunch of keys.

"I'll look forward to cutting back my hours now we have some help." Walters smiled warmly.

Kane opened his mouth to reply but swallowed the retort as a middle-aged woman with dark skin flowed into the office. She shook the snow from a colorful knitted hat, hung it on a peg by the door, removed her coat, then turned toward him and flashed a smile.

"You must be the Deputy Kane everyone is talking about. I see everyone arrived early to meet you." She moved toward him, generous hips swaying. "I'm Magnolia Brewster but *you* can call me Maggie."

"Maggie is our receptionist." Jenna's face broke into a warm smile. "Dial nine-one-one and you'll get Maggie during office hours. Other times, emergency calls go straight to the officer on duty."

Kane stared at her in disbelief. "You handle all emergencies? Fires, paramedics—everything?"

"Yeah, and I've asked the mayor for a twenty-four-hour call-out service but the small volume of calls we receive isn't worth the cost involved." Jenna drummed her fingernails on the desk. "Get the evidence logged, and if you're sitting in on Sarah Woodward's interview, ask Walters to start the DMV check. When he has a list, compare it to everyone I arrested within the last six months, in case they own a similar vehicle."

Kane nodded. Jenna was all business in the office. "Copy that. Anything else I should know?"

"Rowley will fill you in on the details. He's on the ball." She smiled. "Maggie will arrange for the paint samples to go to forensics. Walters is more than capable of overseeing that task."

When Kane opened his mouth to ask another question, she glared at him.

"You'll have plenty of time to talk shop with my deputies, *after* you take me home."

Back at the office one hour later and dressed in his crisp new uniform, Kane supervised the release of Billy Watts. Rowley had found no evidence to prove the man had stolen money. The deputy had also hunted down blue pickups owned by people he knew but had found none with any recent damage. Kane put him to work interviewing Sarah Woodward and moved his attention to the younger deputy, Pete Daniels. Confident Daniels could handle the paperwork, Kane turned away to evaluate the young woman Rowley was interviewing in his cubicle.

Sarah Woodward reminded him of his sister at the same age, and his protective instinct surged to the surface. At approximately eighteen, she was far too young to be conducting her grandmother's investigation alone. Her porcelain skin and blonde hair would be like putting up a "come get me" flare to the crowd of young men arriving for the hockey game. Out for a good time, they would flock to an innocent, naive girl like bees to honey.

Kane pulled a chair into Rowley's cubicle to listen in on the interview with her. He introduced himself and sat down. "Are you traveling alone?"

She blinked cornflower-blue eyes at him, surprised as if he'd just materialized in front of her.

"Ah... yes, I am." Her lips trembled into a smile. "I intend to find my grandmother, so I won't be alone for long." She twisted her fingers in a blue knitted scarf. "I have a few leads."

Kane leaned back in his chair making it creak like an old man's bones. "What new evidence have you discovered?"

"I called my mom. She couldn't recall any specific places Grandma had visited but she had some of her letters. You must understand my mom hasn't been the same since my pa died. The medication affects her memory so I figured the best thing to do was to ask her to send me Grandma's letters." Sarah gave him a sunny smile, all dimples and white teeth. "The letters came by special delivery yesterday afternoon. I haven't read all of them but the third one I opened mentioned speaking to the local real estate broker. Grandma wanted to purchase a small ranch in the area. A place where we could all live far away from the city." She lifted her chin. "I thought I'd go and speak to the real estate broker and ask if Grandma made inquiries."

"You should leave the investigating to us." Kane flicked a glance at Rowley. "Give the real estate office a call and find out what the broker remembers about Mrs. Woodward." He smiled at Sarah. "Can I get you a drink while we wait? A soda or coffee?"

"Yeah thanks, a soda would be nice." Her cheeks pinked as

she unzipped a bright yellow windbreaker. "It's quite warm in here."

As Rowley moved away to make the call, Kane noticed Deputy Daniels in his periphery. The rookie waved Billy Watts toward the door then loitered outside Rowley's cubicle. Kane turned to Daniels. "If you're not busy, grab a soda for Miss Woodward and I'll have a coffee, strong, sweet, with cream."

"Okay, boss." Daniels sauntered toward the kitchenette.

Kane cleared his throat to get Sarah's attention. "You must be close to your grandmother to travel so far to find her."

"I'm very close to her." Sarah took a deep breath. "My mom is sick and I need to find her."

"I may have a lead." Rowley raised his eyebrows, closed his phone, and sat down. "I spoke to the owner of the real estate office, John Davis, and he recalls a woman making inquiries some time ago. He offered to show her properties for sale in the area but recalled her asking for a list so she could do a drive-by. Mrs. Woodward said she'd return if something caught her interest and make an appointment for a viewing but she was a no-show."

"Did you ask him for a copy of the list of the properties he gave her?" Kane rubbed his chin. "It might be worthwhile retracing her steps and checking with the owners."

"Yeah, I asked but he said he'd need time to go through the listings for the last three months. He'll send a list as soon as possible, probably Monday as he is closing at noon to take a couple to look at some properties in town."

Kane waited for Daniels to deliver the drinks then turned to Sarah. "The moment I receive the list of properties, I'll go and speak to the owners. Someone must have spoken to your grand-mother. If you could read the rest of the letters and let me know if you find any clues, you can reach me on this number." He reached for his wallet, took out a card, and handed it to her. "Where are you staying?"

"The Black Rock Falls Motel." She grimaced. "It's pretty noisy since the hockey crowd came to town. It was party central there last night."

"They're a rough crowd out for a good time, and if they bother you, call nine-one-one or me. The Black Rock Falls County Sheriff's Department has a deputy on call twenty-four-seven." Kane stood and escorted her to the door.

"Thank you." Sarah gave him a small smile and stood. After throwing the strap of a bright pink purse over one shoulder, she headed toward an old blue sedan parked at the curb.

"If she needs someone to follow her home—" Daniels moved to his side and stared after her with a silly grin. "—I'd be happy to volunteer."

Kane turned and glared at the young man. "Does the term 'serve and protect' ring a bell with you? Keep away from her. That's an order."

"Aw, come on." Daniels grinned like a baboon. "Didn't you see the way she looked at me? Girls like her love men in uniform."

Oh, great, now we have a predator in the making.

NINE

Alarm gripped her and she stared out of the kitchen window in dismay as her vehicle disappeared into the distance. "Where are you taking my pickup?"

"I sent it away to be repaired." The insolent man in cowboy boots gave her a slow smile. "You won't be needing it."

The strange, cold look in his eyes sent shivers up her spine and she stepped away until her back hit the edge of the kitchen sink. "I didn't give you permission to touch my pickup."

"I don't *need* your permission."

The contemptuous way he looked at her, the curled lip, and self-assured posture made her skin crawl. Something was mentally wrong with him, as if he had two people inside him. This persona was not the nice man who'd encouraged her to move in and get a feel for the area. This was another brutal, savage personality she had no chance to reason with. Drink made him worse and the empty bourbon bottle and glass on the kitchen table frightened her. "You know darn well, I'm leaving in a few days. How do you expect me to leave without a vehicle?"

"Maybe I *want* you to stay?" Cowboy Boots moved a few

steps closer; his dark eyes raked over her, dead eyes without a shred of compassion. "The house is nice and clean and I like a home-cooked meal."

Terrified but determined to stand her ground, she folded her arms over her pounding chest to hide shaking hands. "I *said* I would stay for one month to get a feel for the area. I can't stay forever."

"You *will*, if I say so." He placed one muscular arm either side of her, resting his large hands on the counter. "Problem is, I need money to pay for the repairs to your vehicle. If you want it back, it's gonna cost you five hundred. If you give me your card I'll go into town and withdraw it for you."

His bourbon-smelling breath burned her nostrils, and, disgusted, she turned her face away. "Why don't you drive me into town when the repairs are finished and I'll pay the garage?"

Agony blinded her for a moment. She'd not seen his fist coming. Eyes watering, she stared at him in shock. The next blow sent a metallic taste over her tongue. She held up both hands to shield her face. "Stop it. Why are you doing this to me?"

"I *said*, give me your card and I'll go get the money from town." He grasped her neck in his grubby hand and squeezed. "Or are you deaf?"

Trembling with fear, she nodded in agreement. What other choice did she have? Miles from town without a vehicle, and at his mercy, she had to comply. Perhaps when he left, she could use the phone and call for help. "I'll get it for you."

When he followed her to her room and waited at the door, she couldn't think straight. Her head throbbed and she sat trembling on the bed.

"I'm waiting, or do you need more encouragement?" His mouth twitched into a cruel smile.

Eyes blurry, she stared at him. "Okay." She took her purse from the bedside table, took out a card, and gave it to him.

Unable to remember the PINs to her cards, she'd listed them in her address book.

"The PIN?" He glared at her and stepped closer. "Give me the number." He took a notepad out of his pocket.

When she fumbled the address book, he scooped it up and laughed. "You keep the number in here?" His cowboy hat dipped as he searched through the pages. "How many cards do you have?" He grabbed at her purse and emptied the contents on the bed. "Three?"

Ears ringing, she looked up at him. She couldn't believe he'd hit her. No one had ever struck her before. The room swam in and out of focus and she gripped the side of the bed, trying not to spew.

Pain shot through her as he struck her again. "Stop hitting me. You have what you want." She clutched her throbbing head. "I have three. Take them."

"I will." He headed for the kitchen.

Moments later, she heard his boots on the floor outside her bedroom. She glanced up through swollen lids to see him holding the telephone.

"You can try to run but you won't get far in this weather." He waved the phone at her. "This is coming with me. Have dinner ready when I return or I'll beat you senseless then lock you in the root cellar. It's cold down there and the rats will eat you alive. Your choice."

She heard him whistling and his footsteps echoing down the passageway followed by the roar of an engine as he started his vehicle. Hopelessness engulfed her. She'd do whatever he wanted to survive but he had to sleep sometime. Maybe she could steal his vehicle and make her escape. Who was she kidding? He was as cunning as a fox. *I'm trapped and he'll never let me go.* She lay down on the bed and pulled the blankets over her. Memories of her family drifted into her head and a comforting darkness surrounded her.

TEN

Kane glared at Daniels and forced his mind to concentrate on the job at hand. "The other missing person, John Helms. Have you run a check on his credit or debit card transactions and his phone?"

"Not yet, the man wasn't reported missing until Friday. I guess we can wait until Monday and see if he shows up and then get a warrant?"

"No need to wait." Kane rubbed his chin. "The sheriff informed me Helms went missing some time ago and his phone is not responding. We need to find out why and if he failed to make payments. Start organizing the necessary papers to obtain a warrant. I want a list of the calls he made in the last two weeks, then do the same to get his bank transactions."

"No worries, boss."

Kane returned to Rowley's desk and sat down beside him. Daniels' overfamiliar arrogance with Sarah Woodward disturbed him but he would soon bring him into line. He took a deep breath and reached for his coffee then blew across the steaming liquid, glad his head had stopped pounding. "When did you last hit the practice range?" He swallowed a mouthful of the rich brew and sighed.

"Sheriff Alton takes us down once a month, so two weeks ago. She is one tough lady and runs this place like boot camp." Rowley tapped away at his computer keyboard then lifted his gaze to him. "I've entered notes of Miss Woodward's interview into her file. If you don't need me for a while, I usually take the first lunch break."

"I'll come with you. Walters is still making a list of pickups in the area so I might as well take a break now too. We can take my truck, but before we eat I'd like to speak to the real estate agent before he leaves for the day." Kane drained the cup and stood. "So far, he is the last person to have contact with a missing person. Do you have a photograph of Mrs. Woodward on your phone?"

"Yeah, I do. We've been searching for her. I printed up some flyers. I've showed them to the local ranchers and posted them in the general store and post office without much luck." Rowley signed out of his computer and jumped enthusiastically to his feet. "What's your take on this case?"

Impressed by Rowley's down to earth character, Kane smiled. "Right now, we're assuming Mrs. Woodward spoke to the local real estate broker about properties. We'll need to interview everyone Woodward came into contact with before her disappearance." He grabbed his coat from a hook by the door then led the way outside to his vehicle. "I'm an observer of people's reactions, and showing the real estate guy a photograph of our missing person might trigger a repressed memory."

"And you'll pick up if he's hiding something." Rowley shrugged into his coat and followed. "Would you consider him a suspect, as he appears to be the last person to see Mrs. Woodward?"

"Maybe, but for now all we have is a missing person, not a victim of foul play." Kane shivered and pressed the button on his key fob to unlock the Beast. "Does it ever stop snowing here?"

"Not at this time of the year." Rowley nimbly sidestepped a couple of kids, rounded the hood, then slid onto the passenger seat. He fastened his seatbelt then pulled on his gloves. "The snow hangs around until April sometimes."

Kane recalled passing the real estate office on the way into Black Rock Falls. The snow had eased a little but the wipers labored under the drift on the windshield. He waited for a break in the traffic and headed downtown. His mind moved between the cases Jenna had outlined: two people missing without a trace was unusual in a small town. An attack on a sheriff even more bizarre. Spotting the real estate office on the left, picturesque with its roof heavy with snow and icicles hanging from tree branches, he pulled into the small parking lot outside. He stared at the frost-obscured photos of properties for sale and rent. *Who looks at properties in this kind of weather?* "Let me do the talking. You take notes as necessary and bring up the photograph on your phone."

"Sure. Can I ask a question?" Rowley turned in his seat then continued at Kane's nod. "How do you keep all the cases in your head? You seem to jump from one to another without so much as checking your notes."

Kane pulled his woolen cap over his ears. "I treat the cases like TV programs. I'm sure you watch many different series in one night and you remember what happened in the last episode, right? It's the same thing only these are real people, so instead of waiting until next week's thrilling episode, I need to know what's happened now."

"I think I'm going to need my notes; one mistake and the sheriff will have my badge." Rowley grimaced then took out his notepad and pen. "Ready?"

"Oh, yeah." Kane slid from the vehicle and an arctic blast hit his face. He walked around a woman carrying a kid with a dripping red nose and headed for the door. *I'm crazy to take this job. I don't need the money. I should buy a nice little house and stay home, reading a book, in front of a fire.*

The bell on the door clanged their arrival and Mr. Davis emerged from the back room holding a steaming cup.

"What can I do for you, Deputies?" His eyebrows rose in question and the hand placing the cup on the desk trembled a little.

Kane looked down at him and caught a whiff of brandy drifting from the beverage. "Mr. Davis? I'm Deputy Sheriff Kane. I'm aware you have an appointment soon but I need to ask you a few questions."

"Okay, the clients are due at noon, so I have a little time to spare." David dropped carefully into the office chair behind his desk as if in pain. "Please take a seat. Looking up at you makes my neck ache."

"Sure." Kane sat down on an exceedingly uncomfortable wooden chair, unearthing unpleasant memories of sitting in a principal's office. He pushed the image from his mind and gathered his thoughts. "I'm investigating the disappearance of Mrs. Samantha Woodward."

"I've told Deputy Rowley everything I recall about her and I haven't had time to go through my files for a list of the properties." Davis rolled his eyes to the ceiling as if seeking divine intervention. "It takes time and I'll get them to you as soon as possible."

"I understand and appreciate your help." Kane smiled in an effort to relax the man but from the beads of sweat forming on his brow, it hadn't worked. "I figured seeing a photo of Mrs. Woodward might jog your memory."

"Here, look at this image." Rowley held out his phone. "Do you remember meeting her?"

Davis leaned across the desk and squinted at the image, then flicked a concerned gaze in Kane's direction.

"I have a ton of people dropping by asking about properties." He slumped back in his chair and sighed. "I do remember one woman who mentioned selling her home and wanting to retire here. She wasn't looking for a big place, just something she and her family could manage alone."

Kane straightened. "That's a good start. Do you remember discussing any particular property with her?"

"Vaguely. We'd likely have discussed suitable properties and arranged an appointment for a viewing but I have no recollection of taking an elderly woman to view ranches." He drummed his fingers on the desk. "None at all."

"Did she mention anything about where she was staying?"

"I really don't remember." He spread his hands. "Really, Deputy, I can't tell you what I don't know." He ran a hand through his hair. "I feel like I'm being harassed. This is the second time you've spoken to me in less than an hour, and a young woman came by asking the same questions. She showed me her ID and insisted I tell her where I sent her grandmother. I'm giving you the same answer. The moment I find time to search the old listings, I'll send them to you, but right now I have to leave."

Looks like Miss Woodward is still doing a little investigating of her own. Kane pushed to his feet. "No harassment intended. You must appreciate we have to follow leads, and if you supply me with a list of the properties as soon as possible, we can do our job." He took a card from his wallet and placed it on the table. "Thank you for your time." He led the way out of the door with Rowley close behind.

"Now can we eat?" Rowley rubbed the end of his red nose.

Kane absently rubbed his stomach. "Oh, yeah."

Consumed by the sheer delight of Aunt Betty's chili, all thoughts of the Woodward case slid into oblivion. When

Rowley cleared his throat, Kane's brain snapped back into action. He pushed the empty plate away and reached for his coffee. "That has to be the best bowl of chili ever." He grinned at Rowley.

"I agree." Rowley appeared uncomfortable and moved the salt around the red and white checkered tablecloth like a chess piece. "Ah, the paperwork for a transaction check on Mrs. Woodward's credit cards hasn't been started yet. I don't have her phone number either." His cheeks flushed. "I thought you should know."

Kane's respect of Rowley multiplied tenfold. He appreciated professionalism and honesty. He leaned back in his chair and met his troubled gaze. "I spoke to the sheriff this morning about Mrs. Woodward. Her granddaughter insists she was old-school and didn't own a phone; she wrote letters. We know she banked money in town and picked up her mail." He sipped his coffee, eyeing the relief spreading across Rowley's expression. "She gives the impression of a woman who uses cash rather than a card, *but* as we know she has an account at the local bank, it would be prudent to file the paperwork for access to her records." He gave him a nod of approval. "I appreciate your honesty. Giving me this information means we cover every angle of Mrs. Woodward's case."

"Thank you, sir." Rowley let out a long sigh. "I'll get on it first thing Monday morning."

"No, I need this information now. Daniels should have the documents ready to file for the Helms case by the time we get back to the office. It won't take you long to do the same for Mrs. Woodward. We have probable cause for court orders and warrants for both cases. All I need is a judge. When we get back to the office, I'll sign the paperwork and you'll have to interrupt the local judge's weekend. I'll need permission to do a search ASAP." He finished his coffee and placed the cup on the table.

"I'll get on to it right away." Rowley frowned. "I can't

believe anyone would try to kill the sheriff. She is well respected in town."

"I'm very concerned about the sheriff's safety and if we're going to find the maniac that tried to kill her, I'll need everything you can remember about her cases over the last month or so." He noticed a flush spreading over Rowley's cheeks and smiled to reassure him. "Sometimes it's the little things, the word on the street and the attitude toward her. People hold grudges for stupid reasons and the accident could have been an opportunistic pay-back."

"There's been nothing apart from the arrest of Josh Rockford and Dan Beal. They resisted arrest and Rockford had a few words to say to the sheriff. He's a real jerk and when she rejected his womanizing, he started to push his status as the mayor's son." Rowley smiled. "The sheriff had him up against the cruiser and handcuffed before he knew what had hit him." He chuckled and his eyes sparkled. "When she patted him down, he made the usual smart remarks about giving her an excuse to touch him."

I can't wait to meet this guy. Kane raised a brow. "What did she do?"

"She threatened to call in a doctor to give him an internal examination, said he must be on drugs and carrying if he believed she was interested in him." Rowley's mouth spread into a wide grin and he refilled his coffee cup from the pot on the table. "If that happened, his teammates wouldn't let him live it down. He's the captain of the Larks hockey team and it's a respect issue. You should have seen the look he gave her— annoyed doesn't come close."

Motive enough to frighten her, if he wanted to put her in her place. "I see. I'm going to pull up all the information you have on Josh Rockford and Dan Beal. When the sheriff released them on Friday, did anything unusual happen? Words exchanged, or threats made?"

"Oh yeah, they were giving her the stink eye. She refused to release them before ten." Rowley dug a spoon into a plate of golden-crust apple pie *à la mode*. "They complained, saying they must be at the stadium by eight or their coach would skin them alive."

Kane shook his head. "I expect they had some explaining to do. In my day, arriving late would mean a season on the bench. It would seem being the mayor's son has benefits after all." He met Rowley's amused gaze. "The sheriff mentioned the home game is this weekend."

"Tonight." Rowley grinned. "I'm looking forward to going."

"Has anything else unusual happen of late? What about during the door-to-door you did for Mrs. Woodward?"

"Nothing came up during my investigations. You'll have to ask Daniels about the visits he made with the sheriff to the ranches last week." Rowley shrugged and glanced down, hiding his expression. "He hasn't mentioned anything unusual and he loves to gossip."

Susie, the waitress, came to the table with a paper sack and handed it to Kane.

"One slice of apple pie to go." She gave him a long look, as if trying to gain his interest. "Is there *anything* else I can do for *you*, Deputy Kane?"

He dropped the bag on the table and smiled. "No, thank you. I'd like to stay and try every item on the menu but we have to get back to the office."

"Well then, enjoy the pie." She turned and walked away.

The corner of Rowley's mouth twitched.

"I guess she's looking for a date for the dance tonight." He grinned. "She's sure taken a shine to you, sir."

Note to self. Don't ever come here alone. Kane stood, dropped bills on the table, and grabbed the pie. "Not one chance in hell." He could see Susie out of the corner of his eye, twisting a lock of hair around one finger. *You are way too young for me.*

Rowley gave him an appraising stare. "Don't you like girls?"

Kane shook his head. "Nope. At the grand old age of thirty-five, I prefer *women* over twenty-one." He strode toward the door, keeping his gaze anywhere but in Susie's direction.

ELEVEN

Jenna threw more logs on the fire and stared at the sparks rising in the funnel of smoke and disappearing up the chimney. The recent call from Deputy Walters had her head spinning. Her new deputy sheriff had taken over the moment she'd left and had her deputies working flat-out all day. In two minds about the idea of having a powerful deputy in charge in her absence, she considered the pros and cons. Having a deputy sheriff with considerable experience would mean the workload would lessen, but she would need to make it clear who was in charge. Countermanding her orders without consultation would be something she'd have to speak to him about, and soon. Kane had canceled the twice-daily patrols she'd scheduled during the Larks home-game weekends to ensure the visitors pouring into town noticed a strong sheriff's department presence. The hockey game came with a bunch of out-of-town troublemakers attending the match and her office was understaffed. Her deputies would have to pull double shifts tonight, although it did not take any persuasion to ask Rowley and Daniels to watch the game in uniform.

The after-match dance organized by the mayor at the town

hall went off without a hitch most times with Deputy Walters stationed on the door. Her problem would be the men crowding into the Cattleman's Hotel to drink after the game. Around closing time, she'd need to count on Rowley to help her keep order because inebriated men often refused to take direction from the fresh-faced Daniels.

She dashed a hand through her hair and her mind slid to Kane. *He would have my back, I'm sure of it.* His solid presence by her side would make an impression on the crowd but how could she ask him to assist her? He'd be exhausted after pulling a long shift with little or no sleep. She chewed on what was left of her fingernails, forcing her mind out of panic mode and into a modicum of order. The attempt on her life had unnerved her, and going back out there was wreaking havoc with her nerves.

If one of Viktor Carlos' men found her out on the street, she might as well paint a target on her back. She doubted the locals would lift a finger to help her, not after the previous home-game debacle. After making a point of using diplomacy in disputes, she'd pulled her weapon to keep control during an argument between two rival crowds of supporters in the Cattleman's Hotel parking lot. In the end, Rowley and Daniels had pulled their nightsticks to gain control. The move caused an outcry of police brutality. *It's not as if I discharged my gun.*

The buzz of the alarm on the front entrance broke into her thoughts. She moved down the hallway and peered at the bank of screens in her office. The sight of a black truck with tinted windows had her reaching in the desk drawer for her backup weapon. The vehicle moved toward the house then veered off and slid into Kane's garage. *I'm an idiot. I should have recognized his truck.* She pressed one hand to her pounding heart and caught sight of her reflection in one of the blank flat-screens. Special Agent Avril Parker no longer existed, and in her place stood a younger, more vibrant person.

She'd worked hard to perfect her new body. Six months of

grueling exercises to change her body shape. After reconstruc-
tive surgery, her new face had a straight nose and fuller lips, and
the fine wrinkles she hated had disappeared. The cosmetic
surgeon had insisted on the addition of fake breasts and had
somehow made her eyes appear wider. She wore a new hairstyle
and now her own mother wouldn't recognize her. She'd turned
thirty on her last birthday but the face looking back at her
appeared five years younger. Her commander's voice drifted
through her mind.

*You'll be safe. A new identity, a new face, and hiding in
plain sight works. Don't worry. Enjoy your life.*

Don't worry. What a load of horseshit, as if she could trust
every man in her department. No matter how high up, people
had their price. Her attention moved back to the screens to see
David Kane trudging through the snow toward her house. She
slipped the gun back into the desk drawer and moved down the
hallway to greet him at the front door.

"Hey."

He kicked the snow from his size fourteen boots and lifted
his gaze to her. "Mind if I come in? I have a few things to
discuss with you about the current caseload."

Jenna tried to stop the frown without success. "I hold a
meeting every morning to keep my officers informed and delegate tasks."

"I'm sure you do, but as I took charge of the office today, at
the moment you're out of the loop." Kane stared at her expressionless. "I've made significant progress today."

I somehow knew you would. She stepped to one side. "Of
course. Come in. How was your first day?"

"Fine." He raised an eyebrow and shrugged. "I've never
have a problem fitting in. I moved around during my career."

Jenna strolled down the hallway into the kitchen. "You
came at a good time. I have cookies fresh from the oven, and

coffee." She turned at the door and took in his bemused expression.

You're professional all the way. I'd bet you've been on the job for so long, you find any form of nicety suspicious. She'd not had a real partner for years and craved the company of intelligent conversation. The kind where she could speak her mind, talk shop, and not feel like a Mother Superior. Backpedaling, she chuckled. "Don't tell the other deputies. They don't know I have a feminine side."

"They wouldn't believe me." Kane's mouth quirked up into a genuine smile. "You should show people this side of you more often." He wiped his feet on the mat and reached for the zipper on his jacket. "This will take a while, and coffee and cookies sound like heaven, thanks." He turned and hung his coat on a peg in the mudroom.

TWELVE

Kane gave Jenna a rundown of the day's developments then sat back in his chair and sipped a steaming cup of coffee, waiting for her response. The bruise on her forehead had a dark blue hue and the shadows under her eyes worried him. Even though he'd known her for less than twenty-four hours, he respected her grit.

He glanced around the deliciously warm kitchen and inhaled the aroma of freshly baked cookies. *She acts like military. Everything in its place and spotless.* He tasted a cookie and flavor exploded in his mouth. With a sigh, he closed his eyes in bliss and heard her chuckle.

"So, you are human." Jenna pushed fingers through her tousled hair. "You work like a machine. Do you ever get tired?"

A memory stirred of his wife saying the same thing and Kane's heart twisted. He opened his eyes and frowned. "I do what's necessary to get the job done."

"Okay, if you want to talk shop, we'll talk." Jenna viewed him over the rim of her cup. "What makes you think the real estate agent has anything to do with Mrs. Woodward's disappearance?"

Kane shrugged. "Nothing yet but I have a niggling feeling he's not telling us everything he knows." His phone chimed and he held up one finger. "This will be the files I've been waiting on from Deputy Walters."

A few moments later, they scrolled through Mrs. Woodward's debit card statements for the previous three months. She'd made substantial withdrawals recently. He glanced at Jenna. "From the debit card withdrawals, she's moving around. The last time she used her card was a few days ago at the 7-Eleven out of Blackwater. It appears she's left Black Rock Falls."

"Yeah, but she must have made a purchase in the last two weeks, and from the statement she hasn't spent a cent. All the withdrawals are at ATMs, and going on the previous months, this isn't her usual behavior." Jenna's forehead creased into a frown. "This looks suspicious. From what Sarah told me, before she arrived in Black Rock Falls, she'd mentioned all the towns she visited on the way. Why would she stop using her card in stores and gas stations now? It doesn't make sense."

Allowing the case to percolate through his mind, Kane thought for a beat. "Maybe, she experienced a health issue." Kane shrugged. "It happens. People suffer from dementia or Alzheimer's and wander off without a trace."

"I'd imagine people suffering from either of those illnesses would forget their PIN. It's a steady decline not a sudden onset, and the family would have noticed something was wrong with her." Jenna's eyebrows rose in question. "Sarah said she was very careful with money, so why the sudden change?"

Kane sipped his coffee and placed the cup back down on the table. "That's a valid point, and this morning Sarah told me she'd received a batch of her grandmother's letters via her mother, so perhaps she'll find a reason for the change of behavior in one of them." He leaned back in his chair. "If not, from the evidence, Mrs. Woodward has left our county, and it's time to hand this investigation to the Blackwater Sheriff's Department."

"I'll contact them on Monday." Jenna waved at the screen. "Anything else you need to see? The other file looks like bank statements from a different account."

"Might as well." Kane scrolled down the page and blinked. "Hello, what do we have here? Woodward withdrew a cashier's check for twenty thousand, and from the date, it's not long after her visit to the real estate office. John Davis sent her out to do a drive-by viewing of properties in the area. He hasn't mentioned receiving any offers from Woodward." He rubbed his chin. "Although, Sarah did mention her grandmother planned to purchase a property; perhaps she found a place she liked and drew the check to put down a deposit?"

"Then we'll need to contact the bank and see if the check has been cashed—" Jenna drummed her fingers on the table "—or if someone local has deposited it into their account."

Kane rubbed the heels of his hands into his eyes and bit back a yawn. "I'll get Walters to follow that up on Monday."

"I want you to call Mr. Davis again to remind him about the list of properties he gave Mrs. Woodward." Jenna worried her bottom lip, turning it red, and met his gaze. "Some of the abandoned ranches for sale are in remote areas; anything could have happened to her."

Kane picked up another cookie from the plate and shrugged. "She can't be in two places at the same time, can she? We know from her debit card statement she was miles away *after* her visit to Davis' real estate office."

"True, but maybe she visited real estate offices in other towns and then returned to Black Rock Falls. This is the point, we don't know her movements, and without a phone, it will be impossible to trace her." Jenna rubbed her temples as if warding off a headache. "I think we should lean on Davis."

Liking her ideas, Kane nodded. "I agree. We'll talk to him

again but if the check hasn't been cashed by him, there's no evidence that points to him as a suspect." He nibbled the crumbly delight and sighed. "I'll contact the sheriff's office in Blackwater and ask them to put a be-on-the-look-out call out on her, and I'll call the real estate offices just in case she dropped by. I guess Sarah will have to submit a missing persons' report there as well." Yawning, he shook off the dragging fatigue and peered at her. "I should go. Can we pick this up later?"

"Sure but before you leave—" Jenna placed a hand on his arm. "—did Walters get a list of the other Ford pickups in town? I have the ones Rowley hunted down."

"Not yet but he'll send what he has before he goes home." Kane turned in his chair to face her. "I need a list of suspects ASAP. I'm flying blind here. Can you make a list of anyone you've had problems with no matter how trivial? I'll crossmatch them to the vehicles on the list?" He rubbed the back of his neck. "I'd like to go over your movements for the last six weeks. When you did the house-to-house—or should I say ranch-to-ranch—looking for information on Woodward. Could you have stumbled into an illegal activity?"

"I don't recall anything unusual unless there's a statute against horse breeding. I seem to make a habit of showing up during mating season or foaling." Her cheeks pinked. "I might live here but I'm not a country girl. I couldn't kill a chicken to save my life."

Chuckling, Kane wiggled his brows. "I wondered why you had no livestock and no dog either. Do you have a problem with animals?"

"I'd probably forget to feed a dog." Jenna lifted her chin and her expression turned serious. He'd stepped on a nerve. "Getting back to business. I hope you've sent someone out on patrol this afternoon. I like to give visitors the impression we're around during the home games."

Kane nodded. " I sure did. I sent Rowley to patrol the area

in his cruiser before heading home. I'll need to grab a meal and get some rest before my next shift."

"I don't expect you to pull another shift. Consider yourself off-duty."

"Thanks, but I'm fine." Kane emptied his cup, placed it on the table, and stood. "What time?"

"The game starts at seven and Rowley and Daniels get to the stadium at six thirty." She smiled and her gaze moved over his face. "Our shift starts around ten."

"Okay, I'll pick you up at nine-thirty." He strolled for the door, grabbing his coat along the way.

The freezing chill slapped his face and seeped into his clothes. The last fall of snow had frozen like the icing on a wedding cake and he crunched his way back to the cottage, huffing out great clouds of steam. He didn't like leaving loose ends, and so far the cases in Black Rock Falls had more frayed edges than his favorite pair of jeans.

THIRTEEN

Kane set his mental alarm for three hours. The training received during his varied career gave him the capability to sleep anywhere at any time. Although, since the surgeon installed the plate in his head, the pain he endured was unbearable at times, and the nightmares—long, drawn-out horror stories—were par for the course, but now, for some reason, he couldn't get the image of Jenna pointing the gun in his face out of his mind.

Her kill-or-be-killed expression haunted his dreams. She had been calm; too calm for a normal person following a near-death experience. The overkill of surveillance and security on the property could mean only one thing. Someone had threatened her or she had something to hide. He considered witness protection but the United States Marshals Service wouldn't allow her to become a public figure. To get the treatment he'd received—a new face and a new life with an unquestionable background—was a luxury only granted to a few. *Who are you, Jenna?*

. . .

At nine-thirty on the dot, Kane pulled the Beast outside Jenna's door and sounded the horn. The floodlight over the steps spilled across the driveway and illuminated the steam curling from the engine. Although Jenna had tried to dismiss his worries, he refused to ignore the attempt on her life. If he could gain her confidence, she might open up to him but he doubted it. Her expression told him she wore a shield around her of pure titanium. He drummed his fingers on the steering wheel and stared at the front door. *She doesn't trust me yet but she will.*

The door opened and Jenna appeared and then turned to set the alarm. After pulling the hood over her head, she closed the door behind her, gripped the handrail, and trod with care down the snow-covered steps. She rounded the hood and climbed in beside him with agility, bringing with her a gust of freezing air.

He turned to her. "Where to?"

"The Cattleman's Hotel." Jenna's hood obscured her face as she buckled up and leaned back in the seat. "The hockey crowd drifts out around ten. Rowley and Daniels have parked the cruisers out front and will arrive soon." She smiled. "At least it appears we've been there all evening."

Kane pulled into the space beside two cruisers in the "Reserved for Black Rock Falls County Sheriff's Department" slot and, leaving the engine running, turned to her. The accident remained fixed in his mind. "Do you pin the week's duty roster on a noticeboard or is it by word of mouth or email?"

"It's on the noticeboard beside the kitchenette. Why?"

He rubbed his chin. "So it's accessible to the general public?"

"It could be. Where are you going with this?" Jenna gave him one of her long stares, as if trying to read his mind.

He shrugged, acting as nonchalant as possible. "I believe the driver of the Ford pickup planned your accident and knew you'd be alone on Friday night. Who apart from the deputies could have read the duty roster?"

A flash of apprehension crossed her face but she smothered it with an obviously practiced smile.

"No one is trying to murder me." She chuckled and waved a hand dismissively. "I wrote up the weekend roster for the home game on Thursday. Everyone in town knows I only work on weekends during a home game."

He examined her face, trying to read her, but she was a consummate professional at hiding her emotions. "So you don't post a duty roster for after-hours call-outs during the week?"

"It's not necessary; we alternate. This week it was Rowley and me, next week it's Daniels and Walters." She let out a long sigh. "This week, I removed Rowley from Friday night and posted it on the board. I guess anyone going to the cells or bathroom could see the list—if they could decipher my writing in a couple of seconds. I think one of us would notice if someone stopped to read the noticeboard."

Mind working overtime, Kane stared at her in disbelief. "The bathroom is used by the public, and anyone passing by would be able to read a roster; it only takes seconds." He shrugged. "Why did you remove Rowley from Friday night?"

"He needed some personal time." Jenna dropped her gaze. "His cousin is in town for the game and he wanted to meet up with him."

Kane snorted. "How convenient." *I'll add him to my list of suspects.*

With a snort of disgust, Jenna rounded on him, her eyes flashing with anger.

"Don't you dare say another word about him." She glared at him. "Jake Rowley is the most professional deputy I've had the pleasure of working with since arriving in Black Rock Falls."

Holding up both hands in surrender, Kane met her angry

gaze. "Okay fine, so he's untouchable." He narrowed his gaze on her. "So where else have you worked? The last place must have been a nightmare."

"That's none of your business, but as a professional courtesy, I'll tell you. I came to Black Rock Falls after a stint as a detective in Los Angeles." Jenna flicked him a glance with zero emotion. "I wanted to get away from the city. I'm a small-town girl at heart and the city is like a pressure cooker—something is always getting ready to explode."

Kane stared out the window. "Crime is like water—it levels out no matter where you live." He kept his gaze on the road. "Don't tell me Black Rock Falls is any different. From the court records I scrolled through earlier, you've been busy."

"Yeah, but all were petty crimes, nothing comes close to the murders, drug busts and drive-by shootings I've dealt with in the past." She sighed. "Here, DUIs plus the odd domestic disturbance take up most of our time. We have increased crime rates during the influx of visitors into Black Rock Falls, and trouble follows the rodeo circuit like flies on horse dung. The cowboys come through town like a cattle stampede and the young women flock to them."

Kane chuckled. "Oh yeah, girls love rodeo cowboys. I'm guessing the guys on the circuit clash with the local boys?"

"Every time. Although we have a few locals on the circuit, most from the outlying ranches. There's a ton of whooping and hollering when they arrive home." Jenna waved a hand toward the Cattleman's Hotel. "The bar is already packed."

Kane scanned the area, taking in the overflowing patrons. "Where are the other deputies?"

"Walters will be at the dance." She took a pair of gloves from her pocket and pulled them on. "Rowley and Daniels are at the stadium. After they drop the cruisers here, Rowley's father takes them to the game." She pulled out her phone and glanced at the screen. "They'll be dropped by in a few minutes."

Not wanting to take charge, Kane and waited for instructions. He'd have to bite his tongue if he wanted to fit in, and after commanding special agents, coping with Jenna would be a challenge.

FOURTEEN

The ruckus inside the bar had spilled out onto the footpath. As the men staggered away in small groups, Kane hoped walking into the Cattleman's Hotel and making his presence known would avoid potential trouble. Waiting in the truck was a waste of time. He swallowed his frustration and cleared his throat. "Does the department have a drunk bus?"

"No." Jenna shot him a look to freeze Niagara Falls. "It's not necessary and who would drive it?"

"So what happens if twenty or so drunks get behind the wheel? There are only three cruisers available and my vehicle isn't equipped to transport prisoners." Not wanting to rile her, he softened his voice. "Perhaps if we went inside now, they might think twice before attempting to drive. Does Black Rock Falls have a designated driver program?"

"No to the last question, and yes, but I usually go inside when the deputies arrive. I agree, seeing us is a good incentive to avoid driving under the influence but I'm only one person." Her lips thinned in annoyance. "The sheriff's department presence does work. Many stay here overnight or at the motel, and they can walk from here." She waved a hand toward a line of cabs. "They often share a cab, not that the four cabs operating in town are enough, but some people are prepared to wait."

"Okay." Kane thought for a beat. "I'm here now, so if you want to go inside, you don't need to wait for the others." He killed the engine and unclipped the seatbelt. "Do you want me to contact Rowley for their ETA?"

"No. I'll manage." She gave him a cold stare, reached for the radio attached to her belt, and made the call.

The reply came through loud and clear to inform her the deputies had left the stadium. Kane couldn't imagine why she'd risk using the radio after an attempt was made on her life. A police scanner could pick up the signal and pinpoint her position. She'd made a potentially fatal error. He slid from the seat and shut the door behind him. Wondering how to introduce the subject of her security, he leaned on the hood of the Beast and waited for her to come around to meet him.

It was bitterly cold and freezing air sent a bolt of pain into his temple in a constant reminder of the lunatic who had murdered his wife. He pulled the woolen cap over his ears and noticed Jenna regarding him with a compassionate stare. Straightening, he tapped the Black Rock Falls Sheriff's Department logo he'd sewn onto the front. "I know my hat isn't the official uniform and the badge is from one of my shirts, but I need to keep my head warm and my Stetson just doesn't work."

"Not a problem. We'll make it official. Many of the other counties supply them for their officers." Jenna gave him a curt nod. "I think we could all do with one of those hats in this weather. I have a drawer filled with official cloth badges in the office and the hats aren't expensive."

Steam came out in a cloud as Kane sighed. "Thanks."

"Okay, what's wrong? Spit it out, I know you have something on your mind." Jenna moved around to face him, her eyes flashing. "Tell me."

Kane gestured toward the device on her belt. "The radio.

Anyone on the frequency can listen in. Every time you use that thing, you're giving out your position. It would be better to use your phone. It's more secure. Have you considered speaking to the mayor about earbuds and power packs? I have a friend in DC who can do me a great deal." When she lifted her chin in annoyance, he shrugged. " Maybe consider using your phone until we catch the person who tried to kill you."

"I think the person who caused the accident was a coward who gets his kicks preying on women alone at night." Jenna's head turned toward a noisy group of people leaving the hotel. When they walked down Main and headed in the direction of the motel, she turned her attention back to him. "He wouldn't have the guts to try anything with you here."

I can't stop a bullet from a sniper. "Okay." Kane conceded defeat and rubbed his cold hands together. "So what's the usual procedure? I can't imagine the management appreciates the sheriff's department interfering with their business."

"We usually hang around the foyer." Jenna headed nimbly up the steps toward the entrance to the Cattleman's Hotel. "They employ two security guards but they patrol the bar area." She opened the door and strolled inside. "At least it's warmer in here." She unzipped her jacket then removed her gloves and rubbed her hands together.

Kane followed and scanned the area for potential threats and noticed Jenna mirroring his moves. She stood with her back to the wall. The position gave her a clear view of the parking lot and foyer. He took a spot on the opposite wall and moved his attention to the reception area. Placed behind a set of glass doors, the long service desk sat in front of an impressive mural of a Wild West cattle stampede. Bulls with flaring nostrils charged across a prairie in a cloud of dust while cowboys riding hell for leather galloped behind with six shooters raised. He had an appreciation of art. In fact, he had left an impressive collection of pictures and bronzes in storage after his wife's death.

Pushing down the urge to open the doors and move closer to inspect the exquisite artwork, he shifted his gaze to the patrons moving around inside the building.

Two receptionists served a line of guests. An attractive young woman and an older man with graying hair wearing tailored black jackets stood behind the polished oak counter displaying practiced smiles of tolerance. *Hmm, high class for such a small town.* The place spelled *Money* with a capital *M*. Polished, wooden floors shone throughout, and for a small town the Cattleman's Hotel surprised him with its opulence. Signs directed customers to the bar and restaurant on opposite sides of the foyer.

He dragged his gaze away and looked at Jenna. "This place is a surprise. High class and not what I would expect in a small town."

"Yeah, it's owned by a very wealthy family." Jenna leaned against the wall and yawned. "They have a private gaming club in the back and the place is popular." She shrugged. "They stick to the rules and are rarely a problem."

Kane leaned against the wall. "Are there many wealthy ranchers in the area?"

"Yeah, a ton of big cattle ranchers, and then there are the professionals, teachers, and of course the medical profession. They all avoid town and live opposite Stanton Forest." Jenna's lips twitched up into a smile. "We have a hospital and the college campus on the other side of town."

Surprised, Kane rose both eyebrows. What he'd researched hadn't come close to the real thing. "I had no idea Black Rock Falls is spread over such a large area."

"Yes, well it is a county, and with four deputies and me to watch over the entire place you'll find the job is harder than you think." Jenna's stare moved over him. "I figure you need to keep busy. You act to me like you're a man who doesn't like sitting around doing nothing all day."

He straightened and rested his hand on the butt of his pistol. After ten years in the secret service, it would take time to get used to wearing a weapon on his hip rather than a service pistol nestled in a shoulder holster. Jenna's words percolated through his brain. Black Rock Falls had a ton of rich people ripe for fleecing, and as the gaming world was a nest for corruption, it would make sense for underworld criminal syndicates to negotiate a deal with a local authority figure. Refusal could lead to "accidents". He cleared his throat. "Have you had any dealings with the proprietors of late?" He leveled his gaze on her, gauging her reaction. Man, the way she instantly blanked her expression, she'd survive waterboarding without giving up information.

FIFTEEN

Jenna had observed Kane's movements from the moment he entered the hotel. *He is making a list of suspects. Like a dog after a bone.* "Yeah." A vehicle engine rumbled outside and glanced through the glass door. "Here comes the cavalry. Rowley and Daniels will take one of the cruisers and park it at the rear entrance. There's a walkway to the parking lot from there, so they can keep an eye on anyone trying to sneak out."

"Good idea." Kane's head moved toward the two men huddled in conversation beside the elevators. Every so often, they would glance at him as if evaluating him. He tipped his chin toward them. "The two men you had in the lock-up Thursday night are acting suspicious. What do you figure Josh Rockford and Dan Beal are planning?"

"I'd say Rockford is trying to get to his vehicle without being caught." She frowned. "His team won tonight, so he'll be strutting for the next few days."

"Maybe I'll find a reason to impound his truck." Kane narrowed his gaze and appeared to grow taller. "I've seen too many young guys like him killed in wrecks. They think they're invincible."

"No need to impound his vehicle." She headed through the glass doors into the hotel. "I usually put him in a cab. He likes to be the center of attention, so ignoring him is the best put down."

Jenna walked to the two men with Kane at her side. When Josh Rockford gave her an arrogant smile, Kane straightened and glared down at him. Rockford was either too drunk or stupid to recognize the threat Kane posed and dismissed him with a wave of his hand.

"Do you have a room here tonight or is the mayor giving you a ride home?" Jenna addressed Rockford in a tone of authority then turned to Dan Beal. "And what about you, Mr. Beal?"

"We're not staying and we do need to get home." Dan Beal gave Jenna a salacious wink. "Josh here thought *you* might like to give us a ride in your cruiser?"

"Yeah." Josh Rockford bent to whisper in Jenna's ear but his gaze remained fixed on Kane. "But leave the gorilla behind."

Jenna ignored him but the next moment, Kane stepped forward, placing his body between Rockford and her. "You've had too much to drink. Hand over your vehicle keys. You'll be taking a cab home tonight." He held out his hand. "Now! Unless you would like to spend another night in the lock-up? I'm giving you a warning. Next time I find you drunk and disorderly in public, you'll be my guest in the lock-up."

"You need to control that jealous streak, man. Moving into Jenna's cabin doesn't make you her keeper." Rockford grinned at him. "The sheriff likes me fine, don't you, darlin'?"

"I don't see her jumping into your arms. Maybe she prefers someone a little more mature." Kane's expression had turned to stone. "Give me your keys." He held out one hand.

"My father *owns* you." Rockford sniggered. "He'll have your badge if you charge me."

"Do I look like I care?" Kane dropped his voice to just above a whisper. "Trust me, you don't want to be locked up overnight on my watch. Now hand over your keys or I'll tip you upside down and shake them loose."

The look of pure hatred Rockford gave Kane made the hairs on the back of Jenna's neck stand to attention. The spoiled brat had moved to the top of her list of suspects. She waited for Kane to collect the keys and escort the men to one of the waiting cabs. How they had managed to become intoxicated in a relatively short time intrigued her. Binge drinkers didn't usually captain winning teams, although add Josh's daddy's influence into the equation and anything was possible.

She waited inside as Kane watched the taillights of the cab disappear into the darkness and then returned to the hotel, weaving between the patrons heading home. Some singing the team song, couples held hands. Overall, the people of Black Rock Falls behaved better than expected.

"You shouldn't have to put up with idiots like those two." Kane brushed snow from his jacket and frowned at her.

"I can handle Rockford." Jenna smiled at him. "Although, I have to admit it was nice having someone on my side for a change."

"I'm just concerned for your welfare." Kane sighed as if needing to make his point. "Someone tried to kill you and if you're not being threatened then something else is going on." He shrugged. "Two people are missing without a trace and my instinct tells me there's a connection. Indulge me by running through your movements over the last couple of weeks."

Jenna gaped at him and tried to remember pertinent details of the last two weeks. What did her accident have to do with a missing grandmother? Inquiries on the other man, John Helms, had been superficial at best, and her deputies would be working on his case the following week. Worried there might be a link to the disappearances, she chewed on her bottom lip in an effort to make sense of Kane's reasoning. A flood of customers drifted out of the restaurant and she spotted Mayor Rockford and his wife coming toward the foyer. She nodded at the couple and the mayor paused to speak to her.

"I gather Duke Walters is keeping the peace over at the dance again this evening?" Mayor Rockford smiled indulgently.

Jenna returned his smile. "Yes, he is. I prefer to keep him out of the cold if possible."

"Yes, yes, he is forever singing your praises for being considerate." Rockford pulled his wife's hand into the crook of his arm and patted her fingers. "Well, I better get my lady out of the cold too. Goodnight, Sheriff."

"Goodnight."

Jenna waited for them to leave then pushed away from the wall to move closer to Kane to avoid anyone overhearing her. "I've told you everything that happened but I'll indulge you again. Sarah Woodward came by and made a missing persons' report about her grandmother. I sent the deputies out to the local guesthouses, banks, and post office to make general inquiries. When we couldn't locate her, we took her photo around to some of the ranches in the immediate area as well, just in case she'd decided to use an alias."

"I gather you all went to different ranches?" Kane flicked a glance over her shoulder at the parking lot, then moved his attention back to her. "Which ranches did you visit?"

"The ones on my side of town. We did a door-to-door and covered all of them. Many of the ranchers I know personally, including Parker Lom, the Daniels, and old Zack Smith. His place is way out in the hills and he hasn't had anyone dropping by his place for years." She had the odd feeling he was interrogating her, and her guard went up. "I had a coffee with Parker, and Zack took me out to show me the new bull he purchased. Everyone I met was friendly and I wasn't threatened."

"Daniels as in Pete Daniels' family? The two guys you mentioned at Aunt Betty's?"

"That's right, Pete's brothers. They own the ranch." She

shrugged. "Pete isn't into raising cattle or horses and has a place in town but spends the odd weekends helping out at the ranch."

"So why go out there? Deputy Daniels would have recognized Mrs. Woodward if she'd been working for him."

"Pete was with me when we went by to ask his brothers if Mrs. Woodward had asked them for work. Like I said, Pete lives in town, he rarely visits his brothers. They're not close." Trying to keep her voice steady, she took a casual stance. "They were no different to the other ranchers I visited and acted as laid-back as usual."

"Okay, Rowley mentioned Rockford caused a problem at the office before you released him." Kane looked interested. "Tell me what happened. Right from the arrest."

"Rowley got a call around nine from the manager about a fight in the card room. I met Rowley here and we dealt with the problem. Three men under the influence and causing trouble. Those three spend more time in the lock-up than most of the troublemakers in town. I separated them and kept them in custody overnight after Josh Rockford accused Billy Watts of stealing. Rockford tried to throw his weight around, threatened to call his father and have me fired. He does the same song and dance routine every time I arrest him. He might be a loudmouth but I don't believe he's a threat. I doubt he has the guts to throw a punch and is more likely to run to daddy to complain." She sucked in a deep breath and let it out with a sigh sending a cloud of steam into the crisp night air. "I've run every scenario through my mind and come up with zip. I've dealt with everyone fairly and the attempted murder theory you have makes no sense at all."

"I don't agree. From what I saw, and the facts from the accident scene, it was a deliberate attempt on your life. I intend to find the culprit and discover the motive." Kane lifted his chin toward a group of men heading out of the bar. "Heads up."

The patrons of the Cattleman's Bar gave them little trouble.

The five or so intoxicated men strolled by, climbed into the cabs, and vanished into the night. They waited for everyone to leave the building or take the elevators upstairs to their rooms before heading out into the crisp, dark night.

Jenna turned to Kane. "I'm going inside to use the bathroom, then I'll head out the back door and come back around the front to check for any stragglers."

"Rowley and Daniels should be covering that area." Kane's lips formed a thin line.

She patted him on the arm. "Stop being so overprotective. I'm a big girl and I can pee on my own."

SIXTEEN

After using the restroom, she moved through the deserted foyer and headed out of the back door. The icy chill sent shivers down her spine as she followed the gravel pathway winding through ornamental shrubbery, heavy under a blanket of snow. Turning a corner into shadows, she glanced up but the area was so dark she had difficulty making out the light posts usually illuminating the area. She made a mental note to report the problem to the manager and reached for the flashlight on her belt. Finding the space empty, she cursed under her breath. She must have lost it during the accident and somehow failed to notice it missing. *The accident has shaken me more than I realized.*

Ahead, the snow-dusted pathway seemed to glow in the dark, and the well-lit parking lot would only be a few minutes away. As she turned another corner, the *crunch, crunch, crunch* of footsteps came close behind her. Moving into the trees, she waited for the person to emerge from the shadows. "Rowley, is that you?"

The footsteps stopped and no reply came out of the night.

Heart thundering in her chest, she lifted her jacket and rested one hand on the butt of her Glock. Snowflakes fell over her face tickling like butterflies' wings, but apart from voices in the distance, not a sound came from the pathway. Drawing a deep breath, she edged her way along the path in the direction of the parking lot. Her pulse throbbed in her ears and her footsteps sounded loud in the still night. Maybe she'd been mistaken.

Keeping her hand firmly on her weapon, she moved along the path. The garden appeared sinister at night and snow-piled bushes stood out dark and menacing like gargoyles waiting to pounce. Darkness greeted her around each bend and the winding trail seemed endless. Fear had her by the throat and the sheer stupidity of being scared of the dark alarmed her.

Convinced she had allowed her imagination to get the best of her, she turned the next corner and marched toward the parking lot. The end of the pathway could not be much further away and both Daniels and Rowley would be close.

Crunch, crunch, crunch.

Terrified, she spun around to face the danger but only darkness stretched out before her. She turned again and edged her way further along the trail.

Crunch, crunch, crunch.

Sliding the Glock from the holster, she peered into the darkness but only shadows moved across the snow-covered pathway as the trees moved in the small breeze. "Is somebody there? This is Sheriff Alton. Come out and show yourself. I'm armed."

Panting out huge puffs of steam, she strained her ears. A sound came from behind her.

Crunch, crunch, crunch.

Oh God, he's behind me. A sinister chuckle came from the dark void somewhere to her left. She lifted her weapon. A sharp blow to her wrist knocked the pistol from her hand and it slid into the bushes. A dark, smelly bag dropped over her head. Blind and weaponless, she staggered forward, and before she had time to react, a large hand covered her mouth, pressing the foul fabric against her lips and ground it cruelly into her teeth.

A muscular arm locked around her chest, pinning her arms to her sides. A thick leg slid between her thighs, lifting her onto her toes. Immobilized, she couldn't move or scream. None of her expert training would get her out of his grip. A deep, whispering voice came close to her ear, sending ice-cold fear marching up her spine.

"I have a knife. A *very* sharp knife and I'd be happy to see you bleed. Scream or call for help, and I'll cut your throat." His grip tightened around her chest, making it hard to breathe. "Nod your head once if you want to be a good little sheriff."

Bile rushed up the back of her throat and she nodded her head in agreement. The hood moved and the cold tip of a sharp blade pressed against her throat.

"See how easily I could kill you? But that would be no fun, would it?" The man's voice, raspy and obviously disguised, vibrated against her cheek. He laughed again. "Call off the big dog and I might allow you to live a little longer."

She pushed back into his chest, trying to gauge his size, and inhaled but the foul-smelling hood masked the man's smell. "I don't know what you mean."

"Things were going nice and smooth and you had to bring in a big-city cop." The knife pricked her throat, and rather than stiffen to make the cutting easier, she relaxed against him. "Keep your mouth shut and your dog on a leash or I'll show you exactly what I'm capable of doing."

Panic bubbled up in a gasp of terror but before she could reply, he cuffed her around the head and shoved her hard into the bushes. She fell to her knees, tangled in the dense brush. Disorientated, she dragged off the hood and stared into the shadows. Footsteps pounded off into the night in the direction of the Cattleman's Hotel. Head pounding, she pressed her earring to alert Kane. Trembling with fear, she crawled on hands and knees onto the pathway, searching around for her pistol. *Oh my God, what is happening to me?*

SEVENTEEN

Footsteps crunched on the pathway moving fast in Jenna's direction. Sheer panic grasped her and years of training melted into terror. *Get a grip.* Staggering to her feet, she took a fighting stance. With her back pressed against the bush, she caught sight of the bouncing light from a flashlight. "Who's there? Show yourself!"

"It's Kane." A dark form came into view. "You okay? Did you press your earring?"

She blinked as Kane's flashlight moved over her. Trying to make her voice come out as casual as possible and not like a frightened child, she took a deep breath and stepped into the beam of light. "Yes, and am I glad to see you. Some guy jumped me and I've lost my weapon." Sensing his desire to chase after the man, she touched his arm. "Don't waste your time, he's long gone."

"*What?*" Kane strode past her, headed along the pathway, then turned back. "Did he hurt you?"

"Only my pride. I can't believe he got the jump on me." She moved to his side. "I'm not sure how that happened. I'm convinced the footsteps came from behind me but when I turned to look in that direction he grabbed me." She rubbed her throat. "He dropped a bag over my head, disarmed me, and then held a knife to my throat."

"Are you okay?" Kane moved the flashlight over her.

"Yeah, just shaken." She stared along the path toward the hotel. "Did *you* hear anyone running away?"

"Nope." Shadows obscured Kane's face as he swung the light back and forth. He bent to pull her Glock out of the snow. "Did he say anything?" He handed her the weapon.

She explained, wiped the snow from her pistol, and slid it back into the holster. "One thing for sure, he thinks *you're* a threat. I'm confused. I have no idea why I'm supposed to keep you on a leash."

"Did he touch you?"

Jenna swallowed the lump in her throat. She could still feel the pressure of the man's hard thigh against her, and the stench of the filthy bag clung to her nostrils. She wanted desperately to get into a hot shower and scrub her attacker's touch from her flesh. "He pushed his thigh between my legs. He's strong and muscular, maybe one-eighty pounds and six foot, maybe taller. The description fits many of the men in town, including you." She grabbed his arm, turning him to face her. "I want to keep this incident between us for now. If it gets out I lost my weapon, I'll never live it down." She stared into his shadowed features. "Please?"

"Sure, but if this is the same person who tried to kill you, we should be sweeping the area for clues. I don't like this one bit. You're letting him get away with assaulting you, which means he wins."

She squeezed his arm. "But I won't be calling you off, will I? I'm not hurt, and overreacting could make things worse. *Please* just let it go."

"You're my superior officer and if you order me to stand

down, I have no choice but to obey." Kane's flashlight lit up the bushes. "Where did you throw the hood?"

"In the bushes." Jenna watched Kane retrieve the hood. "It can't be the same man who caused the accident. This guy could have killed me but I figure he only wanted to frighten me. I saw the way Josh Rockford looked at you before. It could have easily been him or Dan Beal; they're both strong men."

"Yeah, if a cab dropped them close by they could have doubled back." Kane shrugged. "It would be a stupid thing to do, it's easily checked. I'll speak to the cab company."

The shadow-lined pathway closed in on her, dark and threatening. *I have to get out of here.* Jenna moved ahead along the trail. "Okay. Let's go."

"Sure." Kane took her arm and shone the flashlight along the pathway. "You're trembling. Is there anything you're not telling me?"

Jenna pulled her arm from his grip. "I'm freezing. I'm angry too. I should have fought back harder."

"I don't think so. He had you immobilized with a knife at your throat." Kane snorted. "In the same position, I would have remained calm and tried to reason with him too."

She glanced up at him and moved closer, glad of his company. "It was a warning to call you off and I figure the accident was a warning too." She blew out a huff of white steam. "You have to be tied up in this somehow."

"*Me?* The question is *why* they believe I'm a threat. I'm living in your cottage; maybe they figure I'm a rival." Kane sighed and she heard a rasping sound as he rubbed his chin. "Rockford did mention where I am living, but frightening you isn't something a man usually does out of jealousy or to get a woman interested in him. It has to be something else."

"Then we have zip." Jenna sighed with relief as they entered the floodlit parking lot and made their way to the front of the hotel.

"No, we have the hood." Kane pulled an evidence bag out of his pocket and held it up like a trophy. "I'll get this to the lab ASAP and see what they find. He could have grabbed it from the trash; it sure smells bad."

"Yeah, I know. I had the filthy thing rammed in my mouth."

She found Rowley and Daniels leaning on the cruisers. Making an effort to appear casual, she smiled at them. "I came around the back way to check the parking lot. Did you report the lights are out to the management?"

"The lights round back are turned off after closing. They keep the parking lot floodlights on all night and here in the driveway." Rowley's face creased into a frown. "Kane wondered what had happened to you. It's pitch-black on that pathway at night. Did you get lost in the dark?"

"Not at all. I'm fine. I was making sure no one was hiding back there." She avoided Rowley's scrutiny by glancing away.

A few moments later Walters checked in to inform her he was on his way home. For once, the home game and dance had gone off without a hitch. She sucked up the worry gnawing in the pit of her stomach and smiled at her deputies. "Good job. I'll see you Monday morning."

"Just a minute." Kane raised an eyebrow at her then skirted his truck and jogged back toward the parking lot.

Jenna stared after him then noticed Billy Watts leaning into the window of a yellow sedan. She turned to her deputies. "Is that Sarah Woodward's vehicle? I didn't notice her leaving the building."

"Yeah, I did. She came out the back door earlier." Daniels smirked. "I've had her all wrong. I didn't think she was the type to hang around a bar."

"She's not and she's not old enough to be drinking. Wait here." Jenna zipped up her jacket and headed toward the parking lot.

She arrived in time to see Kane pop the hood of Sarah's

vehicle and peer at the engine. A few minutes later, the vehicle rattled into life. Moving closer, she caught the young woman's attention. "What are you doing at the Cattleman's Hotel?"

"I went for dinner and waited to see if there was a room cancellation. I don't like staying at the motel." Sarah gripped the steering wheel. "It wasn't my lucky day. All the rooms are taken so I'm heading back to the motel. I guess the noise will die down now the game is over."

"You won't have to stay here too long. We have reason to believe your grandmother has left town." Jenna smiled. "She may be in the next county."

"No, she's not." Sarah worried her bottom lip and gave them a baleful look. "I have a letter mentioning her interest in buying a ranch somewhere in Black Rock Falls."

"All done." Kane slammed the hood and moved toward her with a confident smile. "Drop by the office on Monday and we'll take a look at the letter. I'll send someone out to check the property." He moved closer. "Do me a favor and leave the investigating to us. Driving around in this old vehicle in bad weather is dangerous."

"Okay." Sarah met his gaze and frowned. "It's just you don't seem to be doing anything and I'm really worried about her."

"You have my word we're following leads to hunt down your grandmother." Kane smiled warmly at her. "Our main priority is to keep you safe and I'm sure your grandmother would feel the same. I'll tell Deputy Daniels to follow you to the motel just in case your vehicle breaks down again." His hard gaze moved over Billy Watts and his mouth formed a thin line. "We'll take it from here." He waved him away.

Jenna bent to speak to Sarah. "You should get your vehicle serviced. Kane is right. Breaking down at this time of the year could be life-threatening. Miller's Garage is very reasonable and they have loaners."

"I've been meaning to get it serviced. I'm staying home this weekend but I'll stop in at the garage first thing Monday morning." Sarah beamed at Kane. "Thank you for your help."

"My pleasure." Kane turned and strode off toward Daniels.

"He's a nice man." Sarah's face pinked.

Jenna watched Billy Watts' truck fishtail over the patches of ice on the way out the parking lot as she pulled on her gloves. "He's very efficient." She indicated toward Daniels' cruiser; the engine was running and spilling clouds of white vapor into the still night. "Off you go. My deputy will see you safely to the motel."

When the vehicle pulled out at a snail's pace, Jenna trudged back through the gray frozen sludge to Kane's truck. He stood chatting and laughing with Rowley as if he'd known him for years. They both stopped talking and turned to look at her as if waiting for instructions. She turned to Rowley. "Head off home and get some rest." She grimaced at Kane. "Are you ready to leave? I'm freezing to death."

"Yes, ma'am."

Jenna climbed into the truck, glad to find the interior warming from the heater. The incident had upset her more than she cared to admit. No man had ever caught her off-guard before and she usually had the skill to take down the largest man with ease. *Oh boy, was I mistaken.* Although armed, the idea of walking into her empty house alone disturbed her. Perhaps she could entice Kane in for a hot drink. When he climbed in beside her, she offered him a smile. "Oh, you've heated the truck for me. Is that a ploy to get hot chocolate and cookies?"

"Yeah, well, I guess after working me so hard and making me swear to cover up a potential crime, you owe me." Kane turned the Beast toward home.

"Okay, but I refuse to discuss the incident tonight. There's nothing to discuss until I figure out who he is and why he's threatening me. Maybe the hood will give us a clue but for now that can wait. I'm exhausted." Jenna leaned back in the seat. "I've had enough excitement since you arrived in town and I need some downtime." She wiggled her eyebrows at him. "What do you say?"

"For your chocolate chip cookies? Let me think..." Kane smiled at her. "Deal."

EIGHTEEN

Nerves at breaking point, Jenna paced the house into the early hours of Sunday morning, constantly checking the locks on windows and doors like someone with OCD. At the sound of snow sliding down her roof and hitting the ground with a plop, her heart pounded. She grabbed her weapon and slid along the wall, turkey-peeking around each corner. Convinced someone wanted her dead, she opened her laptop and scanned each case file, checking every minute detail for anything she'd missed, but came up with zip. All her cases had been straightforward.

Living in constant fear should be a thing of the past, and if one of Viktor Carlos' men found her, she wouldn't get a warning. Death would be instantaneous. What had changed in Black Rock Falls since David Kane had joined the department? Perhaps someone had committed a crime and believed she'd turned a blind eye—or ignored it until backup arrived in the form of David Kane. *But what crime? What did I miss?*

Trying to think of every angle, she crawled into bed, glad of the warmth, and with her Glock nearby she pulled out a notepad and made notes on anyone who might be a threat to her. Okay, so Josh Rockford had made advances, but if he was

serious why not just ask her out? She had embarrassed him
lately. A man concerned about his reputation with his fans and
teammates might threaten her after a few drinks. Perhaps he
couldn't cope with rejection or had some weird possessive thing
going on with her.

Whose feathers had she ruffled over the last few months?
Her mind went to a nasty cruelty to animals court case over one
year ago. A local rancher, Stan Clough, a man in his early
forties, had blamed aliens for the animals gutted alive and left in
the fields on his ranch. She'd had him committed for psychiatric
evaluation but when the report came back negative, the case
proceeded. During the court case, Clough had not taken his
dead, sunken eyes off her, but there had been no threat.
Although his one-year sentence had been a joke, especially as
the jail released him after six months.

Apart from Josh Rockford, another man, James Stone, had
pestered her since her arrival. A tall, athletic man in his late
thirties, he was also the size of her attacker. The lawyer of the
well-heeled residents of Black Rock Falls was a popular choice
to smooth over their crimes. In truth, Stone practically stalked
her. If he hadn't been such a close friend of Mayor Rockford,
she would have been tempted to have him charged with harassment. It would have been a waste of time as Mayor Rockford
protected his friends. In a local court hearing, she'd have lost the
case and been fired, because she required the mayor's sanction
for her elected position.

She allowed her mind to drift back to the last time she'd
spoken to the outwardly handsome and charming James Stone.
It had been Thanksgiving and, being alone, she'd joined him as
his guest at the Cattleman's Hotel Thanksgiving dinner. His
kiss on her doorstep had been demanding. In fact, he'd not
taken rejection easily, and the angry flash in his eyes had
disturbed her.

Although they often crossed paths, she kept him at arm's

length and refused an offer of dinner from him on the day before Kane arrived. She'd made the excuse of being far too busy settling in the new deputy sheriff to enjoy herself. His vow never to give up suddenly took on a whole new meaning. Could he have taken stalking to a new level? She made notes in her book and then fell back against the pillows.

Telling Kane would be difficult; she found him a little over-protective but many of the agents she'd worked with had a similar work ethic toward their female partners. In fact, all of them would have taken a bullet for her, and she guessed Kane would be the same. Although some women might find Kane's actions a little condescending, she found his caring nature quite charming. She smiled and hugged the book against her chest. "Right now, you can be as protective as you like. I think I need all the help I can get." She gently fingered the earrings he'd altered. Having Kane close by was certainly a bonus.

NINETEEN

Early Monday morning, the persistent ringtone of Jenna's phone broke into her dream of riding a black stallion in the mountains, and she pawed at the bedside table to answer it. Glancing at the clock, she sighed. Being in charge of the nine-one-one service overnight usually meant a sleepless night, but she'd made it to six without being disturbed. "Sheriff Alton. What is your emergency?"

A man's voice rushed through the earpiece in a garbled flow. She sat upright and pushed the hair from her eyes. "Who is this?"

"George Brinks."

Cold air brushed her shoulders and she pulled the covers up to her chin shivering. Brinks ran a landfill business on the outskirts of town. "Okay, take a deep breath and tell me what's wrong."

"I found a dead body."

Dammit! "Okay. Nice and slow. Where and when?"

"At the back of the landfill area at the Saddler's Crossing end. It fell out of a fifty-gallon barrel."

"Fell from where?" Jenna grabbed a pen and notepad from the bedside table. "Did you see it fall?"

"*No, no, it was my fault.*" He drew in a deep breath but the panic in his voice was evident. "*I don't allow that type of garbage—barrels, I mean—in that area, so I moved it with the forklift. When I lifted the container, it toppled over and the lid came loose. The stink was overpowering and I could see part of a body sticking out.*"

Every sense locked into action, the fear of the previous evening melted away, and a professional calm slipped over her. *A murder under my watch?* Jenna slipped from the bed and put the phone on speaker as she dragged on her uniform. "Don't touch anything and keep everyone away from the area. Close the gates to the landfill and don't allow anyone inside. Not anyone. I'll contact the undertaker to collect the body and be there as soon as possible." She waited for him to disconnect and then called Kane.

"*Okay, I'll be there in five. I guess it's just as well I haven't eaten breakfast?*"

Jenna pulled on her boots. "Yeah. I haven't eaten either. The call woke me and I don't have time to brew coffee, so expect me to be cranky."

"*I can meet Mr. Brinks if you want to take some time after what happened last night? I'll give Rowley a call to meet me at the landfill.*"

"Thanks, but we don't have dead bodies popping up every day. I want to see if it has any relation to our missing persons." She yawned and blinked the sleep out of her eyes. "Mr. Brinks mentioned the body stinks, so someone must have dumped it recently or it would have frozen solid. Don't wear a clean uniform; that smell tends to hang around." She straightened and then reached for her belt and holster. "The beginning to another perfect day."

"*Do you have an ME in town?*"

"Well, not exactly, no. The Black Rock Falls Funeral Home uses the undertaker, Max Weems and his son. They've worked for the county in that capacity for ten years." She holstered her weapon. "I'll call them now."

"*I have fresh coffee brewing, and as you've supplied me with a number of to-go cups, would you like me to bring along a hot drink?*"

She smiled at his thoughtfulness. "I would kill for a cup of coffee—thank you."

TWENTY

After asking for directions to the landfill, Kane headed down the driveway. The countryside still resembled a Christmas greeting card under the watery morning sun, but snowdrifts on the roadside had melted and green patches peeked out. "I hope we've seen the last of the snow."

"Not likely." Jenna was clutching her cup with both hands. "But it's good to see the sun today." She glanced at him. "I need to tell you something that might be relevant to the man jumping me on Saturday night."

He met her gaze and nodded. "Okay."

"I went out on a couple of pseudo dates with James Stone. He's a lawyer to the more affluent residents of Black Rock Falls." Jenna's gaze showed her concern. "He only wanted me to be his partner at functions—nothing serious—but I feel like he's stalking me and he fits the size and build of the man who attacked me. I refused a date with him on Friday, but at the time he couldn't have known what you look like or that you'd be living in my cottage. The only person I informed about your position was Mayor Rockford."

Concerned, Kane frowned. "Does this Stone character speak to Mayor Rockford?"

"I guess so. Stone is the family lawyer and a close friend." She looked at him from below her lashes and her cheeks pinked. "The mayor did see me out with him at the Halloween Ball. We spoke to him."

Kane rubbed his chin and stared at the road ahead. "It is more than likely they discussed my position and I gather you informed the mayor that I'd be staying in the cottage?"

"Yeah, he asked me."

"Uh-huh, so if the mayor told Stone, it would be easy for him to hunt down my details. You filed my application with the town council for approval—right?" Kane cleared his throat. "I guess to some guys, I might be seen as a rival but as I said before, threatening harm isn't the way to win a woman's love." He shot her a look. "I know giving me your personal information is difficult but if he's a creep and a possible danger to you, I need to know. I'm placing Mr. Stone on the list of suspects." He sighed. "Anyone capable of holding a knife to a woman's throat is capable of murder in my book. No other suspects?"

"I did have a spooky animal cruelty case involving Stan Clough. He went to jail for six months."

He frowned. "Spooky? Now that's interesting. I'll pull his file and take a look."

"He told the court that aliens had cut up his cattle and pigs, but when I went with Rowley to investigate the complaint, we found Clough covered in blood. He made some excuse about trying to save them." Jenna frowned and her mouth turned down. "He gutted them alive. Problem is, I can't forget the way he looked at me. He has soulless eyes like a demon."

Disgusted, Kane shook his head. "Animal cruelty is a front runner for psychopathic behavior. He'd be a suspect *if* we were investigating a murder." He glanced at her pale face and smiled.

"You know, the majority of killers I've arrested have been intelligent, interesting, and quite good-looking people. I don't think appearance matters when it comes to murder."

"Have you investigated many murder cases?" Jenna turned in her seat to look at him.

"Some." He shrugged. "I think you're jumping the gun a bit about the supposed body at the landfill. In my experience, the moment people smell death, they panic. The drum could easily hold a dog. If it's been stored in fluid, after a time the fur falls out, and it could resemble a person." He waved a hand toward the frozen countryside. "It's been like this for months and the ground is way too hard to dig a grave. The fact the contents haven't frozen isn't a judgment of time either; tons of liquids don't freeze."

"Let's hope you're right." Jenna sipped her drink and sighed in contentment, blowing out a cloud of steam.

By the time they arrived at the landfill, vehicles blocked the approach road, and with Jenna hanging out the window directing traffic, Kane maneuvered around a line of vehicles. Driving on the wrong side of the road, he headed toward two men barring the gate. Horns sounded and people waiting to unload garbage glared at him. He pulled the Beast to a halt and turned to Jenna. "How do you want to handle this, ma'am?"

"Tell Brinks I want to speak to him and we need someone out here to control the traffic. I'll call Daniels." Jenna waved him away in a dismissive gesture.

He strode to the head of the line and spoke to the two men standing out front. "Open up to let the sheriff through then close the gate behind us. If you have any problems with the crowd, move one of the earth movers in front of the gate. Which one of you is Brinks?"

"I'm Brinks." One of the men stepped forward. "Don't worry, I didn't let a soul near the body."

"Are you sure it's a body, as in human and not an animal?"

Brinks raised one bushy gray eyebrow and rubbed at his untidy beard. "I don't recall ever seeing an animal wearing a wedding ring." He grimaced. "The sight scared ten years off my life. I figured I'd experienced every stink known to man working here but that barrel makes noxious gasses smell like roses."

A shiver of unease lifted the hairs on Kane's neck. No murders had occurred in Black Rock Falls in two years, and the moment he arrived, a body turned up. "How many of your employees worked here on Saturday?"

"Just me and Joey." Brinks indicated with a thumb to the man beside him.

A younger man in thick winter clothing with dark eyes and a crimson nose sticking out above a scarf stared at Kane. "There are usually six of us working here on Saturday."

Kane glanced at the row of vehicles waiting at the gate. "This place is busy, so what made you decide to try and manage with two men last Saturday?"

"I didn't expect many people to turn up seeing as the weather has been so bad." Brinks shrugged. "It was too late to call in the other men by the time the vehicles rolled up."

"Did either of you see anyone dumping the barrel?" Kane blinked away the snowflakes collecting on his eyelashes. "Any regulars you recall? Any information you can recall, however trivial, will be useful."

When both men shook their heads, Kane removed one glove and reached inside his pocket for his cards. He offered a few to both men. "When people come by, ask them if they used the landfill last Saturday and if they noticed anything or anyone suspicious. If they know anything, give them my card."

"Will do, but people in Black Rock Falls don't like to get involved." Brinks pocketed the cards.

Annoyed, Kane hardened his expression and Brinks cringed under his scrutiny. "Really? Well, they might change their minds when they discover we have a killer in the vicinity." He waved a hand to the piles of snow-covered garbage. " Show me where you found the barrel and where it is now." He turned to Joey. "The undertaker will be here shortly. Send him over and keep everyone else outside until further notice. A deputy is on the way to control the traffic."

He walked Mr. Brinks to the truck, opened the door, and ushered him into the back seat. The man's body odor near burned his nostrils, and he hoped the stink wouldn't impregnate the leather seats in his new truck. He slid behind the wheel and turned to Jenna. "This is Mr. Brinks. I've questioned him and Joey but they didn't see who dumped the barrel."

"What time did you start this morning?" Jenna's expression was all business as she turned in her seat to look at the frazzled man.

"Five thirty as usual."

"You're required to supervise the loads placed into the landfill so how could both of you have missed something so large?" Jenna's attention didn't leave the man's face as she pulled on her gloves. "Are the gates locked overnight?"

"Yeah, but a ton of people dumped garbage late on Saturday afternoon. It was too busy to watch everyone. The barrel could have been dumped when I had my back turned. Joey was working over the other side of the lot. We had a blizzard and the snow covered everything in minutes. I didn't notice the can until this morning when I cleared the snow to make a path." Brinks' mouth turned down and he shuddered. "I wouldn't have moved it if I'd known what was inside."

Kane started the engine. "Okay let's take a look." He drove through the gate.

The angry crowd had quietened and a few people had gathered on the sidewalk in subdued conversation. He glanced around. One area of the completed landfill bordered a line of forest and he made out a gate in the distance. "Is there access from over there?"

"There's a trail to a back gate but no one would risk traveling through the forest at this time of year, and the gate has a padlock." Brinks rubbed his dirt-smudged chin.

With the recent thick coating of snow, a herd of elephants could have thundered through the fence without detection. Kane turned back to Mr. Brinks. "Have you checked the gate lately?"

"No."

"Okay." Kane surveyed the area. Snow lay in drifts over the landfill with only the newly cleared path to the drop off area visible. "Which way?"

"Over there by the tree stump. I found the barrel beside the fence, next to the mound of soil we use to cover the garbage once the area is full. Follow the smell, you'll find it sure enough." Mr. Brinks gripped the back of the seat and his expression became fearful. "Can you let me out now? I really don't want to see it again. I'll have nightmares for the rest of my life."

Kane stared in his mirror at the trembling man. "Sure. When you get back to the gate, put up the 'closed' sign." He pulled to a halt and allowed Brinks to escape.

The black fifty-gallon drum lay on one side, stark against the pristine white background. In front, a pink patch of ice sparkled in the sunlight. Kane turned to Jenna. "It's a body. Brinks said he noticed a wedding ring." He met her gaze. "From what he said, decomposition has set in even in this weather. I can take a look if you'd rather stay here."

"That's not going to happen. I'm the sheriff and I've seen my fair share of human remains in all states." Jenna huffed out a sigh and her lips thinned. "You're doing it again." She pulled out a pair of surgical gloves and tossed them into his lap.

Bemused, he stared at her. "Doing what?" He removed his thick leather gloves and replaced them.

"Treating me like a child. I'm stronger than you think." She pulled a blue scarf out of her pocket and tied it around her cold, reddened face, covering her nose. "Let's go." She pushed open the door and headed for the body.

Trying hard to understand her logic, Kane hurried after her, his boots slipping in the snow. "You have me all wrong. What happened on Saturday night could have happened to anyone but I don't believe it didn't upset you because as sure as hell if that had happened to me, I'd be looking over my shoulder constantly." He caught up to her in a few strides. "That incident has no relation to what we have here. If someone stuffed a body in a barrel it won't be pretty and I'm more than capable of taking photos and giving you a full report." He pulled a surgical mask from his pocket and pressed it to his face. He always came prepared to a crime scene. "I was offering you an option, is all. Most people would prefer the chance to opt out of witnessing a messy crime scene."

Jenna stopped walking so suddenly he bumped into her. He gripped her arm to steady her but she hadn't moved an inch. Not too bad for a woman weighing less than a hundred and twenty pounds. Trying not to laugh at her furious expression, he let go and stepped back. "I'm sorry, ma'am. I didn't mean to offend you."

"I'm not *most people*. How do you figure I could possibly investigate a murder if I don't examine the body and the scene? I need to catch a killer and I don't believe my psychic powers are up to the challenge." Jenna balled her hands on her waist and her expression turned to stone. "Get a grip, Kane. I'm not your little sister and I *don't* need you protecting me." She moved in so close he could feel her breath on his cheek. "I've taken down bigger men than you and the sight of death has no effect on me, so back off. That's an order."

Kane straightened. "Yes, ma'am." He admired strength on and off the field and Jenna had the makings of a partner he could trust with his life.

TWENTY-ONE

With every step up the small incline of the landfill, the unmissable stench of death increased. The winter's chill and fresh snow did little to obliterate the *eau de garbage* either, and the landfill's stink had a bouquet Kane would be washing from his clothes and hair for a month. He pulled his phone from the inside pocket of his jacket and took photographs of the surrounding area. Following the path made by the tractor, he scanned the ground for clues but found nothing. The overnight blizzard had covered everything with a foot of snow.

"Kane, get down here. I want shots of everything. Look there—" Jenna flicked him an intent gaze then pointed at an indent in the ground "—that's where the lid fell off, and look over there—is that something gold sticking out of the snow?"

Kane walked to her side. "Yeah, I see it." He raised his phone and took the necessary shots. Moving closer, he zoomed the camera to get in closer. "It appears to be half of a gold bracelet. It might have been dropped here earlier."

"It's a torque bangle." Jenna frowned. She pulled an evidence bag from her pocket, plucked the item from the snow and dropped it inside. She held up the bag and squinted at it. "This is old. The design is Celtic probably, Scottish or Irish."

Kane examined the item. "From the size, it belonged to a man."

"It might have slipped off the corpse." Jenna swiped at the snowflakes covering her long lashes and then pushed the bag inside her pocket. "By the trail of liquid, the barrel rolled some ways before coming to rest." She walked away, following the path made by the barrel in the snow.

Kane noticed Jenna kept to the tractor's tracks, and the way her head turned from side to side, searching the snow for evidence. This wasn't her first dance at investigating a crime scene that was for darn sure. He followed her but Jenna reached the barrel before him and pushed one hand to her face and then turned to face him, eyes wide. He reached her in two strides and peered at the corpse. Bile rushed up the back of his throat at the congealed remains hanging out of the rim. Flesh had peeled from the extended arm. The hand and fingers were held together by a few strands of skin. A gold ring hung loosely around one finger on the clenched skeletal fist. The naked body had curled in a fetal position. Kane's attention moved to the victim's head. The face had melted into a mass of pink jelly but dark hair was evident. He moved closer to examine what appeared at first, to be a silver necklace but found the metal strand was a wire pulled tight around the victim's throat. One shoulder appeared to have a faded tattoo in an unusual weave design. Deep open wounds covered the victim's back, cut deep to display underlying bone. Some crazy had tortured the man to death and from the extent of the injuries, it had been a slow and deliberate murder. Torture was a typical way to extract information he'd seen many times.

He glanced at Jenna. "You should ask Brinks not to speak to anyone about this, especially the media. We'll need to keep the details under wraps."

"Obviously." Jenna cleared her throat. "I'll handle Brinks. I figure he's a little scared of me."

Kane held his breath to avoid inhaling the stink and then moved in closer to record the scene. After taking a dozen images, he straightened and turned to her. "There's a garrote around his neck, fencing wire I figure, and if the bangle belongs to him, robbery wasn't a motive. The injuries make a thrill kill out of the question. Most of them are opportunistic, more like kill and run. The murderers usually leave the body at the scene or close by. This victim's injuries look methodical. Either the killer needed to extract information from the victim or they hated him big time."

"I agree." When Jenna indicated toward the gate with her chin, he followed her gaze. "The undertaker is coming. We'll leave him to finish up here. You're assuming the victim is male but we'll need an affirmative on the sex. This could be one of our missing persons. The torque is significant and the discoloration on the shoulder could be a tattoo or a smear of molasses from the barrel." Her gaze lifted to him. "The deterioration of the body is unusual for this time of year. It's freezing, and if this is a recent murder then the temperature would have preserved the body."

They walked away from the horrific sight and Kane shook his head. "No, whoever did this used a chemical to break down the flesh." He indicated toward her pocket. "The bangle might be covered with it too; look at your gloves, they're stained. You might want to take the bag out of your pocket."

"Okay." Jenna pulled out the evidence bag, held it at arm's length, and frowned. "I'll give this to the lab. We're all done here. You can tell the undertaker to remove the body."

"Yes, ma'am." Kane beckoned to the van heading in their direction. When it pulled up beside them, he waited for Weems to buzz down his window and then indicated to the torque. "We found this near the barrel and believe the body is in some kind of chemical. This bangle needs to be transported in a medical hazard box and sent away for testing."

"Sure." Mr. Weems climbed out of the van with slow deliberation, hobbled around the back, and then opened the doors. He pulled out a glass jar, opened it, and held it out for Jenna with a flash of yellowing teeth. "Pop it in here. I'll send away samples to the lab and then wash it and check for engravings. If there's anything to identify the victim, I'll call you."

"Thanks." Kane waved a hand toward the remains. "We're done here so go ahead and remove the body."

"Sure thing." Weems stared at the corpse, raised both dark eyebrows, then waved his son forward. "I'm Max Weems and you must be the new deputy sheriff? Welcome to Black Rock Falls."

"I need you to confirm the sex of the victim and I'll hunt down missing persons." Jenna lifted her chin. "I believe there's a tattoo on one shoulder and it could be crucial to identifying the victim. Do what you can to preserve it and get me a photograph."

"Leave it to me. I'll be in touch as soon as possible." Weems touched his hat.

When Jenna gave Weems a curt nod and without a word headed toward the Beast, Kane trudged after her. It was difficult to figure out his new boss. He'd try to be that person without stepping on her authority, which would prove difficult.

Throwing his gloves into the landfill hole, Kane lifted his gaze to see Jenna leaning against the passenger door, eyeing him with a troubled expression. "How many people use molasses barrels in Black Rock Falls?"

"Hundreds. Why?"

Kane dragged gloves from his pocket and pulled them onto his freezing hands. "There was one tied on the back of the pickup that hit you on Friday night." He shrugged. "What's the chance this one is the same barrel?"

"Do you really believe someone would be stupid enough to risk tangling with me with a body in a barrel tied to the back of their truck?" Jenna snorted and gave him an amused look. "And in front of a witness? What if they'd slid off the road as well?"

Kane removed the surgical mask and shuddered at the wave of stench accosting his senses. "Most people who commit murder aren't exactly sane." He shrugged. "The timeframe is right. Brinks doesn't know when the barrel was dumped at the landfill." He tugged the hood of his jacket over his woolen hat. "The landfill isn't secure. One side is accessible via a gate. We should take a look and see if anyone has tampered with the padlock."

"I agree but it will take some time to get there and I'm not driving through the forest smelling like a rotting corpse." Jenna's gaze moved over the area then rested on him. "I need to take a shower and eat breakfast first."

Kane's stomach growled at the mention of food. Nothing affected his appetite. "Do you figure the victim is one of our missing persons?"

"What motive would anyone have for murdering them? From what I understand, Mrs. Woodward was a nice old woman and John Helms wouldn't have had time to make an enemy in the few days before he went missing." She peeled off her gloves with practiced efficiency and dropped them inside an evidence bag. "I believe we'll need to look further afield."

"I agree."

"Good. I'm done here. We'll head back to the ranch to change." Jenna waved a hand toward the dwindling traffic jam. "Daniels is handling the traffic problem without help." She reached for the door handle to the Beast and then turned to look at him. "And right now, I need coffee—a gallon of it at least."

TWENTY-TWO

Although Jenna had made light of Kane's assumptions, the idea of the barrel being on the back of the pickup involved in her accident concerned her more than she'd like to admit. She pushed down the wave of uncertainty and leaned back in the seat. The big question was why someone in Black Rock Falls wanted her dead or silenced. Had she overlooked a crime during her time as sheriff? The idea disturbed her. Taking one day at a time, she recalled her movements before the accident and came up blank. Nothing significant had happened apart from the Josh Rockford and friends' arrests.

The image of the body in the barrel flashed across her mind and she mulled over the information in the missing persons' cases. Neither report had listed a torque or wedding ring as personal items. The bangle was significant and surely family members would have mentioned such a valuable item. She unwrapped the scarf from her face and glanced at Kane. She valued his expertise at the crime scene. His observational skills matched her own and she could see his mind working the case by his intent stare on the road ahead. "After seeing that carnage do you still want a stack of pancakes and strips of bacon at Aunt Betty's Café?"

"Oh yeah, but you mentioned a gallon of coffee?" Kane grinned at her and his eyes sparkled. "I'd like that too." He turned off the highway and headed for Jenna's ranch.

"Shower first." Jenna lifted the to-go cups from the consol. "And then we head back into town."

"That sounds like a plan." He pulled the Beast to a halt outside her front door. "I'll call Rowley and bring him up to speed. How long do you need?"

"Half an hour max." She pushed open the vehicle door. "Download the images too and email them to him. He can start a file while we're out."

"Okay."

As she reached the foot of the stoop, a wave of apprehension hit her. Pushing it away, she jogged up the steps and unlocked the door. As she pressed the buttons to deactivate the alarm, she noticed Kane waiting for her to enter the house. *He is making sure I'm safe.* She gave him a wave and closed the door. It had been a very long time since someone had watched her back. The image of the body in the barrel flashed across her mind and her attacker's words rammed into her subconscious. She trembled at the thought of ending up tortured and stuffed in a can. *I have to catch this killer before I'm his next victim.*

Kane had read the files on Sarah's grandmother and had the basic information on John Helms. Mrs. Woodward had thick white hair, so he discounted her as the person in the barrel. John Helms, from the description on his driver's license, was five eight, one hundred and forty pounds, with dark hair and eyes. Kane would need to contact Helms' wife or, better still, speak to the man who had reported him missing, Father Maguire.

Why had the priest and not Helms' wife filed the missing

persons' report? If Helms was the victim, it would open up a can of worms. His wife wouldn't be the first one in history to take out a hit on her husband.

His thoughts went to Jenna and her need to have him under surveillance. The hit-and-run and then the attack on her at the Cattleman's Hotel could have been a warning to keep her mouth shut—about what concerned him, but if she was in danger, he'd coax the truth from her.

He glanced at the photographs of the two missing persons and read the backgrounds on each of them. To his trained investigator's eye, they had nothing in common at all. Kane dashed a hand through his hair and stared at the screen. He couldn't find a motive for murder, zip, nada. From what he'd seen of the victim, he'd endured prolonged torture. How long the victim had suffered and what exactly had happened to him would provide vital information. He hoped the local undertaker had the experience to deal with murder.

He checked an email from Walters and then glanced at the time displayed at the bottom of the screen and logged out. Jenna would be hammering on his door at any moment. Before the thought had left his mind, he heard her voice.

"Hey, Kane."

He pushed to his feet and strode to the front door. "Yeah, I'm on my way. I'll just grab my jacket."

He pulled open the door, and the moment he turned away to grab his coat, Jenna stepped inside, stamping the snow from her feet on the mat.

"I expected you five minutes ago." Jenna gave him a once over and the corners of her mouth curled into a smile. "I have coffee." She held up two to-go cups. "Will this hold you for another half an hour or so? I figured we should check on the gate at the back of the landfill before it starts snowing again." She turned and headed out the door.

Kane's stomach gurgled in protest but he nodded. "Yeah,

thanks. Walters contacted me. Mrs. Woodward's bank check has not been cashed." Kane pulled the door closed and followed her to the truck. "I have uploaded everything onto my phone so we can see the overall picture." He opened the door and slid behind the wheel then noticed her regarding him with suspicion. "Don't look at me like that, Jenna. Right now, we have two victims: the man in the barrel, and you. I'm not discounting our two missing persons either."

"There's no evidence to connect any of them, Kane." Jenna rolled her eyes and then placed the to-go cups in the holder in the console and fastened her seatbelt.

Kane fired up the engine and let it idle. "I'm not so sure. If you're convinced there's no major crime in Black Rock Falls and no one is threatening you for whatever reason, then we have two options: either we have a psychopath on the loose, or by the look of our victim, someone found it necessary to extract information by torture. For what reason, I have yet to determine, but the latter will be easier to catch."

"You've made a rash conclusion without one shred of evidence. We have *one* victim and no autopsy report." Jenna turned in her seat and glared at him, her face flushed. "Why do you keep involving me in this? I'm *not* a victim. I agree the accident and the idiot who threatened me shook me up but honestly, I can't figure out why anyone in Black Rock Falls would want to kill me. I'm not a threat to the other candidates on the ballot for the upcoming elections and anyone in my past who might have a reason doesn't know I live here."

That was a slip. So, you do have someone chasing you.

TWENTY-THREE

Kane headed for town, waiting in vain for Jenna to strike up a conversation. After giving directions via a dirt road through a forest to the backside of the landfill, she reached for her coffee, and they fell back into an awkward silence.

He cleared his throat. "I'll need to interview the priest. The file we have on John Helms doesn't have contact information for members of his family. Which deputy wrote the report? The name is missing on the file and they need a lesson on gathering information. For all we know, our missing person is at home, nice and snug in front of a fire with his wife."

"I put Daniels on the Helms case." Jenna flicked him a cool glance over the rim of her cup. "I'm sure he filed the correct information. Perhaps the file is corrupted. I'll take a look when we get back to the office. I back up everything."

"Do you know if Daniels contacted Helms' wife for more information? If the priest alerted her about her husband's disappearance, she should have called the office by now." Kane turned the Beast onto a narrow road protected from the weather by trees, some had become little more than bare sticks blackened by winter. He followed a line of pine trees with limbs bent under the weight of the snow. "I didn't see any mention of her in the notes."

"I'm not sure." Jenna's brow wrinkled into a frown. "I'll call a meeting when we get back to the office to bring everyone up to speed. It's pointless going over everything twice and the others will need to be kept in the loop."

The fence surrounding the landfill came into view and Kane headed the truck toward the gate at a slow speed, keeping a lookout for signs of a vehicle's tire tracks. "The snow would have covered any tracks. I don't figure we'll find many clues here." He pulled the Beast to a stop.

Leaving the engine running, they jumped down from the cab and waded through the snow and then stopped to survey the area. Each post had snow piled up at least six inches high but the gate only had a dusting. Kane surveyed the drift on each side of the gate. On one side, the piled snow indicated the gate's recent opening. Oh yeah, someone had been here in the last few days. He moved closer and found a chain in the snow. After conducting a search of the immediate area using his boot, he located a broken lock. He turned and waved to Jenna. "Someone has used this entrance."

"It looks like they backed a vehicle into that tree as well." Jenna pointed to a raw patch on the trunk of a tall oak. "Take photographs of everything and bag that padlock." She huffed out a cloud of steam. "Now we know how they got into the landfill without being noticed."

Kane took the images and then dropped the padlock into an evidence bag. "I doubt there will be any fingerprints. Only a fool would remove their gloves in this temperature."

Kane caught a flash of sunlight on metal, and taking Jenna with him, dropped to the ground. Coming down hard on her back, he heard the whoosh of air escaping her lungs and a muttered wheeze of a curse. He rolled over her, covering her with his chest and arms. "Stay down."

A crack rang out and a bullet shot over his head and smashed into the tree behind them, followed by a second. The pine tree exploded and a shower of splinters peppered the back of his jacket. He waited for some time but when no more shots rang out he scanned the hillside for any signs of movement and found nothing. *Where are you?* He gazed down at Jenna's pale face. "You okay?"

"I will be as soon as you get off me." Jenna wriggled and pushed both hands against his chest. "Move."

Kane rolled off her, keeping low to the ground. "You're acting mighty calm. I guess people use you for target practice on a daily basis, same as the hit-and-run, right? Who knew you planned to come here this morning?"

"I called Maggie and told her to inform Rowley we'd be checking out the back entrance to the landfill." Jenna rolled onto her stomach and picked leaves from her hair. "She does tend to yell out messages. Anyone in earshot would have heard her."

Kane rubbed a hand down his face. "I'm starting to believe I've joined the Keystone Cops."

Jenna glared at him, her eyes flashing with anger. "I managed fine before you arrived. You must attract trouble."

He narrowed his gaze. "Me? You *are* joking. This is the third time I've pulled you out of trouble in less than a week."

"Right place, right time, is all." She lifted her grazed chin in the direction of the shooter. "It looks like he's gone. Are you going to let me up now, or are you going to go all macho on me again? What's it going to be this time? Are you planning to throw me over one shoulder and make a run for the truck?"

"No." Kane winced. "This time, you're quite capable of walking but I'd advise you to belly crawl to cover before you stand up."

"Fine but before I do that, tell me something. Why do you

refer to your truck as the 'Beast'?" She grinned at him. "I mean —really? Is it that good?"

Amused, Kane nodded. "Oh yeah, it's the best protection outside a Kevlar vest." He rolled onto his elbow and smiled at her. "When it was delivered to me in Helena, the driver said it was a 'beast of a truck' and I told him, yeah but it's *my* beast. The name kinda stuck."

"Okay." Jenna stared back toward the ridge. "Did you happen to see where the shots came from?" She wiped a mixture of ice and leaf mold from her cheek and rolled onto her belly.

Kane nodded. "Yeah, top of the hill at two o'clock. I caught a glint. It could have been from a rifle or maybe sunglasses." *So, not a professional hit.* "Stay here. I think he's gone but if he's still up there, I'll draw him out."

He wiggled on his elbows to a snowdrift on the perimeter of the forest and made a pile of snowballs then pegged them at the bushes in the opposite direction to give the impression someone had run that way. Lying on the freezing ground, he waited; two minutes and then five. No other shots rang out and the birds returned to the trees en masse in squawks of displeasure at being disturbed.

"I think he's gone." Jenna crawled expertly to his side. "It could have been a stray bullet. People *do* hunt in this area."

Perplexed, he narrowed his gaze on her. He couldn't understand her disregard for personal safety. Her attitude must be an attempt to cover an underlying concern because it sure didn't reflect the overkill of surveillance and alarms installed on her ranch. He crawled into the cover of bushes with her close behind and then rolled to a sitting position. Unable to believe his ears, he glared at her. "There's no way the shooter was hunting. We've been here for some time and I haven't heard gunshots. If someone was hunting they'd be continuing now."

She paled, and by the flash of panic in her eyes, she'd come to the same conclusion. "This—" Kane waved a hand toward the tree shattered by the bullet "—was as sloppy as the hit-and-run. Professional hitmen don't miss or drive away without finishing the job. Cleanup guys don't carry rifles that reflect the light, and we wouldn't have heard the shot. A professional would have taken us out the moment we stepped out of the car."

"I'm fully aware of their capabilities and that's why none of the so-called attempts on my life make any sense." She knuckled her forehead. "If it is a local idiot out for revenge, what do you suggest we do? We can't stay here forever."

Oh my God, she's on somebody's hit list. He wet his lips and swallowed the need to ask her for details. He could protect her but getting her to break her code of silence would be impossible. "We'll need to get deeper into the forest." He grabbed her arm and belly crawled to the trees. "This way and keep your head down."

TWENTY-FOUR

Once under cover, Kane continued to scan the top of the hill, pushed to his feet, and offered Jenna his hand. He pulled her behind a tree. "Why don't you tell me what's really going on with you?"

"What do you mean?" She tried to pull away but he gripped her arm tighter.

"It's obvious you're in Black Rock Falls for a reason and it's not the overpowering desire to be sheriff. My guess is you are hiding from someone and it's not an ex-lover. Maybe since you arrived you've taken the odd bribe or looked the other way?" He noticed her expression turn wary and she yanked her arm away from him. He shrugged. "I don't care about your past but when things happen out of the blue, I need to know the person or organization I'm expected to deal with. If you're into something dangerous and you want out, I have friends who can help."

"How many times do I have to tell you?" Jenna fisted her hands on her waist and stuck out her chin. The look she gave him could strip paint. "There are no drug lords or illegal syndicates of any kind in Black Rock Falls. I don't take bribes or look the other way. If I'd stumbled onto anything dangerous, I would have told you. You're way off base."

He'd not missed the look of apprehension in her eyes. He knew she had a secret and wanted to keep it buried. *Fine, have it your way.* He held up both hands in mock surrender. "Then I apologize for overstepping, ma'am." He offered her a small smile. "I just want a quiet life *but* I'm here if you need me, no questions asked, okay?"

"Okay." Jenna's cheeks pinked as she bent to brush the debris from her clothes. "Thanks, I'll keep that in mind. I'll call Daniels at the landfill. He'll be too late to catch the shooter but he might pick up a trail in the snow."

"No, don't. We'll swing by if you like but from what I observed earlier, the road along that fence line is clear and used frequently. We could try searching for a cartridge casing along the tree line but I can retrieve a bullet from the tree. It's snowing and by the time we get there I doubt we'll find any trace of the shooter." Kane touched her shoulder. "Wait here and I'll get the truck. I'll park in the woods and wait ten minutes or so then go back and dig out the bullet." He smiled at her. "Stay alert."

"Roger that."

Kane stopped mid-step and turned to look at her. He'd deliberately added military speak to their conversations over the last few days to validate his suspicions about her. Her reply convinced him she'd at least had basic military training. The way she handled herself under threat impressed him and convinced him she'd been under fire at one time. He shook his head, trying to force his thoughts back to the problem at hand. Jenna's past was irrelevant to the current crime wave and he'd open up a can of worms if he persisted. Right now, she was the least of his problems. They had a killer on the loose.

Using stealth learned over years, he slipped back to his vehicle and backed it along the narrow road through the forest.

Once safely parked in the dense undergrowth, he beckoned Jenna forward. "I have a sniper rifle in the Beast. Can you handle one?"

"Stop treating me like a rookie." She glared at him and her lips thinned. "This is not my first rodeo."

"Sorry." He pulled open the Beast's rear hatch and grabbed the case containing a high-powered sniper rifle. In seconds, he'd assembled and loaded the weapon. He handed the gun to Jenna. "Use the tree for cover and watch for the shooter on the hilltop. He's careless. I caught the glint on the rifle, so watch out for anything that sparkles. It won't take me long to grab the bullet."

"Go." Jenna positioned herself behind a tree.

Kane moved with care toward the fence line, keeping close to the perimeter of the forest, his attention sweeping the top of the hill overlooking the landfill. His boots made no sound and his ears strained to listen for any sounds. He would have a millisecond to react but he had been in worse situations. Using the trunk of the tree as a shield, he then ran his gloved hand over the damaged bark and felt for the bullet. When his fingers closed around a piece of metal, he could not believe his luck and wiggled the projectile until it fell into his palm. He dragged an evidence bag from his pocket and dropped his prize inside. "Got it."

He returned to Jenna's position, waving the baggie, and watched her dismantle the rifle with swift efficiency. She had the weapon stowed away and was inside the vehicle before he climbed into the warmth of the cab. His belly growled and Jenna let out a snort of laughter. Rubbing his stomach, he chuckled, glad to relieve the tension. "I think I'm ready to visit Aunt Betty's Café."

"Me too." Jenna rubbed her hands together and smiled at him. "Cold weather and assassination attempts make me ravenous."

TWENTY-FIVE

Jenna pushed away her plate. "Eating out with you is making me fat. I'll need to find time to work out or I'll be mush by spring."

"Is there a gym in town?"

"No need." Jenna let out a long sigh. "You are welcome to join me unless..."

Kane shot her a concerned glance. "Unless what?"

"Oh, I'm sorry. I guess you don't work out with your injury. I shouldn't have asked you, that was very tactless of me."

"I work out." He leaned back in his seat. "Apart from the cold weather giving me headaches, I'm not impaired. I'm sure I'm fit enough to keep up with you."

"Oh, I *love* a challenge." She grinned at him. "Any time you're ready, let me know."

"I'm a morning man." A slash of white teeth split his face. "Zero six hundred late enough for you?"

"Six it is." She cleared her throat. "Ex-military man, are you? I don't know many cops who use that terminology, or react so fast in an emergency. Special Forces perhaps?"

"Let's make a deal. I won't bug you about your past, if you don't ask me about mine."

"Deal." She turned in her seat. "But lose the military speak, it's a dead giveaway."

"Yes, ma'am."

Kane's companionship over breakfast had settled Jenna's nerves. It had been over three years since she'd seen action in the field and although her training had kicked in, hiding the aftershock from Kane had been difficult. She shucked her coat, and after hanging the damp garment on the peg beside the door, she turned to peruse the information on the current cases added to the whiteboard in her office. Nothing of note had happened in the last months; in fact, apart from James Stone pestering her for a date, her life in Black Rock Falls had been an ordered delight. The attack in the shrubbery at the hotel and the morning's shooting had slammed her back into reality. On the landfill back road with Kane by her side, she'd been careless. *If not for Kane, I'd be dead.*

She glanced out the door, and apart from Mrs. Gilly's high-pitched voice complaining about her neighbor's dog for the fourth time this month, the outer office was quiet. If she called a meeting during the lull, Maggie could handle the front counter. She gathered her thoughts, wondering if she should mention the incident at the edge of the forest to her other deputies. If Kane had been correct on his take of the incidents involving her, the suspect must have been in the office when she'd called Maggie to obtain information of her whereabouts. The amateurish attempts on her life both worried and eased her mind because a local idiot she could deal with. If Viktor Carlos had discovered her whereabouts and identity, she'd have been in her grave years ago. *I've been stupid.* Her fear of Carlos sending an assassin had clouded her judgment and made her believe every threat came from him.

Perhaps Kane was correct, she'd unknowingly witnessed a

crime. Although, in her opinion, the incidents had been little more than an attempt to keep her quiet, but about what? She racked her brain trying to find one reason for someone to go to such lengths to frighten her. Returning to her desk, she scanned the files again, starting from her first week as Black Rock Falls' sheriff. Nothing out of the ordinary had happened at all but she added details to the list of any particular involvement, or problems with people. She stared at the short list, recalling each incident with clarity. No bribes offered, nothing sinister had occurred, no death threats received, and apart from James Stone asking her out to dinner *again*, the only problem she'd encountered came from the mayor's son, Josh Rockford, and his bunch of untouchables.

The stars of the local hockey team figured they owned the town. Josh had the protection of the Rockford name and wealth. The mayor's son was an arrogant pig, but bullies rarely had the guts to attempt murder. Although, he could have paid someone to do his dirty work for him. For this reason, his name went to the top of her list along with the other two men, Billy Watts and Dan Beal. The three men had come very close to threatening her when she'd arrested them. The only problem was the instinctive urge to include James Stone on the list—although he was a pest, had she given him reason to threaten her?

She recalled with a shudder the strength of the man pressing against her, and the intimate pressing of his thigh. Her attacker could have easily been Stone. Was he jealous of Kane? If so, she doubted he would try to kill her in a hit-and-run. At the time of the accident, he wouldn't have even *seen* Kane let alone discovered he'd be living in her cottage. If it was Stone, the two incidents and the shooting had to be separate. *I'll have to bring Rowley into the loop in case anything else happens.*

A knock came on the door and she glanced up to see Deputy Rowley smiling at her.

"Yeah?"

"It's quiet at the moment. Do you want me to grab the others for a meeting?" Rowley straightened with one hand resting on the doorknob.

Jenna nodded. "Yeah, but just you and Kane for now. We have a number of cases to investigate." She lifted her chin. "Did Kane send you the image files from the body in the barrel homicide this morning?"

"Yeah, nasty business. I've printed a couple of images from the files he specified. Do you want me to give them to him? He mentioned they're for my eyes only."

"Yeah, go and get them but hand them straight to me." Irritated that Kane had taken over again, she leaned forward. "In case you're in any doubt who is in charge here, I'm the sheriff, not Kane."

"Is there a problem?" Kane's six-five, two hundred pound plus bulk filled the doorway, blocking the light. He flicked a glance from one to the other. "If you're referring to the evidence we found at the landfill this morning, I figured it would be better to keep it under wraps as this place is leaking like a sieve." He moved into the room and shut the door behind him. "Did you tell Rowley about the attempt on your life this morning?"

Shaking her head, Jenna stared at him. "Not yet. Do I have to remind you who is the sheriff here as well?"

"As your deputy, it's my responsibility to not only watch your back but act on your behalf in your absence. I'm just trying to do my job." Kane's expression hardened into granite.

Jenna took in his posture; the agitation flowed off him in waves. From his impressive references, he'd carried a gold shield in the homicide division in his last job. He was a born leader, and she suspected his cover story offered a minuscule insight into his capabilities. She needed a professional at her side. The fact he had placed his body on the line to protect her during the shooting proved she could trust him. Right now, she needed him onside and had no option but to allow him some slack. "I am fully aware of your position on my team but as sheriff the buck stops here. I've already given you the lead on the attempts on my life but I'm taking the lead on the murder case. If the two cross over and my involvement in any way causes a conflict of interest, then by all means step in. Until then, you'll both follow my orders. Is that clear?"

"Crystal clear, ma'am." Kane's stance was rigid. He glanced at Rowley. "I'd like Rowley with me when we conduct the interviews. I want to know the whereabouts of any potential suspects at the time of both incidents and his local knowledge will be an advantage."

"Yes, sir." Rowley flicked a glance at Jenna, and color filled his cheeks. "If that's okay with you, ma'am?"

Jenna rubbed her temples. "Of course, but you can worry about that later. The attempt on my life pales in significance with the body in the barrel case. Our first priority is the victim." She lifted her chin and stared at Rowley then Kane. "Understand?"

"Yeah." Kane cleared his throat and straightened, dwarfing the smaller man. "I'll interview Rockford, Watts, and Beal while we're waiting for the undertaker to complete his report."

"Fine." Jenna weighed up the idea of informing Rowley about the incident in the bushes at the Cattleman's Hotel. The young deputy had proven to be solid, and not informing him might hamper the case. She met Rowley's gaze. "Before we continue, I need to explain to Rowley why I've changed my mind about the accident. At first, I honestly believed my accident was just that, but on Saturday night, a man threatened me on the pathway out back of the Cattleman's Hotel. When we were at the landfill this morning someone took a shot at me and Kane is concerned the incidents might be linked."

"Saturday night?" Rowley gaped at her, disbelief etched on his face. "Why didn't you mention it at the time, ma'am? We should at least have searched the area for footprints."

Not willing to elaborate on her humiliation, Jenna shook her head. "It would have been a waste of time—at least fifty people used that pathway during the evening. All I have is a general idea of the build and height of the man. What he said made no sense at all and wasn't related to any case on file. His size could fit various men I know, including James Stone and Josh Rockford."

"This information doesn't leave this room—understand?" Kane looked down his long straight nose at Rowley.

"I know when to keep my mouth shut. So our job at the moment is to rule out persons of interest and get the bullet to forensics?" Rowley jotted down a list in his notepad.

Jenna sighed with relief. "*Exactly*, then we can concentrate on the murder case but for now we keep it under wraps."

"That will be difficult. The fact a murder has taken place and the grisly circumstances will be all over town by now. I doubt the owner of the landfill will be able to keep his mouth shut." Kane rolled his wide shoulders. "The moment we step outside, locals and no doubt the media will be asking questions." He grasped the back of one of the chairs in front of the desk and bent forward, staring at Jenna with an intent gaze. "The garrote is a crucial piece of evidence, so is the bangle. If it's okay with you, I'd suggest that information doesn't leave this room." His knuckles whitened.

Jenna snorted. "I *do* know how to run homicide investigations, Kane."

"Yes, ma'am." Kane let out a long, sigh. "It's just that Daniels is as green as spring grass and might run off at the mouth. Walters is far too friendly with Mayor Rockford, going on the conversation we had with the mayor on Saturday night."

"All excellent points." She met his gaze and raised a brow. "Continue investigating the cases involving me but I expect you to keep me in the loop. Are we clear?"

"Yes, ma'am." Kane straightened and his eyebrows raised in

question. "Do you want to discuss the evidence we have so far on the body in the barrel case with Rowley?"

Jenna tapped the end of her pen on the desk. *Oh, he's good.* "Very well, take a seat, gentlemen, and let's get the show on the road." She stood, picked up a small pile of images from her desk, and walked to the whiteboard. "As Kane said, we have to wait for the autopsy report on the victim at the landfill this morning, and from the decomposition of the body, identification is going to be difficult. When the undertaker notifies us about the victim's sex, we can eliminate the obvious by checking the personal effects we collected against our known missing persons' next of kin. If we have no one on file fitting the description, we'll send the information to other counties. Discovering the victim's identity is our first priority."

"If the body in the barrel isn't one of our missing persons, we'll need to keep moving forward on their investigations as well." Kane gave her a thin smile, turned the seat to face the whiteboard, and sat down. "I could delegate the workload between Walters and Daniels. Assuming the paperwork has come back for the warrants to view Helms' phone and bank statements. That would leave us free to contact the next of kin and trace the jewelry found on the body."

"I agree. Keeping the investigation moving forward is essential." Jenna placed the photographs of the missing persons, Mrs. Woodward and John Helms on the board and secured them with magnets. She took the marker from its holder and added their names. "We know the body in the barrel appeared to have dark hair but we don't know what effect the chemicals or the molasses residue had on the victims' hair color. In my opinion we shouldn't dismiss the fact that either of these people could be our body in the barrel. If so, until Weems can determine the sex of the victim, knowing their movements in the days prior to death will be crucial."

TWENTY-SIX

Just as Jenna thought her day could not get any worse, the phone rang. A knot of anxiety clamped her stomach. It was Mr. Weems with the autopsy report. Listening to the gruesome details of the final moments of murder victims had to be the worst part of her job. "Go ahead, Mr. Weems."

"This is only a preliminary report. The victim is male, age at this point undetermined. The body is in an advanced state of chemical decomposition but I've determined the likely cause of death is strangulation as the garrote around the neck cut through to the spine. However, before death the victim suffered horrific torture over a period of time. Bruising is in different stages and a number of the wounds appear to be at least five days old. He has a fractured skull, his back is broken, and his jaw has received considerable damage consistent to a blow by a blunt instrument, likely a hammer. I'm not sure about the tattoo. You'll need to call in the state forensic science team to examine the body and give a second opinion on this case. I'm not qualified in forensics to give an exact cause or time of death." He let out a long sigh. *"I've emailed you photographs of the bangle. There are interesting markings on the outside. I*

can't read them, and you may need an expert in languages as well."

Jenna cleared the lump in her throat. Another time in her life, she would have had a specialized forensics team working with her. "Very well. I'll contact the necessary people. Thank you." She dropped the phone into the cradle and turned to face her deputies. "Forget interviewing Rockford and the others for now. We'll concentrate on finding out if the body is Helms. If he owned a torque, it's the best lead we have." She returned to her desk and accessed her email account. A few moments later, both deputies' phones gave a message signal. "I've sent you the images of the bangle."

"At least it's not Mrs. Woodward." Rowley bowed his dark head over his phone screen.

"I think it would be better if I speak with Father Maguire before contacting Helms' wife." Kane leaned forward in his chair and gave her a questioning gaze. "Don't you agree?" He took a pad from the inside of his jacket. "Do you have his number? I'll call him. I gather he didn't supply any detailed personal information about Helms' situation apart from some domestic problems?"

"He only gave us a brief outline and enough information to file a missing persons' report." Jenna pushed to her feet and went to the whiteboard. "Just make vague inquiries. The victim could be anyone at this point." She jotted down three separate lists of names and heard Rowley's sharp intake of breath.

"Do you believe Josh Rockford is involved in the murder?" Rowley leaned forward expectantly in his seat and clasped his hands together, resting his forearms on his knees. "We went to the same school."

"I'm not sure. I need to have the three cases on the board so we can all see what evidence we have and who we believe is involved." Jenna wrote "*Attempted murder (shooting and accident)*" on the top of one list, "*Missing persons*" on the second, and "*Body in the barrel*" on the third. "Rockford is on the list of suspects for the shooting and my accident. Watts, Rockford, Beal, and James Stone are the only people I've had personal problems with of late. The only other person who comes to mind is Stan Clough. There was a nasty court case after I arrested him for cruelty to animals a year ago, but as far as I am aware, he got out of jail a month or so ago and is living in the back county. Kane mentioned to me he could be a psychopath in training, and after what I witnessed on his ranch, this type of torture is something he enjoys." She cleared her throat. "He sold his ranch, and I don't have a current address."

"I remember the case." Rowley pulled a face. "He said it was alien mutilations. The man is nuts."

"We need his whereabouts and you should have received notification along with his release information." Kane's blue gaze narrowed. "I'll ask Walters; he seems to know the local gossip."

She tapped the single name under Mrs. Woodward's name. "John Davis is the only person of interest we've linked to Woodward's disappearance, and his involvement if any is sketchy at best." She added the names of contacts for each missing person under their names. The column under the "Body in the barrel", she left blank. "I'm not adding the evidence Kane mentioned for obvious reasons but I'll update this entry with a list of suspects as more information arrives."

"What's the motive for the murder? From the images, the body is naked. The killer didn't take the gold from the victim, so it's not robbery. Kinky sex gone wrong?" Rowley's face had turned an odd shade of green. "The bangle is distinctive and would finger the murderer if he tried to sell it, I guess."

"What makes you believe the motive is money?" Kane raised both eyebrows. "There's no evidence to suggest the victim was killed for monetary gain. Not kinky sex either; those deaths are usually accidental, and garroting a person to the spine isn't accidental. This is torture. This type of killer usually starts with animals and escalates, so Stan Clough fits the profile and he's living somewhere in the area. It makes me wonder if he had anything to do with the other missing persons' cases reported before you started work here."

She nodded. "Yeah, I agree. He does fit the profile and *if* all the other missing persons are dead—but we don't know that, do we?"

"You gave evidence against Clough in the court case." Rowley's brown eyes lifted to Jenna's face. "Is he crazy enough to seek revenge?"

"That's a good point. If he is unhinged, he might want to get back at you." Kane gave Jenna a pointed look. "Does he fit the size of the man who attacked you?"

A chill ran down her spine at the memory of Stan Clough's dead, sunken eyes. Although she hadn't seen him for over a year, he had the same build as the man in the bushes. She nodded. "Yeah, unfortunately he does, but I'm convinced these incidents involving me are warnings. If not, why not kill me too? It doesn't make sense."

"Yeah, it does." Kane huffed out an exasperated sigh. "Psychopaths can lead completely normal lives and they don't kill indiscriminately. They can have wives and children and appear completely normal. I can give you three reasons why he didn't kill you. The killer might actually like you, or you don't fit the type of person he desires to kill. The third and most likely—in his sick mind he believes you're protecting him, if you accidently overlooked a crime. Say for instance Stan Clough was feeding a corpse to his pigs the day you arrested him. It would be your little secret but now he is out of jail, he needs to remind you to keep your mouth shut because he plans to kill again."

Oh my God. Jenna swallowed hard. "Then we have to assume the killer and my attacker is the same person."

"We have to *consider* the possibility and look at the whole picture, not just the murder." Kane gave her a worried look. "I'm afraid you might be the key."

"Whoever is doing this knows their way around town. A stranger wouldn't know how to get into the landfill by the back gate or when to avoid the work crew." Rowley's Adam's apple bobbed as he swallowed. "I've lived in Black Rock Falls all my life. I know these people and I didn't think any of them capable of torturing a man to death." He wet his lips. "Roughing up people, maybe... although..."

"If you have any idea who is capable of torturing someone to death—" Kane glared at him "—spit it out."

"After seeing what Stan Clough did to his animals, yeah, he is capable." Rowley moved around in his chair uncomfortably. "I wouldn't rule out Josh Rockford either. He's a jerk and one of the worst bullies I've encountered. I'd call what he did to the younger students at high school vicious. He does have a mean streak. Watch him play hockey and you'll see how much he enjoys hurting people. He becomes a crazy man at the game. If any of the fans give him a hard time, he gets right in their faces." He rubbed the back of his neck as if trying to make sense of the situation. "I don't mix with his crowd but I know he intimidates people and I've witnessed him threatening the sheriff." He sucked in a breath. "Yeah, he'd be capable of running the sheriff off the road and threatening her to prove his superiority, and I wouldn't take him off the list for the shooting either. Two shots close to hitting you is good from that distance, and he prides himself on his marksmanship. Could he torture a man to death? I couldn't say for sure."

"I wouldn't rule him out of the equation just yet." Kane pushed to his feet. He held out one roughened palm to Jenna for the pen and added Josh Rockford to the "*Body in the barrel*" list then turned to face the others. "Rockford surrounds himself with a small group of friends, all wealthy hockey players, and he is quick to retaliate. We know Helms was a fan of an opposing team. Perhaps he abused him during a game and Rockford lost it and killed him."

"Okay, but why is the real estate guy on two lists?" Rowley pointed a finger to the name "John Davis."

"He makes the '*Missing persons*' list because as far as we can determine, Davis is the last person to see Mrs. Woodward. Davis spoke to her in his real estate office and gave her a list of properties to visit." Kane's brow creased. "Mrs. Woodward withdrew a considerable bank draft and cash. So we can't discount money as a motive if she's been murdered."

Jenna returned to her seat. "Rockford has the strength to commit the crime but he doesn't need money. If it's John Helms —and from the color of the hair, we can assume it is a younger man—he could have met Helms at a hockey game and argued with him. If so, vengeance could be the motive and we know he enjoys hurting people. I believe Rockford and Stan Clough are our prime suspects for homicide."

TWENTY-SEVEN

Excited at last discovering a lead on her grandmother, Sarah Woodward turned the rental truck into the driveway and headed toward the ranch house. Ahead, she made out a pickup parked out front with a man rugged-up against the cold, wearing a Stetson and worn cowboy boots. She parked beside the vehicle and slid down her window. "Hi, I'm Sarah."

Cowboy Boots touched his hat. "Ma'am."

Deciding to leave her purse inside the car, she slid from the seat and smiled at him. "Is this the place my grandma was interested in buying?" She glanced at the dilapidated old house. "It looks like a fixer-upper."

"Yeah, that's what she said she wanted." His mouth turned up at the corners. "She told me she wanted a feel for the place and I arranged for her to stay in the root cellar. There's power down there, beds, and a stove. It's nice and warm. The house needs a ton of work before it's habitable."

Looking all around and trying to feel her grandmother's presence, she stared at the old house. "Did she stay?"

"I guess so. I found some of her things down there." He started walking toward the barn. "She could be back anytime."

Excited, Sarah wanted to jump for joy. No wonder no one had seen her grandma if she was staying out here in the backwoods. "Can I take a look? I would recognize my grandma's things."

"Sure, I'll show you the way."

The hum of machinery came from the barn as they headed inside. When he indicated to an entrance cut into the barn floor, she hesitated. Uneasiness crept over her as she stared down the dimly lit stairs. Fat spiders skittled away and dusty cobwebs wafted in the breeze. A shiver slid down her spine. *Never go into a dark cellar.* The warning played on a loop through her mind.

"If you're afraid, I'll come with you." Cowboy Boots pulled a pistol from the back of his belt and smiled at her. "I have this if we see a rat."

Apprehension slipped over her but she gathered her courage. Going into a dark cellar with a man holding a gun was stupid, but, if it was good enough for Grandma, it was okay for her. "Sure."

Taking each step with caution, she moved along a short passageway and then turned into the main room. The only illumination came from a dusty light suspended by a long cord. It glowed weakly above a wooden table and chairs. To one side unmade bunk beds sat in rows with blankets folded on each end. Heat flowed from a stove set in the middle of the cellar. "It is warm down here. You were right about the stove."

She turned away and agony slammed into her brain. She lifted her hand to the pain and dropped it absently staring at the blood dripping through her fingers. "Oh, I've hit my head."

She turned to look at him and a shaft of light fell on his expression and reflected in his eyes. Terror gripped her at the sight of his glowing eyes. It was like staring into the face of evil. She gaped at the gun pointed at her face and staggered back, uncomprehending. "Did *you* hit me?"

"Yeah." Cowboy Boots gave her an evil smile and stepped closer. He pressed the muzzle of the gun to her forehead. "Back up nice and slow until you reach the table and then be a good girl and remove your clothes."

TWENTY-EIGHT

Trying to unravel the evidence they'd collected, Jenna leaned back in her office chair and her attention settled on Kane. "What's your take on the suspects?"

"So far, Rockford is the only suspect with a possible motive, and I'm grabbing at straws here." Kane rubbed the back of his neck. "The evidence is weak and we'll require proof of his involvement before bringing him in for questioning. The same goes for Stan Clough. We should pay him a visit to find out what he's been doing since his release from jail. He appears to be a prime suspect but we still need to discuss the evidence linking Rockford to the crime."

Interested, Jenna tapped her pen on the table. "Go on."

"I saw a barrel identical to the one found at the landfill on the back of the vehicle involved in the accident." Kane gave her a meaningful stare and then moved to the whiteboard. He made a numbered list in the "*Body in the barrel*" column. "One, a pickup carrying a black barrel ran you off the road. Two, we find a corpse in a similar barrel, and if it is Helms, we have the hockey link to Rockford." He turned and stared at her. "Three, we concluded the person who dumped the barrel at the landfill used the back gate, which probably makes him a local. Four, on investigating, someone shot at us. Rowley mentioned Rockford's a crack shot." He pushed a hand through his hair, making it stick up in all directions. "What else can you tell me about Rockford? Why would he try to hurt you?"

Jenna thought for a beat and then frowned. "Rockford is big on getting even. I did bruise his ego in front of his friends. Do you figure that's enough?"

"Unless I'm correct and all three incidents are warnings." Kane scratched the dark stubble on his chin. "Do you recall the attacker's exact words?"

I'll never forget. Jenna pushed down the need to spew and nodded. "He said, 'Things were going nice and smooth and you had to bring in a big-city cop. Keep your mouth shut and your dog on a leash or I'll show you exactly what I'm capable of doing.' Then he cuffed me around the head, pushed me flat on my face and vanished. You arrived a couple of moments later." She moved her gaze from one deputy to the other. "He didn't make any sense, unless, like you said, I overlooked something during Stan Clough's arrest." She rubbed at the pain throbbing in her temples. "If it was Rockford, I did embarrass him in front of his friends and then you did the same when he tried to hit on me." She sighed. "We know Rockford was at the Cattleman's Hotel at the time I was attacked but from the size of the man, it could have been Stone as well. Although I don't recall seeing him there."

"I doubt whoever is responsible just happened to be in the right place at the right time. Someone is monitoring our movements." Kane stared into space. "The question is, how?"

"Oh, darn." Rowley's face reddened. "When Daniels was at the landfill directing traffic, he called in over the two-way asking for you." He winced. "I told him you'd gone to inspect the back gate at the landfill and would be in later."

Jenna sighed and rolled her eyes at Kane. "What did he want?"

"Oh, he said he'd resolved the traffic problem and wanted to return to the office." Rowley shrugged. "I told him to come on back. It wasn't something requiring your permission."

Nodding, Jenna tapped her pen on the table. It seemed that two-way radios were becoming a problem just like Kane had said. "That's fine. It's not your fault, you had no idea what was happening and neither did Daniels." She met his gaze. "But from now on we need to keep my movements off the airways. If you need to communicate with each other, use your phones."

"That only solves one mystery because you're usually at the Cattleman's Hotel after the Larks' game." Kane rubbed his chin. "Either man would only require a scanner to listen in to the cruiser transmissions. That makes three attempts on your life, in my book. So far, Stone has only been a nuisance and we don't know enough about him to believe he is capable of murder, so his name goes on the attempted murder list for now." He drew a line under Josh Rockford's name. "Rockford has threatened you twice, hasn't he, and in front of witnesses? Is there any other reason he would threaten you?"

Running possible reasons through her mind Jenna came up empty. "I have no idea. I've checked my files, and apart from a few warnings and the night in the lock-up, I've gone easy on Rockford. He is a jerk but I've put it down to youthful exuberance. I don't honestly believe I've given him a motive to hurt or threaten me."

"There must be a motive. Okay, the first one might have been an accident but three incidents in one week isn't something I care to ignore." Kane raised an eyebrow. "Are you sure you haven't overlooked something or been in the wrong place at the wrong time when Rockford was up to no good? Maybe he's committed a crime and this time his daddy can't buy him out of trouble."

Doubt flooded her mind in a wave of panic. Had she missed a vital clue to a crime? "Like murder, you mean?" Suddenly she couldn't breathe, and gripped the edge of the table to steady her trembling hands. "It certainly looks that way, doesn't it? This morning, I made notes on the times I've had dealings with Rockford and the others. I can remember every incident but I'm not going to recall something I didn't notice at the time. So we're back to square one." She swallowed the lump in her throat. *I need time to think, just in case I've missed something.* "If you believe he's a person of interest in both cases, check him out, and everyone else on the list, however trivial."

"Oh, I plan to. If Rockford is involved with the death of the man in the barrel, I can identify the pickup, which is a motive for killing me too." Kane straightened to his full impressive height. "And for the record, I'm not afraid of Rockford's daddy."

"If you're correct and the cases are connected, Josh Rockford won't come in easily." Rowley rubbed his chin and stared blankly at the whiteboard. "Holy cow, if he gets wind, we're planning to haul him in for questioning, he'll hightail it out of town for sure."

"I doubt he'll go anywhere. If he'd planned to skip town, he'd have by now. He was at Aunt Betty's this morning sitting at the table right next to me, grinning like an ape." Jenna pushed to her feet. "We'll ask him to come in for questioning and see what happens. If he lawyers up, then we'll know he has something to hide and we'll dig deeper." She looked up at Kane. "As James Stone is his lawyer, I'd appreciate if you would do the honors."

"My pleasure." Kane grimaced. "I'm looking forward to interrogating him too."

"I'm sure you are, but first our priority is identifying the victim. I want you to chase down Father Maguire to make inquiries about the bangle and tattoo. Get the details on Helms' wife and contact her for confirmation. Before you head out, send in Walters and Daniels." When Kane looked at her with a bemused expression, annoyance made her skin grow hot. "What are you standing around for? Get at it."

"Yes, ma'am." Kane strolled from the room, grinning.

Jenna turned to Rowley. "Find out where Sarah Woodward is today and go pay her a visit. Her number is on file. See if she is okay, then get back here, pronto—we have work to do."

"Copy that." Rowley stood and left the room.

Jenna went to the whiteboard and pushed it into the ceiling receptacle. She sat down as Daniels and Walters entered the office. "I'm waiting for information. Which one of you is hunting down the Ford pickup?"

"That would be me." Daniels smiled at her. "Walters said his head was spinning from looking at the screen for so long, so I took over. I have a list but it's not complete."

"Get at it—now. I need it yesterday." She waved him away then noticed the trail of dried mud in his wake. "Hey."

"Yes, Sheriff?" Daniels gave her the sweetest smile.

"Maggie will get mad if she sees you trailing dirt all over the floor; go and clean your boots."

"Sure thing." Daniels peered at his feet then shrugged. "I was out cleaning the driveway early this morning. I didn't have time to change. Sorry, ma'am."

She turned her attention to Walters. "Did you get the paperwork filed for a warrant for John Helms' bank and phone records?"

"Yes, ma'am, I have the warrant but I haven't had time to look at the records yet. I've been dealing with complaints about closing the landfill. Brinks has been on my back all morning. When will it reopen?"

"Not today. I'll tell Maggie to handle the calls. You concentrate on the records; I need information ASAP."

"Sure." Walters turned to leave. "Do you think Helms is the murder victim?"

Jenna drew a deep breath. "I've no idea but I hope not.

With any luck, someone may have picked our town as the perfect place to dump a body."

"I guess so." Walters frowned. "From what Brinks said it wasn't pretty."

Great, Brinks is running his mouth all over town. Jenna stared at him. "I don't have any details and I'm sure Mr. Brinks is prone to exaggeration. As far as I'm aware, he didn't get close enough to the body to make any observations."

"He was raving some on the phone." Walters shrugged. "If he calls again, I'll tell him to keep quiet." He scratched his chin and stared at her. "I can't figure out why an out-of-towner would try and dump a body here, especially at the landfill when it's so busy all the time."

The implications of his words hit Jenna and she raked her fingers through her hair. *If not, we have a sadistic killer in Black Rock Falls and I'm on his list.*

TWENTY-NINE

After calling Father Maguire's number and getting no reply, Kane checked through old files. His attention centered on cases involving the residents of Black Rock Falls before Jenna took over as sheriff. He flagged reports that involved current suspects. During his search, he discovered Woodward and Helms were not the only people to go missing. Three people of vastly different ages had disappeared without a trace the year before Jenna took office. He shook his head in astonishment at the incompetent police work. The files held missing persons' reports filed by family members without follow-up information, as if no investigation had taken place. He read each case with incredulity. The circumstances mirrored the current missing persons' files. Glancing down at Walters' name on the report, he rubbed his chin. Walters had not mentioned there'd been similar cases in the past. He pushed to his feet and strolled to Deputy Walters' desk. "Do you recall working on a few missing persons' cases about three years ago?"

Walters spun around in his chair and observed him over the top of his half-moon spectacles with a surprised expression.

"I do recall filing the reports." His eyes narrowed. "I didn't handle the investigations. If I recall, I was on vacation around that time. I figured the people showed as nothing was mentioned to me when I returned."

Kane leaned one hip on his desk. "Maybe, but there's nothing reflecting the outcome in the files. If they turned up safe and well, someone should have closed the cases. Who else worked here at the time, maybe I can follow up with them?"

"No one alive, I'm afraid." Walters let out a long sigh. "Sheriff Mitcham passed three months before Jenna took over and Deputy Andy Bristow was killed in a boating accident on his vacation summer before last."

How convenient. The link between the current cases was too significant to ignore. Kane shook his head. "Okay, thanks. Another thing—do you recall a man by the name of Stan Clough? He was involved in an animal cruelty case."

"Sure do." The old man shook his head slowly. "Sick SOB. Come to think about it, I saw him in town the other day." He scratched his graying head. "Let me see. The day before you arrived, he was in Aunt Betty's Café. I guess he comes into town to pick up supplies for his stock."

Surprised, Kane straightened. "You're telling me that he's allowed to keep animals after serving time for animal cruelty?"

"Seems so. I heard he was looking to buy a piggery." Walters peered at him over the top of his glasses. "He sold his ranch to pay for his lawyer but he only spent six months in jail. Got time off for good behavior. The sheriff should know where he's living, they send us a notice when prisoners are released."

Kane shook his head. "She doesn't have a current address for him. Can *you* hunt down where he's living? I need to pay him a visit."

"Sure thing." Walters made notes then lifted his head to look at him. "I'm collating the bank and phone information on the Helms case and will have it for you this afternoon."

Kane nodded. "Great." He strolled back to his desk and sat down.

He would need to make inquiries about the previous missing persons. If the people had turned up, fine, but if not, he might have a bigger problem on his hands. He reached for the phone. A few quick calls would put his mind at rest but, before he punched in the first number, he glanced at Jenna's office door and disconnected. *I guess I'd better ask the boss first.* He strolled into Jenna's office. "Is it okay if I check out the old missing persons' files?"

"Delegate." Jenna pushed a lock of black hair behind one ear and frowned at him. "I want you to concentrate on identifying the body in the barrel and then hunt down what Stan Clough has been doing since he got out of prison."

Kane took in her determined glare and nodded. "Yes, ma'am." He strolled back to his alcove.

Okay, I'll delegate. He waved Daniels over to his desk. "There are open missing persons' files from three years ago. Make a few calls and find out if the cases are current. It could be an oversight but I need to know. If they're closed, sign off on them, okay?" He jotted down the file numbers. "If they're still listed as missing, let me and the sheriff know."

"Sure thing. I'll get at it as soon as Maggie returns. I'm on front desk duty at the moment." Daniels took the note and strolled to the front desk.

Kane glanced up to see Rowley hovering by his cubicle. "Yeah?"

"We were scheduled to take lunch over an hour ago. I'm waiting for Sarah Woodward to return my call, so I can slip out now. You coming?"

Suddenly famished, Kane closed down his computer and stood. "Sure. I'm hitting brick walls with the priest as well." He motioned with his chin toward an elderly woman at the reception desk holding a dog dressed in a tartan coat. "I guess we should wait and deal with her complaint? She looks like she's giving Daniels a hard time."

"Walters usually handles her problems. Mrs. Gilly doesn't like speaking to young whippersnappers." Rowley chuckled. "I'm sure Pete needs the experience."

After lunch, Kane tried to reach Father Maguire again without success. He left his name and contact number with a brief message to contact him urgently. He spent the next hour on background checks and creating files for Jenna's list of suspects. He sent copies to himself and Jenna. As he had nothing to occupy his time in the evenings, he'd work on them at home. The heat in the office made him drowsy and he stretched out his legs and yawned. He waited for the files to upload and noticed Rowley leaning back in his chair, staring at his phone. "Did you hear back from Miss Woodward?"

"Nope, the call went straight to voicemail." Rowley stood and ambled over to his cubicle. "I called the motel where she's staying and asked to speak to her. They refused and said she has a 'Do Not Disturb' sign on her door. They said her vehicle drove out this morning and the sign went up sometime after, so they assume she left the vehicle somewhere and returned on foot." He rubbed his chin. "Do you think I should drop by and see if she's okay?"

A prickle of warning raced up Kane's spine. "Her ride broke down on Saturday night and she mentioned taking it to Miller's garage today. Maybe someone from the garage picked it up." He pushed to his feet. "Since people seem to have a habit of going missing of late, we'd better haul ass over there and check. I'm worried about her."

THIRTY

Kane headed for the door, snatching his coat from the peg on the way out. "We'll go in your cruiser." He led the way out the door and down the street to Rowley's police vehicle. The comfortable warm glow he enjoyed from the office vanished with the first blast of arctic wind. The ice-cold blast cut through his clothes and hit the metal plate in his head like an arrow. Gritting his teeth, he pulled on his woolen cap and tried to stop his teeth chattering. He flicked Rowley a glance. "Do you know the owner of the motel?"

"Yeah, it's been owned by the Ricker family for as long as I remember." Rowley slid into the driver's seat then gave him a worried look. "Oh, sorry, sir. Do you mind if I drive?"

"Nope, it will be good to ride shotgun for a while." Kane climbed into the vehicle and leaned back in the seat. "Talking of weapons... I noticed Jenna wasn't carrying a rifle in her vehicle at the time of the incident. You carry a backup weapon, I assume, and vests?"

"No weapons in the cruisers, no." Rowley shot him a glance. "They're in the sheriff's office. In the metal locker at the back of the room."

I'm going to have to take this up with Jenna tonight.

A few moments later, Rowley turned into the motel parking lot and pulled up in front of the office. "I'll go and get the number of Miss Woodward's room."

Snow brushed Kane's cheeks as he climbed out of the vehicle and scanned the immediate area. "We should both speak to the owner."

He noticed the lack of CT cameras and the two cars parked outside the dozen or so motel rooms. The parking lot had seen a ton of traffic over the last few days, going on the coating of gray slush. A blind moved in one of the units and a face peered at him through a condensation-soaked window and then stepped back out of sight. Taking a mental note of the unit number, he strolled around the hood of the cruiser and followed Rowley inside the office. The door shut behind him with a loud buzz and the heavy stink of cigars seared his nostrils. Moments later, a man emerged from the back room in a cloud of smoke. A TV commercial for beer blared out from behind him and a woman with makeup applied with a trowel sashayed past the door singing an old 1960s' rock song.

Kane moved to the front desk, keeping his hands on his waist. No way did he intend to touch the grimy counter. He wondered why the filthy place was such an attraction for visitors. He stared down at the overweight man in his sixties with receding white hair and a full beard stained yellow around the mouth. "Mr. Ricker?"

"Who's askin'?" The man gave him a narrow stare. "Don't recognize you."

"Deputy Kane." He indicated with his thumb toward Rowley. "I believe Deputy Rowley spoke to you about Miss Woodward earlier?"

"Yeah, and I told him she don't want to be disturbed." Ricker took a long drag of his cigar and blew out a sequence of smoke rings. "We respect our visitors' privacy here, especially if they stay long-term."

"So it seems." Kane straightened and rested one hand on the handle of the Glock holstered on his waist. "When did you last see her?"

"Last night. She came by for coffee." Mr. Ricker shrugged nonchalantly. "I don't figure she's left the room and her breakfast tray was outside the door as usual. Like I said, she wants to be alone. That's what the 'Do Not Disturb' sign is for, don't you know?"

"I understand but we need to speak with her and she's not answering her phone or returning messages. What number is her room?"

"I don't have to give you that information, officer." Ricker flicked the ash from the glowing tip of his cigar into an overflowing ashtray and his dark eyes filled with menace.

Kane moved closer to the man and towered over him. "We have probable cause to break down every door in the place to ensure her safety. Your choice."

"Wait a minute." Ricker let out a long impatient sigh then tapped on his computer. "Room twenty-five. It's the one right at the end of the row."

"Grab the pass key and show me. If she isn't answering the door, we'll need to check inside."

"What's going on out there?" The woman he'd heard singing strolled into the reception area.

"Nothing, Milly, the cops are checking on the girl in room twenty-five." Ricker smiled at her and took a jacket from the back of a chair. "Watch the desk. I'll be back soon." He shrugged into his coat then lifted up a partition in the desk, walked through, and opened the door.

A blast of icy wind rushed inside and Kane held open the door, sucking in the fresh air. He turned to Milly. "Mrs. Ricker?"

"Yeah. What's all this nonsense about Sarah?"

"Just routine inquiries." Kane flicked a glance at Rowley, silencing any chance of explanation. "Have you seen her today?"

"No." Mrs. Ricker chewed on her bottom lip as if thinking. "Rosa delivered her breakfast and picked up her tray. I'm sure she'd have said something if anything was wrong."

Kane waved Rowley out of the door. "I'm sure she's fine."

They followed the wobbling figure of Ricker along the footpath in front of the motel rooms. Halfway down the row, two men strode from a room to a vehicle, keeping their heads down and eyes averted before making a dignified retreat. Kane made a mental note of the make and license plate of the car. Beside him, Rowley stared after the vehicle then jotted down details in his notebook. He caught his eye and nodded. *Good man.*

"This is her room." Ricker knocked his grubby knuckles on the door. "Sarah? It's Bob Ricker. The cops are here to speak to you."

Nothing.

Kane used his fist to bang on the door. "Miss Woodward, it's Deputy Kane. Open the door please or we're coming in."

Nothing.

"Open the door, Mr. Ricker." Kane stepped to one side, and when the door swung inward, he held up one arm to prevent Ricker entering the room.

Light flowed through the door, illuminating the destruction inside. Someone had trashed the room and the smell of burned paper drifted in the musty air. He covered one hand with his sleeve and reached to flick on the light. There was no sign of Sarah in the main part of the room. He glanced at the other men and slid his Glock from the holster. "Stay here."

Moving around the piles of debris with care, he edged his way to the bathroom. Finding it empty, relief flooded over him. He scanned the tiny room. Fragments of burned paper with handwriting still visible curled black in the sink. By the marks on the toilet bowl, someone had flushed the rest. *Someone has burned her grandma's letters.* He bent to examine the vanity, hopeful he might be able to pull fingerprints from the charred smudges. What was in the letters for someone to go to such lengths to destroy them? Retracing his steps, he found Rowley waiting outside, wide-eyed and rubbing the back of his neck. Not wanting to discuss the evidence in front of the motel owner, he waved the deputy away. "Go get the cruiser and grab the forensics' kit."

"Yes, sir." Rowley took off at a run, his boots crunching on the gravel.

Kane reached for his phone and punched in Sarah Woodward's number. The call went straight to a cheery message from her saying she was busy and to leave a message. He left his name and a request to call him urgently. Unease clenched his gut. Hours had passed since anyone had heard from her. He examined the deadbolt on the door and grimaced. There was no sign of forced entry. Whoever had searched her room had a key. After pushing the phone back inside his pocket, he turned his back on the door to speak to the owner. "I gather Rosa delivered Miss Woodward's breakfast this morning, so I assume this happened sometime in the last couple of hours. Did you see anyone hanging around earlier?"

"Nope. I tend the counter and don't bother to come out unless the bell rings." Ricker stared at him anxiously and moved from one foot to the other. "Like I said before, I leave the customers alone. People don't like being under surveillance."

Kane nodded. "Sure, I understand." He pulled out his notebook and jotted down a few details. "I'll need to speak to Rosa and I want a list of everyone who stayed here last night, with all details."

"Sure." Mr. Ricker peered around him in an obvious attempt to see in the room. "She's not dead in there, is she?"

"No. Someone trashed the room." Kane folded his arms across his chest. "I'll write a report for your insurance. Now if you could do as I asked. Oh, and could you bring me a roll of Scotch tape?"

"Sure." Ricker waddled in the direction of the office and returned moments later with the required tape. "I'll go find Rosa."

"Thanks." Kane pulled out his phone and called Jenna to bring her up to speed. "No forced entry, and as Sarah didn't know anyone in town, the 'Do Not Disturb' sign was used by whoever trashed her room. I'm worried for her safety."

"We need to locate her ASAP." Jenna was all business. *"I'll track down the location of her phone."*

"Okay. I'll process the scene and look for prints. If I get any info from Rosa, I'll call you back." He disconnected and slipped the phone into his pocket.

Armed with tape and gloves, he walked Rowley through the crime scene procedure, collecting evidence, but found no prints in the ash smudges. Whoever had burned the papers had worn gloves. By the time they'd completed their sweep of the room, he could hear Mr. Ricker speaking in rapid Spanish with a woman he assumed was Rosa. He ushered Rowley outside and pulled the door shut. "Seal the door."

THIRTY-ONE

Standing beside the motel owner was a young woman in her twenties, and from the hushed conversation, she was under the impression he wanted to check her work visa. He offered her a smile to calm her nerves and spoke to her in Spanish. "You must be Rosa? Can you tell me what time you served breakfast to Miss Woodward?"

"Six thirty." Rosa trembled like a rabbit in a spotlight.

Kane leaned casually against the wall. "Did she speak to you at all?"

"Yes, she did and I was surprised she spoke my language. She said she was excited about hunting down her grandmother." Rosa frowned. "She told me the real estate agent had supplied a list of the properties her grandmother was interested in purchasing."

Interested, Kane straightened. "Was that the last time you saw her?"

"No." She waved a hand at the motel room door. "I'd finished cleaning number twenty-four and was going into number twenty-three when I saw her leave her tray outside the room then get in her vehicle. I didn't see her come back."

"What time did you see her leave?"

"I'm not sure." Rosa screwed up her nose. "Maybe seven-thirty. I don't usually start cleaning the rooms so early but the guests in rooms twenty-four and twenty-three checked out at six."

Kane made a few notes and flicked a glance over Rosa. By the way she twisted her hands in her apron, law enforcement scared her. In fact, her fear of him trembled in her voice. He spoke to her using gentle tones to keep her at ease. "When did you notice the 'Do Not Disturb' sign on the door?"

"Much later, after eleven." She shot a glance at Ricker as if seeking his permission. "Mr. Ricker sent me to clean number eighteen. I took clean towels down to Miss Woodward's room and the sign was on the door."

"Did you knock on her door?"

"Oh, no. I don't disturb guests if they put out a sign." Rosa lifted her chin as if considering his next question. "I didn't see anyone. Maybe you need to speak to Mrs. Bolton. She spies on everyone."

Kane recalled the person peering at him through the window. "Would she be in number sixteen?"

"Yeah, and she's one of our permanent guests." Ricker moved forward, looking anxious. "She's an elderly lady and I don't want you upsetting her. It's not good for business having cops snooping around."

"I'll be discreet." Kane cleared his throat. "I'll speak to her then we'll be on our way." He smiled at Rosa. "Thank you for your assistance."

He watched her scurry away and turned to Ricker. "Don't enter the room until further notice. The sheriff will need to look over the crime scene. Police tape is like a brick wall. If you go through it, I'll arrest you. If Miss Woodward returns, I want you to keep her in your office and notify me or the sheriff immediately." He reached in his pocket for one of his cards and handed it to him.

"Will do." Ricker let out a long sigh and shook his greasy head. "Can I go now?"

"Yeah." Kane motioned to Rowley and led the way to number sixteen. "Do you speak Spanish?"

"Yeah." Rowley fell into step beside him. "This looks bad."

"I'll speak to Mrs. Bolton and see if I can get any information. Call the sheriff and tell her what we learned from Rosa, then contact the real estate agent and get a copy of the list he gave to Sarah. Ask him what time she left his office and if she mentioned where she was heading." He snorted. "I'm wondering why he didn't forward one to me as requested."

"I have no idea." Rowley pulled out his phone and grimaced. "Someone sure as hell was after something from her."

"Yeah, my guess is they wanted the information in her mother's letters." Kane knocked on number sixteen and heard shuffling before a white-haired old lady peered through a crack in the door. He smiled at her. "Mrs. Bolton? I'm Deputy Kane. I was wondering if you happened to notice anyone hanging around the motel this morning between eight and eleven?"

"No one unusual. The two men who checked out and you is all." Mrs. Bolton shook her head, making her jowls wobble. "I'm letting the cold in. Anything else?"

Kane shook his head. "No. Thank you for your cooperation."

The door shut and he waved Rowley to the cruiser and listened to his one-sided conversation with Davis. When the deputy disconnected, he moved to his side. "Any luck?"

"Yeah, he's sending the list to my phone and has added the contact details of the owners. He said he dropped by the office earlier and gave the list of properties to Maggie. It must have been after we left for lunch." Rowley pushed the phone in his pocket then pulled a pair of gloves on to his bluish fingers.

"Something interesting—Sarah mentioned she was taking her vehicle over to Miller's Garage. She asked him where she could hire a vehicle to tackle the back roads. He informed her Miller's had rentals." Rowley rubbed his chin and his gaze drifted past Kane to the slush-covered road. "Mr. Davis said he tried to discourage her from traveling in this weather but she insisted on following in her grandmother's footsteps. She intended to show her photo around in case someone remembered her."

"His account doesn't make sense. I already informed her our deputies had interviewed most of the outlying ranchers and hadn't found a trace of her grandmother." Kane stamped the debris from his boots before opening the cruiser door. He slid into the seat and waited for Rowley to get behind the wheel. "She didn't come across to me as stupid. What would you do in her situation, considering Davis has supplied her with a list of properties, the owners' names, and phone numbers?"

"I'd go down the list and call first. I'd ask if they'd shown the property to her grandmother or had any inquiries from her." Rowley pulled his cap down over his cold, reddened ears then started the engine. "I mentioned the same thing to Davis and he said the list he'd given her grandma was a drive-by list. All except two of the properties are occupied and require an appointment for viewing. He made a point of insisting she contact him to arrange visits to properties that interested her. He said he gave Sarah the same information."

Kane drummed his fingers on one knee, thinking through the situation, then turned to Rowley. "Head for Miller's Garage. If the rental has a GPS, we might be able to track the location. What's the range like for phones in this area?"

"There are black spots, closer to the mountains and a patch near the industrial estate but the rest of the county is fine." Rowley drove out of the parking lot and headed down the main street, slowing to allow a large, shaggy, brown dog to cross in front of the vehicle. "I'll be... There's George Pringle's dog off the leash again. We'll have Mrs. Gilly back in the office complaining before long. For some reason that dog stands outside her house barking all night. You'd think the owner would keep it locked in the yard."

Kane shook his head in disbelief. "Don't we have a dog catcher?"

"Nope." Rowley flicked him a meaningful gaze. "Another thing the mayor denied." He turned into Miller's Garage and pulled up outside the office.

Kane snorted. "Then we'll start handing out tickets. That mutt is going to cause an accident." He slid out the vehicle and, zipping his jacket against the blast of freezing wind, headed toward the door.

A blast of heat hit him, laced with the smell of freshly brewed coffee. He inhaled and sighed. His next break could be hours away. A young attractive blonde sat behind the desk staring at a computer screen as if oblivious to their entry. He cleared his throat. "Good afternoon. My, that coffee smells good."

"Well, I'm sure I can spare a couple of cups." The woman stood slowly and gave him a slow, sultry smile. "You must be the new deputy. David Kane, I believe? I've heard so much about you. I'm Mary-Jo Miller. My dad owns this place." She held out a hand tipped with bright red fingernails.

"Nice to meet you." Kane removed a glove to shake her hand, and when she rubbed her thumb over the back of his hand, he raised an eyebrow. "I'll take you up on your offer of *coffee*, thank you." He disentangled his hand and caught Rowley's snort of amusement.

"What else can I do for you? Are you here about the insurance claim? Because I'm sure the company will contact the sheriff direct." Mary-Jo moved with a subtle swing of her hips toward the coffee maker and filled two to-go cups. "I know how Jake takes his coffee. Sugar and cream for you too, Dave?" She flicked him a sultry gaze from beneath mascaraed lashes as she handed out the drinks.

Are all the women in Black Rock Falls like this? "Yeah. Thank you." Kane straightened and removed his other glove. "I'm making inquiries about Sarah Woodward. I believe she rented an SUV earlier today. What time would that have been?"

"I'll take a look. It was early, just as we opened." Mary-Jo Miller tapped on the computer keyboard and smiled. "Just before we opened."

"Thanks. We're trying to contact her and her phone is out of range. Does the vehicle she hired have a GPS tracking system?"

"I've no idea." Mary-Jo stared blankly at him as if he had spoken in Martian. "I'll go ask my dad." She walked to a door at the back of the office, opened it, and called to her father.

George Miller, dressed in stained coveralls, strolled into the room, wiping his hands on an oily rag. "Yeah, I have two rentals here." He tipped his head toward a fire-engine-red pickup parked out front. "Both have GPS, and I can track them on my phone. Give me a second and I'll give you the coordinates." He took a phone from his top pocket and bent his balding head. "She is stationary out near the Old Mitcham Ranch. No need for me to give you directions, that's some ways past the sheriff's ranch. If she leaves now, you'll pass her on the road."

Kane handed Rowley his coffee, took out his notebook, and scanned the pages before jotting down the address. He thought he recognized the name. "As in the late Sheriff Mitcham?"

"Not him, his granddaddy. The ranch house has been empty for fifty years. Locals believe it is haunted and no one will go near the place. As far as I know, before he died, the sheriff divided the land. He added part onto his grandson's property and sold the rest to the adjoining ranches. I'm not sure what he planned for the house and remaining acre or two."

"Okay." Kane shoved the notebook back in his pocket and took the coffee from Rowley. "Thanks for the coffee, Miss Miller."

"Any time, and call me Mary-Jo. Black Rock Falls is a friendly town." She gave him a beatific smile.

Kane escaped through the door, following Rowley's deep chuckle with annoyance. "Do you know the Old Mitcham Ranch?"

"Yeah. It's about ten minutes from Jenna's ranch." Rowley climbed into the cruiser and flashed a wide grin. "Man, you *are* a chick magnet."

"Just drive." Kane gave him the Stare of Death. "Stop at the office. We'll take my truck and I'll drive. You can watch out for Miller's vehicle, in case we miss her."

"Sure. You'd better grab the two-way." Rowley's grin had not faded. "I'm not sure what the reception is like out there." He chuckled. "Man, next time you want a boys' night out, take me with you. I'll be your wingman."

Annoyed, Kane turned around in his seat and glared at him. "Get your mind back on the job and don't worry about the two-way. I have a satellite phone in my truck."

THIRTY-TWO

After picking up his vehicle, Kane headed the Beast into white. After passing Jenna's ranch, they went by the snowplow guy's house and assorted outbuildings. In the distance, a line of blackened trees stood out like sentries along the riverbank against the winter landscape. The isolated narrow road leading to Sarah's current position had a bank of dirty gray slush, and the blacktop showed signs of frequent use. He flicked a glance at Rowley. "Are you sure no one lives out here? This road has carried traffic over the last couple of days."

"This road gives access to the back acres of other ranches but it ends at the river about half a mile past the Old Mitcham Ranch. I'd imagine the ranch owners use it during winter rather than travel overland in the snow." Rowley shrugged. "If the house is on the market, who knows how many people have driven up here to view the property over the weekend." He frowned. "I should have asked Davis if he'd taken any clients out to the place lately." He pointed to an open gate in the distance. "There's the entrance on the left."

A wave of uneasiness pushed Kane's survival instincts to full alert. From the impressions in the snow, more than one vehicle had visited in the past hours. He pulled the Beast to the curb. "How far from the road is the ranch house?"

"Some way—it's in the middle of the lot." Rowley leaned forward in his seat and squinted into the distance. "You can't see the buildings until you drive around the trees."

"Nice and isolated for a drug lab." Kane indicated with his chin toward the cut-up road. "For a dilapidated property, it sure has a ton of visitors. We proceed with care. Will the trees give us cover to observe the house?"

"I think so but I haven't been here since high school." Rowley grimaced. "Some of us would ditch classes and drive out here to scare ourselves. This place has been a local hang-out for kids for years." He gave Kane a sideways glance. "Don't worry. I grew up, and like I said, I don't run with Rockford's crowd anymore."

Jenna was right about you. Maybe you're too honest for your own good. "It might be kids but it doesn't hurt to be careful."

The truck bumped over the compacted snow on the dirt road and turned into a clump of trees. Kane slid out of the driver's seat and moved to the edge of the clearing. A number of buildings surrounded the old dwelling and the remnants of a corral sat beside a tin-roofed barn. The property appeared to be deserted. He listened intently for any unusual sounds. A drug lab would need a generator and ducted ventilation. Scanning the area, he sectioned off each part and made mental notes. He itched to look in the cellar but pushed his mind out of drug-enforcement mode and back to his current case. Sarah's vehicle had to be on the property. She hadn't passed them and wouldn't be easy to miss. He climbed back in his truck and drove along the driveway.

Stopping by the front of the house, he held up a hand to prevent Rowley getting out. The snow outside the barn swirled in a muddy gray slush and to one side a broken branch held remnants of mud as if someone had attempted to hide footprints. *Oh, shit.* Heart pounding, his Glock slid into his palm. He lowered his voice to just above a whisper and reached for the door handle. "Stay behind me."

Moving with caution around the edge of the building, Kane put one hand up to stop Rowley and peered through a crack into the barn. The red SUV sat in the middle, windows wound up tight. He did a visual sweep of the area. "All clear." He slipped inside and checked the vehicle, then did a quick reconnaissance of the barn. "She's not here."

He ran across the small courtyard and flattened against the wall of the house. Bobbing his head back and forth, he took the chance of peering into a window covered with dust and laced in cobwebs. Nothing moved and he waved Rowley to his side then tried the front door. The hinges squeaked, the piercing noise loud enough to alert anyone inside the house. He raised his voice. "Sheriff's Department."

The silence within was deafening. He counted to ten then moved inside, easing down the hallway and scanning each room. The kitchen door stood open, framing an old wood stove, and the smell of candlewax hung in the air. Waving Rowley into position on the opposite side of the hallway, he moved inside and crouched, ready to fire. A few blackened candles sat in the middle of an old wooden table. Piles of trash, mainly soda cans and cigarette packets, overflowed from a rusty bucket and spilled across the floor. He moved along the wall and kicked in the pantry door.

Empty. The place was empty.

"Clear." Kane holstered his weapon. "No one has been here for ages. Look at our footprints in the dust, which means Sarah didn't come inside the house. We'll check outside." He rubbed the back of his neck and stared out of the kitchen window. "Do you know if there's a root cellar?"

"Yeah." Rowley stared out of the front door. "There's one in the barn."

Kane took off at a jog and barreled into the barn. He searched the floor, kicking at the piles of debris to clear the way, then bent and peered under the SUV. "Dammit, the door is under the vehicle."

Using his gloved hand, he pulled open the vehicle door, slipped the stick into neutral and released the handbrake. "We'll push it out of the way." He moved to the back of the vehicle and stared at Rowley. "What are you waiting for? Don't tell me you believe the crap about this place being haunted?"

"Yeah, I do." Rowley walked slowly inside the barn, eyes flicking from side to side. "The curse is real." He went to Kane's side and pushed the SUV the necessary few feet to expose the entrance. "There's no way I'm going into that root cellar, not without backup."

"Right. So you don't think I'm good enough backup. Too bad if someone is dying down there, huh?" Kane gave him a long, hard stare. "I could order you, but if you haven't got the guts to back me up then at least help me open the hatch." He grasped one of the brass handles and Rowley took the other. "On the count of three. One, two, three."

The heavy wooden hatch groaned open and a thick metallic smell burned his nostrils, taking him straight back to a mass murder scene he would rather forget. *Dammit!* " Sheriff's Department. Is anyone down there?"

Not a sound drifted through the stench of hot blood and excrement.

He moved away and pushed a sheet-white Rowley toward the barn door. "Go and get the flashlight from the glove compartment. I'll see if I can reach the sheriff." He pulled out his phone, and finding no signal, he followed Rowley to his truck.

He grabbed the flashlight from Rowley. "I'm heading into the root cellar. The satellite phone is in a holder under the dashboard. Contact Jenna and keep her on the line until I see what's down there."

"Y-you sure you don't want to wait for backup?" The color drained from Rowley's face.

"Kane gave him a long, steady look. "You're my backup. I need you to stay alert. From the smell, whatever's down there is injured and whoever was here has covered their tracks and left." Keeping his expression bland, he gripped Rowley's shoulder. "Brace yourself for the worst-case scenario. It's probably Sarah." He strolled toward the barn, head erect and back straight. Showing fear to a young deputy was not an option.

At times like these, he valued the years of intense training he'd endured during his time in special forces. He had the ability withstand torture, hardship, and graphic bloodshed, yet no amount of dehumanizing deleted the memories. The moment he took the first step into the cellar, the smell of blood engulfed him, sending horrific visions dancing across his memory. The eyes of the dead held secrets. The innocents, the monsters, God help him, he had witnessed murder in every form and had not hardened at the sight of it.

Pushing the ugliness aside, he squared his shoulders and moved down the steps, swinging the white beam before him. A scratching noise came from the void and he reached for his weapon. The Glock 22 slid into his hand, warm from his body heat. He pressed the flashlight along the muzzle and aimed the beam ahead. A pulse pounded in his ears with each step into total darkness. The dark, stinking pit closed in behind him, and the hairs on his body prickled at the threat of danger.

He bit down hard on the inside of his cheek to regain control. The life of a law enforcement officer was not like TV's emotionless, unfeeling robots who strolled into a crime scene without breaking a sweat. Man, he'd seen men's faces after witnessing a gruesome murder and the horror reflected in their eyes. Before his injury, he could walk into danger, remain calm, and force his brain to evaluate a situation in a clinical way even as it screamed commands to run. Now, the constant throbbing in his head reminded him of his mortality. He gripped the handle of his Glock and the small action infused him with courage. One thing for sure, he could trust his aim.

The flashlight hit a long, red-brick passageway. At the end yawned a dark opening covered in torn, dust-laden cobwebs. A layer of dirt had been disturbed, perhaps swept as if to conceal who had entered the room in the past few days. He continued downward and then as if another entrance had opened ahead, a light stinking breeze puffed dust into his eyes. This time a musky overtone like the smell of an athlete's locker room laced the air. Flattening against the wall, he doused the light and waited, listening for any sound and then moved downward. "Sheriff's Department. Sarah, are you down here?"

Nothing but the whistle of wind drifted past him.

At the bottom, the stench of fresh blood hit him like a train. He grimaced at the smell and turned on the flashlight. Easing around the corner into the room, and keeping his weapon raised, he waved the beam around the root cellar. The place was cleaner than expected and lined with shelves carrying bottles of dusty preserves. An old wooden chair sat in the middle of the room in front of a rusty metal table. He made out a pile of folded clothes and a pair of boots placed on one end and swallowed hard, recognizing the distinctive yellow windbreaker Sarah had worn during her visit to the office. He moved the light over a line of bunk beds. The row of four divided the space into two and obscured his view. "Sheriff's Department. Is anyone down here?"

An ice-cold breeze brushed his cheek and he slid the light to the right, illuminating a ventilation shaft. A tar-like substance stuck to his boots, making a sucking sound each time he moved. He froze mid-stride and pointed the light directly at his feet. The black spots under his boots appeared to be blood spatter.

This can't be good. Keeping his back to the wall, he edged toward the beds. The smell increased and anticipation of what he would find cramped his gut. He bit back a moan and then aimed the flashlight across the cellar floor.

It was a bloodbath.

A fall of blonde hair spread on the crimson ground, and blue eyes, so much like his sister's, gazed at him in sightless despair. He recognized Sarah Woodward even though the once pretty face was blood-spattered and bruised. A mixture of anger and despair surged through him and he bit back the need to run to her side. He gathered his senses, fell into the zone he used during his time as a sniper, and took in the scene. He quartered the area searching for evidence, Something moved and he stiffened, his trigger finger dropping into place. Small red eyes reflected in the flashlight's beam, and as if on command, a number of rats turned from their feast and vanished into the abyss. His stomach lurched and he squeezed his eyes shut to ease the revulsion.

With a heavy heart, he moved around the perimeter of the room as close as possible to Sarah, but avoiding the pool of blood to preserve the crime scene. He past the light over her naked body. A wide red smile cut deep across Sarah's slender neck, exposing the spine, and from the deep defensive wounds to her hands and arms, she had fought for her life. He pressed one hand against the wall and then turned, and holstering his weapon, retraced his steps. Bursting out of the root cellar, he ignored Rowley's gibbering and strode out into the fresh air, off the path, and into a snow-covered garden. He sucked in deep breaths and tried without success to push the horrific scene from his mind.

THIRTY-THREE

Desperately trying to clear his mind, Kane leaned against the tree trying to get the taste of death from his mouth.

"You've left a trail of blood behind you. Did you find Sarah?" Rowley appeared at his side, his face pale. "Is she dead?"

The vision of Sarah flashed back into Kane's mind. "Yeah."

"Jenna wants to speak to you." Rowley stuck the satellite phone in his hands.

Kane wiped his boots in the snow and then swallowed the bile rushing up the back of his throat. He lifted the phone. "Jenna?"

"Yeah. What's happening out there?"

Kane cleared his throat. "Sarah Woodward is dead."

"Sarah? Oh, no. Did she have an accident?"

"No, she's been murdered." He rubbed the back of his neck. "It's real bad. We'll need help from the State Forensic Science Division. This murder goes way over the capabilities of an undertaker."

"I've contacted the Montana State Crime Lab about the body

in the barrel case. They're sending people down from the FSD. They'll arrive first thing in the morning."

"Okay, good. Call them back and see if they can get here now." Kane shook his head to dispel the image of Sarah from his mind. "I found her in the root cellar. We'll need a generator and lights on hand for when the FSD officers arrive." He rubbed his throbbing temple, trying to push the images from his mind. "This is no thrill kill. It looks well planned. Whoever did this cleaned the site, and apart from the blood spatter, the place looks spotless. They've even swept the driveway. I didn't make out any footprints or recognizable tire marks anywhere."

"No evidence at all?" Jenna sounded incredulous.

"Not from what I could see with a flashlight in the root cellar but I haven't had more than a quick look around the barn. We found the rental parked over the hatch to the cellar, and my main concern was for Sarah's safety. It's pitch-black down there and I stepped in a patch of blood so I've contaminated the scene with my footprints. Although, I didn't go near the body, I kept to the wall."

"Did you check for a pulse? Try CPR?"

"No. The laceration to her neck goes to the spine and it was obvious she's dead. There was no need to check for a pulse. The blood spatter is over a wide area and I would have contaminated the scene." He paused to gather his wits. The image of Sarah played a re-run reel in his mind. "We'll need to secure the root cellar and we don't have enough men to run twenty-four-hour surveillance. It's not safe for anyone to do single shifts until we catch the killer and I'm not leaving here until forensics have been over the scene."

"No problems with the men and equipment." Jenna let out a long, frustrated sigh. *"I'll grab some provisions and join you."*

Kane gripped the phone and moved away from Rowley. "Bring Walters with you. I don't think anyone should be traveling the back roads alone."

"Do you think it's the same perpetrator as the barrel murder?"

"Yeah. There are similarities, and after being released from jail, if Stan Clough is our man, he'd be anxious to kill again."

He stared into the distance but could not dislodge the image of Sarah's blank stare. "The body at the landfill, and now Sarah. Whoever is doing this isn't going to be easy to profile. Most serial killers are attracted to a certain type of person and these victims are poles apart. If I'm wrong, and we're not dealing with a psychopath, this may be the work of an opportunistic thrill killer. I suggest you make sure our deputies are carrying a backup weapon and rifle in their vehicles."

"Are you saying if you hadn't come along when you did the other night, I might have been dragged off somewhere and sadistically murdered?"

"Yeah, there's a chance, but most likely it was a warning. Psychopaths aren't sane, Jenna. Maybe he believes you know he killed the man in the barrel and decided to keep his secret. When I arrived, he panicked and tried to prevent you from telling me. Remember what that guy said to you? 'Keep your mouth shut and your dog on a leash or I'll show you exactly what I'm capable of doing.' Maybe Sarah is another warning." Kane sucked in a deep breath. "We have another problem. I found three other missing persons' reports dated back before you took office. The last sheriff shelved them without a follow-up, which sends up a red flag. Walters' name is on the original reports but he went on vacation, and the cases were handled by someone else or not handled at all. I asked Daniels to follow up before I left, so he may have something by now. Do you recall anyone mentioning similar cases?"

"No. The place was understaffed and chaotic after Sheriff Mitcham died. I didn't have any communication from the missing persons' families after I arrived. None of the officers mentioned one missing person let alone three. Normal procedure

should have had them listed as current or unsolved." He could hear Jenna drumming her fingernails on the desk. *"It might have been an oversight. When people die, the chain of communication often breaks down."*

Kane paced up and down, his boots leaving tracks in the snow. "Yeah, I guess, but Deputy Andy Bristow was working at the time and he died *after* you took office, didn't he?"

"Yeah, in a boating accident on the river that runs alongside my ranch." A long pause made Kane believe she had disconnected, but then he heard her tapping on a keyboard. *"There's no mention of these files in my current case folder or open case folders going back five years. Where did you locate the information?"*

Kane kicked at a clump of ice and flicked a glance at Rowley, who stood staring at the root cellar door, face ashen as if in a trance. He needed to get him away from the scene. "In the archives, in the year prior to your arrival."

"Found them. Okay, I'll check for an update now."

"Good. Ah, can you get out here ASAP? Rowley needs to be relieved." Kane lowered his voice. "He is sheet-white and I don't want him driving or I'd send him back in my vehicle."

"Sure, I'll be out there as soon as possible."

Kane scanned the area, his gut instinct kicking in to be wary. "Be careful. You don't know who you can trust."

"Careful is my middle name."

Kane swallowed hard. Jenna was in danger and they both knew it.

THIRTY-FOUR

Jenna leaned back in her chair, the creak a familiar reassurance. She pressed the phone to her ear and listened to Kane's calm voice.

"Don't take chances with this animal. His fourth attempt on your life might be the charm."

He was correct. After three attempts on her life, and two homicides in less than a week, she couldn't trust a soul except David Kane.

"I'll make sure I have a deputy with me at all times. I'm not giving him another chance." She sighed. "If the missing persons' cases *are* active, then I'm worried about an inside cover-up. You mentioned the office leaked like a sieve and we don't know who is involved, although Walters is the only remaining officer from that time. He doesn't act suspicious. If Josh is involved and Walters is speaking to the mayor and reporting on everything we do, it would make sense he'd bury the files."

"Yeah, it would, and you're traveling alone with him later." She heard Kane's sharp intake of breath. *"Watch your back."*

"I will, but before I leave, ask the Blackwater Sheriff's Department for backup. I'll give them a call first and then grab my satellite phone and call you when I leave." She glanced at the door and a shiver of worry shot up her spine. "I'll make sure Walters drives and I'll keep one hand on my weapon."

"*Okay. Stay safe.*"

Suddenly glad to have him around, she bit her bottom lip. "Dave?"

"*Yeah?*"

The headache from hell threatened and she rubbed her temple. "Thanks. I'll be there within the hour." She sighed. "I'll chase up the forensics on the hood my attacker used as well."

"*Copy that.*"

Jenna pushed to her feet and strolled into the outer office. Daniels was at the front desk relieving Maggie and she beckoned for him. "Have you made any headway on the old missing persons' files?"

"Not yet. I've been filling in for Maggie." Daniels narrowed his gaze. "I'll get straight on it the moment she comes back from her break."

"No need, I'll look into it before I leave." She smiled at him. "You'll be in charge until Rowley returns."

"Yes, ma'am."

Jenna returned to her office and called the forensics department. "What have you got for me?"

"*We've determined the existence of blood on the hood but have yet to determine its origin. Would you like me to call you the moment the results are back?*"

"Yeah. Thanks." She disconnected then went down the list, dialing the missing persons' next of kin. Hearing the excited voice of a relative expecting to hear she had found their loved one alive followed by the despair at her denial was heartbreaking. She spoke to an elderly woman about her daughter, missing more than three years. "Did you have any communication from

Black Rock Falls County Sheriff's Department after you filed the missing persons' report?"

"*I did, yes. They told me by the bank records, they had reason to believe Jessica left the area and told me to file a report in the next county. I haven't heard a word since.*" She let out a snort of disgust. "*Blackwater Sheriff's Department found no trace of her either and informed me I'd have to wait seven years before she could be declared dead.*"

Jenna winced. "I'm so sorry. I'm the new sheriff and I'll take another look at the case. I will inform you of our findings."

"*I won't hold my breath.*" The line went dead.

All the missing people had apparently visited Blackwater prior to their disappearance and their relatives had received the same information from her office. All had the sudden urge to drain their bank accounts, just like Mrs. Woodward. Jenna jumped to her feet, went to the firearms lock-up, and took out a rifle. Snatching her coat on the way, she strode to the office door and marched up to Deputy Walters' desk. "I need you to check the ATM records for John Helms. Can you tell me if he disappeared immediately after withdrawing money in Blackwater?" She rested the rifle against his desk and shrugged into her coat.

"I'll do a search." Walters stared at the weapon and raised a gray eyebrow and then tapped away at his keyboard. He turned the screen for her to view the results and a frown crossed his face. "It sure looks like it. He was moving around spending money all over. Maximum cash withdrawals each time, just the same as the others."

Surprised Jenna stared at him. "The others? You knew about the bank account checks on the other missing persons?"

"Not until today. I was on vacation as far as I can recall but I found the files in the old archives." He hitched a rough thumb over one shoulder to an old computer. "I transferred everything I found to the new system."

"I had no idea there was a separate archive." Jenna leaned

over and stared at the screen. "What is the attraction in Black-water? Hookers and male escorts?" She ran her gaze down the five-figure amounts and raised an eyebrow. "High class, by the amounts."

"There are hookers everywhere but I don't know of any male escort agencies. If the men needed company, why go out of town? The Cattleman's Hotel here in Black Rock Falls has high-class escorts at the bar most nights, not Blackwater." Walters gave her an inquisitive stare. "You knew that, right?"

"No, I didn't." Jenna straightened and heard Daniels snigger from the next cubicle. "Prostitution is a crime in this state, Deputy, and I intend to enforce the law. My next question is, why hasn't this problem been dealt with before?"

"No proof." Walters shrugged. "We can't prove they're engaging in prostitution, no money changes hands. It's not a crime to meet a woman in a bar or to have sex with her after a date, is it?"

"I'll be looking into this later but right now grab your coat and follow me." Jenna picked up the rifle and headed toward the front desk. She tapped Magnolia on the back then drew her into a quiet space. "I'm pulling in a few deputies from Black-water County. When they arrive, send them out to the Old Mitcham Ranch. I'll be available by satellite phone if you need me. Oh, and if the media contacts you about the case at the landfill or anything else at all, you tell them 'no comment.' Understand?"

"Yes, ma'am, I've been 'no commenting' all day."

"Good." She smiled. "Deputy Daniels will be holding the fort. Walters will be back within the hour with Rowley. Make sure there is plenty of fresh coffee. It's going to be a long shift."

THIRTY-FIVE

On constant alert, Kane stood beside Rowley on the front steps of the old ranch house, rifle in hand. He'd switched his incoming calls to the satellite phone and pushed it inside his pocket. If Jenna got into trouble on the way out here, he could track the device in her earring on either phone, but right now, with a crazy on the loose, her safety was his first priority. He pushed the unease to one side and glanced around. His attention moved to the bank of trees, blocking his sightline to the road, and the idea someone might be watching them played on his mind. In their current position, they would be sitting ducks. He turned back toward the door. "Let's wait inside. I don't like being so exposed."

"Me either." Rowley shot him a fearful look and ducked inside the house. He sucked in a deep breath and shuddered. "The place hasn't changed since I was a kid."

"Yeah? So did you take girls down the root cellar to scare them? With the ghost legend, it would have been the place to be on Halloween."

"Nah, I didn't go near the barn, period. None of us ever went within ten feet of the door and I doubt anyone goes there now, or ever will again. I'd say the chances of selling this place now is zero." Rowley leaned against a wall, disturbing the green peeling paint, which fell over his shoulders like dandruff. "The old man who last lived in this house hanged himself from the rafters after murdering his wife. The legend says he haunts the place day and night. Even his grandson, the late sheriff, wouldn't come near the place." Rowley swallowed and his Adam's apple bobbed. "They say you can hear the rafters creaking as his granddaddy swings back and forth." He stared sightlessly out of the window toward the barn. "The old man had beaten and came close to decapitating his wife. That's why his son divided the property and sold the land surrounding the ranch house. He built a new place over the other side of town but the land backs onto this fence line."

Bile rushed up the back of Kane's throat. "Really?" The image of Sarah's battered body flashed across his mind like a scene from a horror movie. It was as if history was repeating. "Where did they find the old man's wife?"

"In the root cellar behind the bunk beds. Same place as you found Sarah." Rowley lifted his chin and frowned. "Josh went down there on a dare and told us the place was just as the cops had left it, like a time capsule. He said there are still bloodstains on the floor. It freaked me out big time." He barked a laugh as if to cover his embarrassment. "Being about twelve years old at the time, I had nightmares for over a year. I'm not looking forward to staying here overnight, not now, after what's happened. The place is cursed. Now everyone will say Sarah is haunting the place."

"If you plan to succeed in law enforcement, you need to grow up." Kane snorted and shook his head. "It's not a ghost you need to be worried about. We have two unsolved murders, and the killer or maybe *killers* are still at large. I figure whoever murdered Sarah didn't consider the tracker on the SUV and might return to move the vehicle to a different location."

Keeping his back to the wall, he shifted position to one side of the window and glanced outside. Josh Rockford's name drifted into his mind and made him wonder if the overconfident bully was the key player in this macabre play. "Keep a watch outside and stay clear of the window. I'm going to check out back." He grabbed his rifle and strode into the kitchen.

Running the facts through his mind, he scanned the backyard through the dusty kitchen window and then eased away from the wall to recheck the lock on the back door. He doubted the killer would return in daylight to relocate Sarah's vehicle but he would be watching his back just in case. The evidence pointed to a local who knew the Old Mitcham Ranch and the existence of the root cellar. Rockford fit the profile, and Stan Clough more so with a background of cruelty to animals, and both would have relied on the haunted barn myth to keep people away from the root cellar. Yet leaving the rental had been a massive mistake. The vehicle proved Sarah had visited the ranch, and anyone looking for her would have started an immediate search of the area. He wondered why the killer had not moved the vehicle to a different location, especially after making a substantial effort to cover his tracks. *Maybe he didn't have time and planned to come back after dark.*

He slammed his palm against his forehead. *What an idiot.* The killer hadn't run out of time. He had the sense not to relocate the SUV and then risk a long walk back to the ranch to collect his vehicle. If anyone had arrived, they'd have recognized him.

The sick freak had acted alone. It would have taken two men to move Sarah's vehicle, one to drive the rental, and one to drive his truck. It would have been the only way to get away unseen.

Mentally running the list of possible suspects, Kane rubbed his chin as his mind filled with doubt. His brief encounter with Josh Rockford gave him the impression he was a pack animal. As the alpha male, and a typical narcissist, he liked to impress his friends and bathed in their praise, which would mean he wouldn't go on a murder spree alone. As an exhibitionist, he'd want the world to view his kills and would stage his victims for the ultimate shock effect—not hide them in a barrel or root cellar. *Unless* he had planned to return with his groupies to show them the kill, and maybe take some selfies. If the killer believed he was untouchable, aka the mayor's son, anything was in the realms of possibility.

He considered Stan Clough and figured him a better option. His profile fit like a glove but he needed to know more about his case. Had he brutalized animals in the same manner and escalated his killing spree to people? It was a recognized pattern of behavior for a psychopath and couldn't be dismissed. Then there was John Davis the real estate broker. Instinct told him to dismiss him as a possible suspect, although being the last person to see Mrs. Woodward and admitting to have interacted with Sarah hours before her murder should have placed him slap bang in the middle of his radar.

Both murders had the hallmarks of a sadistic killer, who enjoyed inflicting pain and suffering. It would have taken considerable strength to have caused the amount of damage on both victims. He doubted John Davis had the physical capabilities and suspected a much younger, stronger person. The question of motive burned in his mind. Not a hate crime or a frenzied attack, the torture had been slow and systematic, the end brutal yet swift.

He discounted an opportunistic thrill kill. Most in this group of crazies killed and left the body in situ rather than attempting to hide their crime. They discarded their victims' bodies like burger wrappers and tossed them away like garbage. Once the thrill was over, the life gone, they held no value. The chance of Sarah crossing paths with her murderer on this stretch of highway would be remote. No predator would hang out on an isolated back road, especially in winter, in the hope of finding a victim to lure to their death.

The body in the barrel was not Mrs. Woodward, and he'd found no motive for the sadistic murders. *Unless* money was involved and the killer had murdered Mrs. Woodward as well. After all, she too had withdrawn large amounts of cash before she vanished. If someone had murdered her for her money, then that alone would tie in Sarah. She held information in the letters from her mother detailing her grandmother's last-known whereabouts and perhaps Mrs. Woodward had also mentioned the properties she planned to visit. It would make sense for Sarah to check every possible lead. She'd also failed to keep her movements secret, and any number of people in the garage or real estate office could have overheard her plans.

On the back roads of Black Rock Falls she'd have been alone and vulnerable. Had the murderer followed Sarah or lured her to this location? Did she call anyone in the hours before her death? He needed her phone records. If the same killer had murdered both victims, whoever had killed Sarah must have figured the information in the letters would lead the sheriff straight to him.

Kane ran over the timeline. The last person to see Sarah alive as far as he could determine would have been Mary-Jo Miller. Sarah had collected the rental at eight and he'd arrived on scene at four-thirty. The killer had eight hours to murder Sarah, take her motel key, and then trash her room to destroy the evidence. A local would know about the lack of security and check-out time, but how did the killer discover Sarah had the letters? Kane pushed his fingers under his woolen cap to rub the throbbing scar on his head and went over the evidence one more time.

As far as he was aware, apart from her visit to the office, Sarah had discussed her information with at least three people: Rosa at the motel, Mr. Miller at the garage or perhaps his daughter, and maybe she'd mentioned it to John Davis. He cast his mind back to the night her vehicle broke down. She'd informed him about the information she had discovered, and Billy Watts had been right there beside him in the Cattleman's Hotel parking lot. *Another link to Rockford.* Watts had overheard everything, including his orders to Daniels to escort her back to her motel. Watts could have followed her to the motel and discovered her room number. He pulled out his notebook and jotted down a list of people to interview. His main aim would be to discover the suspects' whereabouts between eight this morning and the approximate time of death. For now, he would have to cool his heels and wait for the autopsy report and then discuss his theories with Jenna. He would need her permission to haul in his list of suspects for questioning.

Another chilling thought entered his mind. If the killer concealed the first murder but deliberately left Sarah's body as a display of his brutality for Jenna to see, it would change everything. The words of Jenna's attacker rang in his head like a death knell. *Keep your mouth shut or I'll show you exactly what I'm capable of doing.*

Cold seeped into his bones as if he stood naked in the freezing temperature. The threat against Jenna hung in the air, unspoken but as sure as the sun rising in the morning. *If Sarah's murder is an example of his brutality, the next time it will be Jenna.*

THIRTY-SIX

The satellite phone signaled an incoming call and Kane snatched it from his pocket.

"*Good afternoon, this is Father Maguire returning your call.*"

He dragged his thoughts from his deliberations and cleared his throat. "Ah, Father Maguire, thanks for calling. I have a few questions regarding John Helms. Do you ever recall him wearing a gold bangle?"

"*A bangle, yes. A torque, he called it. I believe it was a family heirloom and he rarely removed it, as I recall. He said the inscription contained a story about his ancestors.*"

The body is John Helms. Kane leaned his forehead against the wall and swallowed a groan. The only connection between the murders had vanished like smoke in the wind. He'd tied up everything so neatly in his mind, and the revelation that he'd made a gaping error in his impeccable deductive skills came as a shock. If the body was John Helms, the motive for Sarah's murder and the burning of the letters had flown out of the window. He sucked in a deep steadying breath. "That's very interesting, and do you remember if he had any tattoos?"

"Yes, a symbol of some kind on his right shoulder. He'd gotten it recently and it was a bone of contention with his wife. He mentioned the argument with her about it before he left. Does this mean you have some news for me, at last?"

Kane stared into the distance, not wanting to give out any information. "Not officially, no. We found a body and can't make a positive ID without dental records or DNA. We can't jump to conclusions and assume the victim is Mr. Helms. I wouldn't want to cause undue distress to his wife."

"I understand completely. How can I help?"

Kane strolled to Rowley's position and peered out the window, relieved to see Walters' cruiser and a truck moving toward the house. "Is it possible to get me the name of Mr. Helms' dentist? I'd rather not contact Mrs. Helms until we have more information. At the moment I'm still conducting routine inquiries."

"There are three in town. I'll have to tell a white lie and say John recommended one to me then I asked his wife for his name. I'll call you back."

"Thank you." Kane disconnected and strolled across the room to stand beside Deputy Rowley. "Stay here and keep watch. I'm going to help Jenna unload the equipment."

"Okay." Rowley straightened. His face remained pale and his voice shook slightly. "Do you want me to keep the details of Sarah's murder to myself? You know Daniels and Maggie will ask what's happening out here."

Kane nodded. "Yeah, say nothing for now other than we're dealing with an incident. For now, apart from me, only the three of us will know the exact details of the murder, and I'm planning to keep it that way. I'm hoping when the forensics team has examined the crime scene and completed an autopsy, they'll be able to give us more information." He placed a hand on Rowley's shoulder. "Often, keeping specifics of a crime secret leads to an arrest. Sometimes murderers like to brag about their kills, and then you have the lunatics who come into the office to confess. It's all in the details, so we keep our mouths shut. Got it?"

"Yeah, no worries."

Kane did a visual scan of the area outside and then pulled open the front door. He hurried to the truck. The door opened with a whine and Jenna slid out, landing beside him.

"Hey." Jenna gripped his arm and her concerned gaze raked his face. "You look like hell."

Pushing Sarah's death stare to the back of his mind, Kane kept his voice to just above a whisper. "I sure came close to hell in the root cellar."

Jenna's eyes showed a flash of genuine compassion. She squeezed his arm. "I'm sorry you had to go down there alone."

Kane shrugged. "Rather me than Rowley, and I needed him to keep watch. I didn't like the idea of someone trapping me down there if the killer decided to return. The idea of blocking the entrance with Sarah's SUV was a stroke of genius. I almost missed it, and if Rowley hadn't known about the root cellar, we wouldn't have found the body." He glanced at Walters and, seeing he was way out of earshot, moved closer to Jenna. "I've just received info on the body in the barrel. Father Maguire confirmed John Helms wears a torque bangle similar to the one we found and has a tattoo on one shoulder. I've asked him if he could send us the name of Helms' dentist. I'll have Helms' x-rays sent to the forensics team to make a comparison before we contact his next of kin." He puffed out a sigh in a cloud of steam. "After this murder, I'm worried about Mrs. Woodward."

Kane glanced at Jenna; he needed to confide his concerns to her. "After the threat from the guy who assaulted you, do you figure killing Sarah was another warning for you to keep quiet?"

"I hope not, but it's possible." Jenna peered at him and a

flash of worry crossed her face. "I believe Mrs. Woodward is dead. We just haven't found her body yet. She could be in a barrel as well and buried in the landfill."

Kane thought for a beat and nodded. "You could be right, but what's confusing me is why someone wanted to destroy the letters and kill Sarah... unless they're involved with Mrs. Woodward's disappearance? No one knows we're close to identifying the body in the barrel or if the murders are connected."

"Unless Mrs. Woodward came into contact with Stan Clough and mentioned she'd told her daughter all about her visit. Maybe we should ask Sarah's mother?" Jenna flicked a glance in Walters' direction and lifted both eyebrows. "We'll talk later in private." As the old deputy strolled toward her, she raised her voice. "There's nothing we can do for her now. We need to get to work and find her killer."

Kane grimaced. "It would help if we had a suspect." He looked at Deputy Walters. "Any luck finding Sam Clough's current address?"

"Not yet. Davis likely sold him a new place but he's out of the office right now. I left a message."

"I have fresh coffee and hot food from Aunt Betty's for you and Rowley." Jenna waved a small hand toward Walters' cruiser. "There's a box of cakes, apple pie, and cookies as well in the trunk. Eat first then we'll unload the truck."

He smiled at her. "Thanks, I'm famished. You should go inside and I'll grab Rowley to help me unload the generator."

"No need. The generator is set up to work from the truck bed." Jenna walked to the back of the truck and pulled out a box of equipment.

Kane peered at the lanterns packed inside a box. "Did you bring floodlights?"

"I've everything we need. There are survival packs in the back of the cruiser, blankets, heaps of food, my coffee machine, and a change of clothes. I even brought a microwave." Jenna gave him a dismissive wave. "I can handle things from here and Walters is keeping a watch out for unwanted visitors. Go and eat before the food gets cold." She lifted her chin as if defying him to disobey her. "That's an order."

THIRTY-SEVEN

The moment Kane returned, Jenna grabbed a halogen flashlight, depressed the button, and then moved down the steps of the root cellar with the extension cord tucked under one arm. Halfway down, the stench leaked through the face mask and her stomach clenched with apprehension of seeing a brutal, insane act of violence. Refusing to allow Kane to witness any weakness, she squared her shoulders. It would have taken guts to walk down the steps alone in the pitch-black knowing death lay in wait. A faint glow of light spilled from the room and she tightened her grip on the flashlight. Breathing through her mouth, she turned the corner and moved the beam around a room cloaked in deep shadows. A single dusty lightbulb hung from a long string in the middle of the cellar swaying in the breeze from the open door.

Gathering her inner strength and professionalism as a shield, she plugged in the cords and bent to attach power to the floodlights Kane held out for her. Straightening, she peered into the intent gaze peering over his mask. She cleared her throat and willed her knees to stop shaking. "You ready?"

"Yeah, power up." As the powerful lights streamed across

the room like sunlight, Kane averted his gaze. "Man, that's bright." He blinked rapidly and then indicated with his chin toward the bunk beds. "She's over there." He pulled his phone out of a pocket. "You'll want our own set of photographs, I imagine?"

Horrified by the scene before her, Jenna nodded absently and stared at the blood spatter extending from under the bunk bed to the wall. She dragged leaden feet toward the body, keeping to the wall to avoid stepping in the sticky, dark, crimson blobs. Glad to have Kane's solid strength at her back, she pressed against the wall to edge around the beds. Kane's description of the crime scene as a bloodbath had been an understatement. Sarah had suffered for a considerable time before her killer had mercifully cut her throat. The blood pattern splashed on the walls and ceiling told of a prolonged, brutal attack. She couldn't dismiss the wave of compassion for the girl staring at her, with blue eyes opaque in death and mouth stretched open in a silent scream.

Stepping outside the brutality before her, Jenna called upon her years of training to observe the murder scene in a clinical, professional manner. She turned and followed the blood droplets back to the entrance and glanced up to examine the blood spatter on the ceiling. "Look up there. I believe she was hit from behind, knocked senseless, and then staggered over here." She pointed to the trail of blood and Kane's footprints. "The disturbance in the dust on the table makes me believe she grasped it to get her balance. There's blood on the floor and a few drops on the table. If the killer had been in this area, he would have wiped it down."

"I agree." Kane moved to her side then pointed one gloved finger to the chair beside the wooden table. "The killer must have threatened her with a weapon to make her undress. Look at her clothes. I doubt he would have bothered to take the time to fold everything. He would have torn them from her. I'd say she folded the clothes to gain time, maybe to get her head straight after the blow. From the precise folding, she wasn't badly injured. I'd say he used the blow as a threat of intent to make her follow orders." He rubbed the back of his neck. "Let's take a step backward. The only place I found evidence of a struggle or injury of any kind is here, not in the barn. Whoever killed her would realize that no person of sound mind would come down here in the dark. The killer is familiar with the layout of the place and had lamps of some kind. I'd say he planned this ahead of time."

"Or he had an accomplice." Jenna met Kane's gaze. "Do you figure two people are involved? One killed her and the other ransacked her motel room?"

"The door wasn't forced. So, someone used her key." Kane stared at the pile of clothes as if in deep thought. "Without the time of death? It's speculation, but she could've been killed *before* the room was ransacked."

Considering the possibility, Jenna glanced around the cellar then moved with care toward the pile of clothes and moved the flashlight beam across the table. "I see boots but where is her purse? Every time I've seen her, she carried a pink vinyl bag over her shoulder. Trust me, a woman rarely goes anywhere without her purse."

"We'll need to do a search of the vehicle." Kane's gaze drifted over her face. He turned around and stared at the body, his brow wrinkled. "I'd like to see her phone as well. Someone arranged to meet her here. I wish she'd contacted me before she'd decided to head off alone."

Letting out an exasperated sigh, Jenna nodded. "So do I, but the reason begs a question. Sarah didn't appear gullible to me, or stupid. Do you think she trusted the man who lured her down here?"

"It sure looks that way." Kane cleared his throat. "It has to be someone she met in the last week."

"Yeah, and it points to someone who frequents this place." Jenna flicked him a glance. "Or whoever made the place ready for potential buyers."

"Nah, the owner would hardly use his barn as a place to commit murder and risk being disturbed by someone coming here to view the property. No one is that stupid. At this point, we have three main suspects. Stan Clough fits the profile but we have no motive. John Davis had plenty of contact with Sarah but this is too neat. At his age, I doubt he'd have the energy to clean up in such a short time. Plus, he sent a list of the properties he gave Sarah to the office. Why would he do that if he planned to murder her? Same goes for James Stone, apart from being a bit creepy he doesn't have a motive, but I'll check him out just in case." Kane took photographs and then moved closer, casting twin giant shadows on the opposite wall. "Then we have Rockford. My worry is Stan Clough, a potential psychopath, whereabouts unknown. Finding him is top priority."

Jenna moved around the cellar scanning for evidence. "I agree, but right now the only people we can positively place in town at the time of Sarah's murder are Josh Rockford, Beal, and Watts."

"From what Rowley told me, none of the locals would come near the barn let alone venture down here. They believe the place is haunted." Kane turned his head to face her, squinting in the bright lights. "The only person who doesn't have a problem with the myth is Josh Rockford. He is a bully and knows the place. He has almost a cult following. If he and his friends are involved, they had plenty of time to kill her and clean up. I suggest you send Walters and Rowley to bring Rockford, Watts, and Beal in for questioning and then impound their cars before they have them cleaned." His dark eyebrows rose. "If Rockford is guilty, we'll find DNA evidence. Whoever did this would have been drenched in blood and have traces of her DNA on them, and in their car."

Jenna nodded in agreement. "We can hold them for seventy-two hours without charging them but the probable cause is weak. We don't have a shred of evidence against any of them so I hope the forensics team find traces of DNA or we have zip. I'll make sure Rowley asks the suspects to go with him to the office, then it's voluntary." She gaped at the pool of blood and her stomach cramped. "There's so much blood. Looks like she bled to death. The killer didn't have too much time to play out his fantasy. This looks like a rush job compared to John Helms' injuries."

"Maybe. What astounds me is how they managed to leave without leaving footprints." Kane's brow furrowed. "If she'd trusted me with her information, one phone call and I'd have prevented this happening."

"You gave her sound advice and told her you'd hunt down all the leads. It was her choice to ignore you." Jenna moved closer to the body, stepping with care between the rivulets of blood. She crouched behind Sarah's battered corpse and surveyed the blood pattern. "Look here. The killer used some-thing to spread the blood to smudge their footprints and here—" she pointed to a small fabric impression the size of a footprint in blood "—the killer used a second blanket or something to step onto to get out of the blood. A blanket would be big enough for them to stand on and wipe their feet. Maybe strip off, if they hadn't already. If this was planned, the person or persons doing this could have been naked, stepped onto a blanket and wiped away most of the blood with a towel, even pulled on socks and walked out. Look, there's a pile of blankets over there." She waved a hand at a shelf above a sink. "Maybe one inflicted the injuries and another helped him clean up."

"So, more than one person?" Kane narrowed his gaze and peered at the ceiling. "Look at those marks on the ceiling. They're even in size and spaced in bunches." His Adam's apple bobbed and he turned to look at Sarah for a long moment. "They used a stock whip on her. Those cuts on her back are similar to the marks on John Helms. It could be the same killer. He must have whipped her to make her divulge the information in the letters. She isn't bound, so I'd bet someone had a gun aimed on her." He waved a hand toward the bunk beds. "I think you're right about the use of blankets. There's something missing from that bunk, something square. Can you make out the patch on the bed not covered with dust? All the beds have folded blankets and quilts. One pile is missing. I'd say that's what they used. It would be easy to step out of the spatter and onto a blanket, and then use it to smear the blood over any footprints. They could have wrapped the soiled towels and bloody blanket in a quilt and taken the evidence with them." He narrowed his gaze. "Look to your right. Can you see those few drops of blood? I bet that's what dripped off the blanket when they transferred it to the quilt."

Jenna turned to look at him. "That makes sense but why didn't they cover her body?"

"Because she meant nothing to them." Kane lowered his phone to look at her, his expression masked in shadows. "She was an object for their thrill, but once the life left her body, she was useless."

"So they stripped off and walked out of here naked? Not likely in this weather. I can only imagine, when they told Sarah to strip, they stripped as well. I gather a man would work up quite a sweat inflicting that amount of damage, and the stove isn't dusty. It's been used recently." Jenna pinched the mask tighter on her nose. "They'd have had blood on them. Look at the scene, they'd have been covered no matter how much they'd removed with a towel."

"They could have washed." Kane moved with impressive care, using his phone camera to capture the scene from every angle possible without contaminating the evidence. "Rowley mentioned there's a river close by, so it would be easy enough to go there to remove the blood."

Jenna shook her head. "Not likely; it's frozen this time of year." She scanned the rest of the room. "This was built to store preserves and protect from storms but there must have been a bunkhouse for the workers. Once upon a time this place was a big cattle farm." She straightened and picked her way back to the edge of the room. "There's not much more we can do here. Forensics will be here in the morning. I think we should check the vehicle for her purse and phone and then see if there is a bunkhouse with a bathroom on the property. With power from the generator, they'd be able to have hot showers and I've seen forensics pull heaps of evidence from drains." She headed for the entrance. "We'll have to get dogs out here to search for the bloody clothes and blankets. They must have discarded them somewhere."

"They'd have burned them by now. If they didn't strip, they'd need a change of clothes. No one is going to drive back to town naked in this weather." Kane switched off the lights and followed her up the steps, his footsteps making no sound behind her. "So this was premeditated."

"Maybe not. An athlete often carries spare clothes or training gear in his car. So Rockford and his buddies are a fit." She changed her gloves and headed for the rental parked in the barn. "I'll take a look inside. Have your camera ready."

She searched the vehicle and peered under the seats. "Nothing. We'll have to check the trash cans from here to the motel in case they dumped her purse. The garbage truck doesn't do its rounds until the morning so we may be in luck."

"I'll get Daniels on it now." Kane reached for his satellite phone and made the call.

Jenna led the way out the front of the barn and scanned the area. She spotted an old building a short distance from the house. "Over there at the end of the path. That sure looks like a bunkhouse."

"And the path has been cleared recently." Kane bent to examine the pathway. "But maybe not by our killer. Cattle have been moved along here in the past day or so." He kicked at a frozen cow pie. "Yeah, that's fresh. It could have been any one of the local ranchers. Rowley mentioned the cattlemen use this property to access the adjoining land."

"Let's take a look, but we'll change the booties." Jenna pulled the blue covers from her boots and reached into her pocket for more. "If we collected trace evidence from the cellar, we'll contaminate the crime scene." She glanced around to see Kane had already removed his booties and face mask and was observing her with amusement. "Sorry. I forget sometimes, I'm not with Rowley."

"So I gathered." He gave her a wry smile. "I spent four years in a homicide investigation division and you mentioned you've had similar experience. If we can't solve this crime together, my head injury has affected me more than I figured." He replaced the booties and then trudged toward the bunkhouse.

THIRTY-EIGHT

Kane's inspection of the bunkhouse left no doubt someone had cleaned up. The strong smell of bleach lingered, deleting any chance of finding trace evidence, and now he had a case of premeditated murder. At least the forensics team would go over the place with a fine-toothed comb and it would only take a couple of hairs to collect DNA and match it to a suspect to identify the murderer. The odor of chlorine cleared the smell of blood from his nostrils, although leaving the root cellar door open to the winter chill had dissipated most of the stench. He'd dreaded going back to the crime scene but his unease at seeing Sarah's body again had fled in Jenna's presence. Her almost cold professionalism had reinforced his usual distant calm when viewing a victim, and by the time they'd walked out of the bunkhouse, his appetite had announced its return with a long growl. He caught Jenna's smile and laughed. "Sorry, my stomach has a will of its own. I need to eat more often than most people even after witnessing crime scenes and attending autopsies. I *did* appreciate the coffee and the food but I'm hungry again already."

"I wasn't expecting you to eat anything." She glanced at the barn and her mouth turned down in an expression of disgust. "I wouldn't have been able to eat for a week if I'd found the body. It would have been a shock, finding her. It was easier to go down there in the light, knowing what to expect, and with you at my side." She frowned at the sight of her deputies leaning against the truck, heads together in deep conversation. "I can't leave them alone for two seconds? Can you deal with them? I need to wash my hands."

"Sure." Kane strolled toward the two men.

He gave them instructions to take Rockford, Watts, and Beal in for questioning and headed toward the house. He'd make time to speak to Mr. Davis as well; the real estate agent was no longer on the top of his suspects list but he might shed light on where Stan Clough was living. A police cruiser came toward him along the driveway and parked beside the house. From the logo on the side of the vehicle, Blackwater County Sheriff's Department had sent two officers to relieve them. He waited on the stoop and after introductions gave the men a rundown of the situation. He followed them inside and met Jenna in the hallway. "Sheriff Alton, Deputies Jones and Clarke from Blackwater County."

"Thank you for coming." Jenna gave them a friendly smile and waved them into the sitting room. "This way, please."

Kane left Jenna to issue orders and strolled into the kitchen more than happy to see a coffee pot bubbling away on the bench beside a number of plastic-wrapped turnovers and other delicious items from Aunt Betty's Café. Jenna had brought enough supplies for a week, including cans of soup and other goods besides the microwave from the office.

After filling two paper plates with a selection of food, he poured two cups of coffee and then grinned at the cartons of milk and cream packed in snow on the kitchen windowsill. He lifted the window, pulled one inside, and added liberal amounts to the steaming brews.

"You make quite the househusband." Jenna nudged his elbow in a familiar way. "I'm surprised no one has snapped you up." She took a cup and plate and dropped wearily into one of the chairs beside the table and then loaded her cup with sugar.

The familiar scene triggered a memory, and his wife's face flashed into his mind. *Annie.* The image of her was usually the same, and not the vibrant woman he loved more than life. His mind tormented him with her death mask. *Push it away. In this life, she doesn't exist.* He placed his cup and plate on the table and then sat down opposite Jenna. His emotions ran high at the thought of Annie and he'd need to cover any telltale signs of distress from Jenna. Sure, on the job he'd talked his way out of difficult situations many a time, but fooling Jenna wouldn't be easy. He lifted his gaze to meet her inquisitive stare and forced his voice to remain steady. "Domestication is a necessary survival mode. If I couldn't cook or take care of myself, I wouldn't live too long, would I?" He sighed, remembering how Jenna had made it her business to keep him fed since his arrival. "I haven't had to rely on someone to feed me—well, up until now, it seems."

"Oh, I see." Jenna laughed and sipped her coffee then smiled warmly at him. "Strong, handsome, and domesticated. Don't you know women dream of meeting a guy like you?"

Stunned, he swallowed a mouthful of scalding coffee. *Oh, I didn't see that coming?* She had turned the tables on him in an instant. *Okay, I can play that game.* He'd show her a glimpse of his off-duty, normal side and see how things rolled between them. Right now, he needed a friend. Living a life filled with bad memories was miserable. He enjoyed Jenna's company and they worked together as if they'd been partners for a long time, but anything else would have to wait. Right now, a gaping, bleeding hole sat where his heart used to beat, but he needed a friend. Maybe a ways down the track, she'd be the woman to cure the ache in his heart. He leaned back, adopting a nonchalant pose. "That wasn't a come-on, was it, ma'am?"

Expecting her to laugh in his face or reprimand him, he picked up his coffee, not moving his attention from her face. Jenna did not blink but met his gaze full on, as if considering her reply.

"Rowley did mention the female attention you've received since arriving in town. He's asked every waitress at Aunt Betty's Café for a date without success and you have them falling at your feet." Jenna observed him over the rim of her cup. "He figures you're gay, by the way you cover your emotions but I see the way you react to women." She shrugged. "It's something else isn't it?"

"Nope." He glanced away, ashamed, as if finding her attractive would be cheating on his wife. "I did tell him I prefer *women*—not girls."

"I'm glad to hear it." Jenna raised an eyebrow. "It's strange. I've only known you a short time but I trust you. It's like an inbuilt instinct, as if we're the same. Same background, same secrets."

"I'm sure we *are* the same in many ways and I trust you too." He reached across the table and squeezed her hand. "Thanks for understanding. I'm working through some stuff right now. Not just my injury. I've recently suffered a very painful break-up. I'm old-school when it comes to relationships. I like stability and long term, not one-night stands."

"That's good to know." Jenna smiled at him. "It tells me you're dependable and I need that in my team right now."

One of the Blackwater deputies stomped down the hallway and they sprang apart. Kane turned in his seat and smiled at him. "Coffee is fresh."

"I'm fine." Deputy Jones touched his hat and looked at Jenna. "Ma'am, I just had a call from Deputy Rowley. The forensics team has updated their arrival since you notified them about the second murder. They're heading to Black Rock Falls by chopper and Deputy Rowley directed them to come here. They've scanned the area and believe they have room to land in the driveway if we move the cruisers round back."

"Do it." Jenna pushed to her feet. "ETA?"

"Ten minutes." Jones turned and headed back down the passageway.

Kane stood. "I'll move my truck. It's going to be a long night." He finished his coffee and moved to the sink to rinse his cup.

"David?"

He glanced at Jenna over one shoulder. "Yeah?"

"I like having you around." She smiled at him.

He turned from the sink, and gave her a long considering stare. "Thanks."

THIRTY-NINE

The forensics team moved like a well-oiled cog. Three hours after arriving, Sarah's body was loaded onto the chopper and the team had completed their investigation. Kane stood beside Jenna and listened with interest to the head forensic pathologist, Simon Duvall.

"I don't believe you've contaminated the crime scene, and I'll use the hair samples we took from both of you for elimination. We have collected Mr. Helms' body and you'll have my full report on both victims as soon as possible. I'll complete a drug screen on both victims as well but from the defense wounds on Miss Woodward, it would indicate she fought for her life." He rubbed one shoulder and winced as if in pain. "I'm not positive but I might have discovered a footprint partially covered by blood. Once we get the pictures back to the lab, I'll have a better idea." He held out a hand to Jenna. "I'll be in touch."

"Thank you." Jenna shook his hand and let out a relieved sigh.

"Deputy Kane." Duvall nodded cordially toward him then headed for the chopper.

Kane stared after him. "He seems competent. Known him long?"

"No, and yes, he is very professional." The chopper's engine started and she turned away and raised her voice. "I hope the Blackwater deputies have our gear packed up and ready to load. I'm looking forward to a long hot shower." She headed toward the house.

Before Kane could follow, a sleek black sports vehicle came around the trees and headed for the house at full speed, the back wheels sliding in the ice. Whoever was driving was in a rage. The vehicle stopped a short distance away and Mayor Rockford climbed out and slammed the door with such force the side window shattered. *So, he's just found out we have his son in for questioning.*

Kane straightened and rested one hand on his Glock. There was no way this idiot was going to browbeat Jenna. He moved to block the front door and waited at the top of the stairs. He heard footsteps and Jenna's voice behind him.

"I was expecting a visit from the mayor. He'll be here to complain about our overuse of resources." Jenna snorted. "Oh, that's right. We have his little boy in for questioning. He'll be lawyered up by now."

Kane straightened; his eyes fixed on the mayor. "Why don't you leave him to me this time?"

"Okay." Jenna walked away.

Kane stood his ground and glared at the mayor. He moved down the steps. "Mayor Rockford, I believe? What can I do for you?"

"You can release my boy, that's what you can do." Rockford's face turned a deep crimson. "Having too much to drink is one thing, but dragging him from hockey training is another matter. If you wanted to question him over the incident at the Cattleman's Hotel, I'd have brought him to the office myself first thing in the morning."

Kane lifted his chin to look down his nose at the irate man. "Your son hasn't been arrested. He's willingly helping us with our inquiries and can leave whenever he wants. He hasn't been charged but I'd like to question him."

"Where is the sheriff? I'm not speaking to a subordinate." Rockford waved a pudgy hand toward the door. "Go get her immediately."

Kane smothered the urge to pick the man up by his expensive tie and throw him back into his luxury car, and gave him his well-rehearsed look of death. "She's busy."

"Not too busy to speak to me. Remember who signs her paycheck."

"I'm afraid you'll have to take your turn. We've been a little occupied these last couple of days." Kane shrugged. "I'm sure we'll get time to question your son first thing in the morning."

"What exactly do you want to know? I'm sure I can clear up any misunderstanding."

Kane rolled his shoulders in a nonchalant, lazy manner, which ignited a flash of rage in the other man's eyes. "It is a routine inquiry and your son and his friends agreed to come in to answer a few questions. Unfortunately, the sheriff and I have been too busy to get back to the office. I'm sure you understand? If you'll excuse me, it's been a very long day and I have to pack up our equipment." He turned to go and the mayor grabbed him by the arm.

"Just you wait one minute." Mayor Rockford increased his grip. "*You're* on my payroll and I demand respect. Remember I can remove you from office with a stroke of my pen."

Kane stared at the man's hand for a long minute and then slowly lifted his gaze to his face. He noticed Rockford's anger change to uncertainty and drew in a deep breath. "Respect goes both ways. If you touch me again, we'll have a problem, and trust me, you don't want to have a problem with me."

"Are you *threatening* me?" Rockford dropped his hand and stepped back.

Kane kept his gaze steady on his face. "No more than you've threatened me." He shrugged. "I do my job and the only person I have to please is the sheriff. She hires and fires, not you. Now, *sir*, Sheriff Alton needs my help. If you'll excuse me?" He turned, marched up the steps, strode into the house, and shut the door behind him.

"By the look on your face, I gather he insulted you?" Jenna flashed him a wide grin and then walked from the kitchen carrying a carton piled with food.

"Nah, he threatened to fire me, is all." Kane chuckled. "He does look like a pig and he snorts when he's angry. I had a hard time to stop from laughing at him."

"What's his problem?" Jenna rested the carton on one hip.

Kane opened the front door for her and glanced outside; the light had faded to black "Rowley pulled his son in for questioning. He's on the warpath. I don't think it will be the last time we hear from him."

FORTY

Jenna drove her truck inside the barn, glad to see the headlights of Kane's vehicle close behind her. Although the sensor lights around the property had activated on their arrival, unease hung over her. It was common knowledge she lived alone, and the accident and double homicide had her nerves on edge. The near miss may have been an accident but her skin prickled at the notion the murders might have been committed as a personal message. She heard a tap on the window and snapped back, reaching for the weapon at her waist.

"Are you okay?" Kane gave her a quizzical stare. "You've been sitting here for a while."

Her hand moved from the butt of the pistol to the catch on the seatbelt. She opened the door and tried to force a smile. "Yeah, I'm fine. It's been a long and eventful day. I was trying to get my head back on."

"I've had a good look around. The way you've set the perimeter lights and the lack of trees would make it difficult for someone to hide." Kane waved toward the electronic barn door. "The barn is like Fort Knox. You've made sure it's impenetrable, right? That just leaves my place and your house. We can do a quick recon and then I'll unpack what's necessary. We can unload the other boxes in the morning."

"Good idea." She moved to jump down from the seat but he grasped her waist and lifted her from the truck. "You didn't have to do that, I'm quite capable."

"Yeah, I did." He gave her a crooked smile that reached his eyes. "You're exhausted. We've been running on adrenalin all day and now comes the drop." He shut the door and placed one palm on the small of her back. "I'll drive you to the cottage and unpack the pies and perishables, and then we'll go and make sure your place is secure."

"Great idea, thanks." She walked outside. Her attention lingered on every shadow as she depressed the button to close the barn door. "You know, after what's happened, living alone doesn't seem such a good idea anymore."

Kane had seen the look of a hunted person many times and wondered what threat lurked in Jenna's background. She was running from someone and he didn't have too much confidence in her cover story. He'd considered her to be an ex-special ops by the way she moved and handled a crisis, but now he was not so sure. If he'd failed to obtain intel on her from his contacts, and they went straight to the president, then she was in deep cover. If so, she likely had the same plastic surgery as him, and in his case removal of tattoos connecting him to the marines and some scars on his face. His cover was solid, impenetrable, and only three people on earth knew his name and location. He moved through the cottage, clearing each room. After collecting the box of food and his personal bag from the Beast, he removed the scanner and swept each room. He smiled at Jenna. "All good." He noticed her shoulders sag and pointed to the well-stocked wine rack under the kitchen bench. "I've got an excellent bottle of Pinot Noir and steaks in the freezer. How about allowing me to cook for you tonight?"

"I'm not sure I'll be very good company." Jenna pulled the knitted cap from her head and rubbed her hair vigorously. "I might fall asleep at the table."

Kane chuckled. "Then I'll put you on the sofa by the fire."

"Okay, that's a deal." Jenna smiled warmly. The professional mask of a sheriff vanished and Jenna's true self emerged like a snowdrop in spring. She yawned. "See you *after* I've taken a long shower."

Kane pulled two steaks from the freezer. "Take your time." He noticed a shadow cross her face. "Just to be safe, why don't you give me a call when you're ready and I'll come and get you? It's too cold to walk."

"I will. Thanks. Are you usually so thoughtful?"

"Ha, most people I've worked with think I'm an arrogant pain in the butt." He led the way to the door. "Sometimes the image has its advantages."

"It's all in the image, they say." She headed purposefully toward his truck, pulled open the passenger door and then her gaze settled on his face. "It's taken me years to gain respect in Black Rock Falls." She climbed inside and once he'd slipped into the driver's seat smiled at him. "It must be working. Not many people argue with me."

Kane drove to her front door and, leaving the engine idling, got out with the intention of opening her door, but she'd jumped out and joined him before his feet hit the ground. He followed her to the stoop. "I'll check inside just to be safe."

"Thanks, but if anyone broke in, they'd have tripped the alarm and it goes straight to my phone." Her lips curled into a smile. She climbed the steps and used her key to open the deadbolt.

Kane noticed the unlit security panel in the hallway at once and dragged her back before she had taken a step inside. He dropped his voice to a whisper. "Get back to the truck. Don't make a sound." He followed her and reversed down the driveway and into his garage. "The generator we used is your backup power for the alarm system, right?"

"Yeah but the front door wasn't forced." Jenna's gaze flashed to him. "Maybe I forgot to set the alarm. I was in a rush when I collected the supplies."

"There's no power to the house." Kane stared at Jenna's house. "When I came to your door the first time, the front light near blinded me. Now the floodlights lining the driveway are the only ones working. Can we get into the house round back?"

"Yeah, I have a key to the kitchen door." She gave him a long look. "I haven't opened it for some time. No need." She sighed and raised a dark brow. "What makes you think the murderer would risk coming here when you live close by? It doesn't make sense. I'm sure it's just a fuse."

Kane waved a hand toward the driveway. "If there's nothing to worry about, why all the security? Why bug my house? You did this way before I arrived. If someone has threatened you, maybe you should give me a name. No one in this town will be able to help you like I can. You know this by instinct, same as I know I can trust you. We're the same."

"Trust me, if the person who threatened me discovers my whereabouts, then God himself couldn't save me." Jenna met his gaze and lifted her chin in defiance. "At first, I thought *you'd* been sent to kill me. After three years, I'd become complacent, and seeing you, in this black truck, looking like a professional hitman, kind of tweaked my nerves. That's why I pointed the gun at you after the accident."

"Ah-huh." Kane smiled at her to break the tension. "I thought you acted a little unfriendly and I was trying real hard to be a knight in shining armor. You sure you don't want to give me this guy's name? I'm not God but I'm the closest ally you have right now."

"If I gave you a name you'd be implicated. Just drop it. *Please.*" She chewed on her bottom lip, making it blood red. "I've told you more than I should have already." She indicated toward the house. "I hope it's not booby-trapped."

Kane opened his door. "If the place is rigged, we have zero chance of discovering a trip wire or spotting anything unusual in the dark." He dropped his feet to the ground and turned to her. "I'll do a recon of the perimeter to make sure no one is lurking around, and we can check the house at first light. Grab my rifle and watch my back. If anyone is here, they'll be on this side of the house and using the shadows around the outbuildings for cover."

"You might as well draw a target on your back." Jenna slid from the vehicle and flipped open the hatch. "I won't allow you to put your life at risk. I'll call for backup."

"I'm not planning on strolling out under the floodlights. Trust me, I've done this a thousand times and under fire, but you're in charge."

"Okay, I guess combat experience comes in handy in situations like this."

"It sure does. Come with me and watch your step." Kane led her to the door at the back of the garage. "If someone is out there, they'll assume by now we've gone back inside." He opened the door a crack. "From here you can see the outbuildings. I'm going to be moving outside the floodlit area. If I flush anyone out, you'll have them covered with the rifle." He turned to face her. "I'll call out if I see anyone. Stay here in the shadows. If anyone comes out of the dark, press your earring and use the rifle. I'll be back in five minutes."

Not waiting for her reply, he pulled his black woolen cap down low on his forehead and pulled up the collar of his jacket to cover his light shirt. He eased his way along the side of the garage and moved in the shadow of the barn to the rear of the other buildings. Moving in stealth mode, he covered the distance without seeing anything unusual. When he rounded the last building and had the back of the house in view, a rabbit dashed across his path making as much noise as a steer before vanishing in the undergrowth. He waited, heart pounding, for any sound of movement but it seemed the place was deserted. From the far north corner, floodlights lit the other side of the house clear to the fence line.

Turning back, he retraced his steps rechecking the shadows. When he arrived at the garage, he paused just outside the entrance. "Clear."

"Thank goodness." Jenna moved to his side, the rifle looking huge in her hand. "Can you drive me into town? I'll take a room at the motel."

"It's late and we're both exhausted. Stay with me tonight." Kane took the rifle and replaced it inside his vehicle and then closed the door. "I'll cook while you take a shower and make up the spare room for you."

"Okay, but do you have something I can sleep in? I can drop my clothes in the washing machine and dry them for the morning." She gave him a tired smile. "Thanks, you're becoming my rock."

He waited for her to come to his side then locked the vehicle. "I hope so." He followed her to his front door. "Someone has to keep you safe."

FORTY-ONE

Later that evening, Jenna curled up on the bed in Kane's spare room and allowed the day to settle in her mind. Satisfied and dreamy from the meal Kane had prepared, her thoughts went to him. She smiled, hearing his light snoring rumbling up the hallway. He'd acted remote and controlling at first but she'd seen another gentler side to him she really liked. She snuggled under the blankets and closed her eyes. As she drifted into sleep, his image came into her mind. *Who are you really, David Kane?*

The following morning, after an early-morning workout and breakfast with Kane, Jenna followed him to the back of her house. The snow hadn't been disturbed; he meticulously checked every possible area for trip wires or sensor pads. His actions reinforced her opinion of her deputy sheriff. He moved like a marine and acted like special ops or secret service. She'd noticed the tiny scars on his face, much the same as she had after extensive plastic surgery, and he'd certainly suffered a head injury. When he came from the shower with his hair damp, the long scar on his scalp was evident. How he'd survived a gunshot to the head without any side effects told her he was one tough cookie.

After spending an hour searching the property for any explosive devices, Kane reconnected the generator backup unit to the house and barn. She shivered and stamped her frozen feet. "What now?"

"I'll check the connector box inside." Kane ushered her inside the house. "Where is it?"

She led the way along the hallway. " It's beside the back door."

"It's not a fuse." Kane's lips curled into a smile. "The cutoff switch was activated. You must have a faulty appliance. It's okay now, so it's nothing you're using at the moment." Kane strode into the kitchen. "I'll grab your things from the car."

Jenna followed him to the front door. "I'll help. I figure it's the toaster. A slice of bread had gotten jammed in it yesterday and wouldn't come out. I had to pry it loose with a knife and I might have bent something down the hole."

"Down the hole?" Kane chuckled with obvious glee. "I guess you had the sense to unplug it first?"

"Yeah, but I didn't use it again before I left." Jenna stared at him then a thought crossed her mind. "It could be the heater in my bedroom too. It's unreliable."

"I'll take a look if you want me to." He raised an eyebrow and then headed to his truck. "From the setup here, I expected you to be an electronics genius."

Jenna followed him. She shrugged as he piled the rest of her gear into her arms. "I know about alarm systems, but when toasters and heaters stop working, I usually just throw them in the trash and buy new ones."

"That would be the best option." Kane hoisted the microwave into his arms and closed the truck's door using his hip.

She moved up the steps before him, liking the way he followed behind her, guarding her back like a human shield. He was certainly different from anyone she'd worked with in the past. Sure, he had a mask of professionalism and treated her with respect, but she sensed vulnerability when he let down his guard. She'd witnessed his despair after discovering Sarah Woodward's body. His reaction was very different to the way he handled the body in the barrel. Kane had suffered loss, and recently.

Although he'd neglected to discuss the circumstances resulting in his head injury, she understood the incident occurred in the line of duty, but she had the strangest feeling he'd lost someone close to him that day. She dumped the box of dinnerware on the kitchen table and glanced at him. Strong and dependable, he'd protected her with his body in the woods. Maybe he'd lost his partner the day some clown had shot him in the head. A man like Kane would believe he'd failed to have his partner's back. If that had happened, it might account for his overprotectiveness of her. *I guess he'll tell me in his own time.*

"You okay?" Kane's concerned expression moved over her face.

Jenna checked the contents of the refrigerator. "Yeah, I'm fine."

"It's freezing in here. You don't need a refrigerator with the heat off." He set the microwave in place and plugged in the cord. The machine beeped and he took the time to set the clock before turning back to her. "Ready to get back to work?"

"Yeah." Jenna took a pair of gloves from her pocket and pulled them on. "Are you looking forward to interviewing Rockford and his friends?"

"Oh, yeah, and I'll be following up with John Davis as well. He might be trying to cover up something." Kane smoothed his hair and pulled on a woolen hat. "I'll be interested to see if any of our suspects are on the list of locals who own blue pickups. I want to know the whereabouts of our suspects and what vehicles they drive. Especially Stan Clough." He gave her a wry smile. "We're going to be busy, and if we find any proof to connect the murders with the attempts on your life, you know you'll need to step back and give me the lead? We don't want lawyers yelling 'conflict of interest' and ruining our case."

Jenna followed him down the steps and climbed into his truck. "I told you before I am happy for you to take charge of the incidents involving me, and if the two cases are linked, I'll stand aside."

"I'm not trying to take over but anyone can see Sarah's murder was a warning directed at you." Kane flicked her a glance.

She stared at him dumbfounded. After seeing him work in the field, his amazing reaction time and ability to keep all the facts of the cases in his mind, he was obviously the best man for the job.

"Okay, but I'm not staying locked in my office like a frightened mouse. I'll work behind the scenes and direct my deputies to make inquiries. They'll be hunting down leads if you're busy." She nodded. "Yeah, I could do with some downtime to chase up the insurance claim for my replacement cruiser. As it's essential, you'd think the company would push it through for me."

"Not when it's part of an ongoing investigation." Kane gave her a thin smile, slid into the driver's seat, pulled on his gloves, and then started the engine. "They like someone to blame and another insurance company to cover half or all the costs. I imagine the claim will take some weeks. Did you give Rowley the hit-and-run case?"

Jenna stared out the window. "Not yet. With everything else that's happened, my priorities are elsewhere. I just want my vehicle replaced."

"It's not like waving a magic wand. It's a large payout." Kane's chuckle rumbled in his chest as he turned the Beast down the driveway. "Haven't you filed an accident report for an insurance claim?"

Jenna laughed. "Oh yeah, but not for me personally, and nothing complicated like my incident. Mostly rear-enders and theft. You're correct about the insurance investigator, and as you're the only witness in my case, I guess they'll be contacting you sometime this week."

"The day just gets better." Kane pulled a face and headed toward town. "So much for a quiet life."

When they arrived, Jenna stared at the locked door and dark interior of the Black Rock Falls County Sheriff's Department office and flicked a glance at Kane. "What's going on?" She pulled the keys from her pocket and unlocked the main door. "We have people in custody. Where the hell are Walters and Daniels?" She pushed open the door and flicked on the overhead lights.

"I'll go and check if there's anyone in the cells." Kane grunted his disapproval and moving ahead of her, checked inside her office, before continuing down the stairs to the cells.

The door opened behind her and she turned to see Magnolia's bright smile. "Good morning. Where is everyone?"

"Mornin' to you, too. You're the first in this morning." Maggie removed her coat and hung it on a peg by the front door. "No call-outs overnight but Jake is trying to contact you." She raised both eyebrows as if waiting for an explanation.

Jenna removed her gloves and unzipped her jacket. Exhausted, she'd turned off her phone last night, and Rowley couldn't have reached her on the landline. "Did he leave a message?"

"No." Maggie took her seat behind the counter and switched on her computer. "I guess he'll tell you himself soon enough." She lifted her double chin toward the window. "There he is now."

Not wanting to discuss the case in the foyer, Jenna strolled into her office as the door to the cells slammed shut and footsteps headed in her direction. She stared at Kane's sour expression. "What?"

"We don't have anyone in custody." Annoyance flowed off Kane as he followed her into the office. "Walters and Daniels should have been on duty overnight. I told them to hold our suspects overnight for questioning. They should have split the shifts. On whose authority did they release them?"

Jenna's face grew hot and she moved to her desk. She cleared her throat and chanced a glance at him. Oh, man, he resembled the sky just before a hurricane. "I turned off my phone last night and apparently Rowley tried to reach me."

"Why didn't he contact me?" Kane lifted both his hands in the air and dropped them in exasperation.

Jenna shrugged. "Why do you *think*? He likely called the house and when I didn't answer a guessed I'd stayed overnight at your place."

"Oh." Kane rubbed the back of his neck and his gaze raked her face. "Yeah, *I see*, but really that's no excuse. You might have been in danger." His attention moved toward the door. "That sounds like him now." He turned and marched out of the office.

A few seconds later, Deputy Rowley strolled into the office wearing an uncomfortable expression. The tips of his ears had turned a bright shade of pink.

"Morning, ma'am." He gazed at Jenna then his feet. "I released the suspects."

"Why?" Kane shut the door behind him then dropped casually into a chair in front of her desk. "On whose authority?"

"Mayor Rockford came here with a lawyer who said he was representing Josh, Billy, and Dan. He insisted I show him the arrest warrants and asked if I'd read them their Miranda rights." He sucked in a long breath. "I explained the sheriff had brought them in for questioning and no charges had been laid. I also told him we had a right to hold his clients for seventy-two hours without charging them. I tried to contact the sheriff but the lawyer insisted I conduct the questioning in his presence or release the suspects. I couldn't quote probable cause or proceed because I wasn't up to speed with the current investigation." He ran a hand through his hair and shuffled his feet uncomfortably. "We didn't get to impound the vehicles either. The lawyer said we needed a warrant. As the only vehicle suspected in any ongoing cases is a blue Ford pickup and none of the suspects own one, I didn't have probable cause."

Jenna folded her hands on her desk. Rowley had followed the rules. "You had no other option." She caught Kane's annoyed expression in her periphery. "Just one thing. Did you ask the suspects to come in for questioning or did you arrest them?"

"I didn't have a warrant for their arrest." Rowley straightened. "I went to their hockey training and when they came out the dressing rooms, after training not before, I asked them to accompany me to the office to answer some questions." He sighed. "Rockford complained about police harassment, and said this was the third time we'd spoken to him in a week. Their coach told them it would be better to cooperate and they came willingly. I didn't put them in the cells or cuff them. Rockford called his father and shortly after the lawyer arrived and the mayor stormed off ranting about having you fired."

"Did you get to question them at all?" Kane leaned forward in his chair. "About their whereabouts during both incidents involving the sheriff?"

"Yeah." Rowley pulled out a notepad from his inside pocket. "I asked Rockford to account for his whereabouts on the night of the sheriff's accident. He said he took Susie Hartwig to dinner and she spent the night at his place." He flicked a glance at Kane and wiggled his eyebrows. "You'll remember the waitress from Aunt Betty's Café?"

"Go on." Kane waved a hand in dismissal. "Did you speak to Watts or Beal?"

"No, I interviewed Rockford. I'm not sure if Daniels got time to ask any questions. I asked him to question Billy Watts." He turned his attention back to Jenna. "I sent Walters home and swapped his duties with Daniels. He volunteered to be out at first light to search for Sarah Woodward's purse. Do you want me to go and help him? I'll work back from the motel to the crime scene?"

A knock came on the office door and she looked up to see Daniels. "Ah, just the person I wanted to see."

"Mornin', ma'am." Deputy Daniels flashed a white smile and approached the desk.

Jenna lifted her pen to make notes. "Did you have time to question Billy Watts about his whereabouts on the night of my accident?"

"No, but I did ask him if he was anywhere near Dutton Road yesterday morning. He said he did visit the landfill but couldn't dump his garbage." Daniels gave her a smug smile. "I know for a fact he keeps a hunting rifle in his pickup. He knows how to use a rifle. I've been hunting with him on a number of occasions."

"Who told you about the shooting?" Kane leaned forward in his chair then shot a cold glare at Deputy Rowley.

"Rowley." Daniels frowned. A bemused expression crossed his face. "He gave us both a rundown on the cases and what questions to ask the suspects. Times and whereabouts mostly. Although, he didn't mention finding Sarah Woodward murdered." He put his hands on his hips. "It wasn't a secret, was it?"

"Yeah, it is, because we need to keep a lid on the details of her death." Jenna glanced at Kane's stony expression. "I couldn't be reached last night and Rowley took the initiative to enable you to question the suspects."

"Thank you, ma'am." Rowley gave Daniels a nod and then turned to Kane. "After three incidents involving the sheriff in less than a week, I think one of us needs to be with her at all times."

Sick of her deputies classing her as a woman first, and sheriff second, Jenna let out a long sigh. "I can take care of myself and if I am kidnapped and lose my phone, vehicle, or weapon, Kane has devised a backup device to track me." She tapped her earring and smiled at Kane. "Our new deputy is very resourceful."

FORTY-TWO

Dumbfounded, Kane stared at Jenna. She'd lost her mind to be informing anyone about the tracking device in her earrings. He caught sight of movement in the hallway and pushed to his feet. Through the open door, he recognized Billy Watts strolling past on the way to the bathroom. He rubbed his chin, concerned one of Josh Rockford's friends had overheard the sheriff's conversation. The sight of Billy Watts triggered an avalanche of coincidental information he'd overlooked. Mind reeling, he cleared his throat and stared at Rowley. "Have either of you spoken to Billy Watts this morning?"

"I have and he's waiting in the outer office." Daniels stopped halfway to the door. "He came in again for questioning, says he has nothing to hide."

Kane nodded. "Okay thanks. When we're done here, ask him to wait and I'll speak to him."

Turning, he raised both eyebrows at Rowley. "The sheriff has given me the lead in the murder case and my main concern is to stop a maniac before he kills again. We'll need to prioritize. Right now, we don't have a positive ID for the man in the barrel. We're assuming the victim is John Helms and I've asked Father

Maguire to find the name of Helms' dentist. If it is him, then I'll request the local police contact his wife." He massaged the plate in his head and winced at the throb of discomfort. "Someone will need to contact Sarah Woodward's mother and ask her to identify the body."

"I'll ask Maggie to make the calls. She's very good at handling delicate situations." Jenna pushed a strand of hair from her forehead. "I wish I had more men. I need an update on the DMV files and someone to help Walters' search for Miss Woodward's purse." She sighed. "Has anyone heard back from Mr. Davis on the whereabouts of Stan Clough?"

"I completed the DMV search yesterday. It's in the file." Daniels lifted his bushy eyebrows. "I'll call my brothers and ask them if they know where Stan Clough lives." He smiled. "Then do you want me help Walters to hunt down Miss Woodward's purse? Do you have a description?"

Kane gave him the description and turned to Rowley. "Interview Susie Hartwig and see if she can corroborate Rockford's alibi."

"Did you find Sarah Woodward's body at the Old Mitcham Ranch?" Daniels gave him a worried look and moved around agitated. "I mean, you're hunting for her purse from there to the motel, so what's happened to her? I am entitled to know."

Kane narrowed his gaze. "Are you now? All you need to know is we found her body and I'm conducting inquiries."

He waved the deputies away and shut the door behind them. He turned to face Jenna. "Why did you tell the deputies about the tracker in your earring? As you're so concerned about a leak in the office, doesn't them knowing defeat the aim?

"I agree it was a stupid thing to do." Jenna shrugged. "It's too late to do anything about it now, so forget it." She straightened. "I can see your mind working. What else have you figured out about the case?"

"Seeing Billy Watts hanging around in the hallway triggered a few things in my mind." He moved to the whiteboard and picked up a marker. "I don't know if he is involved in the attempts on your life but coincidentally, he's been in the right place at the right time to collect information pertinent to one of our other cases."

"Billy Watts? Really? Which case?" Jenna's face creased into a frown. She stood and joined him at the whiteboard. "What makes you believe he's involved? Watts is the quieter one of Rockford's friends; in fact, more of an outsider. Hence the fight over money in the Cattleman's Hotel."

"He could be involved in Mrs. Woodward's disappearance." Kane wrote the man's name at the top of a space on the whiteboard. "Let's for a moment assume he murdered Mrs. Woodward. Watts gambles, so the money motive is a possibility." He added the information to the whiteboard. "He believes he's home free and then Sarah comes into town looking for her grandma. He wouldn't have been aware of her existence, but during my interview with her, he just happened to be waiting in the next cubicle for Daniels to complete his paperwork. He could have easily overheard the conversation about the letters and know her plans." He scribbled on the board. "It would make sense for him to destroy evidence that implicated him. I *did* wonder how he discovered Sarah's room number because the motel's proprietor refuses to give out information on guests." He snapped his fingers. "Then I remembered that Billy Watts was chatting to Sarah in the parking lot the night her vehicle broke down. He overheard our conversation about her plans to search for her grandma on Monday and the intention to have her vehicle serviced. He was five feet away when I ordered Daniels to escort her to her motel. Billy Watts drove out in their direction and could easily have followed her to discover her room number." He added the last incidents to the list. "If Watts is involved in the disappearance of Mrs. Woodward, then I think we might have found Sarah's killer."

"That sounds solid but I wouldn't discount Stan Clough just yet. He is the only suspect we have with a prior conviction."

Kane nodded. "Yeah, but not if the torture was to extract information, for instance the PIN for the victim's bank account. Heck, I've seen kids beaten to death for their shoes."

"I suppose if Sarah's grandmother stayed with Watts, as a housekeeper for instance, and mentioned him in a letter, we'd be able to track Mrs. Woodward to him. Watts lives alone on a ranch not far from the Larks' stadium, which means he could easily have met Helms as well. If Helms was the type of fan we imagine, an invitation to stay with a player would be too good to refuse." Jenna turned to him and tapped her pen on the table. "If Watts is involved in both murders and the motive is money, we'll need evidence."

Kane stared at the whiteboard. "We know both Woodward and Helms apparently left the county and suddenly had the desire to withdraw huge sums of money from ATMs in the same general area. We know Helms was tortured for a reason. If he gave up his PIN then it makes sense for his killer to withdraw money outside Black Rock Falls to give the appearance the victim had left the area. Before you ask, in most smaller towns the ATM cameras are useless. The pictures are grainy and in winter people are rugged up with hats and scarves." He returned the marker to the magnetic holder. "We have the bank records, and if we can place Watts or any of our suspects in those locations at the same time, we have probable cause for an arrest—and for the record, Stan Clough is still firmly on my radar. The moment I discover his whereabouts, I'll be on him like fleas on a dog."

"I'll go and see the judge personally and obtain warrants for as many phone and GPS records as I can." Jenna's lips curled up at the corners. "I'll be safe at the courthouse unless I run into James Stone but I doubt he'd cause a scene in front of the judge." Her blue gaze moved over him. "Great deduction, by the way, I feel like I'm working with Sherlock Holmes."

Kane followed Jenna out of the door, closing it behind him. Billy Watts sat on a chair in his cubicle, hands clasped on his knees and his attention fixed on Jenna. Kane cleared his throat to get his attention and then dropped into his chair spinning it to face him. "Mr. Watts?"

"Billy Watts." The man leaned back in his chair, taking his measure. "Call me Billy." His mouth curled in a cocky, self-assured grin. "My pa is Mr. Watts." He stretched out long, muscular legs clad in tight jeans and rolled his shoulders. "I gather you're Deputy Sheriff Kane?" He chuckled. "How's it feel being ordered around by a woman?"

Kane composed his features to give him a long, bland stare then took a notebook from the desk drawer and dropped it on the desk. "Much like being under the orders of a coach, I guess. I hear he has you on a tight curfew until the finals?"

"Yeah, since the disagreement at the Cattleman's Hotel." Watts snorted. "Man, some people can overreact. There was no need to call the cops. It was a misunderstanding between friends and now we all have to pay."

"People have a right to enjoy themselves without being afraid of jerks losing control and throwing punches." Kane reached for a pen from the chipped coffee cup on his desk, admiring the picture of a beautiful hula dancer on a picturesque beach complete with palm trees. "You're lucky the sheriff let you off with a warning. I'd have charged you."

"Yeah?" Watts leaned forward in his chair and glared at him. "So I gather you don't support the Larks, or did you bet on the other team this week?" His eyes narrowed. "Charging any of us would have left the team without its pivotal players and we don't like to lose."

Kane met his gaze without blinking. He'd interviewed all types and only the stupid tried to intimidate him. He yawned and covered his mouth with one hand, noticing the man's eye-roll. "Sorry. It's been a long few days. Do you mind if we get down to the questions? What make and model of vehicle you drive?"

"I own a Chevrolet Silverado pickup." Watts jerked a dirty thumb toward the front window. "The one with the black diamond paint and tinted windows out front."

"Okay." Kane glanced at the glistening vehicle parked at the curb and jotted down the details. "Give me an account of your whereabouts on Friday night at around midnight."

"I was here in the cells." He chuckled and crossed his cowboy boots at the ankles. "I spoke to you when they released me, on Saturday, remember?"

"Sure, my mistake." Kane stared at the sheet of paper. The inquiry had been a deliberate attempt to give him the impression the interview was a series of routine questions given to everyone. He lifted his gaze. "Do you know a person by the name of John Helms?"

"No." Billy Watts' gaze remained steady.

Kane kept his face expressionless. "Did you visit the landfill between Saturday and Monday?"

"Yeah. I dropped off some garbage on Saturday morning and I went back on Monday but it had a closed sign hanging on the gate. Why are you asking me the same questions as Pete?" Agitated, Watts moved around in his chair. "I didn't dump no body in a barrel, if that's what you're thinking. I dumped a ton of beer bottles on Saturday at the recycling area."

"Did you return home via Dutton Road?"

"Yeah, it's the way to my house." Watts eyed him suspiciously. "Why?"

Kane wrote a few notes and then lifted his gaze. He didn't like this arrogant young man and his gut told him he couldn't be trusted. "We're investigating a shooting incident in the region of Dutton Road around seven-thirty on Monday morning." He leaned back in the chair and tapped the pen on the notepad. "Did you happen to see a vehicle parked in or on the road at the back of the landfill?"

Billy Watts ran a hand through his thick blond hair and stared at the wall for a beat.

"Yeah, now I come to think of it I did see a dark blue Ford pickup, an older model, parked in the trees." He scratched his cheek and nodded. "Yeah, I noticed it on the way to the landfill and it was still there on the way back. I figured someone might be dumping garbage over the back fence." Color pinked the tips of his ears. "It crossed my mind to do the same thing but I had a police cruiser behind me."

Kane inclined his head. "Uh-huh. Did you happen to see the driver of the pickup?"

"Nah, I didn't see anyone, just the vehicle." Watts grinned. "I did see Deputy Walters' ugly face in his cruiser. He came past me doing seventy."

"How do you know Sarah Woodward?" Kane twirled the pen in his fingers like a casino chip. "Where did you meet her?"

"Sarah?" Watts raised both fair eyebrows to the hairline. "What's Sarah got to do with the body in the barrel?"

Kane kept his expression blank. "Just answer the question."

"Like I said, I've got nothing to hide." Watts cleared his throat and gave a dismissive shrug. "Sarah was here being questioned on Saturday morning. I made some comment or other to her outside about the way you guys harass everyone. That night she showed up at the restaurant in the Cattleman's Hotel. The waiter seated her next to my table. I introduced myself and as we were both dining alone I asked her to join me."

Kane wanted to punch the air. Now he had a link between Watts and Sarah. "What did you talk about?"

"Oh, this and that, mostly about hockey." Watts grinned wolfishly. "She'd heard of me and we got on real well."

Kane made notes. "I assume you escorted her to her car?"

"No, I had someone to talk to, so she left alone. I followed a short time later and she called me over when her vehicle wouldn't start." He flicked Kane an annoyed glance. "Then you showed up and spoiled everything. I was ready to drive her home. Maybe I'll catch up with her later?"

"Okay." Kane made a mental note of Watts' relaxed posture. *He doesn't know she's dead. Dammit, another theory out the window. So much for being Sherlock Holmes.* "Did Sarah mention her plans or where she was staying?"

"She was looking for her grandma." Watts huffed out a long sigh. "I know where she's staying and about her missing grandma. I overheard you talking to her."

Kane leaned back in his chair and gave him a direct stare. "Can you account for your movements on Monday after you left the landfill?"

"Yeah, I went to the Larks arena and dumped my garbage in the bin." He shrugged. "Then I called Dan, Dan Beal, and we went to Aunt Betty's Café for coffee and then hit the gym."

Kane raised his pen. "What time was this and what gym?"

"The gym at Larks and it was about eight when we left Aunt Betty's, I think. Some of the players would have seen me there as well and the assistant coach, John Beenie. They'll vouch for me."

Kane pushed the pad and pen toward him. "Give me those names." He flicked his attention over the man's hands; no injuries.

"Sure." Watts complied.

Asking for a DNA sample often caused people concern and Kane got his feet under him in case Watts decided to run. "Do you have any objection to giving a DNA sample?"

"Oh shit." Watts rubbed both hands down his face and peered at Kane through his fingers. "Has something happened to Sarah?"

Kane reached in his drawer for a DNA collection kit and

placed it on the desk. "I'm afraid Miss Woodward was involved in an incident yesterday morning. We're eliminating everyone who met her. All I need is a swab of the inside of your mouth."

"Do I need a lawyer?" Watts had turned sheet white.

Kane leaned forward and raised a brow. "That's up to you, Mr. Watts. As I said, I'm eliminating innocent people from a long list of suspects. If you have nothing to hide, do the test. It is voluntary but I'll get a court order if necessary."

"I swear I didn't touch her." Watts stared at the sealed packet on the desk. "What happened, did somebody hurt her?" He scratched his cheek and grimaced. "I guess it's bad if you need DNA samples?"

"Like I said, she was involved in an incident and I'm collecting DNA from people who met her recently."

"Okay, I'll take the test." Watts frowned. "Can you at least tell me if she's okay? She's a real nice girl—you know, gentle like."

"I'm sorry. I'm unable to give out any information." Kane pulled on a pair of surgical gloves and completed the test. He pushed a form toward Watts. "Sign here."

"What now?" Watts signed the form and rubbed his chin. "Am I free to go?"

Noticing Jenna heading for her office, he waved her over and then turned to Watts. "I'd like permission to search your vehicle." Kane pushed to his feet. "Do you carry a rifle?"

"Yeah." Watts stood. "Search all you like. I have nothing to hide."

"Problem?" Jenna strolled to his side and gave him a questioning stare.

Kane shrugged. "Nah, Mr. Watts has agreed to a search of his vehicle. Would you mind observing?"

"Sure." Jenna's lips quirked into a satisfied smile as she turned toward the door.

After dropping the DNA kit at the front counter for Maggie

to send to the lab, Kane met Watts and Jenna outside. He checked the car, took samples from the carpet, and inspected the rifle. Watts hadn't fired the weapon recently. He turned to Watts. "Thank you for your cooperation. You're free to go."

"Don't leave town." Jenna waved a document under Watts' nose. "I have a court order here to give me access to your phone and vehicle GPS records."

"Do what you need to do." Watts opened his truck and climbed inside. "I didn't hurt Sarah and I hope you find the SOB who did." He started the engine and drove away.

"He didn't kill her, did he?" Jenna's mouth turned down.

"Nope." Kane followed her back inside the office. "Not if his alibis check out, and they will by the number of people on his list. He volunteered a DNA test as well but I doubt forensics will find a trace on either victim. Whoever murdered her knows how to destroy evidence. The bleach used in the bunkhouse would likely have obliterated any viable DNA. I blame the forensic shows on TV. Before they came along, criminals seemed easier to catch." He sighed in frustration. "Dammit, I thought Watts fit the puzzle."

"I'll get Rowley to cross-match his GPS and phone with his statement before you cross him off the list." Jenna didn't wait for his reply and strolled toward her office. "We should ask Rockford and his lawyer to come in for an interview." She glanced at him over one shoulder. "Find Stan Clough."

FORTY-THREE

"Sheriff," Maggie waved at Jenna from behind the front desk. "I have that information you asked for." She held out a piece of paper.

Jenna smiled and strolled to the counter. "Thanks. Any problems?"

"Not really." Maggie let out a long sigh. "Informing relatives their loved ones have passed is very sad. I'm glad I completed a course in grief management." She frowned. "I've made notes against all the questions you told me to ask them. Only one problem: Sarah Woodward's mother can't travel and her uncle is coming to identify the body. He'll be arriving in a day or two."

"Thank you. I don't know what I would do without you." Jenna took the document and headed into her office.

She sat down and scanned the page. Father Maguire had supplied the name of John Helms' dentist. She picked up the phone to contact the forensics department to pass on the information and spoke to the person in charge, Brent Stanton. "I know it's only been a short time but do you have anything for me?"

"The first subject, the man in the barrel, is a Caucasian man in his late thirties, brown eyes, brown hair, five-eight. The examination by your local man was complete. We're currently classifying insects, soil, and vegetation samples embedded in the wounds, which indicate the victim crawled on the ground and slept outside for a time. There are insects and what could be hay or straw fragments in the wounds and hair. Once these are identified, I'll cross-match them to known species in your area. We have a database of soil samples from many areas in Montana, so I'm hoping for a possible match. From my preliminary examination, I'd suggest his murder occurred in a barn. Apart from the soil and insects, there are signs of frostbite in the extremities."

Jenna rested her forehead on the palm of one hand. "Could you let me know if the information from the dentist confirms a match for John Helms? He fits the description. As far as we are aware, he went missing approximately three weeks ago. His local priest came in and filed a missing persons' report. Is it too early to give me an approximate time of death?"

"I would say the killer inflicted the injuries over perhaps a week. There are signs of healing, although as you know, the fluid surrounding the body has washed away the DNA evidence. Although, rather than destroy the corpse, the mixture has preserved it to an extent. I would estimate the victim was placed in the solution no more than five to seven days before you found him." He cleared his throat. *"There are defensive wounds. The victim tried to shield his face from the attack."*

Jenna scribbled notes on a notebook. "I gather the body wasn't in acid?"

"No, I've sent a sample away for analysis but I'd say more like brine."

After checking her notes, Jenna nodded to herself. "Okay, and have you been able to identify the mark on his shoulder? Is it a tattoo?"

"*Fortunately, yes. After removing the top layer of skin, the mark showed up quite well. I'll send you an image.*"

Smiling, Jenna sighed with relief. "That's great! Thank you. What do you have for me on Sarah Woodward?"

"*I'll have a report for you in the morning. I can tell you the photography from the scene shows footprints and not the ones from your deputy. I've sent them for analysis. The killer or killers of Miss Woodward didn't destroy all the evidence after all.*"

Killers? Jenna swallowed the lump rising in her throat. "Are you implying more than one person is involved?"

"*I can't give you a definite answer until we've completed our investigation. The moment we do, I'll send you a full report.*"

"Thank you." Jenna disconnected and stared at the whiteboard in disbelief. *What the hell is going on in this town?*

Mind reeling, she pushed her chair away from the desk and stood. She glanced at the clock and then peered out into the main office. The place was quiet for a change. A few locals waited to speak to Maggie on the front desk and Deputy Rowley sat in Kane's cubicle, no doubt briefing him on his chat with Susie Hartwig. She could slip out for a few minutes to grab a snack and then head over to interview the real estate broker. Unable to go without informing Kane of her whereabouts, she strolled to his cubicle. Both men stopped talking immediately and she frowned at them and then dropped her voice to a whisper. "I've gotten a preliminary report from the forensics team. They're doing tests on fauna, et cetera, on the body in the barrel and think they might have found one or two sets of footprints at Sarah's murder scene."

"Two?" Kane's eyes filled with concern. "That might confirm my theory about Rockford having followers. I mean, think about the Manson cult—it happens."

Repulsed by the idea of a murdering cult in town, Jenna nodded. "We can't move forward until they finish the report."

She sighed. "I plan on being away from the office when you interview Rockford so I'm going for lunch. If I haven't heard back from Daniels about Stan Clough's address, I'm heading over to the real estate office to see if I can catch Mr. Davis."

"Okay." Kane frowned. "Susie Hartwig says Rockford was with her until about ten. He doesn't have an alibi for Friday night after all. I'm expecting him to come in for an interview at two with his lawyer. Daniels called in, he came up with a blank on Clough's residence and Davis hasn't returned our calls. Do you figure he believes he's respecting his client's privacy by not informing us?" He pushed a hand through his hair. "As a parolee, Clough is obliged to inform his parole officer or local law enforcement of any change of residence. If you inform Davis that you could charge him for withholding this information, I bet his memory becomes crystal clear."

Jenna straightened. She could deal with Mr. Davis. "Good idea."

"If Josh Rockford's lawyer is your stalker—" Kane's lips formed a thin line "—do you want me to lean on Mr. Stone as well?"

Jenna sighed. She'd kept her distance from James Stone as much as possible. She'd rather be locked in her office than sit in on the interview. No doubt, if she appeared to be in charge of the case against Rockford and the incident involving her, Stone would cry foul. "Keep Rowley with you and determine Rockford's movements on Saturday and Monday as well. If you can get Stone alone, ask him as well to eliminate him from our inquiries. If you can use your influence in an unobtrusive way to keep him from pestering me, I'd appreciate your help. I'll expect a full report when I return."

"Yes, ma'am. So tearing him a new butthole is out of the question?" Kane's eyes twinkled with amusement.

Rowley's eyes widened so big Jenna thought they might fall

out and bounce around the floor. With great difficulty, she bit back a grin and cleared her throat. "If we discover he is the one who threatened me in the bushes, I might be tempted to do that myself."

FORTY-FOUR

Kane folded his fingers behind his head and leaned back in the chair, making it moan in protest. He stared at the ceiling, noting the cobwebs, and then turned his attention back to Rowley. "I want to speak to Miss Hartwig. It would be good to have her here when Rockford arrives, so he knows we've questioned her." He dropped his hands and cleared his throat. "Can you pick her up on your way back from lunch?"

"Okay." Rowley's phone signaled a message and his brow wrinkled as he stared at the screen for some moments. "The paint analysis from the accident came back as from a 1977 Ford pickup. I already cross-checked all the DMV listings for a blue Ford pickup with local owners. Out of the hundreds in the area, only five fit the model you witnessed. I hunted down the owners to see if they had rap sheets and found two with misdemeanors listed. The other owners include two men in their eighties and a woman in her seventies. I discounted them, which leaves Davis and Mayor Rockford." He shrugged. "I can't say I've seen the mayor driving an old pickup so I gather it's somewhere on his ranch."

Kane snorted. "So is it the mayor or Davis who has the rap sheet?"

"Davis." Rowley paled. "He beat on his wife."

Interested, Kane straightened in his chair. "When did this happen?"

"Ten years ago." Rowley narrowed his gaze. "She dropped the charges."

Kane had seen too many cases of men losing control and beating their wives to death. "I see." He recalled seeing a light-colored late-model truck parked in the driveway of the real estate office. "Davis drives a Dodge truck doesn't he? Does the Ford pickup have current registration?"

"Yeah, and I've seen him drive the old pickup but not for at least six months." Rowley raised an eyebrow. "The sheriff is heading over to speak with Davis after lunch. If we catch her before she leaves Aunt Betty's, she could ask Davis about his pickup at the same time."

The hairs on Kane's neck prickled at the idea of Jenna walking into the real estate office without this vital information. The casual way Rowley had informed him gave him the impression he didn't consider John Davis a threat. He shook his head. "You do know that Davis is a suspect? We figure he has a connection to the victims and he owns a blue pickup. We must consider him a person of interest with two strikes against him. I'll give Jenna a call and bring her up to speed." He reached inside his jacket pocket for his phone and cleared his throat. "Is there anything else I should know?"

"No, but do you think it would be worthwhile checking if Sarah was on Facebook or Instagram?" Rowley pushed a hand through his hair. "People on social media enjoy telling the world what they're doing, who they're seeing, and the like. What if she met someone, or discussed her plans online?"

"Get at it." Kane smiled at him. "Check all the image files.

If Sarah took selfies, she might have posted them. It would be interesting to see who else she met in town."

"Okay." Rowley gave him a curt nod and headed for his cubicle.

Kane called Jenna to apprise her of the recent developments. "You could be interviewing the person who tried to kill you. I think I should tag along just to be safe."

"*I'm outside the real estate office now. It's the middle of the day, the streets are busy, and I'm armed.*" Jenna chuckled. "*If you prefer, I'll make some excuse to see his vehicle and speak to him outside. I'm sure I'm more than capable of handling John Davis.*"

He rubbed his chin, scratching the stubble. If Jenna had received training in special ops or the secret service as he envisaged, she'd be able handle most men with one hand tied behind her back, but it had not helped her in the bushes behind the Cattleman's Hotel. Like it or not, she was vulnerable and he'd proved as much during the couple of morning workouts they'd managed to squeeze into their hectic schedule. He'd decided to show her a few moves and improve her hand-to-hand combat skills. Her insistence he treat her as "one of the boys" rang in his memory and he pushed down his concern. He'd become close to Jenna in the short time he had known her, and his protective side had rushed to the front. Pushing words out between clenched teeth he sighed. "Okay, but I'd appreciate a hand with the Susie Hartwig interview."

Peals of laughter came down the earpiece. "*If you're worried about her hitting on you again, ask one of the deputies to sit in on the interview.*"

Kane cleared his throat. "Walters and Daniels aren't back yet and when Rowley gets back from lunch, he is searching social media for leads. If you're not here by the time she arrives, I guess I'll struggle through on my own."

"*It must be hard, being so darn handsome.*" Jenna giggled. "*Catch you later.*"

Kane stared at the blank screen and pushed to his feet. *She figures I'm frightened of women. We'll, I'll be darned.* Amused by Jenna's take on him, he decided to tackle Susie Hartwig head on.

He stood and poked his head into Rowley's cubicle. "I'm going to lunch now. You'll have to wait until I get back. While I'm at Aunt Betty's, I'll ask Miss Hartwig to come in for questioning at one-thirty. If Daniels and Walters return from their purse-seeking mission, keep them here until I return. You're in charge." He snatched his coat from the peg near the door and stepped out into the arctic wind. A smile curled his lips as Jenna's comment crossed his mind.

Shrugging into his coat, he decided the walk to Aunt Betty's Café would clear his head. Black Rock Falls hummed with people going about their daily lives. He sidestepped mothers with young children and old ladies laden with groceries as he made his way to Aunt Betty's at a brisk walk.

After ordering a bowl of chili, apple pie, and coffee, he leaned back in his seat to observe the locals. From the waves and smiles, it seemed everyone had accepted him as part of the community. When Susie Hartwig came back to his table with his food, he offered her a smile. "Thanks. Black Rock Falls sure is a friendly town. Everyone knows me already."

"Oh, that's because I added you to the newcomers' wall." Susie jerked a thumb over one shoulder. "It's part of our service to the community. We place the photographs of all new council members and cops on the wall."

"I see." Kane narrowed his gaze, wondering where she had obtained his image. "On a different matter, would you be able to drop into the office at one thirty? I'd like to speak to you about Josh Rockford."

"I can tell you everything you need to know." Susie pushed

a lock of hair from her face. "I'm not going out with him. It was just dinner."

Kane shrugged in an effort to appear nonchalant. "Due to a current case, we're making routine inquiries to eliminate people from our investigation. Speaking to Deputy Rowley or me off the record is hearsay. I'll need you to come in and make a statement. Half an hour of your time is all I'll need." He offered her a smile. "Can you drop by at one-thirty?"

"Sure. I'll get someone to cover for me." She returned his smile. "Do you want me to bring coffee, or we'll have apple turnovers fresh from the oven by then?"

"Yeah, that would be great. Five cappuccinos and ten turnovers, we get kinda hungry." He lifted his fork, waiting her to leave. "Just add it to my tab."

"See *you* later." Susie batted her eyelashes at him then strolled away with an exaggerated swing of her hips.

Kane shook his head. *Oh, boy.*

The exchange had caught the attention of the diners at the other tables. Kane snapped his gaze to his plate and rubbed his temple, hoping they'd not assumed he'd tried to hit on her. Perhaps he should ask Jenna to interview Susie. Jenna's grinning face flashed through his mind. No, if he backed out of doing the interview, he'd never live it down. Avoiding eye contact with the other diners, he finished his meal. As he stood, he caught sight of Deputy Daniels strolling along the street in his direction with a plastic evidence bag swinging from one hand.

He headed for the door and waited for Daniels to reach him. "What have you found?"

"Sarah Woodward's purse. Her ID is inside but no phone." Daniels held up the bag and frowned. "The keys for the rental are inside but the motel key is missing."

Kane reached for the evidence bag and peered at the

contents through the plastic. "Where exactly did you find it? Did you take photographs?"

"Oh yeah, I took pictures." Daniels gave him an unreadable look. "Maybe I should discuss this with the sheriff back at the office?"

"Sure." Kane glanced around. No one was in earshot yet Daniels was acting uncharacteristically cautious. "Ask Rowley to go with you and drop it through the evidence chute." He handed him the bag. "The sheriff should be back soon and we'll log it together. Did you inform Walters?"

"Yeah, just before." Daniels gave him a sideways glance. "He's on his way." He strode along the sidewalk, eyes front and his mouth in a grim line. "I found out where Stan Clough is living too."

Kane fell in step beside him. *Yet you didn't call me. Why?*

FORTY-FIVE

Jenna smiled at two elderly women bundled up so well against the cold only rosy cheeks and eyes peeked out from beneath their hoods. "Afternoon, ladies."

She made her way around a pile of gray, refrozen slush with leaves and sticks standing out in all directions and headed to the real estate office. John Davis was sitting behind a desk out front, staring at a computer screen. She pushed open the door and almost gagged at the stink of stale sweat laced with cigar smoke. How anyone conducted business with him without a gas mask, she couldn't imagine. She stood in the entrance, holding the door open with her foot. "Mr. Davis. Do you have a minute? I have a few questions for you."

"Yeah, but close the door. You're letting the heat out." John Davis took a drag of his cigar and, tipping back his head, puffed out a stream of smoke rings.

Kane's warning flashed across her mind and she took a step back. "Would you mind coming outside? I have a problem with cigar smoke."

"Oh, very well." Obviously annoyed, he pushed slowly to his feet. "I'll grab my coat."

She stepped away from the door and waited for him under the shop awning. He walked toward her and the smell clung to him, tainting the crisp winter air. "Sorry to drag you outside in the cold."

"What can I do for you?" Davis stamped his feet on the icy ground. "I already gave the Woodward girl all the information I had on her grandmother and dropped by your office with the list of properties that interested her. I don't know anything else."

Jenna removed one glove and then reached into her pocket for her notebook and slid the pen from the side attachment. "Where were you on Friday night during the hours of eleven and one?"

"In bed asleep." He huffed out a cloud of steam. "I went to bed about ten-thirty. You can ask the wife."

"What about Monday morning?"

"I came into work to meet a client at eight, took them to view the apartment beside the bank here in town. We went to Aunt Betty's for a snack and stayed there until about ten, I believe. It's nice and warm in the restaurant and, like you, the client has a problem with cigars. I took all the paperwork with me and we did the deal in the café." He frowned. "Plenty of people saw me there, why?"

Jenna lifted her gaze from the notes. "Just routine inquiries." She indicated with her chin toward the cream pickup in the driveway. "That your only vehicle?"

"No, I have an old Ford pickup back at the ranch." Davis raised both eyebrows. "I use it to collect the chicken feed from town once a month is all. I don't like stinking up my pickup. I need a nice vehicle to drive clients around to view properties."

Maybe give up smoking cigars would help as well. "When did you last drive the vehicle to town?"

Davis had a look of surprise rather than the expression of someone caught in the act of a crime.

"Last day of the month." He scratched his chin and eyed

her with curiosity. "You should speak to old Mr. Todd at the produce store. He keeps records. I pick up my order same time every month. Is there a reason you want to know about my old truck?"

"Like I said, it's just routine inquiries." Jenna smiled at him. "Does anyone else have access to the vehicle?"

"No, my wife doesn't drive." He rubbed his chin and gave her a worried look.

Jenna made a few notes and then lifted her chin. "Would you mind if I send an officer to take some photographs, to eliminate it from our investigation?"

"Not at all. I'll call my wife and tell her to expect you." He pulled his coat closer around his rotund body. "Did the Woodward girl have any luck finding her grandmother? She said she'd drop by and let me know."

Seeing a natural way into questioning him about the information he'd given Sarah, Jenna shook her head. "I haven't spoken to her since Saturday. Did you point her in any particular direction?"

"Well, Mrs. Woodward didn't want a big place but she had the finances to make an older home comfortable. There are only a few on my books but I do recall suggesting the Old Mitcham Ranch because the owners have kept up the running of the place. It's dusty and kids have gotten inside a few times but it's solid. It has water and it only needs reconnection to the grid."

She blew out her breath in a cloud of steam. "It's a shame you didn't remember about Mrs. Woodward's interest in the Old Mitcham Ranch the last time we spoke to you."

"I remembered her face but it wasn't until I read over the list of properties and my attached notes I recalled our conversation." His brows knitted. "Old age plays havoc with memory. Days turn into years, it's hard to keep track."

Information of the Old Mitcham Ranch would be gold.

Interested, Jenna wanted to see if he'd run his mouth. "I believe you sold Stan Clough's old property before he went to jail?"

"Yeah, he needed the money to pay his lawyer." Davis' expression became closed and defensive. "I can't give you details. I figure I'd be breaking the privacy laws."

"You sold him a new property when he got out of jail as well, didn't you?" Jenna shot him a hard glance. "I don't want to know the details of the deal but you must know I only have to drop by the Lands Record's Office to discover who owns what property. Do you know it would be a violation of his parole if I'm not informed of his current address? You wouldn't want me to arrest him again, would you?"

"Okay, okay." Beaten, Davis dropped his gaze. "I sold him a piggery. He wanted something isolated. After what happened, he isn't too social. The property runs close to the border of the Daniels' ranch on Rocky Mile Road, and before you ask, yeah, there are a couple of properties close by on the list I gave Miss Woodward."

Another thought percolated into her mind. "Just one more thing. Did you mention who owned the Old Mitcham Ranch to Miss Woodward?"

"The owners' names and contact details of all the properties are on the list I gave her—and you."

Had Sarah called someone before her death? She nodded, pushing down her annoyance. "Of course, thank you for sending the list to my office." She pushed on. "When was the last time you spoke to Stan Clough, or noticed him in town?"

"That would be Monday. He doesn't have bars out there and no landline as yet but he does come into town to pick up supplies." Davis paled slightly. "I noticed him waiting out front of Miller's Garage by the gas pumps. He was probably waiting for the store to open so he could fill his pickup."

Jenna frowned. "Are you sure you saw Mr. Clough before eight on Monday morning?"

"I'm sure. Like I told you before, I had to meet a client here at eight and I noticed Miller's Garage didn't have the lights on." Davis gave her an annoyed glare. "They never open before eight in winter." He gave her a pained expression. "Is that all?"

Jenna closed the notebook and slid the pen into its holder. "Okay, that's all I need. Thank you."

"Any time."

A shudder of horror gripped her at the kaleidoscope of brutal images running through her mind. The idea of Clough murdering Sarah slid firmly into place. Holy cow. Davis had placed Stan Clough at the garage about the same time as Sarah had dropped her vehicle by for a service. Stan Clough, the sadistic animal killer, could have overheard her plans for the day and followed her. *I have to tell Kane.*

FORTY-SIX

At his desk, Kane sat opposite Susie Hartwig with Deputy Rowley taking notes in a chair beside him. Not that being alone with the girl concerned him, but the way she smiled at him brought the interview to the attention of everyone in the office. No doubt, Susie had run her mouth about being asked to drop by the office.

After she'd made a big production of delivering the coffee personally to each deputy and Maggie, she raised one penciled eyebrow. "You didn't order one for the sheriff. Maybe it was an oversight or are you two not getting along? I noticed you both ate alone today."

Kane avoided her curious gaze and moved his attention to the arrival of Josh Rockford and a man he assumed was his lawyer, James Stone. When Josh elbowed his companion and indicated toward Susie Hartwig, he bit back a smile. Rockford would be wondering if his alibi would cover for him. Jumpy did not come close to Rockford's demeanor. Observing Susie Hartwig's interview while he cooled his heels in the waiting area would be driving him crazy.

"I asked if you were getting along with the sheriff." Susie gave him an indignant glare.

Kane kept his expression bland. "We're getting along just fine. Take a seat and we'll get on with the interview so you can get back to work."

"Sure." Susie unbuttoned her coat and sat down, crossing her long legs. "Is this about Josh? I told Jake everything I know."

Kane cleared his throat. "Tell me. Start with Friday night." He opened a statement book and looked at her.

"Josh dropped by after training, and asked me to dinner. After working all day, I really wanted to go home, but then he gave me those puppy dog eyes and I agreed." Susie let out a long sigh. "We had dinner and later went to his place. Not his daddy's house, his apartment in town. I went home about eleven."

Kane made notes. "How did you get home?"

"I called a cab." She giggled. "He didn't tell you I stayed the night, did he? That boy is prone to exaggeration. I'm more interested in the more mature type." She gave him a knowing wink. "Josh fell asleep in front of the TV and I called a cab at about ten-thirty."

A cab would be easy to check. "Did you happen to see him on Saturday morning or Monday morning?"

"Yeah, he came into the café real early Monday morning, met up with Dan, ah... Dan Beal and they had coffee. They left around eight." She tapped her chin and stared into space. "Saturday, I'm pretty sure they came in about the same time as you. The day we first met."

Kane blinked away an eye-roll. He jotted down a summary of dates and times on the statement form and pushed it across the desk to her. "Okay, thank you for your assistance. If you will read my notes and sign them as your statement, you can go." He turned to his deputy. "When Miss Hartwig is finished, witness the statement and show her out."

He noticed Magnolia trying to get his attention and pushed to his feet then headed to the front counter. "Problem?"

"No, everything is just fine. The forensic reports arrived. I've put them in the files." Maggie beamed at him. "I knew you'd be anxious to know."

"Thanks, Maggie." Kane glanced out of the glass door to see Jenna marching toward the office with an expression of doom plastered on her face. He strode to the door and opened it for her and then stood back.

"Hold the fort for me." Jenna moved through the office like a tornado and headed for her door. "Daniels. My office now."

Kane stared after her and then strolled toward Rockford. "Mr. Rockford, thank you for coming in. Sorry to keep you waiting."

"This is James Stone, my lawyer." Josh indicated to a man in his forties, fit and wearing an expensive cologne to go with his superbly tailored suit.

Kane offered his hand and the man's strong grip surprised him. "Sheriff's Deputy Kane." He waved them into his cubicle and sat behind the desk.

"I'd like you to take note that my client has come by of his own free will and will only answer questions I deem suitable. Are we clear?"

Kane sat down and opened the statement book to a fresh page. "They're only routine questions. I want to eliminate suspects for cases that may or may not be related." He leaned back in his chair to give a nonchalant pose. "Mr. Rockford, where were you on Friday night during the hours of eleven and one."

Rockford glanced at his lawyer, who nodded.

"I spent Friday evening with Susie Hartwig. I'm sure she told you already?"

Kane jotted down notes. "She gave a statement to say she left your apartment between ten- thirty and eleven. We'll be able to corroborate her story from the cab records. So maybe you should think again and tell me the truth."

"Okay, okay. I woke up in front of the TV about three and she'd left. I assumed she'd been there all that time but if she says different, well it must be true." Josh Rockford shrugged. "I'm darn sure I didn't leave the house."

Kane met his gaze. "Your father owns a dark blue Ford pickup. When was the last time you drove the vehicle?"

"Why the hell would I drive that old wreck?" Josh Rockford snorted in disgust. "It's used by our ranch hands, and has been for about ten years." He glared at Kane. "I don't know if it ever leaves the property. You'll have to ask my father."

Kane rubbed his chin and stared at his notes for a beat. "That's easy enough to check." "Where did you go after leaving Aunt Betty's Café on Monday morning?"

"Do I have to answer that question?" Josh shot an agonized look at his lawyer.

"No." Stone shrugged. "Unless this question is relevant to a murder inquiry and you wish to exclude my client."

Interesting. "Okay." Kane leaned back in his seat and twirled his pen. "How well do you know Sarah Woodward?"

"The cute blonde?" Josh grinned. "I'd *like* to know her better but when I asked her to join me for a drink, she practically ran into the bathroom. That was outside the Cattleman's Hotel restaurant on Saturday night after the game."

Kane took in Josh's demeanor. He was cocky and sure of himself. He hadn't murdered Sarah but did have something to hide. "Did you return to the Cattleman's Hotel after I escorted you to a cab?"

"I'm taking the Fifth." Rockford glanced at his lawyer. "Maybe I had a hot date. I don't have to tell him, do I?"

"No, you don't have to answer any of his questions." Stone's hard gaze bored into Kane.

"I'll move on then." Kane cleared his throat. "Would you

agree to give a DNA sample? Miss Woodward was involved in an incident and I'm eliminating suspects."

"I'd like to give *her* a DNA sample." Josh wiggled his eyebrows.

"You don't have to comply." Stone leaned toward Josh. "Not unless they obtain a court order."

"I didn't touch the girl." Josh shrugged dismissively. "I'll do the test."

Kane completed the test and, keeping his expression neutral, turned back to Josh Rockford. He needed forensics to go over his vehicle and his father's old pickup. "That's all I have for you for now unless you'd agree to a forensics team searching your truck? We'll need to take a look at your father's old pickup as well."

"In relation to what?" Stone eyed him suspiciously.

"We're investigating two incidents and a blue pickup was involved in a hit-and-run." Kane sighed. "We're in the process of questioning people in the vicinity at the time, and Mr. Rockford is on our list."

"Yeah, you can check out my truck. I didn't do *anything* or cause an accident. You'll have to speak to my father about the pickup." Josh got to his feet. "Can I go now?"

Kane slid the statement pad across the desk to him. "Read and sign the statement, Mr. Stone can witness it for you and then you're free to go."

Kane waited for them to complete the process, stood, and offered his hand. "Thank you for your cooperation. Don't wash the car, will you? If you do, I'm sure Mr. Stone will explain the ramifications."

"I'll make sure he understands, and I'll contact you about Mayor Rockford's pickup within the hour. I'm sure he'll want his name cleared as soon as possible." Stone looked down his nose at him as if he smelled bad. "When do you expect the forensics team to arrive?"

Kane pushed to his feet. "In the next twenty-four hours, and I'd like to take a look at the old pickup today."

"Very well." Stone gave him a dismissive stare and turned to usher Josh toward the door.

Kane moved to his side. "I'd like a word in private?"

"Wait for me at the desk." Stone waved Josh away as if he was an annoying fly. "What can I do for you, Deputy Kane?"

Kane sized up the athletic, good-looking man before him. "I have a few questions. Take a seat. This won't take long unless you need to call a lawyer too?"

"Really? Ask away." Stone gave a sarcastic laugh. "Do you need my movements as well? If so, I was attending a conference in LA. I left here a week ago on Saturday and came back on Monday at around ten, I believe. No sooner had I put my bags inside my house, the mayor called and informed me you were harassing the members of the Larks Team."

Pushing the notepad toward him, Kane met his gaze. "I'll need details, if you don't mind."

"Not a problem." Stone scratched away at the pad then signed the bottom with a flourish. "Would you like a DNA test from me as well?"

"Not at this time." He leveled his gaze at Stone. "There is another subject we need to speak about—Jenna."

"Ah, *I see*." Stone gave him a look to freeze an ocean. "I had a feeling you two were involved." He held both hands up and gave him a thin smile. "That's what happens when I encourage women below my class."

Kane gave him his death glare. "I didn't see your name listed in Forbes—didn't make it again this year, huh?"

"Don't worry, she is *all* yours." Stone shot to his feet and strode toward Rockford.

Kane stared after him, shaking his head. *One jerk down.* He turned his thoughts back to the interview with Rockford. He'd dealt with super-cool psychopaths before and Josh Rockford had the ability to hide the fact he'd killed Sarah. Yet something did not gel. His demeanor was wrong, especially the quip about the DNA sample. If he'd been acting the part of an innocent man, he'd be on the list for an Oscar.

However, Kane refused to discount him as a suspect for the attempts on Jenna's life. Josh had been in the area and couldn't account for his whereabouts during the time of both incidents. His father owned the same model vehicle, and he had motive. He would have to examine the pickup for damage and inspect John Davis' vehicle as well. Kane stared down at the list of suspects. He found it hard to believe the real estate broker was responsible and the list was getting shorter. *Take Billy Watts and Josh Rockford out of the equation, and all I have is Dan Beal and Stan Clough.*

FORTY-SEVEN

Jenna removed her coat and gloves then dropped into her chair. "Shut the door."

"This isn't about finding Sarah Woodward's purse, is it?" Daniels frowned down at her. "I dropped it down the evidence chute. Kane said you'd want to log it in personally."

"Where did you find the purse?" Jenna leaned on her desk, clasping her hands. "I hope you followed procedure."

"I wore gloves and sealed it inside an evidence bag." Daniels looked at his hands then over one shoulder at the closed door before dropping his voice. "I wasn't going to bother to look inside your bin but you did say to check every trash can from the crime scene to town. I found it inside your recycling bin."

Jenna gaped at him in astonishment. "In *my* bin?" The recycling bin had been left at the gate since the collection on Friday and it should have been empty.

"Yeah." Daniels pulled out his phone. "I have pictures." He handed her the phone.

After scrolling through the images, she handed him back the phone. "Did you make an inventory of the contents?"

"No, I looked inside looking for confirmation of ownership.

I found her ID, noticed a set of keys but the motel key was missing." He gave her a suspicious look and cleared his throat. "How come it's in your bin?"

"The Old Mitcham Ranch is on the same road as my ranch. Maybe my trash can was the only one left out or maybe leaving it in my bin was a way to taunt me, who the heck knows?" She narrowed her gaze. "Don't for a second think that Kane is involved. I can account for his movements on Monday. He was with me."

"Sure, it must be a coincidence, but yours wasn't the only can left out. I searched four others along that road." Daniels raised an eyebrow. "So they picked yours on purpose. It must be a local to know where you live."

A shiver ran down Jenna's spine but she shrugged it away and lifted her chin. "Talking of locals, why didn't you tell me your brothers live next door to Stan Clough? I had to find out from John Davis."

"I didn't think it mattered."

Sighing with exasperation, she stared at him. "Is there anything else I need to know?"

"Well, I guess." He squirmed "We own the Old Mitcham Ranch. I asked Mr. Davis to sell it. My brothers had nothing to do with it."

Astonished, Jenna gaped at him. "What?"

"I figured you knew Sheriff Mitcham was our grandpa and left us a bunch of land. It's common knowledge around these parts."

Anger straightened her spine "Obviously not. You should have told me. I'm not a local and all this happened before I arrived." She cleared her throat. "Sit down. I want to know everything. When did you decide to sell the property?"

"Oh, about three months ago." Daniels lowered into a chair and stretched his legs before him, looking far too at ease for Jenna's comfort. "I'm the youngest and the only one of us with a decent job. When my parents died, they left debts and we had to sell personal items to pay the bills. We're always short of cash over winter so I put the old place on the market. I didn't tell my brothers, I thought it would be a nice surprise." He grimaced. "When I rang Dean and told him about the murder, he went ballistic and said I was trying to sell part of our family's heritage. He said we could make more money by charging people to visit over Halloween. He called John Davis and had the property removed from the listing." He gave her a chagrined look. "He gave me a tongue-lashing last night on the phone as well. That's the last time I try to do something to help."

Jenna drummed her fingers on the table. "I see."

"I didn't know Sarah's grandmother was planning on visiting the place either until I saw it on the list Davis dropped by."

The image of Sarah Woodward's glassy death stare flashed across her mind and she blinked hard to push the horrific vision away. "I guess if Mrs. Woodward had put an offer on the place, they would have mentioned it to you, especially as they didn't know you'd put it on the market."

"They didn't mention anyone named Mrs. Woodward or an offer." Daniels rubbed a hand down his face.

Nodding, Jenn unclasped her hands. "Exactly how well do you know Stan Clough?"

"Huh?" Daniels stared at her blankly.

"You know Stan Clough, a person of interest in the current murder cases. Why didn't you admit to knowing the man, let alone where he lived? Are you hiding something?"

"I know *of* him, and everyone knows what he did. I *didn't* know where he lived when I spoke to you this morning." Daniels shrugged nonchalantly. "I rarely go to the ranch during winter. There's nothing to do and my brothers are quite capable of handling the stock. They don't need me. Most times I just get in the way." He gave her a petulant stare. "At the moment,

Dean is real pissed with me—oh, sorry, ma'am—*angry* with me about trying to sell the Old Mitcham Ranch, but when I called him on the satellite phone, he mentioned Stan Clough. He told me Clough was living on Rocky Mile Road with a bunch of stinking pigs. He told me not to tell you because Stan doesn't want anyone, especially *you*, knowing where he lives."

Jenna raised one eyebrow. "Oh, really?"

"I guess he wants a quiet life, ma'am." Daniels winced. "I sure do."

Sarah's homicide is looking more like an opportunistic thrill kill. She gave Daniels a long look. He was not law-enforcement material. "Have you thought about a different career away from Black Rock Falls?"

"Oh yeah." Daniels gave her a crooked smile. "I've always wanted to join the rodeo circuit. Those boys play hard and fast. I've never left Black Rock Falls and I'm hankerin' for some fun in my life. This job with the murders and all is depressing."

Perplexed, Jenna shook her head. "Okay you'd better grab Walters and take your break."

She stood and followed him out the door. Noticing Kane was filing a report, she decided to inspect Sarah's purse with Rowley and log the contents but required Kane's key to the evidence room. Marching up to his desk, she tapped Rowley on the shoulder. Annoyed to see him on Facebook, she glared at him. "With me. Bring a notebook."

"Is everything okay?" Kane glanced up from his computer screen.

"Yeah. I'll need your key to the evidence room. I'm taking Rowley with me to make a list of the contents of Sarah's purse." She moved closer and dropped her voice. "Why didn't you inform me Daniels found the darn thing in *my* recycling bin? Plus, he had Clough's address? He has a piggery on Rocky Mile Road. What's going on?"

"In *our* trash?" Both dark eyebrows rose to the hairline. "He did mention he knew where Clough lived but refused to tell me and then insisted the location of the purse was for your ears only. What a jerk. Do you think he believes *I* had something to do with Sarah's murder?" He tossed her a bunch of keys.

"I have no idea." She rubbed the back of her neck then waited for his reaction to her next bombshell. "Did you know the Daniels brothers own the Old Mitcham Ranch?"

"Nope, Rowley gave me a rundown of the history but didn't mention the current owners. I assumed it was part of a deceased estate." Kane took his notebook from his jacket pocket and flipped through the pages. "Yeah, I was going to ask John Davis for the lawyer handling the estate to inform him about the murder. Has anyone told him?"

"Not about the murder." Jenna wet her suddenly dry lips and eyed the coffee to-go cup on Kane's desk with longing. "I don't want anyone running their mouths until Sarah's family has officially identified the body. Obviously, we don't need to speak to the Daniels brothers as Pete has already informed them. Apparently, Dean contacted John Davis and removed the ranch from sale."

"So we've found our leak?" Kane leaned back in his chair and raised both eyebrows.

Jenna sighed. "It sure looks that way. I figure Pete needs a new occupation. By the way, when is Sarah's uncle coming to identify her body?"

"He should be arriving in the morning. The forensics are back and Maggie says they're in the files. I'm guessing you'll want to look at them first?" Kane moved his shoulders and stretched. "Do you want me to go over Rockford's interview with you now?"

Jenna shook her head. "Later, I'm more interested in the forensics but I'll check the purse first."

.   .   .

Jenna unlocked the cage, snapped on gloves, and slid Sarah Woodward's purse out of the evidence bag and onto the aluminum tray on the table. She turned to Rowley. "Take pictures. Every step."

"Yes, ma'am." Rowley took a camera from the shelf and played around with the settings. "I'm ready." He snapped a few shots.

"Driver's license in the name of Sarah Woodward, vehicle keys with a tag for Miller's Garage." Jenna tipped the bag upside down. A few coins tumbled onto the tray, a pink scrunchie, a pen from the Black Rock Falls Motel, and a packet of gum. She searched inside, found a zipper, and opened a compartment. "Bills." When she unfolded and counted the bills, she found a phone number written on a scrap of notepaper from the motel. "Sixty-five dollars." She stepped away from the table to allow Rowley to take photographs.

"No clues to the murderer here." Rowley displayed the shots on the camera screen. "Do you want me to dust everything for prints?"

"Yeah." She smiled at him. "Nice job. I'll chase up the phone number but I'm guessing it's one of the owners of the properties her grandmother visited, or should I say *planned* to visit." She pulled out her notebook and jotted down the number. "I'll look over the list she received from John Davis before I bother anyone."

"One thing. There's a pink scrunchie missing. She had two in her hair last time she came into the office and it's not on the list of personal belongings you found at the scene." Rowley dusted the items and collected fingerprints. "I figure other things are missing, don't you?" He glanced up at her. "There's no hairbrush or makeup. Women usually have tissues, lip gloss, and women's items in their purses." He shrugged. "She was out for the day. Wouldn't she take more than this with her?"

A cold chill slithered down Jenna's spine and the years of

profiling criminals came to the front of her mind. "The killer has taken something personal as a trophy. Something to remind him of the event." She stared at the small array of belongings. "I'll need to see if anything is missing from the clothing left at the scene. When I went over the list of items from her motel room, I noticed she owned matching sets of underwear. Taking a victim's panties or other personal items is usual. The forensic report arrived earlier. We'll need to check if anything else is missing. We could be looking at a serial killer. Some twisted lunatic who enjoys reliving the thrill."

She waited for Rowley to pack up the evidence then locked the room. "Scan those fingerprints into the database then come to my office."

"Yes, ma'am." Rowley stood back to allow her to mount the stairs. "Do you want the other deputies to attend the briefing?"

Jenna shook her head. The purse had revealed more than she'd have imagined. "Not this time."

Too much information made its way from her office and she needed to shut it down. She trusted her men but now assumed all the leaks came from Pete Daniels. He'd likely kept his brothers and girlfriends up to date with the latest cases. He should have realized anyone he told would run their mouths. *Nothing I can do about it now but as sure as hell, it won't happen again on my watch.*

FORTY-EIGHT

Jenna headed to the main office and went straight to the kitchenette. After grabbing three cups of coffee, she strolled to Kane's desk. "We need to talk in private and I'm ready to look at the forensic reports."

"I'm done here." Kane stood and smiled at her. "Are one of those for me?"

"Yeah." She handed him a steaming beverage. "Did you get anything out of Josh Rockford?"

"If their alibis check out, I won't have anything concrete on Rockford or Billy Watts for Sarah's murder but Rockford is so smooth, he could pay people to cover for him." Kane picked up his notebook and his brow wrinkled into a frown. "Apart from knowing Stan Clough's whereabouts at the time of the incidents, the jury is out on the attempts on your life—any one of our suspects could be guilty." His gaze settled on her face. "You can take James Stone out of the equation; he was at a conference and I don't think he will bother you again." His lips twitched into a small smile.

Feeling as if a great weight had lifted from her shoulders, Jenna smiled. "Thanks, I appreciate your help." She did a scan of the room and lowered her voice. "I have information on Stan Clough, but it will wait until we're in my office. What else did you discover?"

"Rockford and Watts didn't appear to know about Sarah's murder, and when I questioned them about their whereabouts, they appeared annoyed rather than guilty." Kane leaned one hip against his desk. "I need to rule out any connection between Josh and the hit-and-run. I want to inspect both pickups. I gather Mayor Rockford and John Davis live on the same side of town?"

Jenna sipped the scalding coffee. "Yeah, we'll drop over as soon as we've read the reports. I'll ask Maggie to lock up and we'll head on home once we're finished."

"The only person I haven't interviewed is Dan Beal but Billy Watts mentioned meeting him at the gym at eight on Monday morning. If he's telling the truth, he wouldn't have had time to murder Sarah or trash the motel and then be at the gym by that time. We can also rule him out of the hit-and-run because he was locked in the cells on Thursday night." Kane let out a long sigh. "I still have a feeling in my gut the murders are the work of two killers. From the injuries I witnessed, it looks like the same person or persons murdered Sarah and John Helms. The scene was too neat. In my opinion, one person wouldn't have the time or energy to clean it so thoroughly in a limited time." He cleared his throat. "Let's see what the autopsy revealed."

Jenna glanced at Deputy Rowley's cubicle. "Have you finished uploading those files?"

"Yes, ma'am, but there's something you need to see." Rowley spun around in his chair. "I didn't find anything interesting on the suspects' media pages but I did find this photo on Sarah's account."

"Well, I'll be..." Kane bent to stare at the screen.

The image depicted Mrs. Woodward leaning on the tailgate

of an old blue pickup. Jenna leaned closer and noticed a torn sticker on the back. She glanced at Kane. "You have to be joking. That's not the vehicle that ran me off the road, is it?"

"Unless one of the others in town has the same torn sticker, I think it's the same vehicle." Kane rubbed his chin. "Why would Mrs. Woodward try to kill you?"

Uncomprehending, Jenna gaped at the image of the smiling old woman in disbelief. "I haven't met her, so no reason at all."

"This is crucial evidence, Jenna." Kane straightened and moved his attention to Daniels sauntering in their direction, and then back to her. His voice lowered to just above a whisper. "We don't want this information getting out and compromising the investigation. We have no idea who Daniels' girlfriends or brothers have spoken to, and if it includes the killer, he'll be one step ahead of us all the time."

Jenna nodded in agreement. "Okay, my office." She turned and smiled at Daniels. "I've filed the GPS and phone records for Rockford and Watts. Check the dates against the withdrawals from John Helms' and Mrs. Woodward's bank accounts. See if either of them visited the other counties at the same time."

"I'm on it." Daniels headed for his cubicle.

Jenna followed Kane and Rowley into her office. Seated at her desk, she looked at her two deputies and relayed the information on Stan Clough she'd received from Davis. "This puts him in the right place at the right time. He's local to the area and so far, the only man who fits the profile of a sadistic killer, plus three people went missing and then nothing. He gets out of jail and people go missing again. It's too much of a coincidence."

"We'll need to pay him a visit and have probable cause to get a warrant to search his property." Kane's eyes narrowed. "Can you obtain the warrant today?"

Jenna nodded. "Yeah, but first we need to see what's in

Sarah's autopsy report." She read the note attached and swallowed hard. "The forensics team has included a report on the hood we sent them from my attack. The blood is from a pig. No wonder it stank."

"That's not good." Kane gave her a worried stare. "Clough owns a piggery."

She opened the file and scanned the details of Sarah's suffering and forced her expression into one of bland interest. Viewing the crime scene had been horrific but knowing the intricate details, no matter how clinically described, cramped her stomach. She'd known this girl and wanted to help her find her grandmother. The image of Sarah's battered body rushed through her mind, and she blinked away the sting of tears at the backs of her eyes. "Okay. I'll read the report."

"Do you want me to handle it?" Kane leaned forward in his chair and his face held an expression of deep concern.

Jenna paused for a beat, took a deep breath and shook her head. "No, I'm fine." She grasped the mouse and scrolled down the page.

"Maybe start with the ME's conclusion and then we can go through the details if necessary." Kane opened his notebook and took out a pen. "I don't need to see the images."

"Sure." Jenna scrolled through the document. "The ME cause of death is blood loss due to multiple sharp force trauma. He mentions a deep incised wound of the neck and multiple stab wounds of the stomach. The upper torso injuries are consistent with the use of a steel-tipped whip." She sighed. "I'll read the report." She swallowed hard. "The sharp force trauma to the neck led to the transection of the left and right carotid arteries. An incision of the right internal jugular vein caused a fatal exsanguinating hemorrhage. Investigation reveals an inconsistency between the sharp force injuries. The sharp force injuries to the neck would be consistent to a serrated-edge knife, or hunting knife. The wounds to the torso measure one-half inch in diameter with a curved tip, consistent with a kitchen knife. Contusions on forearms could be defensive wounds. The blunt force injury to the back of the scalp is superficial and non-fatal." As her eyes moved to the next paragraph, bile crept up the back of her throat. "The victim exhibited signs of recent forced sexual activity. Swabs revealed no DNA evidence, but a match was found for the lubricated condoms with the trade name of Trojan Bareskin."

She glanced up at Kane. "I'll see what forensics found." She took a long drink of her coffee then went back to scroll through the reports. "Here we go. They found one black hair on the clothing left at the scene, and from the list, Sarah's panties are missing." She read and re-read the next sentence. "You're correct on the number of people involved. They found two sets of footprints in the blood. One sized ten and one eleven. Leather soles." She turned her screen around. "Look."

"This isn't proof we have two psychopaths loose in Black Rock Falls. These people have an allure. We could have one killer and a follower he convinced to go along for the ride." Kane gripped his cup and stared at her with an annoyed expression. He turned to Rowley. "Not a darn word leaves this room. Do not speak to anyone about this evidence. Understand?"

"I understand." Rowley scrubbed both hands over his face. "I can't believe the animals raped her as well."

"And John Helms. Did they find anything else?" Kane gulped down his coffee and eyed her over the rim. "Don't tell me he was raped as well?"

"I'll open the other file." Jenna scrolled through the documents. "Not raped but brutalized. The bugs and seeds they found on him are local to this area. Both murders happened here in Black Rock Falls."

"It's obvious they're locals that know the area. A stranger wouldn't have a clue about the root cellar at the Old Mitcham Ranch but for the townsfolks' teenagers, it's a favorite place to be over Halloween." Rowley leaned forward in his chair. "I'm surprised two men are involved and kept it a secret." He glanced at Kane. "Are you sure you only noticed one person in the pickup?"

"I didn't see the driver at all." Kane drained his cup and placed it on the desk. "Why?"

"Well, it would take a strong guy to lift a dead body and force it into a barrel. Maybe one man could do it okay but not lifting the barrel onto a truck with the fluid and then off again at the landfill. It would take a forklift. I think you can rule out old Mrs. Woodward."

"Most ranchers would have machinery to lift heavy objects and add the liquid once the barrel was on the pickup." Kane leaned back in his chair. "It could have been rolled off the back of a pickup or flatbed truck by one man. The problem is forensics have proved two people were at the crime scene and I have two men using each other for alibis. Billy Watts and Dan Beal both said they went to the Larks gym on Monday morning. I'll give the Larks coach a call as soon as we're finished because if he remembers them, and the other people he mentioned check out, we are back to square one." He thought for a beat. "We also have to consider the second footprint might have been a sightseer. If someone boasted to his friends about the murder, one or more of them might have taken a look see."

Jenna drummed her fingernails on the desk. "We can't prove that one way or the other but you still believe the same people are involved in the murders and the incidents involving me, right?"

"I have from the start. Coincidences are rare, and unless someone has poisoned the Black Rock Falls water supply and we are all slowly going crazy, the chances of two homicidal lunatics in one town at the same time with different agendas would be a million to one." Kane pushed to his feet and went to the whiteboard. "In my opinion, the Ford pickup I saw belonged to Mrs. Woodward. I'm more than happy to go and check the other vehicles but the chance of finding another with the same torn sticker would be remote." He made notes on the board. "Mrs. Woodward loved her granddaughter and went missing well before she arrived. I've checked her rap sheet and she has no priors." He turned to face her, and shrugged. "My guess is Mrs. Woodward is another victim and the killers used her pickup to move John Helms' body, and in an attempt to kill you or send you a warning."

"So you figure her body is lying around somewhere?" Rowley scraped a hand through his hair. "Maybe we should search all the barrels at the landfill."

"Already covered. Brinks has opened every barrel in the place and found nothing, but many are buried under tons of garbage." Jenna finished her coffee. "If that's their usual method of disposal, why leave Sarah in the root cellar?"

"Maybe they didn't want to risk the landfill again." Rowley cleared his throat. "They'd know any barrel dumped there would be checked."

"I agree, and the three incidents involving the sheriff are warnings." Kane moved back toward the desk and sank into a chair and then looked at her. "I know you have no recollection of anything unusual occurring in the last few months but I'd bet my last dollar you've witnessed something." He raised an eyebrow. "Unless you agree to be hypnotized, we won't find out, and I guess that's not going to happen anytime soon."

The hairs on the back of Jenna's neck stood to attention. Somebody had tried to kill her, but unless someone in her past had found her, she had no idea why. She chewed on her bottom lip. "Honestly, there's no need to be so dramatic. I've told you everything I can remember. Trust me. I haven't seen anything unusual happening in Black Rock Falls."

"Okay, allow me to give you my take on the situation." Kane leaned back in the chair, making it squeak in protest. "I'm convinced you're tied up with these murders, however unwillingly. Since Mrs. Woodward arrived in Black Rock Falls, you've interacted with persons unknown and witnessed a crime, or seen something someone wants kept secret. If you didn't see anything other than animal brutality at Clough's farm, it must have occurred during your investigation into Mrs. Woodward's disappearance as that was the only time you did a door-to-door."

Horrified, Jenna shook her head. "I can't believe you figure something I supposedly ignored caused two horrific murders. I didn't carry out the investigation alone and I've retraced my steps. If I missed it then so did Rowley. *Nothing* happened. I'm not some rookie. I'd have noticed anything unusual."

"I'm not saying you're at fault but law enforcers have turned a blind eye many times for locals they like, especially in small towns. People here are like family. Then seemingly out of the blue, you started to crack down on the local jerks." Kane shrugged. "Next thing you know, someone is running you off the road and shooting at you." He opened his hands. "The moment you take one step alone, you get a warning to keep your mouth shut."

Jenna stared at him. "What has that got to do with the murder of John Helms and Sarah?"

"Ah, when we found John Helms, they panicked. The shooting was another warning but when I started pulling people in for questioning, they grabbed you at the Cattleman's Hotel. I guess they figured eventually you'd crumble and inform me." Kane gave her a long meaningful stare. "You thought you heard two sets of footsteps, didn't you?"

Annoyed Jenna let out a long sigh. "Yes, but I don't *know* anything. I would tell you if I did, you know that, right?"

"Oh, I believe you." Kane pushed a hand through his hair. "I doubt Mrs. Woodward was their first victim as we have three other missing persons. Up to her murder, they'd covered their tracks, then you became sheriff. I guess when I arrived they figured you'd brought in reinforcements, but you ignored their threats, and Sarah's murder was a stern warning as in, 'Look what I can do if you tell Kane what you know.'" He leaned forward in his chair. "We'll go through your day book for the last six months or so and then visit all the ranches again, starting with Stan Clough's old place, and see if anything triggers a memory, no matter how insignificant."

Anger welled and Jenna shot to her feet. "We'll do no such thing. I haven't seen a thing or I'd have told you *however insignificant* as you so eloquently suggested." She pointed to the door. "Go and check out Watts' and Beal's alibis and then go and inspect the blue Ford pickups so we can eliminate the owners from our list of suspects." She pushed back her chair. "Don't bother picking me up on the way back. I'll find my own way home."

"Jenna—"

"That's Sheriff to you." Jenna glared at him. "Shut the door on your way out."

"I meant no disrespect, ma'am." Kane stood and shook his head slowly. He straightened and headed for the door.

She glanced at Deputy Rowley. His face resembled a crushed flower. She realized Kane was his idol, the epitome of the perfect officer. Too bad, he would have to learn the hard way, if he dared to doubt her word. "Listen to me, I know for a fact Pete Daniels is repeating everything that happens here to his girlfriends and brothers. They in turn no doubt run their mouths all over town and the criminals know our every move. You must not discuss any of our cases with him or Walters. Keep the conversation to traffic violations and minor infringements. Do you understand?"

"Yes, ma'am." Rowley's face had turned a deep shade of red. "I do think Deputy Kane has a point. What he said makes sense." He hugged the coffee she'd made him like a life preserver.

Jenna sucked in a deep breath. "Investigations take time." She liked Rowley and he had a good sense of the job. "I'll get the paperwork filed for the search warrant for the Clough ranch and we'll check him out. The forensics team will hunt down the brand of footwear used by the killers and find any DNA evidence. Everything will be resolved. Killers make mistakes and we'll nail who did this but it might take a little more time. Don't jump to unsubstantiated conclusions like Kane; be patient and work through the clues." She moved around the desk and patted him on the back. "Solid police work is all we need. Now, go and ask Daniels if he's matched up the movements of Josh Rockford and Watts with the bank withdrawals from Helms' and Woodward's bank statements."

"Sure." Rowley indicated toward the whiteboard with his thumb. "Do you want me to hide the board if you'd rather Daniels doesn't know the details about the current investigation?"

Exhausted and drained, Jenna dropped into her chair. "Good idea."

"Can I get you another cup of coffee?" Rowley pushed the board up into the wall recess.

"Thank you, I think I need a gallon."

FORTY-NINE

Chagrined, Kane dropped into the chair in his cubicle and stared at Jenna's office door. What part of discussing a case didn't she understand? He followed his gut and right now his gut told him there was a connection between the attempts on her life and the murders.

He desperately wanted to pay Stan Clough a visit, and speaking to him was a priority, but a search warrant would be an asset if he noticed anything suspicious. The idea the man owned a piggery worried him and knowing the voracious appetites of pigs, it wouldn't be beyond reason to believe a psychopath would feed his victims to his swine. A pig will devour a carcass, bones and all, and DNA-testing their feces often proved useless.

He rubbed the back of his neck, deep in thought. Did Clough have a family or close friend? If two men were involved in such brutal killings and lived in Black Rock Falls, they would have committed more murders in or around the county. Both Sarah's and Helms' deaths told him the killer had escalated his need to murder. If he assumed the missing persons from two years ago had been victims, he had reason to believe the killer's pattern had been disturbed—and Clough had been in jail for six months.

He would need to contact other counties for a list of missing persons. Psychopaths often moved around collecting victims but kept within a comfort zone of places they knew. Relatives might have reported people missing, but how many people without family and friends disappear without a trace? *This maniac could have been doing this for years.*

He glanced at Jenna's door and decided to get back to work. Pulling out his notebook, he scanned the witnesses Billy Watts had named. The coach would be the best witness and he would ask the manager of the Larks' gym. He called both numbers and wrote down the time the witnesses remembered seeing Watts and Beal arrive and depart. As the times coincided within a fifteen-minute span, he crossed both suspects off his list. He stared at Josh Rockford's name and couldn't dismiss him. He needed to check his father's old Ford pickup.

He opened the DMV files on his computer screen and jotted down the locations of the Ford pickups he wanted to inspect. Still new to the area, he would have to rely on his GPS to guide him. He reached for his phone and punched in John Davis' number. "Ah, Mr. Davis. I'm on my way to inspect your pickup. Do you need to let your wife know? I don't want to worry her by showing up unannounced."

"*I'm finished for the day. My ranch is set back off the road and might be difficult to locate. If you stop here on the way, you'll be able to follow me.*"

Kane frowned. "Yeah, thanks. I'll be there in five minutes." He removed his sidearm from the holster and checked the clip.

"Problem?" Deputy Rowley stopped by his desk, coffee cup in hand.

"Nah." Kane smiled at him. "I'm just being careful."

"Don't worry about the sheriff." Rowley gave him an apologetic shrug. "Her bark is worse than her bite, as they say."

Kane shrugged. "I'm not worried."

Rowley's face pinked and his Adam's apple bobbed. "Of course not. Oh, by the way, none of the dates for the cash withdrawals coincides with Watts' or Rockford's movements, according to the phones or GPS. When he's not with the Larks, Rockford seems to move around town at odd hours, as in overnight, and he spends a ton of time online."

"Okay." Kane holstered his weapon and pocketed his notebook. "I'm heading out to inspect the pickups and then I'm heading home. I'll see you in the morning." He glanced at Jenna's office door. "See she gets home safely."

He met John Davis outside the real estate office and followed his vehicle out of town and into the hills. The landscape resembled a moonscape under the thick coating of snow and night was coming on fast. The light had started to fade by the time he stopped beside the blue pickup. The moment he opened the door, cold seeped through his clothes and snowflakes brushed his cheeks. He pulled up the hood of his jacket and slipped from the seat. Grabbing his phone, he moved around the old pickup, snapping shots. Convinced this pickup was not the one he'd seen the night of Jenna's accident, he gave John Davis a wave. "All done. Thank you for your cooperation."

"Not a problem." Davis moved to his side with a bunch of excited dogs circling him, their footprints disturbing the pristine coat of snow. "I have to ask, has something happened at the Old Mitcham Ranch?"

Kane weighed his reply. "We have reason to believe a crime was committed in the area." Holding up a hand to prevent Davis from questioning him, he smiled. "I'm sorry, as it's an ongoing investigation, I can't give you any more information." He glanced up at the sky and winced at the sight of gray clouds heavy with snow. "I'd better be going, the snow is getting heavier and I need to inspect Mayor Rockford's vehicle before I call it a day."

"Okay. If you drive through that gate," Davis pointed to a dirt road recently cleared of snow, "it takes you directly to the back of Rockford's barn. He keeps the vehicle inside. I'm in a deal with Rockford on feed so we keep the road clear for deliveries. It will cut your traveling time in half. I'll leave the gates open, if you sound your horn on the way back, I'll come down and close them."

Kane nodded and followed him back to his truck. "Thanks."

The trip to Mayor Rockford's ranch had been a waste of time. The old pickup had evident rust in the tailgate and no sign of a sticker. Kane headed home with the sound of Jenna's words ringing in his ears. There could be no doubt the pickup used in her accident belonged to Mrs. Woodward. His conclusion about the case had not changed.

When he arrived home, lights blazed in Jenna's house but no floodlights illuminated the driveway. She neglected to arm her security system. A cruiser, one of the older ones belonging to Pete Daniels, was in her driveway. She'd likely borrowed the vehicle but if he'd given her a ride home, she'd have invited him for coffee, maybe with the intention of finding out what information he'd been leaking. Somehow, the idea of Jenna entertaining another man disturbed him, not in a jealous way but more as if a close friend had dumped him.

Kane stomped through the snow to the cottage. He needed more information, more insight into the happenings in Black Rock Falls. Josh Rockford had something hidden behind his outgoing persona, and who was Stan Clough? Who would be better to bring him up to speed than the town gossip? Reaching for his phone, he found the number. "Hi, Mary-Jo, this is Dave Kane. I was wondering if you'd be free for dinner tonight?"

When she gushingly agreed, he disconnected and then secured a table at the Cattleman's Hotel restaurant for eight. He hadn't been on a date for five years but had played the part of a doting companion on assignment many times. *It's only business.* After shrugging away the nagging voice in the back of his head and ignoring the instant grip of betrayal in his gut for his dead wife, he whistled a tune and headed for the shower.

FIFTY

It was pitch-black outside when Jenna noticed the headlights of Kane's truck heading out of the gate. A wave of panic hit her along with the sinking recollection she neglected to reinstall the floodlights to her security system. With Kane close by to keep her safe, she'd not made the job a priority. Never mind, he'd likely be back after dinner, and in the meantime she'd keep busy.

She glanced at the clock and, seeing it was after eleven, strolled to the front door and armed the security alarm. She peered in the direction of Kane's cottage. The porch light illuminated the doors to his garage. They stood wide open and the inside was a gaping black maw. "Out on the tiles, are you, Kane? Hmm, and after you told me you had suffered a bad breakup. Men!"

Walking back to her bedroom, she flicked off the lights on the way and lay down on her bed. She tried to sleep but the argument with Kane kept coming to the front of her mind. After midnight, her phone disturbed her and it took some moments to realize the beep was the border alarm. "So, you decided to come home, did you?"

She waited for the sound of Kane's truck and the flash of headlights. After nothing happened, she lifted onto one elbow and peered through her open bedroom door to the windows at the front of the house. The green light on the house alarm glowed but no vehicle's lights bobbed up her driveway. Perhaps an elk had wandered on her property, or some other creature looking for a warm place for the night. She turned over in bed and dozed.

Sometime later, a sound jerked her awake. Not moving a muscle, she flicked her gaze around the room. The air was hot rather than cool, and she'd kicked off the blankets during her fitful sleep. The noise came again, soft footfalls on the stoop and a slight rattle as if someone was moving from window to window looking for a way inside.

Three flashes lit up the room.

Frozen with terror she slid her gaze toward the window. A figure loomed in the darkness. Holy shit, someone was taking photographs of her in bed. Her sleep-drugged mind fought past the paralyzing fear and she forced her body to relax. As the man crept away, she heard the familiar creaking of the floorboards and sucked in a deep breath, readying her limbs into action. Heart threatening to burst through her ribs, she slid her gaze down the hallway and made out the shadowy figure of a tall man with broad shoulders. *Someone is at my front door.*

She slid one hand to her ear. One press on her earring would summon Kane; her fingers slid over empty lobes. Shoot! She'd left them on the bathroom vanity. At least she'd honed her hand-to-hand combat skills with Kane and could use them as a backup. Grabbing her weapon from the nightstand, she dove for the floor. The handle of the front door turned with a whine.

Oh my God, he is trying to get inside the house.

Had she locked the door? Lying flat on the floor, she aimed around the bed, waiting for the intruder to enter the house. The door held, but the house alarm failed to send out a piercing scream. Like a vehicle alarm, any tampering with her front door should have triggered the system. Panic gripped her as the footsteps came again as the shadowy form moved along the porch. Pulse running like a freight train, she rolled across the floor and closed the door then slid the heavy bolt into place. The carpenter had laughed at the reinforcing on her bedroom door the day he'd installed similar locks on all the internal rooms. She needed safe rooms, and the heavy doors would give her a few moments' valuable time to deal with an intruder. As the floorboards creaked under the man's steps, she forced her mind into combat calm. She'd never allow someone to creep up on her again, and if this lunatic thought he had the jump on her this time, he would learn the hard way.

Oh my God! He is coming back. Keeping one eye on the bedroom window, she scrambled for her phone and hit Kane's number. His message to call back later made her chest tighten in panic. *You pick now to stay out all darn night when I only have Walters to help me?*

She punched in Walters' number and he replied with a yawn.

"Anything wrong, Sheriff?"

Jenna whispered into the mouthpiece. "Yeah, I have an intruder and Kane has turned off his phone. Can you come at once? No lights or sirens, I want to catch this creep."

"I'm on my way."

When the footsteps paused outside her window, she rolled onto her knees, grabbed the Glock in two hands and aimed at the shadowy figure. Walters would take about ten minutes if he left at once and drove fast. *Long enough to murder me.* If the intruder made one more move to get inside her home, she would shoot and darn the consequences. A tremble went through her and she tightened her grip on the weapon, not moving her gaze from the dark figure outside. The outline of a hand wearing black gloves appeared in the glass, then the outline of a face.

Pushing down fear, Jenna rested both elbows on the bed and her finger slid to the trigger. She raised her voice as loud as possible. "This is the sheriff. Put your hands on top of your head —now!"

A flash of light dazzled her. The man was taking more photographs. Jenna aimed and squeezed the trigger. A loud bang and the window shattered, flinging shards of glass in all directions. Moments later, the man fell with a thump on the porch and made a low moan. Ice-cold wind blasted into the room as she jumped to her feet. With one hand on the pistol and aiming at the window, she reached for the bedside lamp and flooded the room with light. Picking her way around the shattered glass, she moved toward the window.

Outside, Josh Rockford rolled in a ball of pain, clutching his left shoulder. He gave her a puppy-dog stare.

"You *shot* me."

Not taking her weapon off him, Jenna glared at him. "I might have guessed it was *you*. Don't move a muscle, you creep. I should have blown off your head."

"I need the paramedics." Rockford rolled into a sitting position and leaned against the porch railing. "Or are you gonna let me bleed out?"

The adrenalin pumping through her started to ebb and her teeth chattered. Keeping the Glock aimed at him, she reached one hand toward the chest of drawers and picked up the handcuffs she kept there. She tossed them at him. "Handcuff your injured arm to the railing, unless you want me to place a bullet in your kneecap."

"Dammit, woman. I'm hurting here." Rockford gave her a baleful look. "I thought you liked me and now you've shot me. Get me a doctor."

Shaking her head, Jenna held her Glock steady. "Do as you are told or bleed out. I don't like you that's for darn sure and right now I don't care what happens to you."

When he complied, moaning like a wounded animal, she made her way around the room and dragged out clothes. Shivering, she dressed swiftly, and then called Daniels and asked him to take a cab to meet Walters at the hospital. Anger raged through her but she followed procedure and pulled on surgical gloves, collected an evidence bag and then went outside to toss a blanket over Rockford. The wound was a through and through and not bleeding excessively. The bullet had lodged in the wood behind him. There was no way on earth she'd risk going near the pervert, and kept her distance. "Slide your phone toward me, and the moment Walters arrives, I'll attend to your wound, but for now you'll just have to wait."

"Can you call my daddy?"

Jenna shook her head and stared into the distance looking for Walter's headlights. It had started snowing again and her front stoop glistened with icicles. "Nope. I'll call Mr. Stone if you like. You are sure going to need a lawyer. There's no way you are getting away with stalking me. Did you think I didn't know it was you behind the Cattleman's Hotel?" She picked up his phone and dropped it into an evidence bag.

"The what?" Rockford dropped his head. "I haven't been stalking you. I had a bet with the guys. Which of us was game enough to get some compromising shots of you to put on the net." He gave her a half-hearted grin. "I don't need to stalk women, they flock to me." His gaze drifted over her. "I was being nice before. You're too old for my taste."

She took the insult by giving him her best sarcastic smile. "I can see the headlines now: 'Old lady takes down Josh Rockford,' or perhaps, 'Josh Rockford the pervert banned for life from the Larks.' I think the second one rings true."

"Go to hell."

. . .

Walters arrived with an overcoat covering pajamas and a deerstalker hat. He gaped at Josh Rockford then looked at her. "What happened here?"

Jenna handed him a pair of latex gloves and the evidence bag. "The phone is evidence. This creep was taking photographs of me in bed. I'm charging him with trespassing on private property and invasion of privacy." She turned to Rockford and read him his rights. "I'll get a med kit and patch him up and then you can take him to the hospital. Daniels will have to guard him overnight. He's meeting you at the hospital. Speak to someone about making him comfortable in Rockford's room and make sure Rockford is cuffed to the bed.

Jenna headed inside the house and took a wad of cotton out of the med kit. She pulled on fresh gloves then went outside to see Rockford on his feet speaking quietly to Walters. Handing the dressing to the deputy, she retrieved the phone and flicked through the images. Anger rushed over her and bile rushed into her mouth. Apart from the images of her sprawled in bed, Rockford had compromising images of very young girls. She lifted her chin, trembling with rage. "Josh Rockford, I'm also charging you with possession of child pornography." She waved a hand at Walters. "Get him out of my sight."

She stood on the porch, arms wrapped around her, and watched Walters' cruiser disappear into the distance before taking out her anger by nailing the shutters closed.

FIFTY-ONE

The following morning, Jenna's attention moved to the empty garage at Kane's house. *Where has he been all night?* The show of male bravado in her office the day before and being incommunicado when she needed his help had grated on her nerves all night. She went back inside and dialed Rowley's number. "Hey, is Kane in yet?" She filled a to-go cup with coffee.

"Nope." Rowley cleared his throat.

She could hear the hesitation in his voice and shook her head. She knew he was covering for him. "Okay, spill the beans. Where is he?"

"I'm not sure."

She had enough to cope with right now without her deputies taking sides. "If you know, tell me. That's an order, Deputy." She added sugar and cream to her coffee. "He didn't come home last night and I couldn't reach him. Where did you last see him?"

"He was off-duty, ma'am."

Jenna sealed the lid, placed the phone on speaker, and laid it on the table. She shrugged into her coat. "I don't care where he was last night. I need to know where he is now. He's not answering his phone. Josh Rockford tried to break into my house last night and I shot him; he's in the hospital. I figure he's involved in something serious." She sighed. "I've already spoken to the DA. The evidence we have is enough to keep him on remand until they set a date for his trial. The judge is rushing through his hearing at nine this morning. The prosecutor won't need me until the trial."

"What? Are you okay?"

Jenna ran one hand down her face. "I'd be better if I could get in touch with Kane. Where the hell is he?"

"He's still at the Cattleman's Hotel. I noticed his truck in the parking lot out front on my way past this morning."

There had to be more to this story. Impatient, Jenna tapped her foot. "What do you mean, 'still there'?"

"I dropped in for dinner with a couple of buddies last night. They have the special on ribs. Ah... Kane was there with Mary-Jo Miller."

Gathering her wits, Jenna stared at the phone. Kane had said he wasn't ready for a relationship yet he took Mary-Jo Miller out on a date. Why did the idea annoy her? *Oh no, I'm getting feelings for David Kane.* She swallowed the lump in her throat and sucked in a deep breath. "Okay, thanks. I'll be leaving soon. Put on a pot of coffee, I think this is going to be a very long day." She disconnected.

Pushing her mind away from the thought of Kane spending the night with Mary-Jo, she headed for Daniels' cruiser. He'd not been too happy to hand over the keys but his apartment was walking distance from the office and she needed her independence back. Planning her day put everything in perspective. She'd send Walters to relieve Daniels at the hospital. Daniels could take Walters' cruiser and keep an eye on Stan Clough's movements for an hour or so. When Kane decided to arrive, he and Rowley could head to the piggery with the warrant to interview the suspect and, if necessary, conduct a search.

Going over the facts in the Sarah Woodward homicide, she swallowed hard remembering the phone number she'd found inside the woman's purse. After reading the autopsy reports, chasing up the number had slipped her mind. She would cross-reference the number with the list of properties John Davis had given Sarah. Likely, the number belonged to someone she'd spoken to in the hours prior to her death, and that person might have information on Sarah's whereabouts before the murder.

She slid into the driver's seat, placed the to-go cup in the holder, and glanced up to see Kane's black truck driving past and heading for the cottage. The urge to get out and march over to speak to him flashed across her mind, but instead, she started the engine and turned up the heat. When Kane got out of his vehicle wearing a dark blue suit sans tie with his short hair mussed, she gaped at him. He looked gorgeous. Oh yeah, he was her type, but obviously she didn't rate in *his* top ten. Without thinking, she revved the engine and fishtailed down the icy driveway in a cloud of steam. Glancing in her mirror, she caught him staring after her with a grim expression on his face. Slowing the cruiser, she took control of the vehicle and her emotions then headed for the office.

Kane watched as Jenna turned onto the highway and ground his teeth. He'd planned to be home before she woke but the chance of a hot breakfast in a very comfortable hotel had been too much of a temptation. He hurried inside to dress for work, wondering if Jenna had discovered he'd taken Mary-Jo to dinner. He recalled seeing Jake Rowley at the Cattleman's Hotel and grimaced. Oh yeah, her untouchable deputy would have been in her ear, and to make things worse, now she'd believe he'd spent the night with a woman ten years his junior. The problem was he liked Jenna but Annie still owned his heart. Perhaps the loyalty he had for Annie would fade in time.

． ． ．

He arrived at the office three minutes before the start of his eight-thirty shift and made his way to his desk. His attention moved to Jenna's office door and he wondered if he should offer her an apology for the day before. He rubbed the back of his neck. Trusting his gut instinct had gotten him out of more trouble than he cared to remember. Beside him Rowley cleared his throat and the familiar yet annoying squeak of his chair meant he was looking his way. Turning to look at him, he raised an eyebrow. "The boss isn't in a very good mood this morning, is she?"

"Well, considering she tried to call you for backup when Josh Rockford broke into her house and she had to shoot him, I gather you're not on her BFF list this morning." Rowley leaned back in his chair and linked his fingers over his waist.

Kane gaped at him. "*What?* She *shot* Josh Rockford?"

When Rowley explained about the photographs Rockford had taken and the kiddy porn on his phone, Kane rubbed his chin. "Is she okay and who's guarding Rockford at the hospital?"

"No one. Mr. Stone pulled the judge out of bed in the early hours and produced some type of order to allow Josh to be released into the custody of his father." Rowley avoided his gaze. "She wasn't too happy about that either, but Rockford's hearing is set for nine. Walters will attend but it's not necessary with the evidence, It's unlikely Rockford will get bail. The sheriff said the phone evidence alone will be enough for the DA to proceed to trial."

Kane rubbed both hands down his face in disbelief. "Then what happened?"

"She came in barking orders and told Daniels to head out to Stan Clough's piggery. He's to keep him under surveillance until she obtains a search warrant for his property." Rowley grinned in obvious glee. "Pete radioed in to say he'd arrived and it was as quiet as a tomb but if the guy made a move toward him, he'd call his brothers for backup in case the guy tried to feed him to his pigs." He chuckled. "I guess he forgot there's zero bars out there."

Kane ground his teeth. Sending a rookie out alone on surveillance of a murder suspect was not a move he would have made. How could so many crazy things happen in the short time since he'd left Jenna alone? "Is she in her office?"

"Nope. She left about twenty minutes ago and took off without a word."

Kane frowned. "Did you ask her where she was going?"

"Ah... no, but she had a folder with her and she's likely speaking to the judge." Rowley grimaced and gave him a look of incredulity. "I didn't dare ask her where she was going." He heaved a long sigh. "She did the Spanish Inquisition act on me earlier. Once is enough for me."

Kane glared at him. "I gather that was around the time you threw me under the bus?" He waved a hand toward Jenna's door. "You told her about my date with Mary-Jo, didn't you?" He sighed at Rowley's nod. "It wasn't a date as in romantic. It was a fact-finding mission. She's the town gossip and I needed information."

"Did you get any *information* out of her?"

Kane rubbed the back of his neck. "Nah, only that Rockford is a bit kinky. Apparently, he liked her to dress up as a kid."

"That makes sense." Rowley grimaced and shook his head slowly. "The man's a darn pedophile. After the sheriff caught him taking pictures of her, she seized his phone and found images of young girls. He likes to sneak about at night and take pictures of them." His expression darkened. "The sheriff is trying to obtain search warrants to seize all his computers as well. From the texts and images on his phone, he's involved in some nasty stuff."

"*Jesus.*" Kane let out a long sigh. "No wonder Jenna is mad."

"So why stay out all night?"

"After I took Mary-Jo home, I hung around the bar listening to the local gossip in the hope of hearing something. I decided to stay because I'd had too much to drink. I had no idea about Rockford. I figured Jenna was angry because she believed I'd spent the night with Mary-Jo. Not that what I do off-duty is any of her business."

He turned on his computer. "While we are waiting for the search warrant for the Clough ranch, I'll go through the files again and see if I've missed any clues. Clough is the most likely suspect so far but who is his accomplice? Over the years I've found it best not to discount anyone until I've check out everyone's alibis."

"It wasn't Rockford who attacked the sheriff in the bushes." Rowley lifted his gaze and smiled. "I managed to track down the driver of the cab that picked him up on Saturday night and took him to his apartment. You had his vehicle keys, so he couldn't have gotten back to the Cattleman's Hotel in time."

Kane nodded and then turned back to his computer. "Okay. I might drop over to speak to John Davis again too. I'd be interested to find out if he had anyone else looking at properties around the time Sarah planned to visit them."

"I'm heading out to give a ticket to a dog owner." Rowley pulled a face. "I'll catch you later." He pushed to his feet and shrugged into his coat.

Kane opened the forensic files on both cases. He needed the details of the footprints found at Sarah's crime scene. He called forensics and left a message. With nothing else to do in the office, he grabbed his jacket and headed out in the driving snow to speak to John Davis.

FIFTY-TWO

Kane strolled into the real estate office and waited patiently for John Davis to finish speaking to a prospective buyer. He listened to the usual salesman's spiel. It was as if they all came out of the same egg, and born with a mission to persuade buyers they could afford something way beyond their means. When the young couple left, brochures in hand, he shut the door behind them and turned to him. "I'm afraid I'm here to notify you about a murder at the Old Mitcham Ranch."

"A murder?" The color drained from John Davis' face and he ran a hand through his thinning hair. "Anyone I know?"

"I'm afraid so. We found Sarah Woodward's body in the root cellar on Monday." He frowned. "That's the reason the Daniels boys removed the property from sale."

"Dear Lord." Visibly shaken, Davis opened his desk drawer and took out a bottle of brandy and a shot glass. "Do you know who killed her?"

Kane rubbed his chin, observing the old man with interest. "Not yet."

"That place is cursed." Davis blinked rapidly.

Why do people blame everyone else but the killer? "I'd ask that you keep this information between us as it is an ongoing investigation."

"Yes, of course." Davis poured a drink and tipped it back with a gasp. "First the old lady goes missing and now this dreadful thing. I can't believe this has happened in Black Rock Falls."

Kane stared at the man's pallid face. "Who else knew the Old Mitcham Ranch was for sale? Did you send anyone else out to view the property?"

"Only her grandmother." Davis sealed the bottle and pushed it back inside the drawer. "I didn't bother putting details in the front window. No local would be interested, and it won't sell now." He cleared his throat. "I'd burn it down if I had my way." He got to his feet and moved around the desk, staring sightlessly out of the window. "Burn it and the darn curse."

"That might be an option you can put to the owners." Kane glanced down at Davis' feet. He didn't wear the cowboy boots most locals favored but polished loafers. "I'd better keep going. Thank you for your cooperation." He turned for the door, pulled on the handle, and strode out into the freezing morning air.

As he approached the sheriff's office, he noticed the cruiser Jenna had commandeered from Deputy Daniels was conspicuous by its absence. He glanced at his watch and, seeing it was ten-thirty, headed past the sheriff department's front door and toward Aunt Betty's Café. If he had to withstand Jenna's wrath on her return, he'd need some comfort food. The fact she'd not called to bawl him out or issue him with a string of orders played on his mind. Jenna hadn't been shy at cutting him down to size in front of Rowley, and her choice not to confront him seemed a little out of character. Maybe she'd taken personal time to cool her anger, although he'd have thought an ongoing investigation of two murders would have negated any reason to be away from the office.

At the door, the tempting aroma of freshly baked cookies made his stomach growl in appreciation. He stamped the snow from his feet and stepped inside the diner. After ordering enough cakes, sandwiches, and coffee for everyone, he collected the take-out and headed back to the office. People he passed in the street greeted him with smiles and nods. Maybe he would find a home in this little town and a modicum of peace. Snow pelted his face and icy rivulets ran into the neck of his jacket. By the time he reached the office, he couldn't feel his feet, and the headache had returned in an uncomfortable throb.

He met Rowley at the front desk. "Got time for a coffee break?"

"Yeah, I've finished everything the sheriff gave me to chase up. Wow! Coffee and goodies. Thanks!" Rowley reached in the box for the to-go cup lid marked "cappuccino" and sighed in appreciation. "Sarah's uncle arrived and identified the body and I have a list of John Helms' personal effects his wife sent. He wore a diamond stud earring. I rang the ME and he informed me he has reason to believe the killer ripped it from his ear after death. Maybe it's another trophy the killer kept." He collected a pile of cakes and shrugged. "And I had a call from the forensics team."

Kane looked up from the box of food. "Did they find anything interesting?"

"More like disappointing." Rowley shrugged. "No DNA trace on that hair they found on Sarah and the footprints of the boots they found are useless. They said that brand of footwear can be purchased at any Walmart."

"Okay, disappointing maybe but we still know the homicide involves two killers." Kane headed for his desk with his food and coffee. "Maybe we've missed something."

"I've read and reread every report until I'm cross-eyed." Rowley dropped into the seat opposite Kane. "Everyone we thought was involved checks out. We don't have any suspects left apart from Stan Clough."

Kane bit into a turkey on rye and sighed. He chewed slowly, milling over the cases. "It would be helpful if the sheriff kept us informed of her movements. I figure she's off on a hunch."

"Would you like me to call her?" Rowley stared at the uneaten cake in his hand.

Kane pulled the lid from his to-go cup and tossed it in the garbage. "Why not? I doubt she'd take my call right now." He sipped his scalding coffee as Rowley tried Jenna's number.

"She's not picking up. Maybe she's out of range. There are heaps of black spots around here." Rowley frowned. "You don't suppose she's obtained the warrants and gone out to the Clough place alone, do you?"

"I doubt it very much, although I wouldn't rule out the possibility." Kane pushed to his feet. "I'll check if she's made an entry in her day book." He strode into Jenna's office and flipped open the book on her desk. The page for the day's date was blank. "Oh, great!"

He marched into the outer office and went to speak to Maggie on the front desk. "I'll talk to him." He indicated to the angry-looking man waiting at the counter. "Get on the satellite phone and raise the sheriff. She's out in Pete's cruiser and we can't reach her by phone."

"Sure thing." Magnolia sat down in front of the radio.

Kane turned to the angry man. "How can I help you?"

"I need to pay a fine for letting my dog run without a leash." He handed Kane a ticket and a check. "It's a joke. The hospital just released me and now I get a fine. How could I keep the dog on a leash when I'm not home? I'm being harassed by the old lady next door."

"I don't think so. I came close to hitting your dog on the road the other day. I instructed my deputy to issue this fine. Keep your dog under control before it causes an accident. Put up a fence so it can't get out of your property." Kane leveled his gaze on the man. "And I'll be personally looking into any further complaints from your neighbor."

"Are you threatening me?"

Kane scanned the document and payment into the system and issued a receipt. "Nope, but you can take it as a warning."

The man snatched the documents from his hand and stormed off, his face flushed with anger. Kane glanced at the waiting area, glad to see it empty for once. Behind him, Maggie repeated the message and then she turned to him. "She must have turned off the satellite phone. She's not answering the radio either." She smiled. "I'll try again in five minutes."

A knot of worry clenched Kane's stomach. "Has she checked in at all this morning?"

"Not so far." Maggie pushed a mass of curls from her round face. "But she left here in a right mood. Slammed the vehicle door fit to break it off the hinges." She frowned. "Shame she took Pete's car, it's the only one without a GPS. We could have tracked her if she has broken down somewhere. That old cruiser is on its last legs."

Kane ran a hand down his face. "Keep trying until you reach her."

The last time he'd spoken to Deputy Daniels was when he radioed in at ten to report all was quiet at Clough's piggery and he was going to his brothers' ranch to grab a snack.

Lunch had come and gone without a word from Jenna.

When the search and arrest warrants for Stan Clough arrived, Kane gaped at them in disbelief. He called Jenna's phone with no luck and then asked Rowley to join him. "I'm not sure what's going on but the sheriff is MIA and so is Daniels. Did the sheriff discover any new evidence and neglect to inform me?"

"Did she mention what we found in Sarah's purse?" Rowley raised one eyebrow in question.

Kane shook his head. If Jenna had found something relevant, she would have told him. "Daniels gave me a rundown: ID but no keys."

"It wasn't what was in the purse but what was missing." Rowley dropped his voice to just above a whisper. "Things like a hairbrush, lip gloss, women's things. The sheriff thought the killer had taken trophies." He cleared his throat. "Also, we found a phone number tucked inside some bills."

"If it was important, she'd have mentioned it to *you*." Kane rubbed the back of his neck to relieve the persistent prickling of the hairs. Something was wrong.

"What about John Davis? Is he still a suspect?"

Recalling the conversation with the real estate broker, he shook his head. "Nah. The news shook him up a little too much for him to have killed Sarah and he'd have needed an accomplice. Plus I doubt he owns a pair of Walmart cowboy boots." He sighed. "We need to get out to Stan Clough's piggery and check on Daniels. Something doesn't feel right to me."

Impending doom tightened his chest. His concern over Jenna outweighed his rigid training and it worried him. Giving himself a mental shake, he listed his priorities. He'd secure his prime suspect then have every boot on the ground working around the clock until he found Jenna. He glanced at his watch. She'd been incommunicado for five hours. If the cruiser had broken down, she'd have walked to a ranch in that space of time. His fear of the killer torturing her, raping her, escalated into a rage he'd not known existed.

Kane forced the panic down and stood. "Let's go." He strode to Maggie's desk. "Keep trying to reach the sheriff. If you contact her, call me. I'm heading out to the Clough piggery with Rowley." He went to Walters' cubicle, glad to see he'd checked in for his second shift. "I want you to go out on patrol. Drive anywhere you think the sheriff might have visited." He let out a long sigh. "Has Jenna ever gone off alone before?"

"All the time before you arrived." Walters shrugged. "She'll be fine. Tough lady, that one, and independent."

Kane straightened. "I'm acting on worst-case scenario. Start searching for her now. If I find anything suspicious at the Clough piggery, I'll do a search and send him back here with Daniels. Right now, Clough is shaping up as our main suspect." He took a deep breath to drop into combat mode. "Concentrate on finding Jenna and let's hope to God she's okay."

"I'm on it." Walters took his jacket from the back of his chair and headed for the door.

Kane marched into Jenna's office and unlocked the weapons' locker. Clough was an unknown quantity and he didn't intend to walk into a potentially hostile situation without weapons. He filled his pockets, locked the cabinet, and turned to go. "Oh, darn."

The office door had swung shut and on the back hanging on a peg was Jenna's satellite phone.

Incredulity slammed into him. He flung open the door and waved Rowley to join him. "How far away is the piggery?" He handed a rifle to Rowley.

"A good half-hour's drive or up to an hour at least if the roads are bad." Rowley's mouth turned down. "Are you bringing these extra weapons because you figure he kidnapped the sheriff?"

If he has, we're probably too late. "Right now, I've no reason to believe she went anywhere near Clough's piggery, and Pete has been watching him all morning so it's unlikely." Kane shrugged into his coat and then pulled his woolen cap over his ears. "We're going to speak to a potential psychopathic killer and taking these weapons is normal procedure."

"I'm nervous about what we might find out there." Rowley's

face paled. "If he is a serial killer, he could have been killing since he got out of jail."

Kane checked his Glock, slid a round into the chamber, and dropped it back into the holster at his waist. "If Clough is our man, he'll have me to deal with and I don't take too kindly to men who brutalize people, especially women."

His phone rang. "Kane."

"*I think I have an idea where the sheriff went.*" Walter's voice sounded jovial.

Kane rolled his eyes. "Where?"

"*I dropped into Aunt Betty's and asked Susie if she'd seen her. She said the sheriff mentioned taking a drive to speak to the Daniels brothers.*"

"Okay, thanks for letting me know." He disconnected and shot a glance at Rowley. "How far is the Daniels' ranch from the piggery?"

"Not far."

Which would place Jenna in the vicinity of a serial killer. Kane's head throbbed and anxiety cramped his gut. There'd been three unsuccessful attempts on Jenna's life and she'd gone off alone without telling a soul.

FIFTY-THREE

After spending hours trying to convince the judge to issue a search and arrest warrant for Stan Clough, and also a search warrant for Rockford's computers, the last thing Jenna wanted to do was return to the office and confront Kane. She'd picked up a sandwich and coffee from Aunt Betty's Café and headed to the Daniels' ranch, relieved to have a professional excuse to visit friends in Black Rock Falls.

She turned off the highway and negotiated the pile of snow outside the Daniels' ranch. The old cruiser's engine sent billows of steam into the air, blocking her view. She slowed and negotiated the winding driveway toward the palatial ranch house. The sweeping front steps reminded her of the old Southern plantation houses, and standing out front, waiting to greet her, was Dean Daniels, the eldest of the three brothers. Happy to see a familiar face, she gave him a wave. After discovering it was Dean's phone number in Sarah's purse, she'd decided to use the excuse for a visit. She doubted the Daniels boys had any information on Sarah Woodward. If they'd spoken to her prior to her murder, they'd have mentioned it to Pete.

In truth, she needed company outside of the Black Rock

Falls County Sheriff's Department. For a while, she'd push the now uncomfortable reality of working in close proximity to Dave Kane to the back of her mind. After all, she got on well with the brothers, and Dean was closer to her age, not to mention strikingly handsome with his collar-length black hair and teasing grin. She pulled the old cruiser close to a snow-covered garden bed and pushed open the door. "Afternoon. Sorry to come by without notice. I need to ask you a few questions but I won't disturb your chores too long."

"I can't believe you're driving Pete's cruiser. I figured it must be at the wreckers after seeing him driving Walters' cruiser." Dean pushed a hand through his damp hair and glanced at the car. "The Cloud Express, we call that heap. It overheats the moment you push it over forty miles an hour." He waved her inside. "Coffee?"

"I'm dying for one." Jenna could see the kitchen down a passageway toward the back of the house. "*Mmm*, I can smell it brewing from here."

"You might as well sit down and rest awhile. Pete's cruiser will need water and time to cool down before you leave. I'll get Dirk to take a look at it while we're chatting."

She moved along the passageway, noticing the lived-in yet clean look of the sitting room. Dirk Daniels was at the table sharpening his hunting knife and both men smelled as if they had just stepped out of the shower. "Hey."

"Mornin'. What brings you to our humble abode?"

The kitchen had dirty plates on the table and she pushed them to one side and took a seat. She examined his wickedly handsome face. This man could charm the legs off a donkey. "I came to speak to you about Sarah Woodward's murder."

"Nasty business." Dirk ran the blade down the whetstone and examined the edge. "I guess you've come here to tell us we'll get the job of cleaning up the mess?"

Uncomfortable by his nonchalant attitude following a

brutal murder, she leaned back in her chair. "I'm sure there are cleaners of crime scenes available. I'll make inquiries if you like?"

"Sure, inquire away, but not many locals will go near the place." Dirk sheathed the blade at his waist then pushed to his feet. "Did I hear Dean mention you came here in Pete's cruiser?"

"Yeah, I'm driving it for a couple of days." She grimaced. "I'm waiting for a replacement but you know insurance companies, it could be a month or so. I wish the mayor would supply the funds for a couple of new vehicles. Trucks would be more suitable. The old cruiser outside barely goes over fifty."

"If you pushed the old girl, she'll need tending." Dirk pulled on a pair of black leather gloves then held out his hand. "Give me the keys. I'll refill the radiator before you leave." His gaze moved from her face to rest a little too long on her chest. "I wouldn't want you stranded out there in the snow." He raised his attention back to her face and rolled his shoulders. "We're a long way off the main highway and no phone coverage. You'd be a popsicle before morning."

"I've already had one close call. I don't need another one, especially as I dropped by without informing my deputies." Jenna pulled the front of her jacket closed and then reached in her pocket for the keys. She dropped them into Dirk's hand and smiled. "Thank you." The memory of finding John Helms' battered body flashed into her mind and she wondered how much Pete Daniels had told his brothers about the case. "Did Pete mention the other murder? John Helms? Apparently he was looking for work in the area."

"Pete chatters like a monkey every time he visits. I tend to turn off most times." Dirk shrugged. "People don't drop in here looking for work. I told you that the last time you came by. We are a little too isolated for casual callers."

Jenna remembered the visit and Dean's problem with a

horse. The poor thing was making an awful noise. "How is the horse now? The one giving birth and having a hard time?"

"Dean put it out of its misery." Dirk flicked a glance at his brother then back to her. "I told him you'd be asking after that horse. Darn shame, it was fun to ride."

Mortified, Jenna frowned. "I'm so sorry."

"Don't worry. I'll have a new one for him real soon." Dean turned from the bench to look at her over one shoulder. "How do you like your coffee?"

"Make sure you give her our special blend, not the instant garbage." Dirk's mouth curled at the edges. "I'd say she likes her coffee strong and sweet."

"You're right about sweet, I'd like three sugars, please, and cream if you have it?"

"Sure do." Dean gave his brother a meaningful look and indicated toward the front door with his chin. "I'll sit and chat to Jenna while you check out the cruiser."

"I'm not sure about leaving you alone with an armed woman." Dirk wiggled his eyebrows at her. "She might be more than you can handle."

Jenna grinned at him. "I'm sure I can control myself for the next ten minutes or so."

"Go, or we'll be here all night." When Dirk headed for the door, Dean slid into the chair opposite. "Now what's all this about slipping away from the office without telling anyone? Had a spat with Mr. Tall, Dark, and Efficient?"

Jenna took the steaming cup from him and smiled. "Sort of." She leaned back in her chair. "I just needed to get away from the job for an hour or so."

"So, what brought you to our doorstep? You mentioned the girl, Sarah, someone?"

"Yeah, Sarah Woodward. She had a list of properties her grandmother apparently visited, and your contact number was on a piece of paper in her purse. I wondered if she called or dropped by last Monday." She sipped the coffee and sighed. The rich brew slid across her taste buds and she took another drink. "Man, this is nice coffee. It's like a warm hug."

"Is Sarah the name of the murdered girl?" Dean inclined his head, watching her closely. "Some woman called. She didn't give her name but asked if we'd shown an old woman a property we had for sale. I thought she had the wrong number." He shrugged. "I had no idea what she was talking about until Pete called me on Monday about the murder at the Old Mitcham Ranch. He told me he'd put the place on the market as a surprise. Of course, I called John Davis and removed it from the listing." He shook his head. "You know, for a deputy, Pete is stupid. I mean, what idiot does something like that without discussing it with the family?"

Jenna peered at him over the rim of the cup. "He is a little naive. I guess most people are at his age."

"Like Pete? Nah, we are the complete opposite. He's soft like our mother, a useless excuse for a man. You should have seen him when she died, man, he cried like a baby. I don't know how you cope with him. You are aware he tells us every intimate detail of your life? He doesn't know when to keep his mouth shut."

Taken aback by his anger toward his brother, she blinked in surprise. "I had some idea he relayed information to you but he's young and inexperienced. I'll soon whip him into shape."

"I think Pete is past help." Dean turned his cup around on the table then lifted his gaze to her. "Getting back to the Old Mitcham Ranch, I expect it will be some time before the forensics team has finished their inquiries?"

"No, it's all done and you can arrange for the cleaners—if you can find anyone to venture down into the root cellar. I doubt you'll have much luck selling the place." Jenna sipped again and a warm glow started from her toes and spread.

Lethargy spread over her and she yawned. "Sorry. I didn't get much sleep last night."

"Drink the coffee. It will make you feel better." Dean smiled at her. "Do you have any leads? Pete mentioned you think Josh Rockford might be involved, and Stan Clough too."

"I can't give you details, *sorry*, but whoever killed Sarah knows how to cover their tracks. Forensics didn't find a thing." She held a finger to her lips and giggled. "*Shh*, don't tell Kane I told you." *What is wrong with me?*

FIFTY-FOUR

Kane pulled up behind the cruiser parked behind a clump of bushes not ten yards from the gate to Clough's piggery. When Deputy Daniels didn't get out of the vehicle to greet him, he slid from the driver's seat, and with one hand on the handle of his Glock, strode toward the vehicle.

The cruiser was empty.

He glanced toward Rowley and raised both eyebrows. "You don't think he went in alone, do you?"

"Nah. He's not brave enough."

The hairs on the back of Kane's neck stood to attention. He pulled Rowley behind the cruiser and did a visual scan of the area. The snow around Pete's cruiser appeared undisturbed but the road to the piggery twenty feet away was clear of snow from recent traffic. "I don't like the look of this. If Pete had wanted to speak to Clough alone or with the sheriff, he would have driven, not walked."

He moved to the back of the Beast to retrieve his rifle. He wanted it close by, just in case. "We'll go in on foot and take a look around. Keep your eyes open and watch me for signals."

"Yes, sir." Rowley followed him from the truck, keeping low.

The front of the house appeared deserted, with no vehicles parked outside. Clough had recently cleared the snow from the driveway leading to the main house and barn. Kane held up one hand to stop Rowley and listened. He could hear the *clink, clink, clink* of a chain passing through a pulley and the grunt of a man doing heavy labor. He pointed at the barn and placed one finger to his lips to keep Rowley silent. Stealthily, he headed for the outside of the building and, keeping his back to the wall, edged toward the entrance. He bobbed his head around the corner, but instead of seeing Clough, a pool of blood dripping from a line of pig carcasses met his gaze. Clough used the area as a killing shed. He listened but only the sound of pigs grunting nearby reached him. Turning back to Rowley, he shook his head. "Clear. Noise carries through these huge sheds; I heard a man using a pulley before. It must be coming from the piggery. We'll go round back of the barn and use the tree line for cover."

"Okay." Rowley jogged the length of the barn then paused at the corner and peered around. He glanced back over one shoulder. "Clear."

Kane ran through the snow, giving Rowley the lead, and then pulled him up before they reached the open stretch before the piggery. He pointed to a line of tire tracks running from the perimeter of the fence close to the highway and dropped his voice to a whisper. "We'll go round back." Sticking to the tree line, his feet sunk deep in snow as he led the way slowly toward the back of the piggery. Kane examined the area, taking in escape routes and possible ambush positions. He turned to Rowley. "Cover me."

Keeping low, he dashed across the open space and waited a few seconds before waving Rowley to his side. They moved toward the entrance and Kane pointed out footprints in the snow. He handed Rowley his rifle and pointed to the door. With care, he reached for the handle and turned it slowly, wincing at the sound of rusty metal grinding. He pushed the door open and a rush of warm stink hit him. *More fresh blood.* His stomach rolled and he pushed down the sudden rush of apprehension clawing at his guts. Keeping his back flush to the wall, he raised his voice. "Black Rock Falls Sheriff's Department, I'm entering the premises. Come out with your hands up."

He heard a man swearing and the sound of something heavy hitting the floor. Turkey-peeking around the door, a wave of terror smashed into him at the sight of a naked body curled on the blood-spattered cement floor. His gaze traveled over white buttocks covered in gore to a massive steel hook sunk between the shoulder blades. He pushed his rifle into Rowley's hands and met his gaze. "We've found our killer. Cover me."

Disgust gripped him as he moved into the opening and took a defensive stance, holding his Glock in both hands and aiming at the man standing over the body like a predator protecting its prey. The man with dead sunken eyes gaped open-mouthed at him in surprise. He gripped a chain in his filthy hands. From what Kane could see, he had been using the block and tackle to lift the body into the pigpen. Disgust and rage rolled over him. "Get your hands up or as God is my witness, I'll blow off your head."

To his surprise, the man dropped the chain and complied. Aiming his weapon at the man's chest, he scanned the surrounding area. Apart from the pen filled with noisy pigs, the man and the blood-soaked body, the area appeared to be empty. Kane eased inside the piggery with Rowley close behind. "Keep your weapon aimed at him and shoot him if he moves a muscle."

He took a few steps toward the body and crouched to check vital signs. He rolled the body over, and bile rose up the back of his throat at seeing Pete Daniels' sightless gaze. "It's Pete."

Face battered and bruised, Pete's head hung on a strange angle. As Kane made sense of the brutality before him, he realized someone had broken Pete's neck. The cause of the blood was one single wound under the ribs. Keeping his Glock trained on the man, he straightened.

"He's dead." The quivering man with the sunken eyes stared at him. "They said they didn't have time to play with him, he died real quick."

Crushing the need to open fire and kill the simpering animal standing before him, he waved Rowley forward. "Cuff him."

Rowley had not moved.

Kane turned his head to look at the white-faced man beside him. Rowley's face held an expression of sheer terror. "Rowley, look at me. We can't do anything to help Pete now and I need you to keep it together. Is that Stan Clough?"

"Yeah, and he killed Pete." Rowley's finger dropped onto the trigger of his pistol. "He needs to be put down."

Kane laid a hand on Rowley's arm. "I agree, but if *we* kill him, we'll never know what happened here and there has to be more people involved."

"I *didn't* kill him." Clough opened his hands wide. "Why am I always the one you blame? It wasn't me. It was the aliens."

"Right." Kane holstered his weapon and moved toward Clough, turned him around, and patted him down then cuffed him. "You're standing here with the dead body of one of my deputies and you're not to blame."

"The aliens said I could feed him to the pigs, like the others." Clough blinked at him like an owl in the sunlight. "I didn't kill him. No, sir, that wasn't me."

Kane shoved him hard against the wall and glared down at him. "If it wasn't you then who killed Pete Daniels?" The man stank of sweat and blood as if he had not washed in months. "Do the aliens have names?"

"No way." Clough moved his sunken eyes to Kane's face. "They'll kill me. Send me back to prison if you want, but I'm not ratting on them."

The delusional man believed aliens brought corpses to him to feed his pigs. "How many more people have they killed?"

"I don't keep count."

Anger flared and Kane grabbed Clough by the collar, lifting him to his toes. "Did you kill Sarah Woodward? A young, blonde woman?"

"I didn't kill any of them." Clough shook his head. "Why won't anyone believe me?"

Kane glared down at him with the image of Sarah's staring dead eyes at the front of his mind. Psychopaths were creatures of habit. "Do you have a root cellar?"

"Yeah, in the pantry. You really don't want to go down there." Clough let out a long pitiful whine. "They'll be angry with me. This—" he pointed a filthy finger at Pete's body "—is nothing compared to what they can do to a man. I'm in danger, you need to protect me."

"Shut your mouth before I forget I'm a deputy and do something I might regret." Kane dragged Clough to a metal hitching post and, using his spare cuffs, attached him securely; then using flex cuffs he tied his ankles together. He lifted his gaze to Rowley. "This animal isn't going anywhere and we'll need to check the house, but first I'll call it in and get the ME out here." He grabbed the satellite phone from his belt and contacted Walters then turned to Rowley. "Okay, come with me."

He took off at a run toward the back of the ranch house. The back door had a small porch and he moved up the stairs, opened the door, and aimed his Glock into the mudroom. "Sheriff's department, is anyone there?"

No sound came from inside. He closed his palm around the butt of his Glock and moved up the stairs. The back door opened silently. "Sheriff's department, I'm entering the premises."

The silence within was deafening. He walked into the kitchen, waved Rowley inside, and checked the filthy house.

"Clear." He strolled back into the kitchen and indicated toward the pantry. "He said the root cellar is in there."

"Yeah. I see a hatch in the floor at the back." Rowley moved inside.

Kane followed. "Watch my back, I'm going in."

"You'll need a flashlight." Rowley frowned. "I'll open the hatch." He holstered his weapon then bent and tugged on the metal loop in the floor.

The entrance swung open with silent ease and Kane pushed Rowley to one side. He peered into the darkness and listened. A soft humming came from below. He dropped his voice to a whisper. "Can you hear that? A motor of some kind is running down there."

"Sounds like a generator running in the cellar." Rowley raised an eyebrow.

Kane glanced around the pantry. Shelves littered with rat droppings ran along the walls. The odd can of beans and a loaf of bread were the only food in the disgusting place. Beside the door he noticed two switches and flicked on one and then the other. Light flooded the cellar, illuminating a wooden staircase. No other sound came from below. He glanced at Rowley. "Stay here. Keep your back to the wall and your weapon aimed at the door."

"Yes, sir." Rowley pulled his weapon and complied.

Kane moved down the steps, waiting for the click of a gun or the sound of someone moving, but the room was empty apart from a few boxes of supplies piled in one corner and an ax leaning against the wall. The humming sound came from a chest freezer secured with a lock and chain. He stared at the freezer and unease clawed at his gut at the sight of a slick of blood on the white surface. The idea of opening the lid and finding another corpse made his skin crawl. He holstered the Glock and pulled a pair of surgical gloves from his pocket. If this turned out to be a crime scene, he couldn't risk contamination, not twice in one week.

He examined the substantial padlock. Someone had gone to a ton of trouble to prevent someone opening the freezer. "Okay, let's see what you have hidden inside." He grabbed the ax and, in two blows, smashed open the lock.

Rowley's worried voice came from the top of the stairs. "You okay down there?"

"Yeah. Stay there and keep watch. I don't want any surprise visitors." Kane dragged in a deep breath, lifted the lid, and reeled back. "Shit."

A battered, frozen face of a woman stared at him. Blood had dripped from her nose and frozen in hideous red icicles. The victim's bloody fingers had clawed at the walls. Kane swallowed his disgust at the cruelty inflicted on this person. The killers had beaten her to a pulp and then frozen her alive. He went to shut the lid to preserve the evidence and stared in disbelief. Under the frost, he could make out words scrawled in blood. With infinite care, he brushed away the layer of ice crystals and gaped in horror. "Oh my God!"

The victim had named her murderers.

Dean and Dirk Daniels.

FIFTY-FIVE

Jenna lifted her cup and emptied it. A wave of euphoria washed over her and her skin heated. Her tongue stuck to the roof of her mouth. Then a wave of nausea hit her and she lost balance, sagging over onto the table. The next moment, Dean had rounded the table and helped her out of her coat. "Thanks, I'm so hot."

"Looks like the flu to me. It's going around. Come and lie down." Dean's strong arms slid around her waist, lifting her. "Another cup of coffee will get you back on your feet."

"Okay." She didn't recognize her slurred speech. Her heavy legs refused to respond and she fought to remain conscious. *What if I'm having a stroke?* She wanted to insist he call nine-one-one, but she could not form the words. Her head tipped back on his shoulder and she glanced at shelves piled with dinnerware, all the same with two blue lines on a white base. The room shifted, as if the edges had folded under. Blinking madly, she fixed her gaze on something pink and out of place sitting on the shelf. She squinted to clear the sudden rush of blurred vision and made out a pink scrunchie. Fear and disbelief slammed into her. Psychopaths took trophies. *Oh my God. That's Sarah's missing hair tie.*

Darkness swallowed her.

Fear had Jenna by the throat as she fought the fog surrounding her brain. She opened heavy eyelids a crack to get her bearings. How long had she been unconscious? Something was terribly wrong and the instinct to remain motionless permeated her muddled brain. She'd trained for capture and torture and endured the best her commander could inflict. As one of the highest-ranked operatives on her team, she'd experienced unbelievable hardship to make the grade. She wriggled to adjust her position but the brothers had hog-tied her. With her face down, knees bent up behind her, she had no chance of escape. She tensed against the rough bindings on wrists and ankles. The movement tightened the rope pressing against her throat like a noose waiting for the hangman to secure before the short drop to death.

Pain thudded a military tattoo in her temples and she swallowed to quell the need to vomit. Deep, penetrating cold seeped into her naked flesh and a hard, rough surface scraped her cheek. The room came into focus in frustrating slowness, as if a breeze had blown away a veil of smoke. No, not a bedroom but a dank, smelly survival shelter lit by a humming kerosene lamp. Something else overlaid the odor, the heavy scent of male musk and sex. Could she be in the same place the killers had taken Sarah to rape her before moving her to the Old Mitcham Ranch?

Fear curled in her belly and crawled up her chest, stealing her breath. Inside, she wanted to scream and fight to get free, but acting stupid would get her killed. She needed to harness the fear-driven adrenalin rush to fight these animals. Keeping her lashes lowered, she searched for a doorway, making and discarding plans of escape. Acting drugged for as long as possible would be her only hope.

She heard a deep sigh from her immediate right and moved her head a slow couple of inches. Her skin crawled at the sight of Dean Daniels lounging in a camp chair massaging his crotch with a dreamy expression on his face. She pushed her ear hard against the floor. Pressure on the earring would sound the alarm and bring Kane. The familiar heaviness of the gold earring was missing, and realization hit her like a sledgehammer. She'd told her deputies about Kane's ingenious plan to keep her safe and Pete Daniels had informed his brothers. A wave of despair threatened her resolve. She was alone. *I am such a fool.* Taking off like some lovesick fool and neglecting to inform the office of her whereabouts was a rookie mistake. *Not a soul knows where I am.*

Disbelief of betrayal slammed into her. She'd trusted the Daniels brothers. Dean had been one of the few people to welcome her into Black Rock Falls and Dirk, although the loner of the family, had treated her with kindness and respect. What a fool she'd been to allow the handsome men to trick her, and worst of all, Kane's instincts had been correct. She'd overlooked a clue during her door-to-door inquiries.

The truth slammed into her in a tidal wave of memories. No wonder Dean had prevented her from seeing the suffering horse. She'd interrupted him torturing someone to death, likely John Helms. She wanted to scream in frustration. *Stupid, stupid, stupid.* What an idiot to have dismissed Kane's insight into the case, and then added insult to injury by treating him so badly. *I doubt I'll live long enough to apologize.*

A wave of panic rushed over her and her heart pounded hard enough to break her ribs, but she breathed slow and even. She needed to think, and any change in her posture would alert Dean to the fact she'd regained consciousness. Pushing the throbbing numbness in her hands and feet to another place in her mind, she allowed the painful reality of her impossible situation to register. During training, she'd survived the indecency of being naked, cold, and bound. Now she required a plan to outwit two psychopaths in a confined space, naked, and without a decent weapon. *Yeah, right.*

Raping her hog-tied would be difficult and they'd likely untie her to place her in a more suitable position. If she played possum, once they untied her, she could strike like a rattlesnake. The Daniels brothers had underestimated her and that was a fatal mistake.

The thought of falling into their trap angered her, and her heartbeat picked up as adrenalin surged through her. She allowed the anger to grow, building her resolve to inflict as much damage as possible before they took her down. In remarkable clarity, she remembered the previous visit to the Daniels' ranch, including the uncharacteristic flash of annoyance in Dean's eyes at being disturbed. She'd dismissed his unusual behavior as concern for the horse giving birth in the barn. It had been snowing and he strolled from the barn in his shirtsleeves with a slick of sweat on his brow and spots of red on his cowboy boots. He smelled of sweat and blood. All normal odors if what he claimed had been true.

Without warning, Sarah's death stare flashed into her mind, the horror was stamped in her expression for all time. An uncontrollable tremor hit her and she clenched her jaw. Too late. Dean's gaze zoomed in on her, like an eagle sighting a rabbit. She relaxed and when he bent to slap her cheek, she didn't flinch or make a sound.

"You'll keep." Dean sauntered out of view and she heard him climbing the steps.

Jenna listened intently for his footsteps to disappear then lifted her head, gagging as the rope tightened around her neck. Her captors made sure she would not wriggle free without choking to death. She dragged in a few deep breaths to keep the rising waves of panic at bay. The drug had lost its hold on her and, clear-headed, she could make a better assessment of her situation.

The room was little more than a storeroom with two sets of bunk beds at one end. She made out a small table and chair in front of an old, dusty, two-way radio. A flight of wooden steps led into shadows and a gun cabinet held an impressive array of rifles; the drawers below had labels attached from familiar ammunition boxes.

Uppermost in her mind was following her training and not panicking. Keeping positive and solving the problem was her only option. The brothers had not disabled her physically, which was a bonus. Not having discussed her past life with anyone, the brothers would have no notion of her capabilities. No position was hopeless no matter how difficult, and she'd survived worse.

If they untied her with the intent to rape her, she'd have a very slight advantage, but any move against two strong men would require split-second timing. With her legs and arms numb, not to mention muscles stiff from cold, she would need every ounce of strength. If her plan worked, her rigid routine of brutal early morning workouts would pay off in silver dollars.

She stiffened at the sound of footsteps walking on the wooden floor above her head. Dust leaked through the floorboards, glittering in the glow from the lamp. Hinges creaked then light streamed through a door at the top of the steps, illuminating jean-clad legs and grubby cowboy boots. She clenched her jaw, willing her muscles to stop twitching, and closed her eyes. A rapid pulse throbbed in her temple as two sets of footfalls clattered down the steps. As they moved closer, she could smell them. The heavy stink of male musk and stale sweat accosted her nose. Heavy breathing moved her hair and a warm hand ran up her leg from ankle to knee.

Dean's voice seemed to echo in the small room. "She awake yet?"

Rough fingers pried her eyelid open and Dirk's face came into view.

"You gave her enough to knock out a horse." Dirk scowled down at her. "She's cold. I told you to put her on a mattress. It will be like having sex with a corpse. I'll turn up the heat."

"Fine. I'll get the roll of plastic. I'm not planning to leave any DNA. That new deputy is on the ball. One mistake now and they'll pin the others on us." Dean dragged the plastic from a shelf and dropped it with a thump beside her.

"They'll never find them. Apart from the old lady and Sarah, the pigs ate them, bones and all." Dirk's voice came close to her. "We'll have to get her out the freezer but she won't thaw out in this temperature. Maybe pigs like popsicles."

"We'll drop her in the pen with Jenna. Once they smell blood, they'll soon tear them apart, frozen or not. I'll put on the Halloween mask and tell Stan not to feed them for a few days." Dean grabbed her hair and glared at her. "Wake up, bitch. I'm going to make you hurt real bad. You'll beg me to cut your throat." He chuckled. "I hope you're as fit as Pete reckoned because I plan to keep you for a time and have some fun."

"She can't hear you." Dirk kneeled down beside her and slapped her cheeks. "I don't like it when they're unconscious. I want them to fight and scream." He slapped her so hard, bright lights flashed behind her eyelids, and the metal taste of blood coated her tongue. "How much did you give her?"

"No more than usual." Dean let out a long sigh. "She drank the coffee faster, is all. Give her time and you'll have your fun."

"I want to make this one last." Dirk chuckled. "No one knows she's here. Pete's cruiser doesn't have a GPS so they won't be able to track her, and I've nuked her earrings. They'll think Pete kidnapped her and we can say he bragged about grabbing her in the bushes."

"Good idea, then we can take our time and enjoy her." Dean moaned. "Hit her until she comes around. I don't want to wait."

Pain shot like needles in her cheeks and fear came in uncontrollable rushes as her survival instinct came into play. With effort, Jenna rolled back her eyes and forced her muscles to go slack. They must not discover she had regained consciousness. Her only hope was to take them unawares. A rustling came close by then rough hands lifted her and dumped her onto a plastic sheet. A heavy weight landed on her back and air rushed out her lungs in a gasp. Face pressed against the plastic, she sucked in tiny breaths, enough to keep her going. Remaining relaxed when everything inside her was screaming, "*Danger, run, you're going to die,*" took every ounce of willpower.

"Untie her. I want to see her face when she wakes up and feels me inside her."

"Why do you get to go first all the time?" Dirk tugged at the ropes.

"Because I'm the eldest."

Blood rushed into her hands in a painful surge and the rope around her neck slid away, burning her skin. Jenna clamped her lips shut to prevent crying out in agony. As the cords pulled away, she slid onto the mattress. She needed to remain lifeless and breathe steadily to keep up the charade. Dirk had moved away but she sensed someone close and opened her eyes a slit. As Dean moved into in her line of vision and started undressing, a deathly chill slithered down her spine.

Dean stood over her, big and menacing. He ripped open a condom packet with his teeth and grinned at Dirk. "Now roll her over and hold her down. I'm going to wake this bitch up, Dean style."

FIFTY-SIX

Pulse racing fast, Kane shut the freezer lid and sprinted up the steps. He slammed the hatch shut then turned and grabbed Rowley by the shoulders. "What's the quickest way to the Daniels' ranch?"

"There is a gate along the fence line. It leads to a road across the back acres of their property."

He sprinted for the truck with Rowley at his side. "I want to know everything about the layout of the Daniels' ranch, especially if they have any root cellars."

"They have one in the barn and a survival shelter out back." Rowley slid into the passenger seat and buckled up.

Kane started the engine then spun the Beast around and accelerated toward the open gate in the fence line. Ahead, the muddy frozen road split into two. "Which way?"

"Straight ahead. They use this track as a shortcut into town so it will be clear all the way. It takes about ten minutes longer but they won't see us coming." Rowley flicked him a glance. "What happens next? They'll be armed—the place is built like a fortress."

Kane slammed his foot down on the gas and the back

wheels screamed before gripping. The Beast's powerful engine roared as they sped along the icy road. He drove at breakneck speed, and pine trees and fences heavy with snow flashed by in a blur of colors. "They won't be expecting us, so we have that in our favor."

"They won't come easy, and if they have Jenna, we'll have a hostage situation." Rowley cleared his throat. "Should I contact Walters for backup?"

Kane slid the vehicle around a tight bend in the road, fish-tailed around a tree, plowed through bushes, then bounced back onto the track. "He's on the way to secure the prisoner and crime scene. We're on our own."

"Have you handled this type of situation before?" Rowley gave him a worried glance and gripped the edge of his seat.

Kane snorted. "Oh yeah. Many times. If they're holding Jenna against her will and have touched one hair on her head, I'll take them down." He swung the vehicle, barely missing the gatepost, and accelerated. The back wheels hit ice and the vehicle drifted around a bend. He spun the wheel, sending snow flying, and took a shortcut through a row of pines before hitting the road. "Consider them dangerous. Draw your weapon and use it if you're threatened. Most important—stay behind me."

"Roger that."

Tree branches lashed the sides of the Beast as they bounced and slid along the uneven trail. Clues fell into place like completing a Rubik's cube. "One thing." Kane cleared his throat. "During the door-to door inquiries, the sheriff visited the Daniels' ranch with you, is that correct?"

"Nope it was Daniels." Rowley frowned. "He wanted to see his brothers so asked to go with her."

Kane slowed to take a ninety-degree turn into another gate, his attention locked ahead on the treacherous, winding road.

"Can you recall Jenna mentioning anything about the visit when she got back to the office?"

"Nothing specific." Rowley tensed and gripped the door. "The next morning, she asked Daniels if the horse giving birth in the barn was okay. Apparently, it was still having a hard time."

Someone was, I bet. Although it was below freezing, a slick of nervous sweat trickled an annoying path down Kane's back. After seeing the trail of battered corpses, instinct told him Jenna was in the hands of monsters. Alone, even with the extra moves he taught her, she'd only be able to fight them for so long. He had to get to her—now.

"But why would they kill Pete?" Rowley 's face was sheet white.

"If he mentioned he'd told us where to find Stan Clough and was guarding the place this morning, they killed him to set up Clough for the murders. They'd know we'd find Mrs. Woodward in his freezer." Kane slowed the racing vehicle to a crawl to get around a tight bend. "They cut out his tongue because he talks too much."

"I can't believe it." Rowley shook his head. "The Daniels brothers are the last people I thought capable of torturing someone to death."

"No doubt Jenna is of the same mind." He wet his dry lips. "She insisted they were okay. So much for intuition."

The Beast skidded around the next turn, brushed against a pine tree, and then continued along the icy road. Kane gritted his teeth and spun the wheel, gaining control, then pushed the engine to its limit. "I figure the Daniels brothers arranged to meet Sarah at the Old Mitcham Ranch with the intention of torturing her to get information about what she'd discussed with the sheriff's department. They would have gone there fully prepared to rape and kill her. Leaving her body was another warning to Jenna to keep her mouth shut."

"And now they have Jenna." Rowley scratched his dark hair. "Slow down. The ranch house is around the next bend."

Kane pulled to the side of the track. "Any cover?"

"Yeah, this line of trees runs parallel to the house."

"Grab the rifle and follow me. Shut the door real quiet." Kane snatched his rifle from the back seat and dropped out the door. "Keep close. Any sign of trouble, fall back into the cover of the trees." He moved out and, ducking into the woods, ran toward the ranch house. He recognized the two vehicles parked by the house but the cruiser Jenna had driven was missing. "We'll try the house first."

He approached the house from the side and edged to the back door, keeping under the windows. Rowley stuck to him like glue, and from the way he handled himself, Jenna had taught him well. The back door had three steps leading up to a small porch. He waved Rowley to one side then rapped on the door and listened. No sound came from inside. He grasped the door handle and turned. It swung open silently on a mudroom and he peered through into a warm, modern kitchen. "Mr. Daniels, are you there? This is the Black Rock Falls Sheriff's Department. Can we have a word with you, please?"

No reply came from inside; no footsteps echoed on the polished wooden floor.

"I'm coming in." Kane motioned for Rowley to watch his back, rested his rifle against the wall, then moved through the mudroom and into the house. "Mr. Daniels, this is Deputy Kane." He stopped mid-stride at the sight of Jenna's jacket and hat tossed onto the kitchen table, then turned back to Rowley. "She's been here. I'm going to check the house. Stay alert and watch my back."

He drew his weapon and, pushing open each door, searched the rooms with speed. Nothing. He ran back to Rowley. "It's clear but her coat is here. Where's the root cellar?"

"In the barn." Rowley pointed across a cleared area to the

right of the house. "The survival shelter is under that building." He indicated to a hut about twenty feet in the opposite direction.

Kane needed more time, and every second counted. "Okay, if you needed room to torture someone, which would you use?"

"Heck, I don't know. It's been years since Pete showed me around the place. They're about the same size, I guess." The expression in Rowley's eyes turned frantic and his hand shook around the rifle. "The root cellar would be freezing at this time of the year and filled with provisions. My bet is the survival shelter. It's concealed in a dugout under the hut and sound-proofed."

Kane pushed him in that direction. "Go."

He took off at a run, his attention moving in all directions. Six hours, *six* long hours, Jenna had been missing. How long she had been here made little difference. It took seconds to kill someone. Her only hope lay in the awful truth that these monsters enjoyed playing with their victims.

FIFTY-SEVEN

At the idea of Dean raping her, a rush of anger surged through Jenna. The circulation in her hands and feet came back in a painful throb but she pushed back the need to clench and unclench her fingers. She'd endured spousal abuse by the son of a drug lord and survived to bring them down because she'd proved her worth to them. This time she was disposable. The Daniels' other victims had endured prolonged torture before the *coup de grâce*, but was the cruelty part of a ritual or had these men sought information as well?

The heat from Dean's muscular thighs burned into her flesh. She quashed the first instinct to move away and fight because his pleasure came from seeing fear, hearing his victims scream in terror. If he skinned her alive, she wouldn't give him the pleasure. Opening her eyes a slit, she glanced down at his muscular body and noticed he'd removed every hair from his flesh. He obviously didn't plan to leave any DNA evidence but had overlooked the trace elements from the lubricated condom. She read the name on the condom packet he tossed next to her on the plastic sheet and it was the same brand, a Trojan Bareskin.

Terror marched a path down her spine. Trapped in the lion's den, alone and defenseless, she had to act with deadly force and time her attack to the second. When Dean pushed up her knees and spread her thighs, she clenched her jaw and didn't resist. The fool had done her a favor by placing her in a fighting stance. It would take a slight roll of her hips to deliver a death-blow kick to his throat. He moved closer and kneeled before her. Bile rushed up the back of her throat in disgust. She could smell him, and his male scent hung over her in a cloud of disgusting stench. When he fondled her with his rough hands, she wanted to scream, but her unresponsiveness had produced a negative effect on his virility.

"Dammit." Dean sent a stinging slap across her cheek. "Wake up."

"You've overdosed her and she's probably in a coma." Dirk peered into her eyes. "She should be awake by now." He lifted and dropped her arm. "She's out of it."

"Get a bucket of water and pour it over her head. It's freezing enough to wake the dead." Dean moved on his knees to the edge of the mattress. "Don't get any of it on me."

Heart pounding, Jenna waited for Dirk to get to his feet and walk out of her periphery. When Dean's attention moved to his brother, she bunched muscles and rolled. The kick landed under Dean's jaw, with a satisfying crack snapping his head back and crushing his larynx. He sprawled on the floor with his eyes rolled up, showing white. His body jerked and he let out one gurgling sigh. As Dirk turned around, she sprang to her feet and fell against the shelves. One hand closed around a can of beans, and she turned and took a fighting stance. "One down."

The look of pure evil etched on Dirk's face chilled her to the bone.

"I'm gonna slice you to the bone, and then feed you to the pigs." Dirk advanced toward her, drawing his hunting blade from the sheath at his waist.

She pitched the can at his head and missed. The missile bounced off his broad shoulder with as much impact as a feather. He gave a soft, menacing laugh and tossed the knife from hand to hand, regarding her with amused interest.

"That all you got?" Dirk made a figure eight with the blade. "I'm so gonna enjoy making you scream."

"Bigger men than you have tried." She moved her hands in an effort to distract him. "Your brother didn't do so good, did he?"

"Listen to you, all mouth." Dirk grinned as if enjoying a drink with her rather than fighting to the death. "Keep going, you're making me hot, and when Dean regains consciousness, he'll keep you alive for weeks to make sure you enjoy the full Daniels brothers' experience."

He hasn't realized Dean is dead. I must keep him talking. "Kidnapping and torture is a hobby, is it? You like to rape both men and women?" She snorted. "And I thought Pete was all talk."

"Pete?" Dirk shook his head. "That boy didn't have the stomach to kill a chicken. Why do you think he lived in town?" He met her gaze and his lips curled into a predatory smile. "But before I cut out his tongue, he told us all about *you.*"

Shit. Poor Pete. The shock of his confession must have registered on her face.

"Yeah. He started squealing with the first punch." Dirk chuckled and Jenna recognized the laugh as the one she had heard in the bushes the night at the Cattleman's Hotel. "Like he squealed to you about us."

No wonder I heard two sets of footsteps. "Pete didn't mention you at all. You've killed him for nothing."

"And now it's your turn." Dirk waved the blade. "You know, if I slid this knife in just the right spot in your spine, you wouldn't die but you'd be paralyzed. We could have so much fun and you'd have to lie there and take it."

Jenna needed to keep him talking and his attention on her. "You like hurting people, don't you, and raping women—but why Helms?"

"Jenna, Jenna, Jenna." He shook his dark head slowly. "You figure because we own all this land we're rich, but when we killed our daddy he left us a mountain of debt. We needed cash and picked rich, lonely people to befriend. We'd ask real nice for their PIN but if they refused, we used a little more persuasion." He rolled his shoulders. "When we don't need money, we look for something younger, some entertainment to pass a long night."

Keeping him talking was her only hope. "So which one of you started torturing and raping women first?"

"You talk too much, but when Dean wakes up, we'll give you a very personal demonstration. You'd be surprised how long a feisty woman like you can survive. Men last maybe a week but even girls Sarah's age fight until we tire of them." He gave a deep, sinister chuckle and smacked his lips. "Sarah enjoyed it too much and we'd have kept her for a long time but we wanted to show you what would happen if you didn't stop meddling." His lips turned down. "We believed we had an understanding with you."

Astonished, she gaped at him. He actually looked sorry. "I figured we were friends."

"Exactly, and friends don't squeal on friends." He waved the knife as if cutting her throat. "Now you have to die."

I must catch him off guard. "I didn't discuss you with anyone. I told Kane that you're my friends."

She noticed him relax and needed to deal with him before he noticed Dean's wasn't getting up again. She must get off the mattress. The uneven surface was a disadvantage, but that would mean advancing naked on a lunatic with a knife. Attack was the only option and he wouldn't be expecting it.

"It's too late." Dirk ran the tip of his rough thumb down the blade. "You're here. You know we killed Pete and Sarah." His lips curled into a satanic smile. "And I want to cut you and hear you scream."

Trembling with fear, she gritted her teeth. *I'm not going down without a fight.* On her right, she caught sight of Dean's discarded T-shirt, and taking a step backward, she snatched it and wrapped it around her left arm. Since training with Kane, she excelled at hand-to-hand combat, but in a confined space, she'd be against Dirk's superior strength. Keeping eye contact, she shuffled to the edge of the mattress, took a deep breath, and lunged at him.

Surprise gave her time to grab his wrist and slam the palm of her right hand up under his nose. The blow designed to push the cartilage into the brain would be a death blow to most people, but Dirk was as strong as a bull. He shook her off as if she was an annoying fly and staggered back with his back to the mattress, spraying drops of blood from his shattered nose.

"Bitch!" He lifted the knife and ran at her.

In the open, she had room to move. She spun and kicked out, landing a solid chest blow. He let out a bellow, staggered back, tripping over the edge of the mattress, and fell into the shelves. Cans of beans toppled from the shelf, peppering his back, and rolled across the floor. She lunged for a shovel leaning against the wall but not in time. One beefy arm locked around her chest, pinning her arms to her sides, and the cool edge of a blade pressed against her throat. He'd caught her in the bushes with the same move. A warm trickle of blood ran down her chest. She gasped and went limp, hoping her dead weight would unbalance him.

"Sheriff's Department." Kane dropped into her line of vision, with his Glock 22 aimed at Dirk's head. "Drop the weapon."

A shot shattered the silence and a hot sticky mess splashed over Jenna's face. Ears ringing, she staggered as the hand holding the knife fell away. The next second, Kane moved in to drag her against his solid strength.

"It's okay. I have you." Kane's comforting voice filled her buzzing ears. "Rowley, check the body on the floor for life signs."

"They're both dead." Rowley's voice came through the confusion. "I'll call the paramedics. Here, wrap her in blankets."

Warmth surrounded her but shock set in fast and she trembled against him. She stared into Kane's compassionate expression, wanting to tell him she was okay and they hadn't hurt her, but her mouth refused to form words. Leaning into him, she grasped handfuls of his jacket and allowed the tears to flow.

He'd found her.

FIFTY-EIGHT

Kane sat beside the hospital bed and shook his head. "You'll stay here until the doctors say it's okay for you to leave."

"I don't need tests or a psych evaluation. I was slapped a few times and drugged, no big deal." Jenna's eyes flashed with anger. "Come on, you can see I'm fine. It's been three days. How much longer can they keep me here? Can't you see I'm going nuts and the food is awful?"

His gaze moved over her bruised cheek, split lip, and the three stitches in her neck. He shook his head. "You'll stay. Why do you think the DA banned me from visiting you before now? He wanted to make sure we're not in collusion. Although, I'm not sure how that could happen with Rowley as a witness but, hey, we needed proof of a righteous kill."

"They think what? Really? Two psychopaths kidnap me and they want proof of self-defense? Give me a break."

He nodded in agreement. "I told them you took down Dean Daniels in self-defense and I shot Dirk before he slit your throat. You have the stitches to prove it and Rowley's statement. The DA wanted absolute proof of what happened. When we brought you in, the drug would still have been in your system. I found bottles of pills in the kitchen and a coffee cup with your prints. The evidence is with forensics now. Then there's the brand of condoms that matched those used in Sarah's murder and her pink scrunchie." He sighed. "We have plenty of evidence, and the moment I told Stan Clough his aliens were the Daniels brothers in Halloween masks, he started talking. His statement backed up what Dirk told you. He said they'd been killing for some years, and when he owned the other ranch, his pigs had eaten the bodies too." He rubbed his chin. "He will be charged for unlawful disposing of multiple bodies and will probably end up in a mental institution."

"I'm still shocked." Jenna gave him a worried look. "If you hadn't brought me up to speed with our morning workout sessions, I might be dead."

"Nah, you never lose the training. It's inbuilt. I just gave you a nudge to get it back on track." He smiled at her. "Don't think I won't have you working your butt off the moment you get clearance from the doc either."

"The way they are fussing over me, that will be sometime in the fall." Jenna flopped back on the pillows.

Kane squeezed her hand. "In the meantime, do you want to know the motives your hardworking team of deputies have confirmed beyond reasonable doubt for the murders?"

"Oh, doh!" Jenna pulled a face then winced in pain. "Go on then, give it to me. So far I only know what Dirk told me."

Kane gave her the conclusions he'd relayed to Deputy Rowley concerning Sarah's death and the attempts on Jenna's life on the way to the Daniels' ranch. "The abuse the Daniels brothers suffered as kids likely triggered the psychopathic behavior, especially when mental health issues are in the family history. It's possible the father murdered their mother and maybe Pete survived because he left the environment as a baby." He sighed. "The mutilation of the cattle might have preempted the murder spree but it could also have been a way to control Clough. It's likely that being so isolated, they've been acting out their fantasies on animals since childhood."

"After you found Stan Clough with Pete's body, what made you keep looking? He was our prime suspect."

"The forensics found two pairs of boot marks at Sarah's crime scene and Clough kept on insisting *they* did it and he was afraid of *them*. I didn't believe him but secured him and then searched the house looking for trophies or evidence." He sighed. "When I found Mrs. Woodward's body, she'd written the Daniels' names as her killers in blood, and all the pieces fell into place." He let out a long sigh.

"How did you find me? The bunker is well hidden."

Kane smiled. "If Rowley hadn't told me about the survival shelter on the Daniels' ranch, we wouldn't have found you in time. By the way, you sure trained Rowley well; he didn't falter once. Shocked and horrified maybe but as solid as a rock."

"Yeah, he's a good, dependable deputy and a very nice guy." Jenna rubbed her temples, and her forehead wrinkled into a frown. "I can't believe the Daniels brothers had the brains to use Mrs. Woodward's pickup to cause my accident. I guess the BOLO we put out on the vehicle hasn't panned out yet?" She fingered the dressing on her neck, and her eyes reflected her pain.

Kane nodded. "Yeah, it did. Walters found the pickup parked in plain sight in the Cattleman's Hotel parking lot." He smiled. "Rowley is taking paint samples from the damaged front panel as we speak."

"That's good. I gather they had time to dump Pete's cruiser to make sure they weren't implicated in my kidnapping?"

Kane shrugged. "It looks more like they planned to put the blame on me."

"You?" Jenna stared at him wide-eyed. "Why you?"

"The new kid in town was their biggest threat, I guess." Kane rubbed the back of his neck. "They dumped Sarah's purse in our trash bin and I found a lock of her hair and the missing underwear in my garage. They didn't have time to dump the vehicle. We found it under a tarpaulin in the Daniels' barn and it's with forensics, so we are two patrol cars down at the moment." He met her annoyed gaze with a grin. "Don't worry, I've spoken to the mayor and he has a rush order on two brand spanking new trucks to replace them. We'll have them soon."

"That's wonderful. How many of his arms did you have to break?" She giggled and the sound filled him with relief.

"Not one." He wiggled his eyebrows. "I used my charm."

"Well, you have that in spades." Jenna sighed. "It is hard to believe they murdered John Helms or poor old Mrs. Woodward for money. Dirk told me they had a heap of debts after they murdered their father. They befriended lonely people and tortured them for their PIN. He spoke about it as if it was like getting a new job to pay their bills. The way he validated murder was chilling." She shuddered and rubbed her arms. "Both Dean and Dirk admitted to raping and murdering Sarah, but from what Dirk said, they've killed quite a few victims. Problem is that it's hearsay. If forensics don't find a stash of trophies, we'll have nothing to go on." She grimaced. "Although you have to admit, feeding the victims to Stan Clough's pigs was a stroke of genius."

Deep in thought, Kane rubbed his chin. "Maybe Clough can explain why they stopped killing for two years, and then started again. The behavior doesn't follow the usual psychopathic murderer pattern."

"As you said before, they'd need a fix, and we have no idea how many bodies are rotting away in barrels, do we?" Jenna leaned back in the pillows and yawned. "We should consider every missing persons' case in surrounding counties from the time they killed their father." She let out a long sigh. "Won't that be fun?"

"Don't worry. Once we're talking serial killers, we hand it over to the FBI." Kane patted her hand. "The state forensics team is out at the ranch. If the Daniels brothers kept trophies, they'll match them against any missing persons throughout the state."

"I feel like an incompetent fool. We still don't know how Helms met the Daniels brothers in the first place."

Kane stood and filled a glass with orange juice and handed it to her. "Yeah, we do. I finally managed to speak to his wife. Her story was pretty close to Father Maguire's account. The couple had marital problems and Helms needed a break. He decided to hit the road to follow his favorite hockey team and attend all their games. His vehicle broke down in Blackwater and he had it towed to a garage. He told his wife he'd met two men out of Black Rock Falls at the garage. They'd offered him accommodation plus a lift back to town to collect his vehicle for a few days' work on their ranch. As his vehicle was going to take a week to repair, he agreed. He must have been out of earshot when he used his phone; the Daniels brothers obviously didn't know he'd called her."

"So, you're sure it was the Daniels brothers he met?"

Kane smiled. "Proof positive. They made the mistake of speaking to Helms at the garage in front of the owner. They ordered spare parts for Dean's pickup and left their contact number. The mechanic remembers them leaving with Helms."

"Why didn't his wife tell all this to the priest?"

"I asked her the same question. She didn't speak to the priest until he asked her about the dentist; apparently he didn't mention anything about lodging a missing persons' report on her husband." Kane shook his head. "When I questioned the priest, he told me the wife wasn't mentally stable and he didn't want to worry her."

"That doesn't account for not being able to contact her for ages." Jenna met his gaze with a frown. "Did you ask her where she'd been hiding?"

Kane nodded and sat on the edge of her bed. "I did. When Helms told her he was excited about meeting new friends and was looking forward to an adventure, she packed her bags and went to her mother's house. She was angry at Helms and turned off her phone. She didn't turn it back on again, hence the reason we couldn't locate her. When the priest visited her and asked about the dentist, he told her the phone was out of order." He sighed. "She did seem very vague at times and couldn't understand why her husband had decided to drive around in freezing temperatures rather than work out their problems." He snorted. "She had a point. Why anyone would travel alone to Black Rock Falls in the middle of winter to stay with strangers, with or without the hockey game, defies explanation."

"*You* came here." Jenna pushed a lock of dark hair from her forehead and her lips curled into a smile.

He grinned at her. "Yeah, I did. But after four homicides, four attempts on your life, and discovering the star hockey player in town is a potential predator *before* I've received my first paycheck... I'm not so sure if Black Rock Falls is the quiet town I imagined." He gave her a long look, noting the apprehension in her eyes. "Yeah, the DA did question me about why I left a lucrative position and came here. I explained, but now they want me to take the psych evaluation along with you."

"At least I'll have company." She frowned and pleated the edge of the white sheet. "How did the Rockford hearing go?"

"He's currently in the county jail awaiting trial on a ton of charges." Kane cleared his throat. "Even his daddy won't get him out of this and I doubt the mayor will be elected for another term either; the townsfolk are not impressed." He sighed.

"You'll be up to your neck in court cases for the rest of the year. Man, those Daniels brothers were a class on their own."

"Have you ever come across this type of psychopathic killer before? I thought most of them worked alone?" Jenna raised both eyebrows. "They had different types of victims, and that's unusual, isn't it?"

"Not necessarily. We're talking about two different men here. Say Dirk took most of the abuse from his father. He'd likely have the desire to torture men and make them pay for what happened to him as a boy." Kane pushed a hand through his hair, worried this kind of discussion might upset her after her experience. He would keep it simple. "Then Dean might have believed his mother allowed his father to hurt them and his focus was on hurting women. Rape and torture aren't sexual; it's punishment." He sat on the edge of the bed and watched her reactions carefully. "I believe the initial motive was money, as you said, and the Daniels boys used their brains. They only wanted cash—tortured their victims for their PINs and then cleaned out their bank accounts. My guess is they started slow, and inflicting pain triggered the psychopathic behavior. The prolonged torture and rape of their victims came later. Psychopaths escalate, and each kill is more extreme to feed the thrill."

"But Mrs. Woodward was seen banking cash. They kept her for a time before killing her, didn't they?" Jenna sipped her drink. "I wonder why?"

He shrugged. "As far as we can tell we believe they discovered she had a variety of bank accounts and a fortune hidden away. My guess is she called them about purchasing the Old Mitcham Ranch. She likely wanted to get a feel for the area and I figure they suggested she stay with them. I found her purse in a drawer in a bedroom in their house. She likely offered to work around the place as a housekeeper for practically nothing and at first they paid her in cash."

"So why kill her?"

"Ah, well, I believe she'd have told them she had the money available to buy the property outright. We know she obtained a nice fat cashier's check as a deposit. She was the golden goose and they wanted to clean out all her accounts. Once they did that, she was useless to them."

"Okay, you have proof to connect them to Samantha and Sarah Woodward's murders, and Pete, of course." Jenna looked at him expectantly. "Have you found anything else to link them to Helms' murder?"

"We found an earring matching the one missing from Helms' body with the earlobe still attached in the Daniels' barn. I'm guessing they took him home and didn't waste any time torturing him for his PIN." He sighed. "Their phone records and the GPS in Dirk's pickup match every withdrawal date and time for both Helms and Woodward. We think Helms went in the barrel because Clough hadn't set up his piggery in time."

"Anything else I need to know?"

"Yeah." Kane rubbed his chin. "As of one hour ago, the investigation is out of our hands. Like I mentioned before the FBI will be checking files from other states as this involves serial killings."

Jenna's face drained of color and she placed the glass on the table then lifted her chin.

"I have a confession to make. I *did* miss something the day I went to the Daniels' ranch." She cleared her throat and a pink flush spread over her cheeks. "I heard a whining noise like something... some*body* in pain. When I asked Dean, he said his mare was giving birth." She met his gaze. "He had blood spots on his boots and stank of sweat. I should have checked or at least remembered. Helms and Sarah are dead because of me." She leaned back and closed her eyes. "I used to be a good judge of character and I actually *liked* Dean and Dirk. I figure my profiler training was a complete waste of time."

He considered her confession for a few seconds then shook his head. "You're not to blame; you accepted the explanation of two men you trusted, and if you'd discovered them torturing John Helms, they'd have killed you and Pete. They had a good scheme, and being psychopaths, they wouldn't have thought twice about killing the pair of you." He sighed. "Charm is a gift psychopaths have in spades. Trust me, they could fool the best of us. Think how many people Jeffrey Dahmer and Ted Bundy deceived?"

"You know," Jenna opened her eyes and looked at him as if seeing him for the first time, "underneath that tough, no-nonsense image lies a gentle heart. You're a kind and generous man and it has been an honor working with you."

Kane smiled and squeezed her hand. "Thank you. I like working with you too. I just have to keep reminding myself who is the boss." He chuckled. "Which I have to admit has been a *big* adjustment for me, but I'm a quick learner."

"And I need to respect your experience and work *with* you." Jenna sighed. "I'm used to rookies." Her lips twitched into a smile. "It's been amazing having someone to trust. Do you think we'll ever find a replacement for Pete?"

Kane chuckled and moved his thumb over the back of her hand. He'd contacted HQ to find a suitable replacement—someone *he* could trust. "Yeah, we'll find someone. Why don't you leave that chore to me?"

"Do you *really* think Black Rock Falls is interesting?" She gave him a blank stare.

He nodded. "I sure do. I'm wondering what will happen next."

"Oh, I figured with the new deputy arriving, you'd ask for a transfer—and I wouldn't blame you." Her eyes misted over and she swallowed hard.

Amused, Kane cleared his throat. It just so happened he liked living in Black Rock Falls. "Do you really think I'd leave my cozy cottage, fresh-baked chocolate chip cookies, and seeing my boss in pink slippers?"

"So will you stay and help me fight the bad guys?" She chewed on her bottom lip and her gaze drifted over his face.

What? Leave her alone in this backwoods town? *Never.* He smiled down at her. "Yes, ma'am."

A LETTER FROM D.K. HOOD

Dear Reader,

I am delighted you chose my novel and joined me in the exciting world of Kane and Alton in *Don't Tell a Soul*.

If you want to keep up to date with all my latest releases, just sign up at the following link. Your email address will never be shared and you can unsubscribe at any time.

www.bookouture.com/dk-hood

Writing this story has been a thrilling adventure for me. Delving into the lives of ex- secret agents and serial killers was a dream come true. I love forensic science and enjoyed researching every aspect of the crime scenes.

If you enjoyed my story, I would be very grateful if you could leave a review and recommend my book to your friends and family. I really enjoy hearing from readers because when I write, it's as if you are here with me, following the characters' stories.

Writing a novel is a very isolating business and I would love to hear from you—so please get in touch on my Facebook page or Twitter or through my website.

Thank you so much for your support.

D.K. Hood

KEEP IN TOUCH WITH D.K. HOOD

http://www.dkhood.com
dkhood-author.blogspot.com.au

 facebook.com/dkhoodauthor
twitter.com/DKHood_Author

ACKNOWLEDGEMENTS

To Dan Brown for the brainstorming sessions and inspiration.

To Dave Kentner, Dana Frye, Judith Leger, and all the great people at the ERA and Asylum Group for your support and advice.